The
Ravi Lancers

Also by John Masters

NIGHTRUNNERS OF BENGAL
THE DECEIVERS
THE LOTUS AND THE WIND
BHOWANI JUNCTION
COROMANDEL!
BUGLES AND A TIGER
FAR, FAR, THE MOUNTAIN PEAK
FANDANGO ROCK
THE VENUS OF KONPARA
THE ROAD PAST MANDALAY
TO THE CORAL STRAND
TRIAL AT MONOMOY
FOURTEEN EIGHTEEN
THE BREAKING STRAIN
CASANOVA
THE ROCK
PILGRIM SON

The
Ravi Lancers

JOHN MASTERS

LONDON
MICHAEL JOSEPH

First published in Great Britain by
MICHAEL JOSEPH LTD
52 Bedford Square, London, W.C.1
1972

7181 1044 7

Printed in Great Britain by
Richard Clay (The Chaucer Press), Ltd,
Bungay, Suffolk

*For Sandy Richardson, who
had the idea, and faith*

Foreword

IN THIS BOOK the reader will encounter a great many Indian names. It will help to remember, first, that Hindus do not use surnames, and second, that many of them share the same final honorific. In a name such as Himat Singh, for example, Himat is the man's real name; Singh means 'lion'—indeed *all* male Sikh names end with Singh. Thus there are innumerable Singhs, Dasses, and Rams, etc., who are not related to each other. Fathers and sons do not have the same names, thus a man called Puran Lall might be the son of one called Nathu Ram. When reading this book it might make it easier to ignore the final part of a man's name and think of him solely as Himat or Puran or Krishna.

A second problem for the reader unfamiliar with the old Indian Army is the class of men known as Viceroy's Commissioned Officers. The ranks of King's Commissioned Officers were the same as in other armies, i.e., general, major, captain, etc.

The ranks of non-commissioned officers can be directly translated. In the Indian cavalry and infantry, with which we will be dealing here, the equivalents were:

	Cavalry	Infantry
Private, trooper	Sowar	Sepoy
Lance-corporal	Acting Lance-Dafadar	Lance-Naik
Corporal	Lance-Dafadar	Naik
Sergeant	Dafadar	Havildar
Sergeant Major	Dafadar-Major	Havildar-Major

Between the true officers and the NCOs, however, there existed (and still exists) in the Indian Army a unique class of men who, having come up through the non-commissioned ranks, received commissions not from the King but from the Viceroy of India. They

7

wore swords, were addressed as 'sahib', received salutes, and had powers of command and punishment over all Indian soldiers; but they were subordinate to all officers holding the King's commission. In those days, when all the King's Commissioned Officers were British and all the enlisted men and NCOs were Indian they were the vital link between the two. Their grades, to which there are no equivalents in other armies, were:

Jemadar (cavalry and infantry): wore the same badges as a second lieutenant
Rissaldar (cavalry), or *Subadar* (infantry): wore the same badges as a lieutenant
Rissaldar-Major, Subadar-Major: wore the same badges as a major.

In this period there was no confusion between rissaldars and lieutenants because the latter would be young men with white faces, wearing sun helmets or peaked caps; the latter would be grizzled men with brown skins, wearing turbans.

In the cavalry, rissaldars and jemadars commanded troops, or were seconds-in-command of squadrons, and also assisted in various staff duties. The quartermaster (a captain or lieutenant), for instance, would be assisted by a Jemadar-Quartermaster; the adjutant by a Jemadar-Adjutant (in the cavalry this man had the mysterious title of Woordie-Major, 'the Uniform Major'); and the colonel was advised on all matters to do with the men's religions and customs by the Rissaldar-Major.

The private armies belonging to the Indian princes, which were known as Indian States Forces, were a special case again. Here all officers, of whatever type, would receive their commissions from their own ruler. If an Indian States Force regiment was incorporated into the regular army arrangements would have to be made to give the Maharajah's commissions the same validity as King's and Viceroy's commissions. In the Great War one Indian States Force regiment, the Jodhpur Lancers, did actually go to France, and I should make clear that neither that regiment nor the State of Jodhpur has any relation to my purely imaginary Ravi Lancers and State of Ravi.

Finally, the non-military reader might reasonably wish to be informed that a regiment was a homogeneous cavalry unit of about 600 men commanded by a lieutenant-colonel, the cavalry equivalent of an infantry battalion. The regiment was split up into squadrons of about 125 men and they into troops of about thirty. Regiments or battalions were grouped by threes or fours into brigades; and three brigades, with added artillery, engineers, signallers, etc. made a division.

This book is wholly a work of fiction, and no reference is intended in it to any person, living or dead, except for the few obvious historical characters mentioned.

I gratefully acknowledge the enormous help given me by Lieutenant-General Moti Sagar PVSM, late Colonel of the 4th Gorkha Rifles, and by Lieutenant-Colonel George Shipway, late of the 13th Lancers.

J.M.

The
Ravi Lancers

January 1914

'**44**TH BENGAL LANCERS ... will march past! Regiment will advance in squadron column from the right ... Walk march!'

The colonel's voice came faint on the morning breeze to the extreme left of the line, where Warren Bateman sat erect on his charger in front of D Squadron. Fainter yet as his squadron completed the wheel he heard the voice of George Johnson ordering A Squadron to halt. The ranked lances ahead began to thicken as the squadrons, each in line, closed up on the leader. In their turn he heard Tinsley and Sheridan order their squadrons to halt. He eyed the distance to the rear of C ... thirty paces, twenty-five ...

He raised his sabre straight above his head and shouted, 'D Squadron ... *halt*!'

The regiment stood in a dense mass, six hundred bamboo lances resting vertical by the riders' knees, six hundred steel lance points glittering, six hundred red and white pennons fluttering. It was January 1st, 1914, and, as on every January 1st, the Army in India was parading to proclaim, once again, that the King of England was the Emperor of India. Here at Lahore, one regiment of Indian cavalry, one battery of British field artillery, one battalion of British infantry, and three battalions of Indian infantry, were now gathered in full dress, ready to march past the major-general commanding the district. It was eight o'clock in the morning, the low sun beginning to melt the frost off the sere grass round the huge parade ground.

Warren glanced round to see that his squadron were in line and no one's turban had fallen off. They were a magnificent sight. The full dress of the 44th Bengal Lancers was a long tunic of dark blue, faced with scarlet and piped with gold. Round the waist officers

13

and men wore a cummerbund ten inches deep, the officers' being made of brocaded gold silk, which cost them a hundred pounds each out of their own pockets, and the men's of a bright yellow silk. The breeches were of white drill, the boots of black leather, the spur chains of gilded metal (the officers' of gold); and the officers' scabbard slings of gold brocaded cord. On their heads officers and men alike wore a turban wound of dark blue silk, with a gold spray fan rising on the left side. The sowars held in their right hand the lance, its foot set in a leather socket on the toe of their right stirrup iron. All officers, both those holding the King's and the Viceroy's commission, carried a drawn sabre in a yellow-gauntleted right hand, the back of the blade now resting on the right shoulder, gold sword knot wrapped around the wrist, the acorns dangling loose.

Glancing towards the saluting base Warren saw that the massed bands were not yet ready. There would be a few minutes wait before the march past began. Behind his squadron the artillery battery was already in position. Behind it the Royal Oxford Fusiliers were marching up, and the Indian battalions stood ready to follow. He shifted his weight in the saddle as he heard his rissaldar hurl a vicious word of abuse at some man near the right of the line. He still felt stiff from yesterday's polo match. He saw the members of the Dragoons' team, yesterday's opponents, on the saluting base, in mufti. It was good of them to come and watch the parade, after a riotous night, when they might have been in bed. They were a good team, twenty-two goals, and it had been a hard game, though not as hard as against the Ravi team the week before. That old Bholanath, the Rajah's brother, was a really good player, and rode like a demon.

The massed bands reached their allotted position. The infantry were formed in close column of companies. It wouldn't be long now. The 44th looked good. He could actually see the pride of the squadrons in front of him, and feel the panache of his own behind him. The men were hard and fit, thoroughly disciplined, well trained. Every man could ride perfectly, and the horses were as good as any in the Indian Army. But—to what end? Was the goal of all this splendour, all this efficiency, just more cold-weather manoeuvres, such as were due to start in three days' time, and would repeat themselves every successive cold weather until his retirement? And, once every ten years, perhaps, a half-hour scrap against ragged-arsed tribesmen on the North West Frontier? Polo tournaments, pigsticking, and endless talk about horses, horses, nothing but horses? He liked horses well enough himself, but could secretly sympathize with Joan when she said that his brother officers were no more intelligent than their mounts, and a lot less handsome. She was up there now, under the shamiana beside the saluting base, with Diana and the children. He thought he could just see her big hat through the forest of lances.

He heard his colonel's long-drawled order and the 44th Bengal Lancers moved off in column of squadrons, all together, the black horses' necks curved, heads tossing and champing, bits jingling, curb chains chinking. The massed bands were playing the 44th's regimental march, the Triumphal March from *Aida*. The squadrons advanced in order: A—Punjabi Mussulmans; B—Punjabi Mussulmans; C—Jat Sikhs; D—Rajputs. Behind the Lancers the 41st Field Battery of the Royal Artillery was moving too, the 18-pounders grinding along behind teams of matched bays, the British gunners riding the wheel horses or sitting upright on the limbers. Dust rose like haze over a morning sea, and the bodies of the horsemen seemed to rise out of it like seaborn gods, floating inexorably forward in a dense phalanx, scarlet and blue and gold, flashing steel above and the distant city rose-red in the morning light ahead.

Warren Bateman came level with the saluting base and shouted, 'D Squadron, eyes ... right!' He turned his own head and circled his sabre round and down. Major-General Glover raised his hand once more to the peak of his plumed cocked hat, and then was hidden by the right hand men of the squadron's front rank. There were Joan and Diana and the children, waving to him. He counted ten and shouted, 'D Squadron, eyes ... *front*!'

One part of the parade over without disaster, he thought, remembering the time Sowar Chattar Singh fell off his horse slap in front of the Viceroy, or the time George Johnson rode his squadron into a battalion of infantry.

Up in front A Squadron was forming squadron column to the left. The rest would follow in turn, until the regiment was tracking the boundary of the parade ground back to its original position, while the infantry marched past. The artillery was clear of the saluting base now and the Fusiliers coming on. The bands switched to their regimental march, *Lillibulero*.

Warren stifled a yawn. After his years with the Burma Military Police peacetime soldiering with the regiment lacked any real incentive. One did the same things over and over again, and of course in the end did them perfectly ... but that was boring, and who could be sure they were doing the *right* things? One certainly had more independence than in the British service, but all the same, for a captain of thirty-four, with fourteen years' service, to be worrying about how to account for two lost stirrup leathers, worth 8 rupees 4 annas, was ridiculous. The officers were a band of brothers, all right, trusting one another to the hilt, but ... the mental horizon was narrow compared with his lonely years with Joan in Burma, when there seemed to be no limit to the discoveries they could make about the country, and its people, and even about themselves. He'd tried to range as far here in India but—from inside the regiment—it was difficult. Perhaps he'd retire and study Indian history and literature. But what would he live on? Joan kept on saying it didn't matter, something would turn up, she would make a fortune writing poetry or painting pictures ... alas, none of that could be relied on to educate Louise or send Rodney to Wellington.

'C Squadron ... *halt!*'

He started, and hurriedly shouted, 'D Squadron ... *halt!*' He had almost repeated George Johnson's gaffe. Major Boyd-Carter was shouting at him from behind the squadron, 'You went too close, Captain Bateman! Hold back when the gallop past begins, to your proper distance.'

'Yes, sir,' he called.

He wheeled Ploughman round and surveyed his squadron, while the big black gelding shifted and fidgeted under him. The line was good. 'Look to your stirrups and girths, lads,' he called out in Hindustani. The men transferred their reins to their lance hands and felt under their saddles, first on one side then the other, to make sure girths and stirrup leathers were secure and tight. A gallop-past by a full regiment of cavalry was an exhilarating affair to take part in and an awesome spectacle to watch, but it was also damned dangerous. It was twelve years since a slipped girth had thrown a sowar off during a gallop-past, but everyone knew what had happened to him: instant death under the hoofs of the rear rank.

'*Sab thik hai, rissaldar sahib?*'

'*Sab thik hai, sahib,*' the rissaldar responded from behind the squadron.

The bands were playing *Lutzow's Wild March* at a hectic speed.

The green-clad mass of Gurkhas, who marched at that pace, was approaching the saluting base. Five minutes later the bands fell silent. Artillery and infantry lined the left side of the parade ground, a wall of blue and scarlet, Frontier-drab and Rifle green.

Colonel Woodward sang out the long-vowelled orders: '44th Bengal Lancers will gallop past! By the right, walk ... march!'

The band again struck up *Aida*. Ploughman's powerful quarters tensed and he began to move as though he had understood the colonel's distant order. The sun was a hot arm across Warren's shoulders now, and dust blew away in dancing spirals down the length of the parade ground towards the city.

'Trot!'

The squadrons jingled into a trot, and Warren thrust himself deeper into the saddle. The bands changed into the *Light Cavalry Overture*.

'Canter!'

His legs squeezed Ploughman's flanks and the huge horse bounded forward. Ahead the rigid lines of the squadrons bent, and at once straightened again, like bow strings. The dust towered higher than the horses' heads, the thunder of hoofs blurred the blare of the bands. Quarter of a mile to go, his black-mustachioed Rajputs galloping shoulder to shoulder behind him, the bearded Sikhs ahead. Now he was racing past the stand, the frenzied trumpets of *Light Cavalry* loud in his ears. He felt a momentary exhilaration ... But this was all make-believe. Would he ever see enemy ahead, the lances lowering, his sabre slashing down?

The commands filtered down ... *Trot! ... Walk march! ... Form troop column!* The review was over, the regiment riding back to its lines. The sun was high and he had a tolerable thirst on him.

An hour later he was sitting at the head of the dining-room table in his bungalow, dressed now in dark grey flannel trousers and a light-weight tweed jacket, with a white shirt and the tie of his old school, Marlborough. A copy of the day's *Civil & Military Gazette* lay beside his plate and the *khitmatgar* was helping him to grilled kidneys, bacon, and fried eggs. His wife Joan sat on his right and his sister Diana on his left, both already eating. The children sat in high chairs at the foot of the table, with *ayah* standing between them, helping them to eat.

'That was a wonderful thing to see, Warrie,' his sister said. 'The gallop past. But it was frightening, too.'

'And probably quite useless,' Joan said, lifting her tea cup. 'The army always gets ready for the last war but one.'

Warren said, 'Oh, I don't know. There'll still be cavalry charges.'

Joan said, 'Tribesmen aren't going to stay and be charged at, and any European army would have guns and machine guns. But let's not talk about war. It's such a *bore*, almost as bad as horses. What time are we going to Shalimar?'

Warren pulled out his watch, and said, 'Noon? Is that all right?'

Joan nodded, her mouth full of bacon. The two women were as different as could be: Joan tall and long-nosed, willowy, dressed now—as on the parade ground—in a diaphanous white gown gathered high under her bosom, her hair down, loosely controlled by a broad scarlet ribbon. She looked like a Greek poetess or a prominent courtesan of the French Directory, anything but what she was, the wife of a captain of Indian cavalry. Diana, two years younger, was built more like himself, not short but giving an impression more of solidity than of height, her dark brown hair neat, her clothes inconspicuous in browns and dull greens, her rather large hands now resting on the table. She'd spent six months with them now, here in Lahore and in the hill station of Dalhousie, but no luck. Most of the eligible bachelors weren't attracted, seeming to want something more flashy; and to the only one who showed any interest, Diana was polite but distant. 'She doesn't really want to get married,' Joan had said to him one night, 'not unless she can find another Warren.'

'Oh, nonsense,' he'd replied; but perhaps there was a bit of truth in it. Diana had always worshipped him.

A small brown fox-terrier face, with a white eye patch, peered round the open door from the hall. Warren pointed his finger and said, 'Out, Shikari! You know you're not allowed in the dining-room.'

The face disappeared. Diana got up, 'I'll take him for a little walk ... and Louise and Rodney. Come on, children.'

The *khitmatgar* stood motionless against the wall behind Warren. Joan gestured for more hot water and he silently disappeared. Warren said, 'We'd better start thinking about what you're going to take home. There'll only be a fortnight after I get back from camp ... You're going to find Shrewford Pennel rather lonely, I'm afraid. No one to talk to. Not your sort of people, I mean.'

Joan said, 'There's Ralph. He was hardly more than a boy when I met him, but he seemed interesting ... unusual, anyway.'

'He's unusual, all right,' Warren said.

He spread marmalade on his toast, while the *khitmatgar* put the fresh pot of hot water on the table. Ralph Harris was a queer one, sullen and boisterous by turns, sometimes rude, sometimes over-polite, often withdrawn into himself. One could hardly blame him. His situation wasn't his fault. Still, it was a pity that Joan found Diana so dull. There was a lot they could have done together, even in the depths of Wiltshire, if they shared the same enthusiasms.

He got up, wiping his mouth, 'I think I'll take a look at the stables, dear. See that the carriage is cleaned up. We don't want to go to Shalimar looking like a party of Southend trippers.' He bent and kissed her hair.

They drove back from the picnic lunch in the great Mogul gardens after three o'clock, the children dozing fitfully between *ayah* and Diana on one seat, himself and Joan opposite, the *khitmatgar* in full livery smart on the box beside the *syce*, the fox terrier Shikari sitting proudly between them. Shalimar was very beautiful, Warren thought. All the works of the Moguls had a great strength and calm, at least the early ones. The Taj Mahal felt flashy and somehow foreign after one had really absorbed Fatehpur Sikri and the Red Fort. He had tried to point out to Diana some of the special graces of Shalimar. She listened, because he was her brother—he could tell that she was not really interested; but the crowds of Indians in the gardens had held her attention. After six months she could barely tell a Sikh from a Muslim, but that didn't matter for it was always the children that absorbed her—they, and the marks of poverty and disease, which were prominent enough even in this rich capital of a rich province.

The carriage rolled past the garrison cricket field, and Warren saw that a match was in progress. He said, 'Who's playing?'

'The Club against Ravi State,' Joan said. 'I saw the announcement last week but didn't tell you in case you decided to play instead of taking us to Shalimar, as you'd promised.'

Warren laughed. 'Naughty puss ... Well, I think I'll watch for a bit. Might as well doze in one of the chairs here as at home.'

The children woke up. 'Daddy, Daddy, can we watch too?'

'No,' he said. 'You go home with Mummy. *Idder rokna, Afzal*

... No, Shikari, home you go, a cricket field's no place for an inquisitive little dog. Do you want to spend an hour or so here, Diana? Good ... See you about five, dear. We'll walk back.'

He waved briefly as the carriage rolled away. It was no use even asking Joan whether she would like to watch the cricket. She wouldn't.

He found empty chairs among those set up outside the pavilion, and greeted a few friends. 'Who's batting?' he asked his neighbour.

'Fellow at the crease is Krishna Ram, Yuvraj of Ravi. He's the captain, of course, though he's only twenty-five or twenty-six. Couldn't have a subject ordering his prince about, could they? Don't know the fellow at the other end's name. Doesn't matter, for he won't be there long, I can see. But the Yuvraj ... oh, good shot!'

The lithe figure in white bent, the bat swung powerfully, the red ball whistled along the dried grass past the pavilion. Diana clapped heartily. Warren settled down to watch, and was rewarded with half an hour of grace, during which the young Indian prince scored forty runs. Two wickets fell and then the Yuvraj, seeming to grow careless, hit across a good-length ball and was clean bowled.

'That's the trouble with these people,' Warren's neighbour muttered, 'no perseverance.'

The Yuvraj was walking back to the pavilion, his bat under his arm, taking off his batting gloves. Everyone was applauding politely, except Diana who was on her feet, clapping enthusiastically. The prince glanced at her and acknowledged her with a little nod and a touch of his hand to the long peak of his yellow and white cap.

'He looked as though he knew you,' Warren said.

'In a way. He was standing next to us at the parade this morning. We didn't speak, though.'

'Well, we could now. They're taking tea.'

Diana at his side, he strolled under the awning set up behind the pavilion. The Yuvraj, divested of pads and cap, came in rubbing his hands. Warren said, 'A pretty knock—except the last stroke.' He smiled.

The Yuvraj said, 'I know, sir. I ought to be ashamed of myself.'

'You're the Yuvraj of Ravi, aren't you? I'm Warren Bateman, 44th Bengal Lancers.'

'I recognize you from the parade this morning. I thought your squadron was the best. Of course that may be because they are Rajputs, like us.' He laughed lightly, a fresh boyish laugh.

Warren said, 'This is my sister, Diana. She's staying with us.'

'In the fishing fleet,' Diana said with a smile, 'though I haven't caught anything ... or is it me who's supposed to be caught?'

The prince was the same height as Warren, about five-foot-ten, but slimmer, his skin the colour of wheat, his hair shining black and wavy, his eyes dark brown and deep set under strong straight eyebrows. He was bowing awkwardly to Diana, obviously a little ill at ease with her. He wouldn't have much knowledge or experience of European society, living up in that remote pleasant little kingdom nestled in the foothills of the Himalayas.

'Where did you learn your cricket?' Warren asked idly.

'My grandfather employed an English professional when I was a boy. Then I had a tutor, Mr. Charles Fleming. He played for Oxford. Have you heard of him?'

' 'Fraid not,' Warren said. 'Well, whoever it was taught you well. You could be another Ranji, if you put your mind to it. And time, of course. And went to England.'

'I'd love to,' the young man sighed, 'but ...'—he spread his hands—'My grandfather says my place is in Ravi, with our people. If my father were alive, perhaps I could, but he is dead, so I am the heir.'

They sipped tea. The prince looked surreptitiously at Diana when she looked somewhere else. Twice Warren thought that he was trying to frame some polite remark to her, but didn't know how. He remained silent. Diana smiled at him and he smiled back.

Suddenly he blurted out, 'I'll be seeing you at Ratanwala Camp, sir.'

Warren said, 'Oh? Of course, I forgot, the Ravi Lancers are coming down to act as enemy for us. But I didn't know you were serving in them.'

'Yes, sir. I'm a major, the Second-in-command.'

'Then for heaven's sake don't call me "sir". I'm only a captain and should be calling you "sir".'

'Yes, sir ... Captain Bateman.' The prince smiled again. 'But you know I'd only be a subaltern in your regiment ... if I were allowed into it.'

'I wish I could come to Ratanwala, too,' Diana said.

'We don't allow camp followers in the Indian Army—haven't for a long time,' Warren said, grinning.

'And afterwards I'll be going home ...'

'Are you going home?' the Yuvraj said, his face falling.

'On February the 4th,' she said.

The prince said, 'I was hoping ... I was going to ask Captain Bateman if you would all like to visit Ravi. It is very beautiful. Of course, it is only a small state, and our capital, Basohli, is not much more than a village. But ... we have very good snipe shooting ... some duck ... cricket ... polo ...'

Warren shook his head, 'Very kind of you, Yuvraj, but there just isn't time. Now, Di, we'd better be getting back. Goodbye, Yuvraj. See you at Ratanwala.'

'Goodbye, sir. Goodbye, Miss Bateman.'

'Goodbye, Yuvraj,' she said. She smiled and held out her hand. He took it and bowed awkwardly, the pale gold of his skin suffusing with a blush.

They walked away round the edge of the ground. The sun was low over the distant trees and the blue smoke of cooking fires rose from the hidden bungalows of the cantonment to mingle with the dust from trotting carriages and exercising horses.

'Seems a nice chap,' Warren said. 'Though I don't envy these princes at all ... raised as petty gods to find when they grow up that they really have no responsibility. I believe Ravi comes under the Agent to the Governor General for the Hill States ... A lot of them take to drink, or worse. I can't say I blame them.'

'It's a shame we can't visit it,' Diana said, 'but it can't be helped.'

'No ... When you get home, let me know at once if there's any trouble between Joan and Mother, won't you?'

'Oh, there won't be!' Diana exclaimed. 'No one quarrels with Mother.'

'No, but Joan has her own ideas about so many things—the way the children ought to be brought up ... this Harz-Goldwasser method ... the way she dresses, eats, acts ... It looks pretty odd sometimes. Mother might not approve.'

'Don't worry, Warrie,' his sister said, taking his arm. 'We'll all get along famously until you come home in August. And I'm so sorry you wasted so much time and trouble trying to find me a husband. I'll just have to reconcile myself to dying an old maid, won't I? ... By the way, are you going to take Shikari to camp?'

'I thought I'd have to. Joan never sees that he's properly exercised ... but you'll be here, won't you? I'd rather not take him unless I have to.'

'I'll exercise him, Warrie.'

'Good. He's a nice little dog, but ... well, *I* don't think a manoeuvre camp is the place for dogs. Except retrievers, perhaps.'

'Ooh ... darling ... aaah!' Warren groaned in Joan's ear, his weight bearing rhythmically down on her. Her legs were twined round his back, her head twisted, the fair hair a cloud on the moon-lit pillow. The bed creaked faster. Her teeth met gently, then suddenly sharp, in his ear. She began to moan, muffling the sounds against his throat.

Afterwards, he went to the bathroom and disposed of the contra-ceptive which she always insisted that he used. The damned thing turned the act of love into something vaguely unnatural and de-grading, and it didn't feel so good, physically; but that wasn't of much importance compared to Joan's peace of mind; and they certainly should not have another child, partly because of the expense and partly because she had had such a bad time giving birth to Rodney three and a half years ago.

He lay down again beside her, and she curled up in his arms. 'I wish you were coming back to England with us,' she said.

'So do I,' he said.

'Oh, I don't know,' she said. 'I think you'd miss the manoeuvres, the parades, the sowars.'

He said thoughtfully, 'Yes, I would, but I shall miss you more. One can't have everything in this world.'

She lay silent against him for a while, then said, 'I wish your family lived in London.'

'H'm,' he said non-committally. He liked London well enough, to visit as a young man, or on leave, but—to live in the Smoke, as the cockneys called it? What was it that woman said in the Shaw play? *Not bloody likely!* And it was no use pretending to Joan about it.

'I'm starving for art,' she said, 'theatre, music, people who *think* and *talk* instead of clumping about on stupid great horses. People with their brains in their heads not in their behinds.'

'You could spend some nights in Uncle Rodney's flat—he has a spare room, I know—and do some things from there ... as much as we can afford.'

'It's difficult for a woman alone,' Joan said. 'She gets stared at, which I don't mind. And pestered, which I do ... Oh, well, you'll

23

be back in August, and perhaps I can persuade Ralph to take me up once or twice.'

Warren kissed her and turned over sleepily. 'Yes, that's an idea. You may be able to bring him out of his shell ... persuade him the world isn't all against him.'

January 1914

WARREN AND HIS brother officer, George Johnson, walked slowly round the Ratanwala *jheel*, the village headman beside them. 'I should think four guns is the maximum here,' Warren said. 'We could have a shoot tomorrow, unless old Rainbow's got something planned for us.'

Johnson shook his head. 'No, there's nothing till the day after. Some of the infantry have to march out into position, that's all.'

Warren said, 'All right.' He told the headman what he wanted done about the snipe shoot. The headman said, 'It will be done, sahib,' salaamed twice and walked away across the fields to his village. Warren and Johnson set off down the road to the camp, both smoking pipes as they strolled along. It was four o'clock on another perfect cold weather afternoon in the northern Punjab. The tents of the Lahore Brigade stood in long rows among mango and oak trees on a gentle slope ahead, the mud-walled village of Ratanwala to the north, the shallow lake, Ratanwala Jheel, reputed to provide some of the best snipe shooting in India, in a depression to the east.

At the entrance to the camp, they met a group of officers all of whom Warren knew from the club and previous manoeuvres— Upchurch of the Oxford Fusiliers, Moore of the Gurkhas, and Corelli of the 8th Brahmins, keen shooters all. Upchurch said, 'Been arranging that shoot we were talking about, Bateman?'

Warren nodded, 'Yes. It's all fixed. Four guns. Let's draw lots for the places this evening, and then another four can take the *jheel* on Sunday.'

'Good enough,' Captain Corelli said. He looked up the road, 'Here, what's this? I thought your lot were the only cavalry going to grace these manoeuvres with your presence.'

Warren, looking along the dusty road which bordered the camp, saw the glitter of lance points to the north. 'It'll be the Ravi Lancers,' he said. 'They're going to act as enemy.'

'Indian States Forces?' Moore said. 'That ought to provide some comic relief.'

'I've heard this lot are good,' Warren said. 'They have a damned good polo team, anyway.'

The lances were advancing. Ahead of them rode a tall thin man in a heavy pith helmet. 'A British officer?' Corelli muttered.

Warren said, 'Yes. Colonel Hanbury. He was Central India Horse, re-employed by the Rajah.'

The column came on, the thin colonel at the head sitting stooped in the saddle, looking neither to right nor left. The watching officers, all in mufti, raised pith helmets or battered felt hats as he passed. He glanced at them then, and touched his right hand to the peak of his topi. A trumpeter rode to his left rear and a sowar bearing a yellow guidon to his right. Now he was reining in his charger, halting, turning round so that he was stopped at the side of the road, his back to Warren and the others. The leading squadron, led by an Indian wearing a khaki turban, wheeled left into the camp. A fat Indian captain, riding like a sack of potatoes, trotted out of the camp, turned his horse alongside the leading squadron commander, and began pointing and gesticulating. Now came the sowars ... horses well groomed, coats healthy in spite of the dust covering all of them, Warren noted. In the rifle buckets they were carrying the old carbine, but the buckets were well dubbined, everything tight fastened, nothing flapping, girths tight, no horse lame or pecking ... they were better looked after than the men. Not that the men were badly turned out, but they lacked the polish and expert management obvious in the horses: their turbans were not all equally well tied, nor their puttees well fastened, and they didn't sit alike—this man proud and erect, that one like a stuffed doll in the saddle. The lances were slung, where most regiments rode into camp at attention, but the men looked alert, untired, and cheerful. There was some laughing in the ranks, and Upchurch muttered, 'Lots of talky-talky, eh?'

Corelli exclaimed, 'Look!' Warren stared. Elephants, by God! Down the road came a string of twenty elephants loaded with tentage. They entered the camp. Small parties of men cantered up from the rear of the column, and an old Indian with fiercely upturned white moustaches, who had ridden up to sit easily beside the British colonel, gave them orders. Warren recognized him as Bholanath, the polo player. As the elephants shambled across the area allotted to the Ravi Lancers for their camp, every few yards a man on top would throw down a rolled tent. Oxcarts came now, gaily decorated, with un-uniformed men, ordinary peasants, naked but for loin cloths, perched on the yoke.

'I'll bet those carts are normally full of women,' Moore muttered.

'Of course,' Upchurch said, 'can't expect those fellows to do without their home comforts.'

The carts wheeled into the camp, axles screaming. That was good management, very good, Warren thought, for oxcarts moved at barely two miles an hour, less than half the rate of cavalry, and to have both arrive in camp together was a feat of timing. Also, the carts must have started out very early.

Another squadron arrived, headed by two men riding side by side. One of them was a captain, the other a sowar, carrying a lance. As they passed Corelli stifled a guffaw and Upchurch said— not very softly—'Good God, bloody Wog pansies?' Warren saw that the officer and sowar were holding hands as their horses walked together.

'That explains why they haven't brought any women,' Moore of the Gurkhas said. 'They don't need them.'

Warren stared after the couple, not sure whether to smile or frown. He knew that there was homosexuality among many Indians, as Oscar Wilde's trial had shown that there was among Englishmen. He knew it was more prevalent among some Indian peoples than others. An officer commanding Sikhs would be more aware of it than one commanding Dogras or Rajputs, such as these men; and an officer commanding Pathans would have to develop a broad tolerance and follow certain well-defined rules, for among them it was almost universal. But in the Indian Army it would never be flaunted on parade, nor would such a relationship be accepted between an officer and a sowar or sepoy. Colonel Hanbury must have seen, but had said nothing. Well, this was the Ravi Lancers, not the Central India Horse or the 44th of the old Bengal Line.

The other watching British officers drifted away. Warren and Johnson headed for their mess. As they walked, a squadron of Ravi Lancers wheeled into a column of troops directly in front of them, and its captain called out in Hindi, 'This is our place, rissaldar-sahib. Allot the tents.'

Nothing happened. The squadron commander wore spectacles and did not sit his horse well. He was now fidgeting about, looking right and left, while a rissaldar and two jemadars had a heated argument nearby. One of them called, 'There are not enough tents for my troop, captain-sahib!'

'Yes, there are!' the rissaldar snapped.

The captain spurred forward, saying, 'Don't argue, please! Come. Gather here.'

Warren thought, there's a man with no confidence in himself. If the rest of the officers were like that, the regiment wouldn't be much use. George Johnson relit his pipe, glancing back over his shoulder. 'How would you like to command that lot, Bateman?'

Warren said, 'Not a bit ... but there'd be compensations.'

'Women,' Johnson said, grinning. 'Baksheesh. Perks. Five rupees for every promotion to lance dafadar, twenty to dafadar, and as for jemadar ...'

Warren said seriously, 'I meant, one would be part of an India that only exists in the Native States nowadays—the India that our forefathers knew.'

'You can have it,' Johnson said. 'Y'know, I believe I'm on to a better way to treating bog-spavin in the early stages. What I say is ...'

They walked on towards the mess tent and the immaculate mess dafadar saluting outside. Warren remembered that he hadn't seen the Yuvraj of Ravi arrive with his regiment. Well, you couldn't expect a prince to suffer the boredom of a route march, could you?

As his horse trotted in under the shade of the trees by the well, Warren eased it back to a walk, then to a halt. George Johnson was already there, sitting on the brick surround of the well munching on a sandwich, his orderly holding the two horses, watched by a knot of naked children. Warren slipped to the ground, gave his reins to his orderly, Narayan Singh, and sat down at Johnson's side. He pulled out his own sandwich, peered into it, muttered, 'Cold mutton. Can't that bloody *khansamah* think of anything else? ... They've got quite a bold plan, George. It could end in a disaster —a real one—but that's their business.'

'What are they going to do?' Johnson asked, his mouth full.

'Send two squadrons to swim the Ravi behind your right rear

and probe in from that side, while the other two squadrons hold you in front.'

Johnson munched, shaking his head. 'That'll give Rainbow fits. He thinks the river is protecting his flank.'

Warren passed on more details of the Ravi Lancers' plan as they ate. Round the right sleeves of their khaki drill tunics both men were wearing the white armband of an umpire. Johnson was the chief umpire with the infantry brigade which, with one squadron of cavalry, was advancing into 'enemy' territory in a small exercise; the Ravi Lancers were the 'enemy' who were trying to stop them. The village well at this tiny hamlet ten miles north of Ratanwala Camp was the prearranged rendezvous where the umpires met and exchanged plans so that each would know where to place himself and what information to give the commanders as the action unfolded.

An hour later Warren rejoined the Ravi Lancers in their bivouac to the north, arriving at the same time as a large open car, covered with dust, drove in from the opposite direction. As he dismounted near where Colonel Hanbury was sitting on a folding camp chair, the Yuvraj Krishna Ram leaped out of the car, saluted the colonel, and said, 'I'm sorry I'm late, sir, but the Privy Council wasn't held till this morning. Have I missed anything?' He was wearing a perfectly cut drill uniform with a single long yellow and white medal ribbon on his left breast, and immaculate field boots, gleaming like the sun. He noticed Warren then, and saluted again with a smile, 'Hullo, sir.'

Colonel Hanbury said, 'You haven't missed anything, but you're just in time for an interesting job which I was going to give to Major Bholanath ... if you feel up to some swimming.' He smiled a frosty little smile at Warren—'I am putting the Yuvraj in command of the flanking force.'

The prince saluted and turned to hurry off, but the colonel said, 'Wait a minute. You're not moving off for two hours yet. Get something to eat and then come back here and I'll give you the details ... Would you care for a bottle of beer, Bateman?'

'No, thanks, sir. I think I'll have a nap, though.'

Two hours later the flanking force set out. The two squadrons allotted for the task were C and D. Old Major Bholanath, the polo player, who was a younger brother of the Rajah, commanded C, and a fair-skinned, handsome Captain Sher Singh—the one holding hands with a sowar as they rode into camp—commanded D. The two hundred lancers headed south-east towards the Ravi River across a scrub-covered plain dotted with patches of cultivation, dun-coloured villages, and isolated trees. A column of dust traced their movement as they marched at the alternating walk then trot, walk then trot, of cavalry. Warren wondered whether the British force would see the dust and note its direction. But they were at least ten miles away, and the air was thick from the steady cold weather wind blowing off the thin topsoil. They would see nothing.

An hour before dark the force reached the right bank of the Ravi. The river was half a mile wide, flowing in two or three channels: it was hard to tell whether there were one or two long, low sand islands in the middle of the river. The near bank was a steep sand slope, the far one a low beach littered with bushes and tree trunks stranded from the floods of last monsoon. The squadron commanders gathered round the prince, and he said, speaking in Hindi, 'Let us cross at once. You go first, uncle. I'll follow with Sher Singh.'

Major Bholanath said, 'It would be best to give men and horses a little breathing space, Highness. And to look to the girths.'

'Very well, uncle,' the Yuvraj said, 'fifteen minutes.'

Warren dismounted and walked to the bank. The horses would enter the river almost at a jump, the bank was so steep, though barely six feet high. The water swirled deep and fast here. Anyone who was unseated in that first scramble might be swept away and drowned. It was the sort of risk that would obviously be taken in war, but in peace time manoeuvres? ... A British officer commanding regular troops would think twice in this situation. Was it worth the risk to men's lives? And, if anything happened, he might be reprimanded, or worse. Obviously such considerations didn't worry Krishna Ram or the two squadron commanders. They might drown twenty men, and their Rajah wouldn't raise an eyebrow.

When C squadron entered the old major went first, easing his horse down the steep bank to a final plunge, then he was out, the horse swimming strongly, his white hair gleaming under his turban. By then his leading troops were in the water, three abreast, all swimming, the sowars leaving the reins loose, holding to the horses' manes with one hand. At Warren's side the prince watched them go, smiling. 'My uncle's a wonderful man. He's my great-uncle, actually ... He doesn't hold his rank because he's the Rajah's brother, you know. He's the best officer we've got.'

Warren nodded—'One of the old school. And a terrific polo player—rides as hard as anyone I've ever seen.'

Bholanath's horse was kicking up out of the water, the major turning in the saddle, his arm waving in the twilight.

'Here we go,' Krishna Ram said. He edged his horse, a beautifully paced hunter, towards the bank. His orderly, a squat sturdy dark-skinned ape-like man, rode behind him, and two sowars who carried sabres instead of lances rode close, one on each side. Warren followed close, with his orderly, and almost together they all plunged into the river. The current carried them downstream and they reached the sandbank at the same place as C Squadron had; but by then C was entering the second channel, wider but shallower, where every now and then the horses' flailing hoofs found bottom. Behind, D Squadron were coming across, the horses' teeth bared in apparent snarls, as their powerful legs thrashed the water.

The prince and his group followed C Squadron into the second channel. There were no others, Warren was relieved to see, for some of the horses were stumbling as they struggled out on to the far bank. They looked tired—and the force was going to cross the river again, back to the right bank, ten miles farther downstream. As the rissaldar at the tail of D Squadron urged his horse up the bank and reported, 'All across, sahib,' the Yuvraj said, 'We'll rest here an hour, and take the evening meal.'

Warren dismounted. No cookers were accompanying the force so the men would be eating cold chupattis and *dal* from their mess tins. He himself would be eating the same, for when Colonel Hanbury had offered him mutton sandwiches he had decided to take the sowars' food instead.

The Yuvraj came towards him, holding a bottle, 'Whisky, Captain Bateman?'

Warren said, 'What about you?'

'I don't drink. I had my bodyguards bring it for you.'

Warren took the bottle. 'Well, that's very thoughtful of you. Wouldn't Sher Singh and your uncle like a drop?'

'They have their own.' He sat down beside Warren on a dried tree trunk half-buried in the sand. 'Do you think we did that all right?'

'Very good,' Warren said. 'You may have a little more trouble at the next crossing, but ... no regiment could have done it better.'

'Thank you ... We're really good, you know. Not like most States Forces.'

'So I can see,' Warren agreed. One of the prince's bodyguards handed him a collapsible silver cup and poured some whisky into it. 'Hanuman, *pani*,' the prince said, and the ape-like orderly poured water from a large silver flask into the whisky.

Warren raised the cup. 'Your good health.' He drank appreciatively. He had half expected to be served the whisky brewed in the Simla hills, but this was genuine Scotch, and a good one.

'I am really so sorry that you and your sister cannot come to visit us in Basohli,' the Yuvraj said, 'and Mrs. Bateman, of course.'

'So am I,' Warren said.

'I told my grandfather about you. He said he hopes you can come another year. Your regiment will still be in Lahore when you return from furlough, will it not?'

'Probably not,' Warren said. 'We've spent three years here, earmarked for divisional troops of an infantry division, and the powers-that-be think it's time we were put into a cavalry brigade —probably Secunderabad. But I'll remember your kind invitation.'

'Please!'

The twilight thickened to a cool smoky dusk. Warren drank, refusing a second whisky. They knew how to look after themselves, he thought. The silver flask and cup and whisky were nothing special: he knew some regiments of Indian cavalry where a table would have been set up long since, the officers sprawled in camp chairs, and mess orderlies in full regalia serving cold champagne; but the atmosphere here wasn't like that of regular Indian cavalry. The men offering him more whisky were not soldiers dedicated to their regiment, but personal servants dedicated to protect the Yuvraj's life with their own. Krishna Ram did not command by experience or rank, but by divine right, and all this gave the gathering in the dusk at the river's bank a mysteriously feudal atmosphere ... but he was glad to note that he had misjudged the young man, in at least one respect. It wasn't idleness but his responsibilities as heir apparent that had prevented him riding down to Ratanwala Camp with his regiment.

It was full dark when the force moved on, riding now down a dusty track that led south half a mile east of the river. They rode through a village where dimly seen women ran for the huts as they heard the hoofs, and here and there a man stood in a doorway, silhouetted by the dim oil lamp behind him, peering out as the horsemen passed. Near midnight they turned right and again headed for the river. The half moon, just risen, shone on a broad expanse of water. Warren involuntarily shivered. It was a long way, and here there were no islands to break the passage. They would have to swim it all in one.

'As before, fifteen minutes, and then we go,' the Yuvraj said. Soon, 'We are ready, Highness,' old Bholanath said, and the Yuvraj said, 'Go then, uncle,' and the old man called, 'Come, children! ... The far bank will come no closer by looking at it.'

He walked his horse into the water. Warren thought, he's right; but to plunge into a crossing like this without knowing what the other bank was like—it was a darker line of shadow, nothing more, barely distinguishable—that was risky. Still, this was the cavalry spirit that everyone was supposed to strive for, so who should complain? Krishna Ram and his bodyguards were going in and Narayan Singh was waiting at his side, Warren walked his horse into the river.

Ten minutes later, after a crossing when twice he thought he would be swept away, both times the horse finding ground underfoot in time, he reached the far side. Now the force was once more on the right bank, the side up which the British brigade was advancing. Unless they had misread their maps they were about five miles behind the right rear of the enemy. Now the prince could either advance at once and occupy the ground before the British knew he was anywhere near, or wait till light. As he turned to Major Bholanath, Captain Sher Singh loomed up out of the moonlight. 'Highness,' he said, 'we have a sowar missing. Mangla Ram.'

'What about his horse?' the Yuvraj asked.

'That's here. He must have slipped off somehow during the crossing. No one saw him.'

This was what he had been afraid of, Warren reflected. At that, they were lucky not to have lost more. And Sowar Mangla Ram could probably have been saved with better discipline and supervision in the ranks.

The Yuvraj said, 'Leave a jemadar here with a section—and Mangla Ram's horse. Tell them to search down this bank the rest of the night—send some men over the bridge at Harian at dawn and search the other bank, too—and get a boat and search the

33

islands. If they don't find him or his body by dusk tonight, to go back to camp.'

The captain saluted and disappeared. The Yuvraj turned to Bholanath and said, 'We'll wait here till first light, uncle. At night it's too easy to seize the wrong hill. Put out picquets and rest till five-thirty.'

Warren prepared himself to sleep. So much for Sowar Mangla Ram, drowned that the Ravi Lancers might show to good advantage on manoeuvres.

After three hours' shivering and fitful sleep, inadequately protected against the frost in his greatcoat, Warren got up and spent an hour walking up and down the river bank. Then the advance continued. For an hour the squadrons rode across country in column. Then, as the first light spread in the east, they halted. The officers gathered round and unfolded their maps on their saddles. 'I think we're here,' Krishna said, pointing at a spot on his map. 'That village there—you can just see some smoke rising from it—is Amarganj. The enemy will be somewhere the other side of the rise of land there.' He pointed at a low ridge a mile to the west.

'Then we ought to take that,' Major Bholanath said, brushing up his moustaches.

'I was going to order the squadrons forward in line, well separated,' Krishna said, 'until we made contact.'

'I think we'd do best to seize that ground first, Highness,' the old major said.

Krishna Ram hesitated. He had done very well so far, Warren thought; now would he accept Bholanath's suggestion—which was tactically the correct one—or insist on having his own way?

Krishna said, 'Very well. Take your squadron forward and capture it. But don't show yourselves on top, uncle. I don't want to let the enemy know we are here until we are ready.'

A moment later C Squadron trotted out in extended order across the ploughed fields, now half hidden by tendrils of morning mist, towards the ridge. Soon the leading troops dismounted, took their rifles, and ran on up to the crest on foot. There they lay down. The reserve troop and the horseholders waited in cover a hundred yards back among scattered thorn bushes and low trees. Krishna Ram, Captain Sher Singh and Warren rode forward. Below the ridge crest Bholanath met them. Everyone dismounted, got out their field glasses, and peered west.

Dust was rising two miles to the south-west, and from the dust an occasional flash showed steel reflecting back the morning light. 'Infantry,' Bholanath muttered. 'Where's their cavalry?'

'They'll be ahead,' Krishna said.

Warren, scanning the undulating plain through his binoculars, and knowing the British plan, realised that he was looking at the two reserve battalions of the brigade, which were advancing in column of route, protected, they thought, by the other two battalions spread out on a wide front ahead of them. But they were not; they were very vulnerable, provided the Ravi Lancers got closer.

The Yuvraj said, 'We're almost out of range ... Do you see those two low hillocks ahead there—beyond the village? We can get there without being seen.'

'Good, I'll go,' Bholanath said.

'No, uncle. It's Sher Singh's turn ... Take your squadron that way, keep them behind this ridge until you reach the village, then ride up the hills from behind. C here will move to the village, where I'll hold it in reserve until we see what the enemy do. We may be able to charge them in flank, as they deploy. Or get at their transport.'

Sher Singh hurried back to his waiting squadron. Warren thought, I'd better be getting over to tell George Johnson what's going to happen. He took a last look through his binoculars at the hills which were the Ravi Lancers' objective. The shape of a building on the left hillock caught his eyes, and he said, 'Wait a minute, Yuvraj ... that's a shrine.'

'Not a temple, sahib,' Bholanath said, peering under a shading hand.

'No,' Warren said, 'I can see from the architecture that it's Muslim.'

These people are Hindus, he thought. In Ravi a Muslim would have no rights against a Hindu ... would probably be imprisoned and tortured, as was the rule in Kashmir, if he were found slaughtering a cow—even his own cow; but this was British India. He said, 'I think you'd better not occupy that left hill, Yuvraj. I'll tell the other umpire why not.'

'Thank you, sir. I'd never thought of that,' the prince said. He's very young really, Warren thought as he rode away. The uniforms and rank badges and manoeuvrings were a sort of grown-up Boy

35

Scouting to him, and in that world he was efficient and almost mature; but force him out of the make-believe, bring up something real, like a people's religious susceptibilities, and he showed how naïve he really was. He was a nice young man, a lot in him, and willing to learn. One could only hope that increasing age, wealth, idleness and lack of responsibility would not turn his eager energy towards profligacy and self-indulgence.

Half an hour later Warren was at George Johnson's side when the latter told the colonel of the 8th Brahmins that his battalion, marching in column of route, had come under heavy rifle fire from the low hillocks now close to his right front, and had lost fifty men. On the colonel's order the infantry scattered and took cover. Slowly the colonel—a formal old gentleman due for retirement—sent for his company commanders and laboriously began to make a plan. An hour later runners and flag-waving signallers had finally got the news through to brigade headquarters, and an hour after that Brigadier-General Roland Vernon Rogers, MVO, cantered up in a fine rage. The general was thin, baldish, and tallish, an ex-British cavalryman with large private means, which he had devoted to the wholehearted pursuit of orders, decorations, and medals. He had a slight limp, wore a monocle and considered it a great slight that on reaching general rank he had been given a brigade of infantry—*Indian* infantry at that. He was known throughout the army as Rainbow Rogers, from the rows of bright ribbons on the left breast of his tunic. Not one of them had been earned in action. He leaned down from the saddle now and called, 'What's happening here? What's all this about enemy fire?'

The Brahmins' colonel pointed out the hillocks and explained that he was going to attack to clear them in twenty minutes' time. The artillery was already ranging. Meanwhile they were under heavy and accurate fire from about a hundred rifles.

'You, too, sir,' George Johnson said to the general.

The general said coldly, 'I'm the director of the exercise as well as commanding the troops. Don't be impertinent. What's the meaning of this, Bateman? How can any enemy have got there?'

'They swam the Ravi twice and marched most of the night, sir,' Warren said.

The general was peering through binoculars. 'I don't see anyone on the near hill.'

'No, sir, I told Major Krishna Ram to keep his men off that

because it is mostly covered by the grounds of that old Muslim tomb and shrine you can see from here.'

The general stared coldly at Warren. 'What nonsense is this? Either they occupied the hill or they didn't.'

'In theory, sir, they ...'

'I am not interested in your theories.' He turned on the Brahmins' colonel: 'You attack right away.' He looked at George Johnson. 'They will succeed with no more casualties. And you—' he glared at Bateman—'can tell your rag, tag and bobtail that they've lost twenty men from artillery fire. And the same number of horses.'

'Sir,' Warren said, 'the horses are well down the reverse slope, and it's a battery of 18-pounders in support of the Brahmins here.'

'What's that got to do with it?'

'Only howitzers can hit the horses, sir. The 18-pounders will either burst on the crest or go well over.'

'Don't try to tell me what the guns can do,' the brigadier-general snapped, 'get back up there and pass on my orders. *Orders*, Bateman!'

'Very well, sir,' Warren said, saluting. He mounted his horse and swung away at a canter. Damned old fool, he thought. He's upset because he's been outmanoeuvred, and because Major-General Glover was somewhere in the offing, inspecting the exercise. Still, the Yuvraj's force had held up the British advance for over two hours, and if they didn't waste time now they could still rejoin the rest of the regiment in time to attack and with luck wipe out the sole squadron of British cavalry, which was by now totally isolated from infantry and artillery support. He urged his horse fast up the slope. Krishna Ram was waiting for him over the crest of the hill, binoculars in his hand.

'I think we have killed the general several times over,' he said, grinning.

Warren found himself grinning back. 'Yes, but he's immortal for the duration of the exercise ... You've been under ranging artillery fire for ten minutes, and now they're firing concentrations. You've lost twenty men and twenty horses.'

The young prince said, 'And I can see the infantry coming out of the scrub jungle down there.' He turned to his trumpeter. 'Blow fire and retire.'

A ripple of blank rifle fire swept along the crest, then the cavalry-men ran down the back slope, swung up into the saddles of the patiently standing horses, took their lances out of the rifle buckets and slipped the rifles back in, then cantered away, led by the Yuvraj. By the time the leading infantry reached the hill tops they were a mile to the north, drawing rein on the far side of a squalid village.

'That was a good gallop,' Krishna cried.

'For you,' Warren panted. 'All of us don't have thoroughbred hunters.'

Major Bholanath cantered up and touched his fingers to his forehead. 'Prince, it is unwise to halt here even for a moment. We are still in artillery range and the observers will be up on the hills back there by now. We are in full view.'

'Extended order,' the Yuvraj cried to his trumpeter. 'Trot!'

The two squadrons shook out into a single long line, three files deep, and trotted on across the fields. Rainbow Rogers would say that the artillery was inflicting heavy casualties, if he could see this, Warren thought, but he can't. Fifteen minutes later the squadrons reformed threes, still at the trot.

'Captain Bateman ...'

He awoke from a reverie. The Yuvraj was saying. 'We're having a guest night in our mess tomorrow night. I'd be honoured if you'd come as my guest.'

Warren hesitated, trying to remember whether there was any function he ought to attend in his own regiment. The Yuvraj said quickly, 'We eat Indian style, but there is always European food for Colonel Hanbury.'

Warren said, 'Unless your *khansamah*'s a lot better than ours, I'd prefer Indian food. In any case, I accept with thanks.'

'Oh, good! Of course, we don't really have a mess when we are in Basohli, because nearly everyone is married and lives in his own house, with his family ... like the Guards in England, Mr. Fleming told me ... but on manoeuvres we have one, because my grandfather is very keen that we should be as much like a regular regiment as possible.'

Warren lit his pipe and the Yuvraj a scented Egyptian cigarette. They rode on side by side in companionable silence.

Warren heard the strains of *The Mikado* long before he reached the huge marquee which was the Ravi Lancers' officers' mess. He whistled softly under his breath, for only one regiment of the regular Indian cavalry had a band. These Ravi people not only had a band, it was playing the European music very well. He whistled again when he passed the last row of sowars' tents and came in view of the open sward in front of the marquee, where the band was playing, for they were dressed in full dress of gold and white, their bandmaster wearing gold sash and gem-encrusted sabre. Deep armchairs of leather were scattered over the thin grass at the edge of the grove nearby, and a score of lanterns, hung from the boughs or set on standards, cast a golden glow on silver and crystal and the huge plastron badges of the dozen mess orderlies and a pair of lancers in full dress standing as sentries to either side of the marquee entrance and officers standing in little groups or sprawled back in the chairs, glasses in hand.

Corelli of the Brahmins came up alongside him and muttered, 'Good God, how on earth did they bring all this stuff out here?'

'You saw the elephants and the bullock carts,' Warren said. 'Are you a guest, too?'

'Yes, Colonel Hanbury invited me. He's a friend of my father's.'

They went forward together. As they came out into the light the Yuvraj stepped forward, hand outstretched, followed by Colonel Hanbury. Warren briefly stood at attention and said, 'Good evening, sir.' He relaxed. 'Evening, Yuvraj. You fellows know how to make yourselves comfortable, don't you?'

'What will you have?' the prince asked.

'Oh, a chota peg, please.'

The prince passed on the order in Hindi to a waiting orderly, ordering a lemon and soda for himself. They stood a moment, talking to Colonel Hanbury and Corelli. The drinks came and Warren sipped his as he glanced about him. Everyone except the band and the sentries was wearing blue patrols, the simple high-button tunic and tight trousers strapped over mess Wellingtons that were worn in the evenings in camp. All but Corelli the infantryman wore on each shoulder a large patch of chain mail, with coloured cloth backing—yellow for Ravi Lancers, scarlet in his own case. The Yuvraj wore heavy gold aiguillettes on the right shoulder and a miniature gold sunburst medal hanging from a yellow and white ribbon. Noticing Warren looking at them, he murmured apologetically, 'I'm ADC to my grandfather. And this is the Royal Order of the Sun of Ravi. We're supposed to be descended from the sun, you know. My grandfather insisted on giving it to me when I

39

came of age ... I'd like you to meet some of our officers. Major Bholanath you know from the exercise.'

'Yes,' Warren said, with a smile, 'and, to my cost, on the polo field.'

He shook hand after hand. The names were a blur to him. A few had characteristics already distinguishable to him. This one was Sher Singh, the pansy. This spectacled one, Himat Singh, let his VCOs argue over the allotment of tents. This fat one, looking more like a *babu* than an officer, was the quartermaster. They all spoke English, some not too well—notably old Bholanath, who mangled it terribly and interspersed it with Hindi and Pahari words. Then the band struck up a new tune and Colonel Hanbury guided Corelli into dinner, followed by the Yuvraj and Warren, the rest of the officers strolling behind, talking animatedly.

As he entered the marquee Warren suppressed another whistle. The mess table was polished mahogany, thirty feet long and groaning under such an array of silver and gold as he had never seen except once when dining in the mess of a very old and rich British battalion. He saw at first glance that the plate was not the accrual of decades and centuries, as in that case, but all given at once, probably by the Rajah, in order that his Lancers should not feel like poor relations. Down the centre of the table there were peacocks in silver, elephants in gold, several statuettes of lancers in full dress, a silver gun, goblets, chalices, bowls and vases. Corelli, sitting opposite, caught his eye and almost imperceptibly winked. They sat down.

While Colonel Hanbury and his guest ate through six European courses—soup, fish, entrée, roast, sweet, and savoury—the rest were served with spicy tidbits of meat, egg, mountains of savoury rice, vegetables, curried chicken, and sweetmeats done up in silver foil. Sherry, white wine, red wine, champagne, port, madeira, and brandy followed each other in ritual procession. Some of the Ravi officers drank a great deal, some none at all. All ate with the fingers of their right hands, some gracefully and some coarsely. The band played European music on the grass outside. At one end of the marquee, behind the president's chair, a pair of lances were crossed over a large photograph of the Rajah of Ravi, garishly hand-coloured and ornately framed. In the wrinkled old face, under the jewelled turban ornament, Warren recognized features similar to Krishna Ram's—the same wide level eyes and hawk nose and firm chin.

40

Round the table the talk was in Hindi and English, animated in the former case, stilted and desultory in the latter.

After dinner, when toasts had been drunk to the Rajah and the King-Emperor, everyone straggled out on to the grass again. An elderly lieutenant, who bore the unmistakable stamp of having been a rissaldar of the regular service, belched appreciatively as he walked by. An hour later, after a couple of brandies and sodas, Warren said to his host, 'I'd better be off to my charpoy now, Yuvraj. It's been a delightful evening ... By the way, did you ever find that sowar, Mangla Ram?'

The Yuvraj nodded. 'They found his body six miles downstream, this morning. I'm going to ask my grandfather to give his widow a pension.'

'Oh, wouldn't she get it anyway?'

'We have no pension system. They are awarded as the Rajah thinks fit. It's all rather *kachcha*, I know—' he spread his hands deprecatingly— 'but it's the old-fashioned way, and my grandfather won't have anything else.'

'You're lucky,' Warren said. 'If Mangla Ram had been one of ours we'd be holding courts of inquiry from now till the rains to establish whether he died as a result of military service or not, and who should pay for the lost and damaged equipment ... Well, I hope we'll see some more of you during the manoeuvres. You did Rainbow in the eye yesterday and he'll be after your blood. Look out! ... Good night.' He turned to Colonel Hanbury, sitting a few feet away with Bholanath and Corelli. 'Good night, sir.'

'Good night, Bateman.'

Warren walked away out of the circle of light. The band was playing Indian music and a drunken officer was dancing to it. The sowars were singing softly to the music in the lines, where regularly spaced hurricane lanterns marked the end of each row of tents. A dismounted lines-sentry brought his lance to the salute as he passed. It had been an interesting visit to another world, or rather, to an organism trying to belong to two worlds. He ought to invite the Yuvraj to his own mess for something—a drink at least. But Krishna didn't drink. Dinner, perhaps—though there were those in the regiment who would not take kindly to seeing any Indian sit at table with them, prince or no. He'd have to think of something, because the Yuvraj seemed to realize that for Warren the goal was to have a fuller, deeper appreciation of India and Indians—not the other way round.

The lights were on in the 44th Lancers' mess and he saw some figures through the opened flap of the marquee, but he turned aside, being in no mood for horseplay or horsetalk, went to his tent, where his orderly was waiting for him, undressed, and lay down on his camp bed. Another two-day exercise tomorrow. Then a short one. Then the ride back to Lahore. See the family off. Individual training. Stables. Furlough to England. Secunderabad. Squadron drills ... He fell asleep, yawning.

August 1914

THE ROAD ARROWED north between a double avenue of mango trees. Prince Krishna Ram forced the open car down it through mud and half-dried puddles as fast as the engine would take it. The steady screech of the klaxon, worked continuously by the orderly sitting beside him, made oxcart drivers turn round and stare, perched high on their carts, and hurrying women to step off under the mangoes, their necks supernaturally erect under the loads they carried on their heads. Far behind, journeymen and tinkers, harlots in curtained carts and loin-clothed men carrying a plough on their knotted shoulders, stepped back into the road and trudged on, the hurrying car already forgotten.

The sun was a glaring yellow disc to the left, sinking into the flat fields beyond the Ravi. It was the time of the monsoon and though it had not rained here for three days, heavy rain had fallen in the mountains and the river ran full and brown, swirling in its wide bed. Krishna looked at the gold watch on his wrist, as he had done every ten minutes for the past ten waking hours (for the watch was new), and saw that it was six o'clock. He should be in Basohli by seven. He trod harder on the accelerator. Then he'd have to change before he could present himself to his grandfather. Light grey trousers, a white shirt, tie, and jacket of the new sunproof material, were certainly much more workmanlike than Indian costume, but grandfather didn't like it, and it also made one sweat more on a day like this—it must have been over 100 when he left Lahore, and though the passing of the hours had blunted the edge of the heat, he had sweated and mud had caked on him and he felt rumpled and unclean. 'A good cold shower will make a new man of you,' as Mr. Fleming used to say. He pressed the Daimler's accelerator against the floor boards, and the speedometer crept up to sixty miles an hour. This is life, he exulted silently—speed, and the prospect of war!

A dozen chickens burst into the air like a bomb of bursting feathers from under the wheels. The young man cried out involuntarily, and looked back over his shoulder. He saw four racing chickens, and one bundle of white feathers in the road. 'It is nothing, lord,' the orderly beside him said, 'they have plenty of chickens.'

But Krishna pressed on the brake and brought the car to a standstill. 'Run back, Hanuman,' he said, 'and bring the owner of the chickens to me. I'll pay her.'

The orderly got out of the car, grumbling, flicked dried mud spots off his ornate yellow tunic and turban and walked back down the road. A woman ran out of a hut, picked up the dead chicken by its neck, and hurried forward, her other hand outstretched. 'Murderer!' she cried, 'villain, robber of widows! The apple of my eye, the most valuable of all our hens, a great layer ...'

'Quiet, woman, quiet!' Hanuman said. 'You are lucky. Your chicken has been killed by the august Lord Krishna Ram, Son of the Sun, grandson and heir of our Rajah.'

The woman stared at Krishna and then stooped low, hiding her bowed face behind joined palms. She crept closer, muttering, 'Maharaj ... maharaj.'

'Here!' Krishna felt in his pocket and gave her an eight-anna piece.

She took it and bent to kiss his feet where he had swung them negligently out of the open door and rested them on the running board. She recoiled when she saw he was wearing European shoes.

Hanuman said, 'Go, woman, and be thankful, for thou knowest the chick was not worth four annas.' He gave her a push, climbed up into the car and settled his squat form beside his lord. Krishna put the car into gear and headed north again, but at a slower speed. The sun had set. It was the hour when the world lost its edges, and the eye could not tell whether the looming mountains were nearer or farther than the village ahead, or the lone temple on the far bank of the Ravi. Krishna switched on the headlights but their beams, too, blended into the universal warmth of twilight.

Low hills began to rise on either side, and the road curved into the Ravi gorge below Basohli, his grandfather's capital. He drove slowly through a village, its mud houses set under a cliff along the bank of the great river, among tall trees. Women at the water's edge covered their faces with the ends of their saris as they saw the car approach. Men made low salaams when they recognized the Rajah's yellow livery in the front seat, bowing to the dark-skinned servant in his yellow splendour rather than to the pale-skinned young man at the wheel, who might have been a European. They don't see many English here, Krishna thought; the English go up to Dalhousie and Bakloh to the east or Sialkot to the west, but this road leads only to Basohli ... and what would any English-man want there? Woodsmoke from the evening cooking fires touched his nostrils, and drifts of it trailed like blue scarves across the road. A line of cattle plodded out from among the houses, and Hanuman said sharply, 'Careful, lord!' Krishna sighed, and slowed still more. The cattle were sacred, of course. His poor country would never rise until the people outgrew such superstitions. Even here in the rich foothills of the Himalayas there were more cattle than the land could support. Yet it was forbidden to kill them. Only last week his grandfather had had the right hand cut off a Muslim villager who had been found to have killed a calf and secretly eaten it on some ceremonial occasion, with his family. Superstition ... dirt ... poverty ... disease ... and yet the people so good, so kind. It frightened him to think that one day soon he would rule them. Better to die in battle, for in truth he did not understand the people as his grandfather did.

He fell to thinking of how he should approach the Rajah to get what he wanted. Grandfather was very old—seventy-eight—and very old-fashioned. He couldn't speak a word of English and he could barely read or write Hindi. Sometimes he was cruel and sometimes he was kind. It was impossible to tell what he was going to do because he didn't act according to a definite set of rules, like the English did. It was important not to let him make the wrong decision at first, because although it was not impossible to get him to change his mind, it was not easy. Krishna's goal was difficult, but worthwhile. There was a great opportunity for the State. There was a chance for glory, and for his grandfather's army to outstrip the armies of all other States in experience and efficiency. As for himself ... his thoughts wandered, to London, to tall-funnelled ships, to the ocean he had never seen, to Buckingham Palace and the King-Emperor, a cricket field intensely green, with huge gasometers at one end, just like Mr. Fleming had told him about, and men in Free Forester and I Zingari blazers, here and there a dark blue county cap. And the women, so pale, lovely, aloof ...

Yellow lights began to prickle the dark, the hills fell back and the city spread out ahead, sharp-edged on the left by the black void of the river. He passed the maidan and the twinkling row of lights in the cavalry lines the far side. What excitement there would be over there if they could know what he was going to propose! For a moment he thought of driving across the maidan and telling the quarter-guard the news, whence it would spread in a flash all through the regiment; but Colonel Hanbury would be offended, and in any case it was not settled yet. He must get to his grandfather as soon as possible, for fear another State forestalled Ravi with the same offer.

As he drove slowly into the heart of the city he heard the thud of drums and the wail of chanters and hillmen's pipes. The clash and clink of leg ornaments grew louder under the music, and he remembered that it was the Feast of Vishnu, the ancestor of his race, and the creator of the river and the kingdom. As a child he had loved those feasts and festivals, with the steady shake of drums all through the night, and the flash of women's bangles in the light of the oil lamps, and the red glow of fires reflected in the dancers' faces; but since growing up he had come to think them a little barbarous, surely a waste of the people's time and energy, as much as the fantastic sums a father had to spend on the marriage of a daughter—enough, often, to entail his land to the moneylenders for three generations. Surely his grandfather could do better things for the people than pay for all these musicians and tumblers and dancers and acrobats?

He was about to drive the car round the edge of the square behind the mass of spectators, when he noticed that a great peacock feather fan was waving under the yellow awning that had been erected by the palace gates. That meant his grandfather was there, watching the dancing. He'd better not take the time to bath and change. He stopped the car and told Hanuman to take it into the palace courtyard and unload and unpack. Then he walked round behind the milling people and went in under the awning.

The Rajah of Ravi squatted on a pile of huge cushions, two men slowly fanning him. He was wrinkled, pale skinned, a little stooped forward even in the squatting position, his knuckles swollen where his hands rested on his knees. The three vertical red stripes of a

46

follower of Vishnu were painted up his forehead, and his mouth, lips, and tongue were stained dark red with betel juice. Even as Krishna came forward, passing among the courtiers and followers squatted on the carpet under the awning, and in front of the women in their separate section, the old man accurately spat a stream of betel juice into a brass pot beside him. Then he saw Krishna coming and cried, with a cracked smile, 'Aha, here comes the Young Sahib.'

Krishna knelt and touched his hand to his grandfather's ankle, and then to his own forehead, in obeisance. He said eagerly, 'Grandfather, there is ...'

'Wait, boy, wait! Sit beside me here and watch the dancers. It is the Mahabharata.'

Krishna knew then that he would have to contain himself for a time. The Mahabharata was his grandfather's favourite story—as indeed it was of most Indians—and when the tale was being recited or danced he would always be present. In fact, Krishna could have guessed it was a performance of the Mahabharata as soon as he saw the peacock feather fans.

He squatted down beside the rajah, glad that the British officers he had been playing cricket with in Lahore could not see him now. The ability to squat, they seemed to think, was something an Indian was born with, but no Englishman could ever achieve. He turned his attention to the packed earth of the square, surrounded by a white and brown and red wall of people, which swayed to show that it was human. Above the continuous light tap-pause-tap of the hand-held drums he distinctly heard a distant roll of thunder. 'God be praised,' his grandfather muttered. 'We need the rain.'

They were dancing the long scene of the Bride's Choice. He recognized one of the dancers, whose hands and face were dyed dark blue, and who wore an ornate crown on his head, as the demi-god Krishna, avatar of Vishnu, for whom he himself had been named. They were near the end of the scene, for Krishna appeared only at the end. Various suitors had failed to bend the great bow, and then Karna had succeeded, only to be refused permission to shoot because he was thought to be the son of a mere charioteer, not of royal blood; then kings and princes had tried to bend it and instead had been knocked over backwards by its recoil; and mighty Arjun, the Achilles of the epic, disguised as a Brahmin, had bent the bow and shot an arrow—and only then came dark

47

blue Krishna, beloved of women, to swing around and around the beaten earth while the singers squatted in a row facing the awning and drummers pounded their drums with the flat of their hands and the pipes droned and the dancers' feet thudded.

The singers chanted the tale in Sanskrit:

Krishna knew the son of Pandu, though in robes of Brahmin dressed;
To his elder Baladeva thus his inner thought expressed:
'Mark that youth with bow and arrow and with lion's lordly gait.
He is helmet-wearing Arjun! Greatest warrior mid the great,
Mark his mate, with tree uprooted, how he meets the suitor band
Save the tiger-waisted Bhima none can claim such strength of hand!
And the youth with eyes like lotus, he who left the court erewhile,
He is pious-souled Yudisthir, man without a sin or guile
And the others by Yudisthir, Pandu's twin-born sons are they.
With these sons the righteous Pritha escaped where death and danger lay.
For the jealous fierce Duryodhan darkly schemed their death by fire
But the virtuous sons of Pandu 'scaped his unrelenting ire!'
Krishna rose amidst the monarchs, strove the tumult to appease,
And unto the angry suitors spake in words of righteous peace.
Monarchs bowed to Krishna's mandate, left Panchala's festive land,
Arjun took the beauteous princess, gently led her by the hand ...

The dancers moved to the side, the music died. The crowd stretched and shuffled. The tale of the Bride's Choice was over. Next would come the Imperial Sacrifice, but first there would be a pause—half an hour, perhaps more—while dancers and musicians refreshed themselves. The next spell would last two more hours. All around the square, men squatted against the walls of the houses, relieving themselves. The women were doing the same in the darkness under the palace wall, behind the awning. Krishna felt glad that Miss Bateman had not been able to accept his invitation to visit Basohli. She wouldn't have said anything, of course, but he knew what she would have been thinking.

'Grandfather,' he said, 'I have something important ...'

'Tch, tch, boy, I don't want to hear about it now. The Imperial Sacrifice is one of the best parts of the story. It's a favourite with our people.'

48

Krishna knew that, and knew why. The next part of the Mahabharata began with Arjun, who has won the beautiful Draupadi, returning to his mother, together with his four brothers. They tell the mother that they have won a great prize; before they can tell her what it is or what they mean, she says, 'Enjoy it in common'. The command of a mother must be obeyed, and so Draupadi becomes the wife of all five brothers, not merely of Arjun who won her. The reason it was popular in Ravi was that in the upper regions of the kingdom, where eternal snow swept down to rolling grassland 10,000 feet above sea level, all the brothers in each family did indeed share one wife in common. Looking across the square, Krishna saw a dozen of these Paharis (hillmen), easily recognizable by the homespun wool of their clothes, the rope wound around their waist, the red-bronze Mongolian tint of their skin and the high embroidered caps the women wore on top of their heavy tresses. That was another thing he was glad he didn't have to explain to Miss Bateman—how five brothers could bow down before one woman, share her body, and obey her without degradation to their manhood; for among the Paharis, land and flocks passed only through the female line.

His grandfather had been following his glance and now said, 'Perhaps we should marry you to a Pahari, Krishna. They are good stock, strong and healthy. And beautiful. See that one there, staring at you so proud and haughty. Ai, if I were twenty years younger I'd have her brought to my couch. Why don't you?'

Krishna laughed uneasily. It was barbaric to treat women like cows to be brought to the bull. He said, 'I don't want to share my bride with Hari and Gopal,' naming his younger brothers.

'Of course, you wouldn't have to,' the rajah said, 'we'd find a family where more than one girl had survived. There are some, if they're born at the lucky season.'

Krishna nodded. Among the Paharis girl children were put out naked on the ground for the first twenty-four hours of their life. Most died, leaving the few who survived to be the brides of the men. A girl born at this season, August, was more likely to live than one born in December, when a foot of snow covered the high pastures. More barbarism ... indeed the British treated it as murder, where it was practised in British Indian territory, such as Bashahr.

The music began again, hesitant, gradually picking up volume and confidence. The crowd came back and squatted dense around

49

the square. Thunder boomed louder to the north and lightning began to flicker along the mountain rim. Krishna settled down to watch the dance of Draupadi, won by Arjun but eventually becoming the chief wife of Yudisthir, the eldest son and heir to the kingdom. In spite of himself, he became absorbed ...

His grandfather stirred, 'Now, boy, what is it that you have to tell me?'

Krishna realized with a start that the music had ended. Great drops of rain were falling on the square and the crowd was thinning. Thunder grumbled close around the city. He shook himself out of the glade, where Arjun was marrying Krishna's sister, and the banished brothers were wandering through the forest, and said, 'Can we talk in private, grandfather?'

The rajah struggled to his feet, helped by his attendants. 'An affair of state, is it?'

Krishna nodded and the old man said, 'We will go to the temple, then. The Rawal will be there and I won't have to explain it all to him again, afterwards.'

Krishna said, 'Very well, grandfather.' Inwardly, he groaned. Why did the old man have to consult the Brahmin on everything? What did Brahmins know more than anyone else, at least from the mere fact of being born to Brahmin parents? It wasn't as though a man could *make* himself a Brahmin by educating himself. The rajah was old-fashioned, but there was no way of changing him now.

Krishna followed him out into the rain, along the palace wall and into the shelter of the temple. The Rawal, the chief Brahmin of the temple, came forward to meet them, palms joined, under the whitewashed entrance. Inside, dim oil wicks burned in shallow earthenware dishes, casting a yellow light on the paintings of demons and the daubs of bright colour where offerings of spices lay in front of carved stone figures of gods and demi-gods. The shadows of many-headed, many-armed dancers flickered on the ceiling among the blackened patches made by centuries of smoke from lamps set in the niches among the heavy-lidded gods and the heavy-breasted Apsarases.

The rajah led the way to a dim lit room, where a stone phallus of black stone rose out of a quoit of the same stone. Orange turmeric dusted the knob of the phallus and garlands of broken flowers lay on it and around its base. The three men squatted. There was no door to the low opening behind them, but Krishna knew that no one would come and no one would listen. His grandfather looked at him and he began to speak, using words he had carefully rehearsed on the long drive from Lahore.

'Grandfather! Rawal! As you know, England declared war on Germany yesterday ...'

'We know,' the rajah said. 'The Agent to the Governor General sent me a telegram.'

Krishna said, 'The Viceroy is declaring war on behalf of India. An Indian Expeditionary Force is to be sent to France. Part of that force is to be the Hindustan Division.'

'They'll leave enough troops in the country,' the rajah said. 'Or bring more in before anyone could organize properly.'

Krishna shook his head, shaking off his grandfather's ridiculous idea. He continued. 'Every infantry division contains one regiment of cavalry. The divisional cavalry of the Hindustan Division is the 44th Bengal Lancers. Last night, I learned in Lahore that the 44th Lancers have discovered anthrax in two squadrons. They will not be able to go.'

His grandfather said, 'The better fortune for them. War in Europe is a cold, bloody, brutal business.'

Krishna said, 'I don't know for certain, but the British officers I talked to seemed to think that there was no other regiment available. Every cavalry regiment in the country, British and Indian, is committed to some important role and cannot be taken off it.'

The Rawal, sitting tall and thin and dark, all dressed in white, said, 'My lord Krishna, are you suggesting that ... ?'

'Yes!' Krishna cut in. 'Let us offer the King-Emperor our Lancers for imperial service! It is the best regiment in all the States Forces. The Military Adviser said so after last cold-weather inspection, didn't he? He said it was better trained than some regiments of the Indian Army. He said to me, privately, that there were only three regiments among all the armies of all the princes of India fit to be ranked with the regulars, and our Lancers were the best of those three.'

The rajah said gloomily, 'When I employed that old English colonel, I thought I would just be convincing the British that *we* would do nothing against them ... You are mad, boy! Why should I send my people off to be killed in a British war thousands of miles away? I don't even know or care where France is ... or

51

Germany. Our problem is not the French or the Germans, but the British.'

'Grandfather,' Krishna said earnestly, leaning forward, and realizing suddenly how strange and out of place his trousers and tie and jacket looked against the Rawal's *dhoti* and *kurtha* and the rajah's white robes, with the grains of rice sticking to the painted stripes on both men's foreheads, 'we have trained our Lancers to be the equal of the Indian Army. India is threatened, and we ought to be fighting beside the British. We are soldiers, after all. How can we *truly* compare with the Indian Army if we sit at home, filling our bellies, while they are fighting a real war?'

'You mean that afterwards we will be able to take on the British on level terms?' the rajah said, ruminating. He shook his old head angrily. 'You are being ridiculous, grandson! I have seen my father and my cousins bayoneted to death by British soldiers, on that square outside the palace! There is no more sense in fighting them than in fighting the smallpox. The way to survive is to stay away, keep quiet, out of sight. They will pass, like all plagues, in the wisdom of Brahma.'

'I do not think we should *ever* fight the British,' Krishna said. 'I think we should learn from them. Why is it that they can rule India with 800 officials? And the British soldiers outnumbered two to one by Indian soldiers? It is because they have a superior civilization. We are backward and ignorant. We will always remain in subjection, and will deserve to, unless we learn from them, and improve ourselves. But if we don't fight beside them, they will continue to look down on us. If we do, they cannot refuse to give us what we then will have earned—greater freedom to rule ourselves.'

'One cries war, another peace,' the Rawal said, 'it is like the Mahabharata.' He began to chant:

Ponder well ye gracious monarchs, with a just and righteous mind,
Help Yudisthir with your counsel, with your grace and blessings
*   kind,*
Should the noble sons of Pandu seek his right by open war,
Seek the aid of righteous monarchs and of chieftains near and far,
Should he smite his ancient foemen, skilled in each deceitful art,
Unforgiving in their vengeance, unrelenting in their heart?
Should he rather send a message to the proud unbending foe,
And Duryodhan's haughty purpose seek by messenger to know?

52

The chanted Sanskrit died away and the rajah lowered his palms, which he had joined together to listen respectfully.

Krishna said, 'Yes, but Rawal, when Krishna went to Hastina, there was no war. Now there is. The choice has already been made. It is only a question of whether we act nobly or ignobly, whether we stand by the British, or let them suspect that we are not really their friends after all.'

'I don't see why we should pretend to be their friends,' the rajah said. 'Their vassals, yes. Perhaps they are better overlords than the Germans would be. Certainly better than the Muslims were. But friends? No, no!'

'Highness!' Krishna said. 'I am your grandson. The Lancers are my regiment. I want to take them to war. I will not be able to hold up my head if I do not. Grant me what I ask, I pray.'

'Ah,' the old man said slowly, 'the young warrior wants to win his spurs. And what if you are killed?'

'I have brothers.'

The old man cracked his swollen knuckles and winced. He stared, unfocused, at the darkly looming phallus. 'And my people ... some, many will die. For what? So that their young rajah can prove himself? That is a worthy object. But, to help one lot of barbarians conquer another in a cold land across the forbidden Black Water? No, no!'

'It will only last a couple of months,' Krishna said. 'The officers in Lahore all say it will be over by Christmas. If we don't go at once we'll be too late ... *We have eaten their salt!*' He leaned forward urgently. He knew that would tell, for trueness—not to the spoken or written word, but to hosts, to guests—was a cardinal principle of his grandfather's view of life. Thunder crashed close, shaking the temple and making the dancing shadows waver on the curved ceiling.

'I suppose so,' the rajah said heavily. 'When the Agent set me on the *gaddi* out there, on the very spot where I had seen my father killed, he looked into my face, and, as clear as any message written on parchment, I saw what he did not say, for it was written in his cold blue eyes, *If you forswear this allegiance, the bayonets are ready for you, too.*'

'The rajah is a man of peace,' the Rawal said.

The rajah shook his head. 'I am not. I am a man of fear. That is different. I am terrified of the British, as a man is terrified of rabies, more than of the rabid dog. They are to be feared for what they carry in their hearts and minds. What all Europe carries, I think. Blood. Hate. Something infectious, and fatal. It is not the war that I fear, but the exposure of my people to that fatal disease ... Rawal, what advice do you give us in this matter?'

The Rawal said, 'The speech I quoted just now was made in Virata, when Yudisthir and his brothers were deciding whether to fight or to negotiate for the return of the kingdom which Duryodhan had usurped from them.'

Lightning lit up the outer room and glistened for a moment on the silent phallus. Krishna looked at the ceiling, trying to contain his patience. Why did Indians spend such time going circuitously round and round the point, bringing in old fables and legends that had no more truth than the *Odyssey* and the *Iliad*, and no more relevance to the questions which had to be answered, the decisions which had to be made?

The Rawal said, 'They decided to send an envoy to Hastina, to the court of Duryodhan, to find out his intentions. Peace, or war. Destruction, or preservation.'

The nipples of an Apsaras seemed to move on the wall and Krishna's young loins stirred.

'That is our situation, lord rajah. The war that has been declared is not our war, and we have no need to take part in it. But there is a deeper struggle, between Christian, European ideals which have been imposed on us by force, and our own ancient ways and beliefs.'

'Some of us do not need to be forced to accept the foreign way,' the old Rajah said, with a half-smiling glance at Krishna.

'True, sire,' the Rawal said, 'in any case, four methods are prescribed for us to follow in any such struggle or dispute. The first is *sam*, that is, dialogue, negotiation, discussion. We cannot hold the discussions necessary for *sam* here in India, for we are in a subordinate position and they are not their true selves. Let us therefore send an envoy to them. As the kings sent an envoy from Virata to Hastina, let us send an envoy to Europe. An envoy of the same name—Krishna.'

Krishna said, 'You mean, you agree? That we should offer our Lancers for the Indian Expeditionary Force?'

After a pause and a suppressed sigh the Rawal said, 'Yes, Highness ... but our motive will not be to help the British defeat the

54

Germans, but to aid India in this other struggle I was talking about ... a struggle which is taking place inside you, particularly, Highness, every moment of every day.' He turned back to the Rajah: 'Sire, as I was saying, the first method tried should be *sam*. Let the Yuvraj, as India's envoy, live among the Christians in the heart of their civilization, asking, seeing, observing, discussing, loving ... if he can. At the same time we will be carrying out the second method laid down in our philosophy, the method of *dan*, for surely the act of sending him and so many men to France, as hostages, is a gift, an appeasement.'

The rajah shifted comfortably, while Krishna tried hard to contain his impatience. The rajah said, 'Very good. What of *bhed*?'

The Rawal said, '*Bhed* ... creating a rift in the enemy camp, so weakening him and thus making it difficult for him to win by force. Again, I think that the sending of the Yuvraj, and the regiment's loyal service in the war, will create this rift. They will ask themselves—Can Hindus really be inferior, as we have believed for so long? Is it not only justice, our own justice, to let them go their own way? How can we hold down and despise those who have volunteered to stand up at our side? Can their civilization, which has its own values but is also able to live and fight by ours, really be dismissed or suppressed? ... Questions such as these, asked in the Christian camp, will carry out the method of *bhed*.'

'And *dand*?' Krishna said with sarcasm, 'am I to start killing Englishmen if *sam*, *dan*, and *bhed* fail?'

'It may come to that, Highness,' the Rawal said equably. 'As you know, *dand*—physical force—is only the last resort. Your love of and admiration for European ways will ensure that you, at least, will not resort to physical conflict unless you feel that you have no other recourse ... though I cannot promise the same of all the men who will be accompanying you.'

'I can't imagine that situation coming to pass,' Krishna said shortly.

'I can,' his grandfather said grimly. 'You are young. There are matters beyond your present imagining. I fear that this war will show them to you in a terrible guise. That is the worst thing about your embassy. You will leave here a young man, happy, unscarred ... and come back old, older than I ... So be it, then.'

Krishna said, 'Will you please send the telegram at once, grandfather? There isn't a moment to be lost.'

The old man said, 'We'll have to think of terms—pay, pensions of men killed or wounded, compensation . . .'

Krishna said, 'I suggest that we ask for exactly the same terms as the Indian Army. It will save much time.'

'Very well,' the rajah said. 'Help me up, boy . . .' He embraced his grandson suddenly, and Krishna was surprised to find the old body shaken by a silent sobbing. 'Vishnu preserve you,' the rajah muttered. 'May Vishnu bring wisdom and truth to your soul . . . Your mother told me she wanted to see you as soon as you came back.'

'It is late, sir,' Krishna said doubtfully.

'Not for her,' the rajah said. 'Go, boy, lest worse befall—'

Krishna made obeisance to his grandfather, joined his palms to the priest, and hurried out of the temple. It was raining hard now, pools of water lay in the dark square, lashed by the rain, and the lamps at the palace gate flickered in their niches. A sleepy guard admitted him and he ran down the narrow corridors to his widowed mother's door. He called, 'Mother, it is Krishna. You wanted to see me?'

She answered at once. 'Come, son.' She was talking almost before he was through the door. 'Where have you been? What dangers on the road in that devilish machine? Did you win the ca-ricket? How many rupees did you spend in the Hira Mandi?'

Krishna laughed, hugging her. 'There, mother, now be quiet a moment. Yes, we won the cricket. Dayal Ram is bringing our team back by train to Pathankot tonight. They ought to be here tomorrow. *He* visited the Hira Mandi, of course, but I did not, at all. I took an English captain to tea at Faletti's. Captain Bateman. I met him and his sister in January. And we're going to the war!'

'What war? What are you talking about, son?'

'War in Europe. Grandfather is offering the Lancers to join the Indian Expeditionary Force to France.'

'Oh,' his mother said. She scratched her chin thoughtfully. 'You've been meeting English women, eh? That will lead nowhere. We don't want you marrying a European, like the Holkars. And you didn't go to Hira Mandi? That Fleming Sahib put such puritanical ideas into your head that it'll take some sensible Indian woman half her life to suck them out again. The Young Sahib, that's what you are! Aiiih, my son twenty-seven and not a father! When are you going to get married again?'

'When I fall in love,' Krishna said, 'but there's no danger of that just now. I have more important matters in my mind.'

He had been married as a child to the daughter of another ruling house; but the girl had died of smallpox a week before the marriage was due to be consummated, on Krishna's sixteenth birthday.

'Bholanath's granddaughter,' his mother said thoughtfully. 'She's seventeen now and very pretty. Healthy and strong, too. That's good stock. A cousin of yours, of course, but that's no harm.'

'Mother, I must go.' He kissed her, stopping the flow of words in his embrace, and slipped out while she was still talking.

Hanuman, out of his splendid livery now, lay asleep across the doorway of his room. He rose silently as Krishna touched him with his foot, and said, 'Lieutenant Pahlwan Ram was here. He said one of the dancing girls says she is in love with you. He will send her here if you want her.'

Krishna said, 'I'm tired. And if I didn't take a girl in the Hira Mandi, why should I take one now? Pahlwan ought to know I don't like that kind of love.'

As Hanuman went on ahead of him, yawning and lighting the lamps, Krishna said, 'That will do. I'm going to sleep now ... Do you know, we may be going to France to fight in the war?'

The squat orderly said, 'Whom do we fight?'

'The Germans.'

'Are they white or brown or black?'

'White.'

'Ah. That'll be the first time I ever fought a white man. But my father fought the English in the Great Mutiny time.'

'I know, Hanuman. Go now.'

The orderly shambled out, his long arms swinging, and Krishna heard him lying down again on the mat outside the door. He began to undress. Mr. Fleming looked seriously at him from one of the silver frames on top of his chest of drawers. At the other end of the chest there was a picture of Ranjitsinhji raising his cap to the crowd after scoring a century for England; the picture was autographed by the great cricketer himself. What would *they* think of one of his captains offering him a dancing girl? Well, Ranji must have been brought up in similar circumstances, but Mr. Fleming would be very unhappy. Mr. Fleming had been insistent about the respect due to women, even the most humble, and about the sin of treating lightly what should be a deep, rare emotion.

He got into his pyjamas and climbed into bed. How long would it take the Viceroy to reply? How long after that would they be given to get the regiment equipped for overseas? He felt a pang of guilt as he remembered that he had not told Colonel Hanbury yet. He'd have to do that tomorrow. The colonel was really too old for active service, but the British would probably insist that he accompany the regiment or send another BO to take his place. He saw, in a vision, the Lancers cantering across a green field, the lances swinging slowly down to the horizontal, the steel points shimmering as the horses stretched into a gallop. At their head rode ... Krishna. The demi-god, his face dark blue. Himself.

He turned over uneasily, thinking of the conference in the temple. What would Miss Bateman think of that great phallus in the inner recess? How could she be expected to know that it was a concept of God's immanence in creation? She would believe that Indians worshipped sex, thought of nothing but sex. Superstition, dirt, poverty ... What did the Rawal mean, that he was being sent as an envoy? Nonsense! He was going as an ally. Perhaps after this the Rajahs of Ravi would get a title equal to that bestowed on the Gaekwar of Baroda: Daulat-i-Inglesiya, Faithful Ally of the British Government.

A crash of thunder shook and rattled the new glass window in its frame, and lightning blazed like white fire over Mr. Fleming, Ranjitsinhji, and the small brass statue of the Lord Krishna embracing his mistress, the graceful Radha, on the mantelpiece.

August 1914

'**N**EXT DETAIL, READY!' the rissaldar barked, and the eight sowars snapped to attention on the firing point. 'Number!'

'Detail, lying—load!' The men sprang forward and down into the lying position. The bolts clicked, the rounds crunched home. Warren Bateman, walking up and down behind the raised earth platform of the firing point, heard the buzz of the field telephone. The signaller on duty picked it up and said, '*Butts-men tayyar hain, rissaldar-sahib.*'

The rissaldar acknowledged the information with a raised hand and gave the next order. 'Five rounds grouping—fire!'

Monsoon clouds hung like bloated parti-coloured balloons over the ranges and the muddy fields and green trees that spread all round. Rain was falling on the city a couple of miles to the west and on the cantonments just behind him. Soon it would be raining here, too, and the men would be more depressed than ever. The annual course had to be fired, but Warren thought that in the circumstances it would be better to have postponed it for a time and taken the regiment out on a six-day route march, even though it would have had to be on foot. Anthrax, at this moment above all, when the division was mobilizing with frantic speed, to go first of all Indian troops to the war! And this regiment to be its spearhead, its cavalry arm to search and probe far ahead of the trudging infantry, to protect them against enemy infiltration, to be their eyes and their shield! It was a far more interesting role for the independently minded officer than service in an all-cavalry formation, endlessly practising the charge, endlessly extolling the *arme blanche* ...

And now, a hundred horses already shot and burned, the ashes buried, the others under the strictest quarantine—the 44th Bengal

Lancers had simply been wiped out as a cavalry unit, as effectively as though someone had cut the page out of the Indian Army List. The immediate fact was bad enough, seen in the context of the orders for mobilization received six hours before the outbreak was discovered; but the prospect before them was even more bleak. All the remounts available were wanted for the regiments in the Indian Cavalry Corps, and those on the North West Frontier. What on earth could they do with the men until horses were somehow found?

The banging of musketry continued. The squadron was firing badly, he noted. No good shouting at them—that never helped a man to aim or fire better. They were upset, and it showed.

A sowar carrying a silver-headed cane marched smartly up and saluted. '*Colonel-sahib salaam bholta, sahib. Daftar men.*'

Warren returned the salute, calling, '*Rissaldar-sahib, mujhe daftar-ka jana hai,*' and headed towards the cantonments. It was a mile down a dusty track and the sun was hot and the air damp, for it was nearly ten o'clock. Sweat darkened the back of Warren's khaki shirt and the top of his breeches under his Sam Browne. He wondered what the colonel wanted him for. He couldn't think of any crimes of omission or commission, but in the army one never knew. Colonels saw or imagined things their own way, according to their own rules. But it couldn't be very bad or he'd have been told to appear wearing belt and sabre.

In the outer office the adjutant rose to salute him as he entered and Warren said, 'What does the CO want me for, do you know, Rouse?'

'He'll tell you,' the adjutant said, with a half smile. 'Go straight in.'

Warren opened the colonel's door and walked in. 'You sent for me, sir?'

'Yes. Sit down, Bateman ...' The colonel sat back in his big chair behind the big desk. He was a tall burly man with a stubble of grizzled hair on either side of his broad sunburned forehead. He seemed now to be searching for words. At length he said, 'Damned if I know whether I'm doing you a good turn or the opposite but ... I've been ordered to find an officer for posting to the Ravi Lancers as second-in-command and I've selected you. You stand a good chance of getting command soon, because Colonel Hanbury must be near the age limit.'

'The Ravi Lancers?' Warren said, startled. 'States Forces?'

'Yes. The Rajah heard that we'd got anthrax and offered his Lancers to replace us as Divisional Cavalry in the Hindustan Division ...'

'I bet that was the Yuvraj's idea,' Warren exclaimed.

'Eh? I don't know, but the Chief must have advised the Viceroy to accept, because it's been done ... They're an efficient lot, as States Forces go. We all saw quite a bit of them on cold weather manoeuvres, but mind, it's what is under the surface that matters and there I expect they're what one would expect—discipline and interior economy shaky, plenty of *bhai bundi* and *baksheesh* ... and the Brahmin more powerful than the CO.'

Warren said, 'I am surprised at GHQ deciding to send a States Force regiment overseas, instead of putting them on the Frontier here, and calling down, say, the Guides to replace us.'

The colonel said, 'I agree. But frankly, I think we're laying up trouble for ourselves in sending any Indian troops to France at all. It's a white man's war, and they'll learn to kill white men. The *sepoys* and *sowars* are going to meet white women very different from memsahibs. They're going to see things it would be just as well for all concerned that they should never see. Even the most loyal of them are going to return here questioning, wondering ... Well, all that's in the future. For now I'll just give you some advice. If you don't want these Ravi fellows to run away the moment a German says boo to them ... or land you with the regimental funds embezzled ... or lie around smoking *bhang* when they ought to be inspecting stables ... or bribe the dafadars for small favours ... you're going to have to drive them, take no excuses, show no mercy, right from the beginning. These people are not *our* Indians, but the Indians as they were before we came, the Indians we walked all over at Plassey and Laswarrie ... individually brave, often enough, but idle, corrupt, self-seeking, vicious when your back's turned. Frankly, how in blazes you're going to manage it after Colonel Hanbury goes, I don't know. That's the bad side of the job. The good side is that you'll be promoted major at once, and, as I said, stand a good chance of replacing Colonel Hanbury soon.'

Warren said, 'Yes, sir.' His colonel had twenty-nine years' service, all in India. He knew the men and the country intimately; but when he joined there were men and officers still serving who had seen the Mutiny, and they had passed on their attitudes to him. India was not as simple as that. In some ways it was worse, in some better. He himself was certainly not going to treat all the Ravi officers as scum, but rather would try to find out the qualities and defects of each. It would be a wonderful opportunity to get to know a class of people the British really had nothing to do with—the educated Indians of the upper and middle class. He would get an insight into the soul of another India—perhaps the true India—an India unmoulded by British hands or British attitudes.

The colonel lit a thin cigar. When he had finished he said, 'You are to report to Basohli as soon as possible. The regiment is due to march from there on the 10th, to entrain at Pathankot for Bombay. You might intercept them on the line of march. They are being embodied into the Indian Army on the same terms and conditions as our own men. You will be given the acting rank of major, with pay, at once, and appointed second-in-command. The Ravi officers are being given powers of command, but not of punishment, over Indian and British troops.' He stood up, extending his hand. 'I was ordered to choose a major or senior captain for this job, Bateman. I chose you not because I could spare you the most easily—damn it, your going will break our polo team, if we ever play polo again —but because I think you're the best man for the job. Indian painting and Indian music are more than just children's daubs and cats' caterwauling to you ... which is all they are to me. It's going to be a difficult job. Good luck.'

Warren shook the proffered hand, and went out into the glaring sunlight. The silver-stick orderly leaped up from his chair on the veranda and saluted. Warren put on his topi and walked across the parade ground. His bungalow was just outside the lines on Roberts Road. He was living there still, but eating in the mess; and he had dismissed all the servants except the bearer, the six syces, sweeper, and bhisti, to their homes on half pay as soon as Diana and Joan and the children left in January. He was supposed to have followed long since on his own furlough, but another officer's sickness had stopped that and now ... He'd been wondering whether to stay in the big bungalow, with its four bedrooms, or move into a bachelor's quarter for the rest of the hot weather. That problem at least had been solved for him.

He patted the head of the squirming, barking Shikari, threw his topi lightly at the bearer who came out, salaaming, to meet him, and went into the drawing room. He thought of ordering a drink but decided against it. He had a lot of thinking to do, apart from the packing, and arranging for the disposal of the contents of the bungalow. He called, 'Dost Mohammed! *Nimbu pani.*'

While the bearer was squeezing the lemon, Warren thought, he'd have to leave him behind; but he'd take his orderly, Narayan Singh, if the CO would let him transfer for the duration. It would be good to have one real soldier at his side ... or his back.

He sipped the lemonade, the bearer dismissed, the fox terrier at his feet. Bees hummed outside the closed windows and drawn blinds. The punkah swung lazily in the gloom over his head, worked by the punkah boy half asleep on the veranda by a rope tied to his big toe. The regiment was going to stay here, horseless, rotting, while *he* went to war. War ... with Indians who would be much more like the Indians the British had fought a century and more ago than the sepoys and sowars of the modern Indian Army. Raised under a despotism, religion, superstition, custom would be more important to them than discipline or law. Their relationships, their whole life would be guided by persons, personalities, personal emotions—not impersonal principles.

He shook his head. He would find out all about this soon enough. Now, he must think of the immediate necessities ... but the blue envelope on the mantelpiece caught his eye. That was from his mother, posted five weeks ago, telling him that all was well with Joan and the children. Joan's own letters had become progressively scarcer since she reached England. But there had been no trouble between the women, nor with Ralph, as he had half-expected; in fact, early letters from Diana had been full of how well Joan and Ralph had got on with each other. It was not surprising, really, for they were both intellectuals. He ought to have realized that it needed someone like Joan, so unorthodox and Bohemian, to make poor Ralph forget for a moment that he was the illegitimate son of Warren's father. But now, in this letter, his mother said she had found a good position for Ralph with *Blackwood's Magazine* in Edinburgh, and that he had left to take it up. Edinburgh was a long way from Wiltshire. Pity they couldn't have found Ralph another job in London; yet Di in her letter, enclosed with their mother's, seemed to think that Ralph's going to Edinburgh was an excellent plan. Perhaps it was, for Ralph—but Joan would be alone again in Shrewford Pennel, without any intellectual stimulus, for no one could call good old Di a blue-stocking.

Joan ... the bungalow was still full of her, with her long face and long nose and distant smile, that warmed without warning; and her dresses that made the other memsahibs gasp with astonishment; and her strange unrhymed ecstatic poems in imitation of Swinburne; and her paintings that looked like nothing on earth and yet held the eye so that one was always wondering what they might possibly be; and her habit of smoking a cigar now and then (though it made her feel sick); and letting the children run about naked, without topis, and do what they wanted, and her Harz-Goldwasser Method and her Montessori System. The other memsahibs swore she was ruining the children. Well, there were more things in heaven and earth than were dreamed of by wives of cavalry officers ...

Shikari licked his dangling hand unexpectedly and he looked down to see the dog looking up at him with soft eyes, the stump of a tail stirring. He fondled his ears and thought, what's going to happen to you when I go. He might ask another officer to look after him, but for how long? It would be inhuman to put him down, fit and in the prime of his life. The dog licked his hand again and Warren thought, by God, I'll take him with me! Why not? He had never thought dogs should be taken on manoeuvres, as some of his fellow officers did, and he probably wouldn't have thought of taking Shikari to war if the regiment, his own regiment, was going and he among them. But the prospect of being alone in the Ravi Lancers suddenly made him quail. He bent down and said, 'Shikari, you're coming to France! *Parlez-vous français?*'

As he stood in front of the mirror that evening while Dost Mohammed eased him into the high-collared mess jacket with its rows of gold braid, he thought it was appropriate that there should be a regimental guest night on this his last day with the regiment— his last time for full mess kit, last days as a captain ... so many lasts. In the mirror he saw Joan's line drawing of a nude, that hung on the opposite wall. What a fury of whispering there had been over that, when the other wives saw it, as they were being led through here on their way to the *ghuslkhana* at dinner parties! It was a great pity Joan couldn't come with him to Ravi and the Lancers. She understood much about Hinduism that he could only try to. She found nothing shocking in the sexuality displayed in the temples. 'Shocking' wasn't the right word for his own thoughts about it, but he didn't know what was. 'Degrading', perhaps—for surely it was degrading to equate God with the animal functions of procreation.

64

There must be more to it than that, of course. With luck, he might learn a lot from the Ravi Lancers—at least as much as they were going to learn from him.

He went out, his one miniature medal swinging against his chest, and walked to the mess. The Oxford Fusiliers' band, lent for the occasion, was playing on the lawn and the liveried servants moved about with drinks on silver trays. The rain had passed, and mosquitoes whined around the oil lamps set on high stands. Through the open doors of the dining room he could see the shining mahogany table and the silver trophies and the damask napery set in lotus blossom shape at each place. He had seen it all so many times before, but this was going to be the last time—for how long? The band was playing selections from *The Yeomen of the Guard* and the guests were beginning to arrive: the major-general commanding the district, the Commissioner, officers from other regiments of the garrison.

The Roast Beef of Old England! They sat down to dinner and the sherry was passed. Soup and more sherry. *The Merry Widow.* Fish from Karachi, packed in ice, and sent up on the Sind Mail, with white wine. Meat, tough lamb and roast potatoes, with champagne. *Floradora.* Dessert. More champagne. Savoury, angels on horseback, Port, sherry, madeira.

'Mr. Vice, the King-Emperor.'

Scrape of chairs on stone tiles. Raising of glasses. Port sparkling red, bright against the lamps. The mess dafadar at salute behind the president's chair. The servants in a row against the wall, all at attention.

'Gentlemen, the King-Emperor.'

God Save the King. Drink. Hesitate. But to throw the glass over your shoulder had been forbidden ten years ago as a waste of money.

General Glover was still on his feet, his glass raised. 'Mr. President, I offer a toast. To victory!'

The president rose again. 'Mr. Vice—victory!'

'Gentlemen—victory!'

This time the word, *victory*, rumbled along the table, and the general himself was the first to throw his glass over his shoulder. It smashed against the wall and the pieces fell tinkling to the floor. Twenty glasses followed with a sound of crystal bells.

In the anteroom Warren found himself sitting next to the Commissioner, who was wearing white tie and tails, the collar of the Star of India around his neck.

'I hear you're going to the Ravi Lancers, Bateman,' he puffed. He was fat and bald, with shrewd sharp dark eyes. 'Have you ever served with Rajputs?'

'No, sir ... But I thought Ravi was a Dogra state.'

'Dogra is a purely geographical term. The people who live in that area are of various castes. The men you are going to serve with will call themselves Rajputs. Are you looking forward to it?'

Warren said slowly, 'Yes, sir. I think so. It's not going to be easy. My CO wonders whether it's really wise to send any Indian troops to France, and I suppose that would apply even more strongly to States Forces.'

The Commissioner said, 'I know what he means, but there's a more subtle danger than that. A danger to the Indians. In exposing them to the power of alien gods, if you like. The gods of Europe do not speak Hindi. They have nothing in common with the gods of the *Mahabharata*. The right sacrifices and mantras may not work there. The men will feel isolated, out of their depth, alone. They will need comforting more than disciplining.'

An interesting idea, Warren thought, and different from what his colonel believed. The Commissioner said, 'If I may venture a word of advice, Bateman, I would go slowly, go cautiously. React rather than act. We civilians have to deal with the Indian more as he is, less than with what we can make him, than you do in the army. We have learned that methods which will work with Englishmen, won't necessarily work with Indians. It's what outsiders would call deviousness, but often it isn't devious, it is just ... Indian. They have their own ways of thought, you know.'

'Yes, sir.'

'Well, I thought it would do no harm to mention it ... So you are going to do battle under the walls of Troy, with Lord Kitchener as Achilles and the Kaiser as Hector. I wonder what would represent Helen in this modern *Iliad*?'

Warren said, 'Belgium, I suppose? ... I have thought it's more like the *Mahabharata*.'

'Oh,' the Commissioner said, surprised, 'you know the *Mahabharata*?'

'Yes, sir. And the *Ramayana* ... The *Iliad* always seems to me to be about a war where it will not really make any difference who

66

wins, because there's no difference between the two sides. The *Mahabharata* gives me an impression that it is not only about a war between nations, but between ideals, between good and evil, almost. More like *Paradise Lost*.'

'Yes,' the Commissioner said thoughtfully, 'and in that other war, *all* the fighters are on one side, *all* the thinkers, the questioners, on the other. So war itself is turned sideways and becomes both less tangible and more sensible. I am an old fogey and a man of peace, but I wonder, after this German war is settled, what will be left of what we were fighting for.'

'It'll be over by Christmas, a lot of people say,' Warren said. 'Our cavalry people—the ones who are going overseas—are afraid they won't get there in time.'

'And what do you think?' the Commissioner said, his beady eyes gleaming.

Warren said slowly, 'I think it will be long ... and unpleasant, sir. And not like anything we have been practising and training for.'

'You *are* a heretic, aren't you?' the Commissioner said. He leaned forward and lowered his voice. 'But you're dead right.'

'Victory, victory!' a young man shouted at the other end of the room, waving a brandy glass.

'Victory!' the others chorused.

'Spurs off!' a voice rose. 'High cockalorum! ... Come on! Ned, Fowler, Tommy, Rouse ... line up here. Other side there ...'

Crash, a picture fell from the wall as the line of young bodies formed up against it. A grinning mess servant ran in to sweep up the mess. All the bearers and waiters were peeping round the heavy curtains to watch the sahibs at play.

'Off with his bags ...'

'Hold tight, they're coming.'

'Go!'

The rich embroidered jackets were hurled into corners. The shirt-sleeved young men ran across the room, leaped into the air and crashed down on the other side. Sweat began to run. A chair broke. On the lawn the band was playing selections from the works of Johann Strauss.

'Come on, Warren!'

Warren put down his glass, it was the last time, and these were his friends and comrades, his brother officers, fellow Englishmen.

But it suddenly seemed childish, as Joan had always thought these mess antics were. The demi-gods and heroes of the *Mahabharata* didn't act like this when they were, so to speak, between wars: they spent their time seducing milkmaids ...

'Go on. Enjoy yourself,' the Commissioner said, raising his glass. 'The Ravi officers won't be the same at all.'

Warren took off his jacket and spurs, threw them into the corner, and hurled himself at the opposite line.

August 1914

WARREN BATEMAN SAT in the back of the jolting tonga, facing sideways, his feet propped against the awning support on the left side, his back against the support on the right, Shikari curled up beside him. The pipe tasted aromatic and fresh in his mouth, the fields were green with growing wheat, and a light rain was falling, the end of a heavy monsoon shower that had lasted half the night and well into the morning. The road stretched behind, pools of water spattered by the falling rain and long ribbons of water marking the ruts in the deep mud. With his orderly, Narayan Singh, perched up front with the *tongawala*, and their valises, suitcases, and bedding rolls under the seat, the pony could manage no more than a fast walk in the heavy going.

Eighteen miles to Basohli, still. Perhaps he'd have done better to hire a horse in Pathankot and ride, but then he would have arrived without his kit, and it was very unlikely that a State regiment would be able to fit him out with decent clothes and equipment. He'd just have to contain himself in patience. He was, after all, in India, not British India but Vedic India ... and this ancient tonga was taking him ever deeper into its mysterious heart. The villages, sprawled low in mud wall under thatched roofs, did not look different from the villages in British India, whose border he had passed an hour ago. The temples were the same, the oxen the same in the fields, the red-bodiced women the same at the wells, the wiry loin-cloth'd men the same in the crops, but there was an unmistakable air of the East, unsupervised. The milestones which, over the border, marked the miles and furlongs in freshly painted English numerals, were now marked in almost illegible Nagri, where the stones were still standing. The trees lining the road had not been trimmed for a century, and the road itself would have been a disgrace to a village track in the poorest province of the Raj, although it was one of the only two carriage roads into Basohli, the capital.

A sizeable village appeared ahead, and Warren called to the *tongawala*, 'Woh gaon kya hai?'

'Kangrota, sahib.'

He saw that the village had a large *maidan* and what looked like a *dak* bungalow or perhaps a State PWD inspection bungalow close to the road. Uniformed men were marching hither and thither about the *maidan*, and now, under the trees ringing it, he saw horse lines, and rows of tents. He had met the Ravi Lancers on the road. He called to the *tongawala*, 'Turn in here. To the *dak* bungalow.'

At the bungalow steps a couple of sowars looked at him doubtfully, and then saluted. Colonel Hanbury came out, accompanied by a tall lieutenant, whom Warren recognized as Dayal Ram, the adjutant. Warren saluted. 'Major Bateman, reporting for duty, sir.'

The shadow of a smile flitted across the colonel's thin, dour face. 'Glad to have you with us. Dayal, please see about getting Major Bateman suitably mounted, and provide him with a baggage orderly —I see you've brought your personal orderly with you.'

The Yuvraj Krishna Ram ran lightly up the steps and saluted. 'Stables ready for your inspection, sir.'

Colonel Hanbury said, 'Major Bateman's arrived ... Stay with me for Stables, Yuvraj, but afterwards take over A Squadron, as we arranged. And you'll have to give up your room in the bungalow, too. You'll be wanting to get settled in, Bateman?'

'I'd like to attend stables, first, sir,' Warren said.

The colonel nodded slightly as the Yuvraj stretched out his hand to Warren, saying, 'Delighted to see you here, sir. We were all so pleased when the colonel told us who had been posted as second-in-command.'

He stepped back and Colonel Hanbury started down the steps, the others following.

An hour and a half later Warren was in his room in the *dak* bungalow, making notes in a little book while Narayan Singh polished his belt and fixed the Ravi Lancers insignia on to his helmets and uniforms. Warren wrote quickly.

Maj. Krishna Ram—A Squadron—likeable, seems younger than his age, 27, because so eager, keen. Very English in outlook and training. Speaks and reads English perfectly. Educated at home by English tutor. Excellent cricketer.

Maj. Bholanath—C Sqn—50—Rajah's brother. Old type Rajput, tough, stubborn, can barely read or write. Very capable. Will have trouble with administration in Europe, and with complicated plans and orders.

Captain Himat Singh—B Sqn—35. Nervous, unsure, poor power of command. Educated Lahore University, BA.

Captain Sohan Singh—35—Quartermaster. Fat, greasy, wears glasses. Little English. Son of Basohli merchant. Probably shrewd, possibly crooked.

Captain Sher Singh—D Sqn—28—Relative of Rajah. Educated Lahore University, failed BA. Good looking, big mouth. Very polite. Hand holder. Worse?

Lt. Brian Flaherty—Signal Section—35—Big, powerful, green-eyed, red hair, half-caste (son of Pahari woman and ex-sergeant telegraph official). Chip on shoulder.

Lt. Dayal Ram—Adjutant—29—Tall, handsome, probably a lady-killer. Not well educated. Very athletic, naturally good at all games according to Krishna.

Lt. Mahadeo Singh—38—CO's galloper—an ex-rissaldar of Hodson's, retired as no vacancy for rissaldar-major for him, and joined Ravi L. Typical old type VCO. Experienced but uneducated. Poor English.

Lt. Pahlwan Ram—Intelligence Offr—27—Relative of Rajah. Dark, ugly, slight squint. Drinks or dopes or both.

2/Lt. Ishar Lall—A—19—Fine looking youth. Knows nothing but seems willing to learn. Also distant relative of Rajah. Has small scar on chin which is only way of telling him from his twin brother ...

2/Lt. Puran Lall—B—otherwise they're indistinguishable in manner and appearance. Cheerful young scoundrels.

Regimental Medical officer—not arrived yet.

He closed the notebook and put it in his breast pocket. They were superficial notes, he realized, made after only a few minutes of conversation and observation, but he had to begin somewhere. Tomorrow he'd start on the VCOs. It was a great pity there was no rissaldar-major at the moment. The previous one had been much respected, according to Krishna Ram, but he was sixty. The Rajah had wanted to send him on active service, but the Government of India had insisted on posting a rissaldar-major from the regular army to replace him, and this man hadn't arrived yet. It would be a disaster, Warren thought, if the newcomer were not an outstanding personality. The VCOs here were a good lot, better overall than the officers, but they lacked a true disciplinary sense. They were too much like elder brothers to the sowars, not their leaders and overseers, responsible for everything they did and did not do.

He was wondering what the men would be doing at this time, when there was a knock on his door. He called, 'Come in.'

Krishna Ram entered, saluting. 'A game of *kabaddi* is just starting, sir. I thought you might like to watch.'

'Thanks, I would.' He got up and began putting on his Sam Browne.

'Oh, don't worry about that, sir,' Krishna said.

Warren said, 'An officer's either in uniform, Krishna, or he's not.'

'I'm sorry, sir,' Krishna said. 'I'll get my belt.'

'It would be better,' Warren said.

The young man ducked out, returning a minute later wearing his belt and sabre. Warren sighed. As they weren't going on parade with troops they didn't need to wear sabres. Well, one thing at a time. 'I'm surprised you haven't organized a cricket match,' he said smiling.

'It's my favourite game, the greatest game in the world,' Krishna said fervently, 'but rain's spoiled the grass here, we couldn't make a pitch ... Do you think there'll still be county cricket in England next year?'

'On account of the war? I imagine so.'

'I'll spend all my leave from the front watching ... if the war's still on then.'

Warren and Krishna stood side by side for half an hour watching the men, naked except for tiny loin-cloths, their bodies oiled, run and wrestle and elude each other up and down the barren land between the horse lines and the nearest wheat fields. Clouds piling higher over the Siwaliks and a livid gleam on the remote Himalayan snows promised more rain for the night. The air was very damp, but it was not unbearably hot. The long lines of horses swished their tails in the 'stables', and sowars wandered about, singing, or squatted on the ground mending their socks, or dozed on the ground sheets spread inside the tents.

Happening to glance round at a moment of inaction in the *kabaddi* Warren noticed a woman gliding between the tents behind him. That was Regimental Headquarters, he knew. The sentry at the end of the row, leaning negligently on his lance, made no move to stop her. Perhaps she was a petitioner come to complain about the troops riding through the crops. She slipped into a tent. Warren thought it was an officer's, for it stood a little apart. The flap closed behind her. Warren turned back.

Women in the lines was a matter that could easily come up in France. He'd better find out from Colonel Hanbury what his policy was on such things.

The game continued. Warren began to light his pipe. A sharp crack in the air over his head made him duck involuntarily. Immediately afterwards he heard the bang of the rifle. 'What the hell ... ?' he began, then another bullet cracked over his head, but closer. The *kabaddi* players had hurled themselves on the ground or were racing for the shelter of the trees. Krishna Ram was flat on the ground beside him. He saw then that in the middle of one of the rows of tents a man with a rifle was taking aim, apparently at him, Warren, across the *maidan*. He was about a hundred and fifty yards away.

'Stop!' Warren shouted. *'Banduq girne do!'* He felt no fear. The man was trying to kill him, but as he didn't know him he could have no real intent. He was drunk, or doped, and would not be able to see very straight. He put his pipe in his teeth and walked firmly across the ground, over the prone *kabaddi* players. Shikari trotted at his side, ears pricked.

'Drop, sahib!' a prostrate figure called up to him. 'He's gone mad.'

He advanced. Another bullet smacked by, then the man ran forward, to get closer. He was swaying as he aimed. The bullet cracked so close that Warren imagined he could feel the wind of its passage. Shikari barked angrily and darted forward. From the corner of his eye Warren saw men running behind the tents to take the marksman from behind. Then he was almost looking down the muzzle of the rifle, and into the man's enlarged red pupils. He snapped in Hindustani, 'Put that rifle down! Attention!'

Slowly a look of puzzlement came over the man's fuddled face. Slowly he lowered the rifle. Warren realized that Krishna Ram was at his side. Men appeared among the tents, led by a lance-dafadar from the quarterguard with levelled rifle.

'Wait,' he commanded them. 'You ... attention, I said.'

The man placed the butt of the rifle by his bare foot and stood at attention, swaying.

'Why were you shooting?' Warren demanded.

'Sahib ... I don't know ... I thought ... I saw the enemy ...'

'*Bhang*,' Krishna said disgustedly, naming the popular North Indian type of hashish. 'I can smell it on his breath.'

'Put him in close arrest,' Warren said. 'Tell the adjutant to see that he comes before the CO tomorrow.'

'Yes, sir ... You were marvellous, sir! I've never seen anything so brave, just walking slowly up to him with your pipe in your mouth. You gave me the courage to get up and follow you.'

Warren said, 'I knew there wasn't much danger ... By the way, whose tent is that?' He indicated the tent inside which as far as he knew, there was still a woman.

'Dayal Ram's sir. The Adjutant.'

'Tell him about the shooting, now, then.' He walked away. Now Krishna would burst in on whatever was going on inside the tent; and then perhaps he, Warren, would learn what the Ravi Lancers did about officers making love to village women at four o'clock in the afternoon in the middle of camp.

As he neared the *dak* bungalow he saw a heavily loaded tonga struggling through the mud of the driveway. Two Indians, one fair and one very black, both in uniform, sat in the back. The tonga stopped in front of the quarterguard, the horse's head hanging. The travellers climbed down. The fair Indian called to the quarterguard commander, '*Dafadar-ji*, where's the adjutant-sahib's office?'

By then Warren was close enough to see that the speaker wore the crowns of a rissaldar-major. The black Indian wore a baggy, ill-fitting uniform and the three stars of a captain: an Indian captain would only be in the Medical Service, so this must be the new Regimental Medical Officer. He walked forward, saying, 'Can I help?'

The black captain turned slowly, looked Warren carefully up and down, as though he were a specimen to be put under a microscope, and then saluted in an ungainly and grudging fashion.

'I am Captain Ramaswami, Indian Medical Service,' he said. 'I am a specialist in gynaecology and working on many important research projects in Madras—important for the women of India—when I was posted to the military side for this European war—which is of no importance to anyone in India.'

Warren introduced himself, thinking that the man was looking for trouble. The sooner they got him back to his gynaecology, the better. 'Were you trained in India, doctor?' he asked.

'No. At St. Mary's Hospital, London. I am FRCS and MRCP.'

The other man was ten years older, and had probably been very slim when younger, but he was thickening now and there was a little bulge under the faultlessly polished Sam Browne belt. The buckle of the belt was a big silver plaque bearing the cipher of Queen Victoria and in raised metal letters the word GUIDES. He saluted briskly and said, 'Rissaldar-Major Baldev Singh, IOM, sahib, reporting for duty.'

Warren said, 'I see you are from the Guides. Were you their rissaldar-major?'

'No, sahib. I was senior rissaldar. My rank dates from yesterday, with this regiment.'

The adjutant, Lieutenant Dayal Ram, came running up. Warren noticed that he had done up his tunic one button awry. He said, 'About the shooting, sir ...'

'Later, Dayal. See that these officers are properly taken care of, and introduced to the CO.'

He turned on his heel and all except the doctor saluted. He went up into the *dak* bungalow. Now, he thought, we are complete. It remained to turn this collection of human material into a proud and war-worthy regiment of Indian cavalry. He pulled out his watch and saw that it only lacked quarter of an hour to durbar time. Durbar—an informal gathering of the regiment to air grievances and discuss whatever came into mind—was an old Indian Army custom. He was glad to see that the Ravi Lancers observed it.

As he strolled across the maidan he saw that the sowars were already gathering. It was with a small shock that he realized they were all wearing uniform. A durbar was a non-military gathering and normally everyone wore mufti. But, of course, they were on active service now, and no one had any plain clothes, except the suitcases which each officer was allowed to take in the baggage, full of civilian clothes and sports gear. It could not be helped, but he missed the comfortable sense of a family conference which plain clothes gave—the loose white shirts and wrinkled tight-fitting trousers, some men with flowers behind their ears, others wearing garlands round their necks. Some of the men here were wearing garlands, he saw, even though in uniform; also many wore *tilaks*, caste marks, painted on their foreheads—something which was not permitted in any regular regiment. But why not? There was no reason why a caste mark should have an adverse effect on a man's efficiency or courage—rather the reverse.

He saw the officers gathered under a tree at the edge of the grove, and went to join them. Colonel Hanbury came down the *dak* bungalow steps and walked across. As he arrived the six hundred men, who had been squatting on their heels, rose to their feet. All made *namasti* towards him, with joined palms.

The colonel said, 'Rest, lads.' The men again squatted and made themselves comfortable, while the officers and VCOs leaned against trees or sat on chairs that had been brought from the *dak* bungalow. Shikari lay down at Warren's feet and rested his head on his paws.

Colonel Hanbury began to speak in slow accurate Hindustani, with little feeling for the language, but perfectly plainly: '*Jawan-log*, I will introduce to you the new officers who have come to join us for the war. Major Bateman ...' he glanced at Warren, who took a few paces forward. 'Major Bateman has come to us from the 44th Bengal Lancers, to be our second-in-command. He is a very good polo player, and has served in Burma and on the North West Frontier. Do you want to say a word?'

Warren said, 'I am proud to have been chosen to serve with this regiment, and look forward to going into action with you.'

The colonel said, 'Captain Ramaswami, IMS, is our RMO. He is from Madras, but trained in England to become a doctor.'

The captain said in English, 'I do not speak Hindustani. My native language is Tamil which none of you here will understand. I did not ask to be sent here, as I am a specialist in the diseases of women. However, now that I am here I will look after you as best I can. My second specialty is the study of Vedic medicine, and if anyone wishes to be treated in the ancient ways, I will do so in order to continue my researches.'

Warren noticed the colonel's frown, and thought, well, why not? If a man wants Vedic treatment, why should he not have it? Why should western ways be forced on him against his will?

The colonel said, 'Here is our new rissaldar-major. Rissaldar-

76

Major Baldev Singh, IOM, from the Guides. He lives at Mirthal on the banks of the Beas. Like you, he is a Dogra Rajput.'

The RM stepped forward. 'I am the rissaldar-major,' he said in a quiet voice, that yet carried. 'I have twenty-six years' service with the Sirkar. I have been wounded once and awarded the Indian Order of Merit. I am *your* rissaldar-major. You will uphold my honour before the *sahib log*, and I will uphold your caste and faith and honour before the world. Any man may speak to me of a cause affecting his honour at any hour of the day or night, but if it touches upon any other man of the regiment he who wishes to speak shall first tell that other that he intends to speak to me. Such is my word.'

He stepped back. The men had hung on his words intently, Warren noticed. The old RM, who had been replaced, had apparently been a tremendous character, and there was nothing harder than to follow such a figurehead at a time of stress, such as now. But this man had a calm confidence, a power that compelled without domineering, that were most impressive. They had been lucky after all, for there was no more important post in the regiment than rissaldar-major.

The colonel said, 'Now ... who wishes to speak? ... You. It is Darshan Ram, is it not?'

'Yes, sahib. Of B Squadron. I have served the Rajah faithfully for thirteen years. I am a marksman and have no punishment on my record. Yet for six years now I have been passed over for promotion. Yesterday my nephew was promoted lance dafadar in A Squadron. My face is blackened.'

The colonel glanced at Himat Singh, who said, 'There is no disgrace ... we cannot all be promoted ...' He seemed nervous, Warren thought. He would do better to say outright that the man did not have the temperament for command, or whatever was the reason. 'Your chance has not gone. You may still be promoted. You are considered whenever there is a vacancy, as is everyone.'

A man in the crowd said, 'It is right that a man's years should be taken into account. We are not babes, to be commanded by boys.'

'Nor by ancient blockheads,' Krishna Ram cut in. The men shuffled and hissed approval, and the colonel said, 'Next ... Gopal.'

'I am Dafadar Gopal of the Signal Section. We are going to Fer-rans to fight for the Sirkar and the King-Emperor. That is good. But we will be among heathen, who know not our gods, and might have no respect for our ways. It is in my heart that we might be given improper food, and there will be no redress. Also that we will be unable to perform prayers and ceremonies in the appointed manner. We are Rajputs, Kshatriyas all, and it lies heavy on my heart that we may return unclean, though we go now pure in our faith.'

There was a murmur of agreement, and Warren said, 'Sir, if I may ... We will be in a division with Sikhs, Mahrattas, Gurkhas, even Brahmins, we shall not be treated differently from them.'

The rissaldar-major stood forward. 'My sons, I have told you, your honour is in my hands, and mine in yours. Save in one matter only, nothing of our law and customs shall be transgressed without agreement in durbar. That matter is—victory. We are soldiers. Our *Pandit-ji* will agree that when it is victory or defeat that lie in the balance, then no law or custom shall prevail except that which leads to victory. For we have eaten the Sirkar's salt.'

Again the crowd of men murmured, but this time as though chanting a low *Amen* to the RM's words.

Next a tall man stood up, palms joined, and said, 'Sowar Daulat Ram, C Squadron. The Lord Vishnu came to me in the night, and bade me give away all that I own and meditate by the banks of Holy Ganga for the next twenty years. I have spoken to the major-sahib asking for my release.'

Old Major Bholanath said, 'And I bade you speak up in durbar that we may all know whether it is the god that calls you, or the war that affrights you.'

Warren listened intently. This you would hardly hear in a regular regiment, and certainly not when the regiment was actually on its way overseas.

Daulat Ram spoke earnestly to the men around him, his hands spread beseechingly: 'I am not afraid, friends. You know me. I was happy as a sowar. My wife and children know nothing of this. But the god has spoken and I must obey.'

'Let him go,' one called, and another, 'He is giving up his pay,' and another, 'Even if it be that he has no stomach for the war, let him go. We would not want his comradeship.'

The colonel listened a few moments longer and then held up his hand. 'You may go, Daulat Ram. See the adjutant tomorrow ...'

Another man stood up. He had just received word that his father had died in the hills and he must go back at once for the burning, and to look after the land, but he would send his brother, who had served five years in the regiment, to take his place ...

Next, there was a rumour that the regiment would not receive *batta* as they were not Sirkar's troops. Was this so?

Could the sowars be allowed to go barefoot when on stable sentry at night as they were much more comfortable that way than in army boots?

'Also,' the fat Quartermaster broke in seriously, 'it will save wear and tear on the boots, which will last longer.'

The men chuckled at that one, and the colonel said, 'Stable sentries may go barefoot as long as we are in India. But not once we land in France. You must remember that there it will be cold and wet much of the time. Also, we will be wearing thick serge uniforms, that are to be issued us when we reach Bombay, together with all our other war equipment ... Next?'

It was over at last, and the sun had set as Warren walked back to the *dak* bungalow at Colonel Hanbury's side. The colonel said, 'A good durbar on the whole. These men need to be handled differently from ours, Bateman. They see no British police, commissioners, soldiers, and of course our law does not run here.' He shook his head, 'I hope General Glover does not insist on too much ...' He did not finish his sentence. He went on, 'As soon as you have had dinner, please get all the particulars of our entraining strengths, baggage weights, and so on. Tomorrow, early, ride to Pathankot to prepare for our entrainment, with the railway authorities. We shall arrive the day after tomorrow.'

He turned into his room, looking tired and old, as Warren saluted.

Late August 1914

WARREN LOOKED DOWN the row of officers seated at a
long table in the officers' dining saloon, nodded at Krishna at
the other end, and began his talk. 'Very well, gentlemen. This is
the ordinary way a table is laid for dinner. Take the glasses first.
The small glass—this one—is for sherry, which is served with the
soup. Then this ...'

The troopship rolled steadily north westward. Warren spoke on,
thinking, most of them know all this already and even if they don't,
why should they be forced to comply with our customs? They were
grown men, part of a civilization considerably older than the European. But yesterday, Brigadier-General 'Rainbow' Rogers, the senior
officer on board, had seen Lieutenant Mahadeo, the ex-rissaldar,
eating rice with his hand, and had told Colonel Hanbury to get his
officers house-trained without delay. They were taking it very well,
thanks mainly to Krishna Ram's attitude—all except Flaherty, the
Anglo-Indian, who was staring with a surly mien at the empty
plate before him, his head bowed.

'... Take up knife and fork, like this ... Not like a dagger,
Ishar Lall, more like a pencil ... Try it, Flaherty.'

'I'm not a *desi*, sir,' the big man said sullenly. 'I know how to
use knives and forks.'

'I'm sure you do,' Warren said, 'and so do other officers here.
Now please join us in our little exercise.'

He smiled slightly and Flaherty picked up his knife and fork with
an ill grace. Warren thought, why is it not possible to work out
behaviour proper to *Indian* gentlemen and see that the officers con-
form to that? Old Bholanath was muttering in Hindi, 'This is a
silly way to eat ...'

The prince broke in sharply, 'You must not speak Hindi at table, uncle. Otherwise those of us who are not fluent in English will never become so.'

'I'm sorry, Yuvraj,' the old major said sweeping up his moustaches. 'I am as stupid as a water buffalo.' He spoke in Hindi.

Captain Sher Singh leaned across the table and said officiously to Puran Lall, 'You should eat, even pretending, with the mouth *closed*, like Major Bateman-sahib showed us.'

'Yes,' Krishna Ram said, 'but although the VCOs and men use the word "sahib" of us, we do not use it of ourselves.'

'Very good, sir,' Sher Singh said obsequiously, half bowing. Warren had noticed the slip and decided to speak to Sher Singh about it privately; but Krishna couldn't stand the fellow, and now that Warren had known him for three weeks he could see why. Sher Singh, besides being effeminate, was a man who said yes sir, no sir, you're marvellous sir, to your face, and the opposite behind your back. He and Pahlwan Ram were the problem officers of the regiment.

The SS *Nerbudda* ploughed on up the Red Sea. The temperature was 105 in the shade and the humidity 99 per cent. The *Nerbudda*'s speed through the water was eleven knots, which was precisely the speed of the following wind. The black smoke from the single funnel hung in a dense pall over the ship, cutting out the sun without reducing the heat. The hot-weather drill uniforms had been handed in at Bombay, and cold-weather serge issued. The results were so intolerable that even General Rogers, however grudgingly, had had to give permission for all ranks to appear in shirt sleeves at all meals and parades except officers' dinner at night. Even so, large dark stains showed where everyone round the table was sweating, though the fans whirled noisily overhead.

The lesson in table etiquette finished, Warren said, 'Now, gentlemen, we have a more delicate subject to go into ... how to use the WC. If you'll follow Major Krishna Ram to the officers' bathroom section on the main deck he'll explain why. Carry on, Yuvraj.'

The officers filed out, Flaherty frowning and Mahadeo looking guilty. Warren lit his pipe and sat back, wiping his forehead. The reason for this embarrassing and insulting interlude was that an officer of the Royal Oxford Fusiliers, who were also on board, had complained that he had found one of the lavatory seats covered with shit. It was assumed that a Ravi officer was responsible, for were they not used to squatters? Was it not known that in first-class trains even educated Indians climbed up on to the seat and squatted there, often missing the bowl in consequence? After receiving the general's order, Colonel Hanbury had talked it over with Warren and Krishna and decided to leave the explanations to the latter, as it would come better from him. It probably was Mahadeo, Warren thought, who had perhaps never even seen a seat-type lavatory, for Krishna had told him there were none in Ravi, not even in the palace, because his grandfather would not permit it. So now the officers were being shown how to defecate, and even to urinate, like Europeans. He prayed that none of the Fusilier officers would chance to go to the bathroom section while the lesson was going on. They found the 'black sahibs' funny enough without giving them more fuel for their prejudices.

Shikari stuck his head round the open door of the saloon. Warren pointed the stem of his pipe at him and said, 'Out!' The head quickly withdrew. He's just trying it on, Warren thought. He's intelligent enough to know that this is the dining room, where he's never allowed. He was a bit of a nuisance on board, to tell the truth, what with the little special kennel that had to be made for him, the arrangements for his litter, the difficulty of exercising him.

Warren got up and went out, where Shikari was waiting for him. Krishna ought to be finished in the bathroom now, and then there was to be a class in English.

The colonel of the Royal Oxford Fusiliers was walking up and down the deck, his hands behind his back. He saw Warren and called him over. 'No, don't put away your pipe ... You have some playful young officers in your regiment, don't you, Bateman?'

Warren said carefully, 'What do you mean, sir?' Privately he thought, what have the Terrible Twins been doing now? The day after the troopship left Bombay they had managed to sound a false-alarm boat drill, and yesterday they had climbed the foremast and spent an hour jammed in the crow's nest with the seaman on watch, to the immense rage of the captain.

The colonel said, 'One of my officers went to sit down in his deck chair this morning, and it collapsed under him. He heard giggling nearby, and thought it was one or two of your people.'

'It might have been, sir,' Warren said. 'Do you want me to investigate?'

'Not officially, or I'd have spoken to Colonel Hanbury. I just

82

wanted to tell you privately that this officer, and others, for that matter, don't like being made fools of by black men. We are a regiment of British infantry, you know.'

'Yes, sir. But ... our people are officers, too.'

'Of course. Of course. But just see that they keep their tricks to themselves, will you? It'll be better for everybody, in the long run.'

He nodded in sign of dismissal and Warren relit his pipe, which had gone out. He'd have to speak privately with Krishna Ram about this. It was a damned shame to treat the Terrible Twins differently just because they were Indians, yet ... there it was. He himself did not quite know how to handle the problems that came up, and he was living in this new situation. How much harder must it be for a red-faced captain of British infantry, long accustomed to think of all Indians as niggers, and even of the Indian Army regulars as Black Horse or Black Foot? He settled himself into a deck chair, first looking to see that it had not been tampered with, and dozed off.

At ten that night, soon after dinner was over, he set off on an inspection of the troop decks, making each squadron commander accompany him in turn. Though it was a little cooler on the upper decks as soon as the sun went down, in the troop decks it seemed just as hot, or hotter. A swell from the port side was making the ship roll steadily. The hot metal groaned rhythmically, and with the metal, the men jammed in the hammocks, all swinging slowly to and fro in the roll. Warren crawled under the rows of hammocks, every now and then sticking his head up between them, to peer by the light of the naked electric bulbs overhead, into the face of a sowar.

'Are you all right, lad? Are you comfortable?'

'I am well, sahib.'

'Are you comfortable, son?'

'It is hot, sahib. Otherwise, I am comfortable.'

'Can you sleep?'

'I have learned now, sahib. At first, I could not.'

'Where are this man's boots, Major Krishna Ram? They're supposed to be on the deck under his hammock, with his lifejacket, in case of alarm.'

'Rissaldar-sahib, where are this man's boots ... ?'

The sweat poured down inside Warren's shirt and off his forehead. A dismal groan sounded from nearby, followed by retching and the sound of pouring liquid. 'There'll be a lot of that tonight,' he said. 'See that the men clean it up themselves, at once. You'd better get the squadron sweepers on duty, too.' To himself he thought, my God, you could cut the smell here with a knife—of digestive gases, garlic and curry farts, and the bodily odours of six hundred men compressed between steel decks barely seven feet apart.

Captain Himat Singh met him at the beginning of B Squadron's area. He was trying to hold down his queasiness, and looked pale green in the light. Warren asked the same questions, made the same points. At the end he said, 'These hammocks seem closer together than A's. Closer than when I inspected the day after we sailed. Have you got some extra men in your section?'

'No, sir.'

'What is it then?'

The pale Himat Singh looked ever more unhappy. 'It's the *gora paltan*, the Fusiliers, sir ... Their company commander said we were occupying ten feet across the deck that was properly his.'

'And you moved back?'

Himat Singh seemed to be searching for words before he finally said, 'Yes, sir.'

They were talking stooped across the body of a sower who may or may not have been asleep, the steel deck tight over their heads. Warren was furious. The bloody weakling, to let himself be bullied like that!

He controlled himself, and said, 'You were wrong to do that. It's not you who suffers, but your men. They hardly have room to breathe.'

'I know, sir ... but he was a major and he was so definite.'

Warren sighed. 'Listen ... you are not Himat Singh, an ordinary man like any other man in the street. You are the commander of B Squadron of the Ravi Lancers. Every time you speak you speak for a hundred men, who have no other voice. In whatever concerns them, speak louder, for they speak through you.'

Himat Singh hesitated a long time and then said, 'Sir ... they have spoken.'

'What do you mean?' Warren said irritably.

'They knew the extra ten feet across the ship really belongs to us, but when my rissaldar ...'

'That's Ram Lall, isn't it?'

'Yes, sir ... When he suggested I should complain to you, the

84

men said No, that the *gora log* needed the space more than they did because they were not born to the heat, as we are.'

Warren said, 'You mean you let your rissaldar and the sowars decide what to do? That's not the way to command a squadron. *You* decide, and *you* order, and *you* see that your orders are obeyed...'

Himat Singh licked his lips and seemed about to say something more, but changed his mind, except to say, 'I'm sorry, sir.'

'Well, I'll sort this out tomorrow. We can't do anything now.'

A gust of air, at first seeming like the breath of a furnace but still welcome as a change from the vomit-laden oven stillness in the troop decks, blew down the ventilator shafts. The ship was circling into the wind, and for the next twenty minutes would steam in the opposite direction, just to blow air through the hold, troop decks, and engine room. The manoeuvre was performed twice each day and twice each night, and without it many men would have died of heatstroke. Two privates of the Fusiliers were already dangerously ill from it.

Warren went on with his inspection of the squadrons. Then to the hold, heavy with the dense smell of manure and horse urine, and the stable sentries vomiting in the corners where the stable refuse was piled to be carried up long steel ladders, and thrown overboard every dawn. Then to the kitchens where the captain of the ship had grudgingly allotted some coal-burning range space for the use of the Ravi Lancers' cooks. At last he had seen every man and every horse of the regiment, and it was nearly one o'clock. He found the officers' saloon open, the blackout curtains drawn. Krishna Ram and Himat Singh were there, tall glasses beside them. He flopped into a chair at their table and ordered a chota peg.

Himat Singh jumped up immediately and said, 'I'm just going to bed. Good night, sir.' He hurried out, his head bent.

Warren stirred his drink and glanced at Krishna Ram. 'What are you having? *Nimbu pani?* On a night like this you need something stronger. Not a damned breath of air, and still a hundred.'

'Sir, I ...'

'I don't mean it, Krishna. I know you don't drink.'

'Mr. Fleming warned me very strongly about the danger of drinking, sir ... My father drank a great deal. He drank himself to death, my mother says. But ... I'd like to drink with you, sir.'

85

'Are you sure? Good. Steward, a chota peg for Major Krishna Ram here.'

When the drink was brought and Krishna had sipped it apprehensively, he muttered, 'It's not at all sweet, is it?'

'It's not meant to be. Sweet drinks are for women ... Why did Himat Singh leave in such a hurry?'

'He was telling me about the affair of the troop deck space, sir. And what he had done, and not done. He is very ashamed of himself.'

Warren drank slowly. 'He has no self confidence, that's his trouble. He seems to be incapable of acting on his own initiative. He has to find out first what everyone else thinks. That's no way to command troops, especially Indian troops.'

Krishna Ram hesitated just as Himat Singh had, at the end, in the troop decks; but he did at last find the words he wanted. 'I think it's our panchayat system. All important questions in our villages are decided by a panchayat, a council of five elders. They are advised by anyone who has special knowledge or interest, and that sometimes means the whole village. We really don't have a single village headman as you do in British India.'

Warren nodded. 'We found we had to have one man to deal with, who could be held responsible, and he had to be given authority to carry out the policy.'

'Of course,' Krishna Ram said hastily. 'I am sure that works better ... but the panchayat is what our people are used to, and it's very hard to make them change their attitudes. These things are in their minds, in their souls, sir, although they cannot easily speak about them—especially in English ... It is a hard job to change such attitudes.'

Warren said, 'We don't want to change them ... at least I don't. I can't see why it should be necessary to abolish your ways. Some of them just have to be put aside for the duration, because they don't fit into a modern army or a modern war. Afterwards everyone can go back to the old ways.'

'If we can, sir,' Krishna Ram said, 'and if we want to. We may have learned the European ways and found them better. I certainly hope so.'

'You really do?'

'Of course, sir. There is much that I would be sad to see the end of ... even panchayats ... but nothing will really change or improve until our ways of thinking are changed. Better education, for instance. Better health and more real medical care, not the old superstitions. Better care of women and babies. Sanitation, hygiene ...'

'You're right, I suppose,' Warren said, 'but when the time comes, be careful, Krishna, will you? Go slowly, or you'll pull up the flowers with the weeds ... I see that the CO's appointed you officers' censor.'

'Yes, sir, but of course I shall not read your letters.'

'I am afraid you must if you are to do your duty.'

'Yes, sir ... Have you seen Ship's Orders for today, sir? General Rogers has ordered that caste marks may not be worn in uniform. As we are in uniform all the time on board, the men won't be able to wear *tilaks* at all.'

Warren said, 'Well, there's an example for you, of what we were talking about. The general's taking another step to change the way you think. A caste mark seems quite normal to the men. To us ... I don't mean myself, you understand, but to the European ... it's a badge, announcing "I don't think the same as you".'

'And, "I don't know how to use a water closet",' Krishna Ram said, smiling.

'I suppose so. Have another drink.'

'Thank you, sir, I think one's enough for me. But I do like it.'

'Well, goodnight. I'm going to get these sweaty rags off and try to sleep.'

The young man stood up at stiff attention, and Warren thought, I must get him to relax more when we're off duty. We're supposed to be like a family then, but he hasn't quite got the hang of it yet. None of them have. Well, they're Indians, he thought, yawning mightily.

Next morning at six Warren went up to the boat deck, where the whole regiment was gathered, dense packed around the funnel, under the boats on their davits and all over the areas marked off for deck tennis and shuffle-board. The sun was a copper ball low over Arabia and the sea had died to a flat oily calm. The wind still followed the ship at just its speed and the black pall of smoke still hung overhead. On all the deck, on the canvas life-boat covers, and now on all the assembled men, there fell a steady rain of black soot.

Under a makeshift awning stretched between two lifeboats and a corner of the ship's officers' cabin structure, the regimental Brahmin sat cross-legged in white *dhoti*, and the long shirt called a *kurta*.

The officers were wearing the peaked service cap which the general had insisted they wear instead of turbans, so that they should not be mistaken for VCOs. The sacred fire burned in a small charcoal stove in front of the Brahmin. Krishna Ram was seated, knees crossed, across the fire from the Brahmin. On Krishna's right was Major Bholanath and on his left the rissaldar-major. Warren took off his shoes, and joined Colonel Hanbury on small cushions specially placed for them level with the sacred fire, but to one side.

It was the Rajah of Ravi's personal sacred day. On this day all the people of his state prayed to God to grant him long life and wisdom, and his regiment were doing the same in the burning trough of the Red Sea. The Brahmin was a fat and frightened priest from the Basohli temple, a cousin of the Rawal's. He had trembled so much as he went up the gangplank at Bombay, his palms joined in prayer and his lips mumbling mantras that Warren had thought he would need help to get on board. Now he had recovered his nerve, or become accustomed to the expanse of the ocean, or perhaps it was the service that he was engaged in, the special privilege of his caste, to communicate between men and gods; now he seemed an emanation of wisdom and calm as he began to chant a litany in Sanskrit.

Warren settled his back against a stanchion, and prepared for a long vigil. The Brahmin chanted for fifteen minutes, now and then rhythmically bowing over the sacred fire. Then a row of sowars on the other side of the fire struck up a hymn, accompanied by men beating hand drums with their palms, and the wail of a lone mountain pipe. The Brahmin started another long mumble. The deck trembled to the deep beat of the engines far below. The soot rained down inexorably from the black cloud. Two white faces appeared at the top of the companion leading up from the main deck below, stared in astonishment, and disappeared.

The Brahmin cast sugar and salt in the fire and it flared up green and yellow. He stood, and walked slowly round the fire chanting the while. He touched the foreheads of Krishna, Bholanath and the rissaldar-major with a white paste and pressed a few grains of rice on to each. Then Krishna spoke a few words, asking the men to pray for his grandfather the Rajah. Bholanath spoke, reminding them that their conduct in battle would reflect directly on their sovereign, who was descended from the Sun. The rissaldar-major stood up and called upon them to bear humility and peace in their hearts

88

even while they wielded the bow of India against the Rajah's enemies. As he spoke a distant shower moved down the western coast and for a while a rainbow, the sign of the god Indra, arched over towards Egypt above the silent sea.

Then they all stood at the salute while Colonel Hanbury and Warren went down the companion to their breakfast of porridge and kippers.

After tea that day Warren went to the first class saloon to read. By unspoken agreement the officers left the small music room on the starboard side to the half-dozen ladies on board, mostly wives of officers going home on final retirement. That left the saloon as the focal point of the officers' leisure time. In the evenings there was always one table of men playing whist and another of auction bridge. By the little bar one or two drank, and in the leather-padded armchairs, now usually dark with the previous inhabitant's sweat, some read. A gramophone was screwed on to a table in one corner, with a stack of records, mostly ragtime or Gilbert and Sullivan, in a rack below.

Warren read on, a fatuous servants' hall novel from which his attention kept straying—to images of Hindu gods—to the poor saddlery in A Squadron—to Himat Singh and how he could instil in him the drive and confidence a squadron commander needed in war—to young Krishna Ram and how he would face battle—to the problem of *bhang*, the use of which was apparently winked at in the regiment, though it was strictly forbidden in the Indian Army . . .

He hardly noticed the music at first because he had heard it so often from the lines of his regiment, or in the Lahore bazaars as he strolled about looking for a bargain, or in the evening at a nautch. It was a *raga* played expertly by *sitar*, *dol*, and drone. Glancing up he saw the Terrible Twins and Pahlwan Ram crowded round the gramophone listening to the record, which seemed to belong to the Twins. He listened appreciatively. He did not pretend to be an expert on Indian music, but Joan had taught him how to appreciate it, and this was a good tune, well played, with a very tricky beat. He let the book fall into his lap, leaned back, and closed his eyes. The music flowed over him like a river, as infinite in its rhythms.

A voice startled him, shouting, 'Turn that thing off.'

He opened his eyes and noticed, a little way from him in another chair, a Fusilier captain. It was he who was shouting at the group by the gramophone. They did not hear. The captain got up and strode towards them. He was a red-faced fellow, burly to the point of fatness. Warren suddenly realized that he must be the same man on whom someone—probably indeed the Terrible Twins—had played the trick with the deck chair. Warren thought his name was Simpson. He reached the gramophone and shouted angrily, 'I said, turn off that bloody wog music. This is an officers' mess.'

He jerked the tone arm off the gramophone, took the record and threw it on the floor, where it shattered.

Warren stiffened. Pahlwan Ram, so small, dark, and ugly he seemed to be an image of the white man's worst thoughts about India, scuttled out of the room leaving the Terrible Twins to face the furious Englishman. They looked alarmed but not frightened, as though amazed that anyone could act so rudely.

The captain said, 'Perhaps that'll teach you to play your dirty Indian tricks with British officers.'

Warren jumped up and called sharply, 'Captain Simpson!'

The electric bells by the door and at various places along the walls burst into a frenetic jangle, loud enough to drown all other sound. The men somnolent in the armchairs, or bent over their cards, or turning to listen to the argument, all jerked to their feet and for a moment held there, heads cocked like an assembly of robots first started, then disconnected in mid motion.

The steward called out, 'Submarine alarm! Boat stations!'

They all ran for the door as the ship's siren began to boom out a series of hysterical short notes while the bells clanged and jangled. Already sowars and soldiers were tumbling up on deck, lifebelts on. Warren forced his way against the stream to his cabin, his mind racing. He'd speak to the Fusilier captain. And the Twins. But now he had to check A and B Squadrons at their boat stations while the CO did C and D. Was there a submarine in this calm greasy sea, where a porpoise would be seen five miles away? Surely there were no enemy submarines in the Red Sea?

Grabbing his life jacket and fastening it as he ran he hurried back up the now empty companions to the main deck. A quick glance down the starboard side showed the men of A Squadron at ease in their allotted places, quiet, Krishna Ram and Ishar Lall strolling up and down in front and the VCOs facing the men. He hurried through to the port side. A mob of sowars was trying to fight its way into the boats now swinging down from their davits on the deck above. Farther along, a company of Fusiliers stood at ease, watching the chaotic scene.

Warren ran forward shouting, 'What the hell's this? Get back!' He began to yell in Hindustani. 'Get back! You will not get into the boats until ordered!'

He gave a young sowar a tremendous cuff on the side of the head. He saw a jemadar there, and called, 'Draw your revolver, sahib! Shoot anyone who tries to get into the boat!'

The jemadar looked astonished but did as he was bid. Warren saw Captain Himat Singh clawing ineffectually at the back of the crowd. Gradually they prevailed. The squadron took up a shaky line on the deck, well back from the rail.

Warren turned on Himat Singh like a tiger, 'What is the meaning of this? Your squadron acted like a panic-stricken mob!'

'They ... they didn't understand, sir,' Himat Singh stammered. 'They thought ... they had to get into the boats ... as soon as they were swung down.'

The ship's siren boomed a long steady note and a passing ship's officer said, 'Stand down. It was a false alarm. The lookout mistook a bit of flotsam for a periscope. No submarines around here.'

Himat Singh said, 'It wasn't their fault, sir. They ... they were not afraid. They didn't understand.'

Warren lost some of the edge of his rage. He said wearily, 'Did *you* understand that they weren't supposed to get in the boats until so ordered?'

'Yes, sir.'

'Then why in the name of God didn't you make it clear to them? You do it now, and then dismiss to the troop decks. In one hour from now I shall call a boat drill for your squadron only. And tell the Adjutant, from me, that you are Field Officer of the Week for the next four weeks running, and confined to the regimental lines.'

'Yes, sir ... Sir, will you tell the men it was not their fault, but mine. Otherwise, they ...'

'By God, I'll do nothing of the kind. You tell them. Don't apologize. Don't explain. Tell them what they did wrong, and tell them what they should do right next time. Then practise it, all day and all night if necessary.'

He turned on his heel, acknowledging the other's salute with a curt finger to his cap, and strode towards his cabin, to restow his lifejacket. An orderly met him, saluting, 'Colonel-sahib salaam bholta.'

He found Colonel Hanbury in the cabin set aside for the regimental office. The colonel said, 'I have been ordered by signal from the War Office to send two officers to London to settle details of the regiment's absorption into the Indian Army for the duration ... pay, pensions, *batta*, promotions, replacements and reinforcements, and so on. I have decided to send you and Krishna Ram. You will go by train direct from Marseilles, where I understand the division will be in camp until it is concentrated.' He nodded in dismissal. As Warren turned to go he added, 'Unless we are hurried into action, you can take a few days leave while you're in England.'

'Thank you, sir.'

Warren set off again for his cabin. What a stroke of good luck! He'd invite Krishna Ram to come down to Shrewford Pennel with him, unless he wanted to have a fling in London. But probably not; he seemed a very well behaved, even rather priggish young man.

In his cabin the pictures of Joan and the children in the leather folder smiled at him from the top of his chest of drawers. He began to undress and after a time found his anger melting. They were good people, really, but what a job he had ahead of him! He took the folder off the drawer, gently kissed all three of them in the photographs, and then went to have a bath.

September 1914

K RISHNA RAM STOOD in the corridor of a South Eastern and Chatham Railway first class coach, staring at the passing fields with an intense awareness that made him see everything with the clarity of a stereopticon. He and Major Bateman had had seats in the compartment behind them, where their suitcases still rested on the rack, but before the train left Dover a lady entered and Krishna Ram had eagerly given her his seat. She was the first English lady he had seen in her own country, and like the country itself she was all that his dreams, and Mr. Fleming, and the books, and the magazine illustrations had promised.

The fields slid by, intensely green though it was the end of summer. Surely they ought to be burned out by now, and ready for the cold weather rains. Tall trees, still rich in leaves, marched in front of bare skylines. A ploughman walked slowly towards the train behind two horses—but what horses! They were huge, stately as chestnut elephants, with heavy masses of hair round their fetlocks and mighty necks curved like heraldic beasts in some temple of the Ganges. Behind them the plough glided through the heavy loam of the land. Now a village appeared, grey stone houses, wheat-thatched, grey walls, a stream with green cress swirling under a grey bridge, a boy with a fishing rod, a pink-cheeked English boy wearing knicker-bockers and shirt and tie and bright school cap. A church steeple raised a slate finger to the clouds from a cluster of dark trees ... a school, the playing fields empty, the goal posts white against the green ... oast-houses, hop fields, orchards red with fruit. The clack of the wheels on the rail joints grew faster, the carriage swayed in long steamer-like rolls. The foreground blurred, a station passed in a stammering blur of sound and vision. Krishna Ram said, a little apprehensively, 'My goodness, we are going fast, aren't we, sir?'

Major Bateman smiled, 'About sixty miles an hour, I should think. It's quite safe. Expresses always go as fast as this in England.'

'I've never been so fast in my life,' Krishna said. He drew a deep breath of the racing air, for the corridor window was open. 'I like it ... It's exciting. Like a galloping horse!'

Soon the houses began to cluster along the line, the paired rails increased from two to four to six, still the train raced on, the exhaust beat of the engine and the clatter of the wheels flung back now by grimy warehouse and pulsing factory.

Major Bateman said, 'Nearly there now.' The train wound like a long snake round severe curves, seeming to feel its way through the maze of shining rails. A dark river appeared, beyond it scores of spires piercing the sky. Krishna recited to himself a poem Mr. Fleming had taught him:

And high over all the Cross and the Ball
And the riding redoubtable dome of St. Paul

They were back in a trench of houses and factories. Now they were rumbling out across the river. The Thames was flowing in from the sea, rushing silently up, dark and iridescent, wooden crates and boxes and bottles floating on it. The train stopped, an unsignalled cessation of motion, under a smoke-grimed glass arch. 'Charing Cross,' Major Bateman said. 'You get the suitcases down, Krishna, and I'll see if I can find a porter.'

'I can carry them, sir.'

'No, no. An officer in uniform must not carry any bags or boxes in public.'

A porter appeared, touching his cap, and five minutes later they were whirling away through crowded streets lined with massive buildings. 'This is the Strand,' Major Bateman said. 'Trafalgar Square. That's the Nelson Column ... The Admiralty Arch. Whitehall. I've told the driver to take us by Parliament Square.'

Westminster Abbey rose ahead like a dream embodied in honey-coloured stone. To the left a huge Union Jack floated over the buildings he had seen in a hundred paintings and photographs—the Houses of Parliament. Helmeted policemen at the gates were saluting tophatted men as they hurried in. Members of Parliament, they must be, rulers of the world, before whom rajahs and maharajahs bowed, kings and presidents quailed.

'St. James's Park and the Horse Guards,' Major Bateman said, as the taxi bowled along one side of a park, the green of the grass unimaginably deep, and there was a lake mirroring the trees, and ducks and swans and little birds hopping everywhere and people feeding them. Another huge building appeared on the left with soldiers marching up and down in front of it. 'Buckingham Palace.' Then there was a high wall on that side but more parkland to the right ... an arch, more acres of rolling park, to the left now, and high-nosed men and women riding thoroughbreds under the dappled shade of long avenues of trees.

The houses closed in on both sides. It was the first time since leaving Charing Cross, Krishna thought, that one side or the other had not been open to the river, or a square, or a park. The taxi stopped. Krishna sat motionless, his mind full of superimposed impressions.

'Come on, Krishna,' Warren Bateman's distant voice said good-naturedly, 'you're daydreaming.'

He scrambled out. 'I'm sorry, sir. I was ... seeing London. It makes Lahore look like a village. And as for Basohli ... !'

'It's a big place,' Major Bateman said, as they followed the hall-porter into the hotel: but Krishna was not thinking now of the size. It was not by size that England held India; it was by discipline, hard work, courage, and justice. It was not the size of London or the busy-ness of the streets that had overwhelmed him, but the sense of majesty, of ease with which this massive power was supported, of grace shown in the parks and the flower boxes.

They had lunch in the hotel and then set out for the West End. First, Major Bateman took him to his own bank to open an account there. The bank was a large-windowed building, solid, its stones dark with grime but flowers bright along the window sills. Inside Krishna wanted to step on tiptoe, for the only sound was the murmur of voices from a far place. Young men in long black frock coats leaned easily over the polished mahogany counter, and the walls were covered with portraits of His Royal Highness the Grand Duke of Something, Her Majesty the Dowager Empress of Something else, with underneath, in every case, the laconic legend *A customer of the Bank.*

'Good afternoon, Captain Bateman, we haven't seen you for three or four years, have we?' a frock coat said cheerfully, holding out his hand. 'Why, goodness me, are not those a major's badges on your sleeve? Congratulations!'

Major Bateman introduced Krishna and asked the frock coat to open an account in his name. 'He has a draft on Bombay to start it with.' Then Krishna was watching the man write easily with a quill pen on large sheets of paper, and later signed his own name, *Krishna Ram of Ravi*, in several different places.

'Is this how you will wish to sign your cheques, sir? Very good. Do you need any cash now? Twenty pounds, I suggest. An officer can't go around with no money in his pockets in England, I'm afraid, as I understand you gentlemen can in the East. A glass of sherry to celebrate ... ?'

Krishna sat in the little private room, fondling the glass. This was another dry wine, but he was getting used to them now. Wine and whisky not only tasted good, but they made everything a little easier. It was a strain sometimes, being so far behind. He felt that he was running with all his might to attain what these people had been born with, or at any rate had held so long that it had become a part of themselves. Here, where millions of pounds were being handled, so easily, so quietly, over glasses of sherry, he felt like the barbarian that this quiet man with the pince-nez probably imagined him to be.

Then it was Sackville Street and Wyricks for three sets of uniform. 'They're our regimental tailors in the 44th,' Major Bateman said. 'We think they're very good.'

The head cutter in Wyricks looked extraordinarily like the frock coat in the bank, perhaps a shade more deferential in manner yet in no way subservient. They sat in comfortable armchairs among bolts of cloth while the cutter, a tape round his neck, brought out rolls of khaki. 'This is the regular barathea of your regiment, Major Bateman. But perhaps, for active service in France you might do better with this one ... It's a whipcord, an ounce or two heavier but a bit stronger. Oh yes, quite a bit stronger. Less liable to tear on thorns and brambles, you understand ... very good. The whipcord.' He put it aside on a table and strolled off to return with another roll. 'This is the cavalry twill for the breeches. You can't get anything stronger that will hold its cut. Three pairs? ... Very good. Now perhaps I had better check your measurements, sir. It's, let's see, over three years since you were here last, I think.'

'You mean, in case I've grown a potbelly, Thompson, don't you? I think I'm in pretty good shape. I've been playing a lot of polo.'

'Indeed, sir? Quite. H'm. No change. Very good. You are to be congratulated. Now, sir ...' turning to Krishna Ram. 'And perhaps

96

a glass of sherry while we put the details into the ledger?'

Krishna fondled the glass. A great wine. Warming, and a little sweeter than the last. Banking and tailoring were run the same way here. And cricket. And war, perhaps. Then he remembered his grandfather describing how British troops had bayoneted the rest of the royal family in Basohli during the Mutiny. Of course the Tommies were the lower classes, but still ...

They returned to Paddington and their hotel and later out to dinner at the Savoy, with Krishna as host. Major Bateman said, 'I had hoped Joan would be able to come up to have dinner and spend the night—I sent her a telegram from Dover, you know—but she's just replied that Louise, that's our little girl, has a bilious attack, so she can't come.' He stowed the pink telegram slip into a pocket. 'We'll have to be bachelors.'

'That'll suit me,' Krishna Ram said. 'I am rather nervous with ladies.' He thought of Mr. Fleming's words of warning, about how fatally easy it was to go wrong with ladies, insulting them either by saying too much or too little, by being too cold or too warm—though he could not understand how a well-brought-up English lady, so cold in her chiselled beauty, could ever expect *more* than a man, in his coarseness, might offer.

They ate by an open window of the Savoy dining room, looking out over gardens heavy with the scents of late summer, the Thames flowing now towards the sea, a river of polished darkness touched by golden lamps along the Surrey shore and the lights of boats gliding upon the unseen stream. Inside, the string band played overtures and light operas during the meal, and the champagne glass at his elbow sparkled like the lights in the chandeliers and the stars spangling the women's long gowns. Their breasts and shoulders and arms were white as alabaster, and barer than an Indian harlot's, and they glided in insolent beauty down the aisles between the tables, ahead of their escorts, fur and silk half-covering, half-revealing pearls and diamonds gleaming at the cleavage of their breasts and in the gold piled on their heads.

'I feel like a boor sitting in here in uniform at this time of day,' Warren Bateman said. 'The staff aren't used to it yet, either. The head waiter had to remember there's a war on before he let us in ... Now, what shall we have? I can tell you that I'm going to order the grouse.'

After consideration, Krishna chose roast beef. Major Bateman raised an eyebrow, but Krishna said, 'The roast beef of Olde England is the best in the world, isn't it?'

'Yes. I was thinking that your grandfather might not approve.'

'I don't care,' Krishna said recklessly, 'I'm in England now ... Europe ... I have to live the European way. This is London, not Basohli.' He drank deeply from the fizzing, cold glass.

Major Bateman smiled and said, 'Enjoy yourself. I won't sneak on you ... But I'd be careful with that champagne, if I were you. It's stronger than it looks, or tastes.'

Krishna Ram nodded absently. He felt good. He wasn't worried about anything, including his grandfather. That was the secret of how the English had conquered India so easily and ruled it with so little trouble. With their sherries and champagnes and whiskies, they didn't worry.

He said, 'The only thing I'm sorry about is missing the cricket. I did hope to see Jack Hobbs bat and Richardson bowl at the Oval.'

Major Bateman said, 'The first class season's over, but if the weather holds we'll get a game. We have a Harvest Saturday cricket match at Shrewford Pennel every year. It's against Hangerton, that's the parish we're joined with. My father was vicar of Shrewford Pennel but as soon as he was dead the Church authorities abolished it as a separate parish—it's Hangerton-cum-Shrewford Pennel now. But they let my mother live on in the vicarage ... the Old Vicarage, it's called now. The vicar of the new combined parish lives in Hangerton.'

'Will I be allowed to play?' Krishna asked, his heart lifting. A hundred times Mr. Fleming had told him that village cricket, on the village green, was the core and heart of the game.

'Oh, yes,' Major Bateman said, 'there are never enough players just in the villages! The Pennels usually have a house party and their male guests form the best part of our team. This time we at the Old Vicarage will do that.' He stood up slowly, dabbing his mouth with his napkin. He was looking at someone standing behind Krishna's chair.

Krishna turned and saw a tall young woman, standing close, one hand rested easily on the back of his chair. A ruby brooch sparkled at the base of her *décolletée*, emphasizing the disappearing curve of the breasts. She wore a heavy bracelet of rubies on her left wrist. 'I'm Harriet Symonds,' she said. 'We're one man short in our party, and we ladies would prefer it to be one man extra. Would you care to join us?' She was about twenty-three, golden-haired, her mouth wide. She smiled down at Krishna and he felt a chill run up his spine. He stared at her, helpless as a rabbit before a weasel.

Major Bateman said, 'This is the Yuvraj Krishna Ram of Ravi, Lady Harriet. I'm Warren Bateman, 44th Bengal Lancers. It's very kind of you indeed, but we've just landed from India, we've been running about London all day, and really are just about to go to bed. Please do excuse us.'

'Very well,' the lady said, 'you'll be on leave again.' She was looking directly at Krishna. 'You'll find me in the telephone book. I'd love to show you London.'

She turned and strolled away, her head high, the movement of her buttocks easily visible in the tightness of the silk across them. The two men sat down. 'I've seen her name and photo in the glossy papers,' Major Bateman said. 'She's one of the leaders of the young set in London, I believe. And quite a wild one, I gather.'

Krishna said, 'Her father is a peer?'

'An earl. The Earl of Hanwell.'

'And she is allowed to talk to men she has never met before?'

Major Bateman smiled—a trifle grimly, Krishna thought—and said, 'In this country there's no way of stopping her ... Well, as we said we were leaving, we'd better do so. I'm quite tired anyway.' He hesitated and said, 'There's no reason you should come, too, you know. They only really need one man.'

Krishna said, from his heart, 'I don't want to stay here alone. I ... I feel out of my depth.'

For a time after they had gone to their rooms at the hotel, and he had undressed and lain down, he could not sleep. The city had a hum and a beat that was rather like the throb of the *Nerbudda*, but quieter, deeper—and bigger. As the ship would not—could not —swerve from its course for pieces of seaweed or sea birds in its path, so Krishna felt that the city would not—could not—swerve from its accustomed and necessary way for the sake of animals or people in its path. If you went with it, at its pace and for its purposes, then it would carry you effortlessly forward; but if you wanted to go another way, or at another speed ... what then? Before he could answer his own question a vision of Lady Harriet Symonds hung before him, its wide blue eyes staring into his own ... inviting? That was not possible! Then why had she told him she was in the telephone book? Why had she come over at all?

The champagne and brandy he had drunk gently submerged him and he knew no more until he heard an insistent knocking on the door and the key turning and the maid in black and white coming in with a tray and a bright, 'Good morning, sir, it's 'alf past eight and 'ere's your early morning tea and I 'ope you like *The Times*, 'cos that's what I've got for you.'

They spent the most of the next day at the War Office where Krishna signed a score of agreements on behalf of his grandfather, and ate dinner at their own hotel. The following morning Krishna found himself in another train.

The engine of this one was dark green and it had a deep band of burnished copper round the top of the funnel. The coaches were chocolate below and cream above. But the countryside was the same, a patchwork of meadows gliding by, so green, dotted with old mansions, churches, hamlets. The train stopped in gentle sunlight for old men to get on and young children to get off, it whistled politely down verdant valleys, and followed fat trout up a winding stream, until Major Bateman leaned across, tapped him on the knee, and said, 'You're daydreaming again, Krishna. We get out at the next stop.'

The train slowed and a platform sign passed: *Woodborough*. A tall young man of about Krishna's own age, wearing a pepper and salt tweed suit and a tweed cap, was standing at the station gate opposite their carriage. Warren Bateman got down, exclaiming, 'Ralph! I thought you were working in Edinburgh.' Krishna detected the surprise in the voice.

'I was, until a week—a couple of weeks ago. Then I left. Got sacked, as a matter of fact. I was too socialist for those feudalists up there ... This is your Rajah, I suppose.'

'The Yuvraj Krishna Ram of Ravi,' Warren corrected him. 'Krishna, this is Ralph Harris, who lives with us. My mother was his guardian.'

The man's hand was out, his eyes looking into Krishna's. He was over six feet, thin and pigeon-chested where Warren was square and sturdy, but their hands and feet were oddly alike in their gangling bigness, and the eyes, grey and deep set, were identical. Krishna thought they must be some relation to each other.

'Let's have your bags, and I'll stow them.'

A few minutes later they were rolling away in a trap. It was the same countryside that Krishna had seen from the train, but now it passed more slowly, more closely. Now the smell of the dust in the road, of the hay in the stacks was added to what he had only experienced through his eyes. Major Bateman and Ralph Harris talked desultorily, the major asking after various people and the other answering briefly. After half an hour's brisk trot in sunken lanes between thick hedges the road swung, revealing a two-storeyed building of grey stone, with many big windows and a flat roof line, facing the road across fifty yards of green lawn, behind a low dry-stone wall.

'The Old Vicarage,' Major Bateman said. 'It's church property. That's the church, beyond. The old graveyard's behind the holly hedge.'

The wheels of the trap crunched on the gravel of the curved drive, and stopped. Major Bateman jumped down, the door opened, and a woman came out, a half-naked boy child running ahead: 'Daddy, Daddy!' the little boy cried. The woman said quietly, 'Warren.' Major Bateman held out his arms. 'Joan!'

Krishna busied himself helping Ralph Harris get the suitcases out from under the seat, in order not to intrude on the reunion. Then he heard another woman's voice, this one older and more musical than the other; and Major Bateman's, 'Mother!'

He turned then and came forward. Warren Bateman said, 'My mother ... Yuvraj Krishna Ram of Ravi, mother.'

She was above normal height, even for an English woman, a little stooped, her black hair streaked with grey, her skin rather sallow. Her eyes were strong blue, and her voice steady as she said, 'Welcome to England, Yuvraj. You have brought lovely weather with you.'

He bowed over her hand, wondering whether he ought to kiss it. Then Major Bateman was saying, 'My wife Joan. You didn't meet her in Lahore, did you?'

'No, sir. Only your sister, Miss Diana.'

Warren's wife was an inch taller than her tall mother-in-law, but slimmer, a willowy body bending as she held out her hand, long blonde hair straying in the breeze. Her face was very different, long, long nose, high forehead, her mouth always moving. Her hands were long, the fingers like the stalks of lilies. At her skirt, which was of gipsy cut, the little boy stood with legs apart, staring up at Krishna, his hands thrust into the pockets of his only garment, a pair of velvet shorts.

'I'm Rodney Bateman,' the child said. 'I'm four and a half. My sister's been sick again.'

A tall strongly built man, not more than twenty-one years old, came round the corner of the house. He was deeply sunburned, with a powerful throat rising from broad shoulders. His fair hair stuck out in dense curls at the back and sides of his cap. He was wearing a labourer's corduroy trousers and shirt, with no coat. 'Is 'ee finished with t' trap, Ralph?' he said and Krishna caught the flitting frown on Warren Bateman's face, at the familiar address from a man who was obviously a servant of some kind.

'Yes, Sam ... unless you want him to give a hand with the suitcases, mother?'

'No, no,' Warren said. 'We can manage them ourselves.' The trap disappeared round the corner and Joan Bateman said, 'Come up and see Louise, Warren. She's furious at being kept in bed.'

The clop of hooves on the gravel made them all turn. A bay gelding came trotting up from the road, ridden by a woman wearing breeches and sitting astride, her short hair blowing around her face. A black and white cocker spaniel trotted at heel. Krishna's heart gave a bump, as he recognized Diana Bateman. She swung down in one easy motion and, still holding the reins, threw her arms round her brother's neck. 'Oh, Warrie, I thought you were going to catch the 12.43! I've been exercising Mr. Harcourt and Fudge on the Plain. They're both getting pig fat.'

She had seemed tall in Lahore, when Krishna's eye was still unaccustomed to English ladies, but she seemed almost short against Joan and Mrs. Bateman. In Lahore, too, he had thought her very white and pale, but now her complexion was brown and rose under a layer of dust, and standing beside Joan, her nose looked snubber, her chin more rounded.

She turned to Krishna, her hand out-thrust, and again he could not help noticing that it was as big as his, or bigger. The spaniel jumped up and she said, 'Down, Fudge! This instant! ... Hullo, Yuvraj. What a pleasant surprise to see you again ... and here!'

He stammered, 'I'm ... deeply honoured,' then blushed, thinking it was too flowery a phrase for the occasion. Mr. Fleming had so often told him to be polite but not effusive. It was not done. Old Mrs. Bateman saved him by leading into the house, saying, 'Now you'll want to wash after your journey.' The house smelled of furniture polish, and cut grass from the lawn, and a little whiff of horses in the stable, and something boiling on a coal fire. He thought: This is what Major Bateman means when he talks of Home.

Going up the stairs, Joan Bateman said, 'How long is this awful war going to last, Warren? You know, I've lost my father and Harry already, in less than six weeks.'

Major Bateman stopped short. 'Joan! What happened?'

'Harry was killed at Mons with his regiment. My father died two weeks ago of a heart attack. The Admiralty had re-employed him to open a destroyer base in Scotland.'

'I wish you could have let me know.'

The tall woman shrugged. 'What was the use? They were dead and you were on a ship, heaven knew where ... The casualties are terrible. How long can it go on?'

'Until we win,' Major Bateman said, and led up the stairs. 'Come on, Krishna, I'll show you to your room.'

Next day, after a lazy morning and a light lunch Krishna met Warren Bateman and Ralph Harris in the hallway, all three wearing white flannel trousers, white shirts, and blazers. As they were about to leave the house Joan Bateman called downstairs, 'Wait for me!'

Warren turned his head up, '*You* want to watch cricket? What's come over you?'

'Oh, what else is there to do?' she said, appearing at the head of the stairs, the children behind her.

'Well,' Warren said dubiously, 'I don't know how much Louise and Rodney can stand ... but you can always bring them back.'

At the cricket field half a dozen men were already gathered, most wearing corduroy trousers held up by braces, farm boots, and wool shirts. Two more were driving half a dozen shorthorn cows out of the field with expert cries and gestures. Major Bateman introduced Krishna Ram to the men as they came up. Most touched their forelock with a smile as they said, 'Afternoon, Mr. Warren, so 'ee's back from India, eh?' And to Krishna again the touched forelock and, 'Pleased to meet 'ee, zur,' in an accent that, when they were talking among themselves, Krishna could barely understand.

As Ralph Harris and Joan Bateman wandered away together, a man of about Major Bateman's age came up, wearing white flannels, silk shirt and proper white cricket boots. He said, 'I heard you were home, Bateman. On leave?'

'Three days,' Major Bateman said briefly. 'This is the Yuvraj

Krishna Ram of Ravi. Paul Hutchinson. He's by way of being squire of Hangerton. And captain of their cricket team, naturally.'

Krishna could tell from the other's accent that this was another gentleman, and noted also that he made no attempt to shake hands but greeted the introduction with an offhand nod. Now he said to Warren Bateman, 'Are you playing Fuller?'

Major Bateman said, 'I asked him to play last night, but he had a previous engagement.'

'Just as well,' Hutchinson said. 'On all counts, he's a really top class bowler ... much too good for most of our fellows on a pitch like this.'

He strolled away with another nod, and Krishna said, 'Who's Mr. Fuller, sir?'

Major Bateman hesitated before answering. 'He's a man ... a gentleman ... who lives in the village.' He hesitated again. 'There was a lot of unpleasant talk about him ... about unnatural vice ... Personally, I am not sure that the accusation was just, and I am also not sure that it is Christian to cut someone off from society like that, even if it were. But you know what people are. This is a very small community. Fuller's retired into his shell. Doesn't see anybody ... Come on. It's time for the toss. And by the way, call me Warren off parade.'

Major Bateman won the toss for Shrewford Pennel and put his team in to bat. Krishna settled in one of the rickety deck chairs on the rickety verandah, with his pads on, for he was going in first wicket down. His turn came soon enough, for the opening batsman only made five before swinging across a ball that failed to rise more than six inches, having slid in an old cowpat trace, and was bowled neck and crop. Krishna walked out with his bat swinging lightly, and his shirt sleeves rolled half way up his forearm, just the way Ranji wore his. The church and a corner of the Old Vicarage were just visible on the low rise of land beyond the road, where the Green Man's inn sign swung to and fro in a light breeze. Two heavy copper beeches towered over the pavilion, their leaves beginning to speckle the grass with a coppery glint.

He took middle and leg, glanced round at the field, and waited. The ball came a shade slower off the pitch than he had expected. He thought, even with this dry weather the ground here is nothing like as hard as the matting in India. He watched the ball very carefully for the rest of the over, leaned on his bat for the next over while the sturdy farm boy at the other end hit two fours, and then again faced the fast bowler. He began with a straight drive over the bowler's head for six, followed by a late cut off a rising short one for two, and then another drive, this one past cover point, for four more. Each time a thin ripple of applause reached him from the pavilion, and for the two boundaries, all the Hangerton players applauded too.

For forty-five minutes he batted as well as he ever had before one of Hutchinson's leg breaks had him caught in the slips off the edge of his bat. He swung round with a grin, tucked his bat under his arm and started the walk back to the pavilion, all in one motion. All the Hangerton players were clapping and as he passed Hutchinson the latter said, 'A nice knock, Yuvraj. *Are* you a relative of Ranji's?'

Krishna shook his head, smiling. 'No, sir. I wish I was.'

Then he was back in the pavilion and everyone was clapping and Major Bateman said, 'Well played, Krishna. Pity you missed your century.'

'What did I make?'

'You mean you don't know? Eighty-four.'

Ralph Harris went out to bat. Joan Bateman watched him walk out, a peculiarly distant expression on her face. She was wearing a flowing yellow silk scarf, the colour of Krishna's blazer, a magenta dress, and a wide-brimmed black hat. As Krishna was taking off his pads he heard Warren Bateman say, 'Look what the children are playing with, Joan!' his voice sharp. Glancing up, Krishna saw that they were using cowpats as modelling clay.

'We mustn't stult their creative impulses,' Joan said firmly, 'there's nothing wrong with cow dung ... Is there, Krishna?'

Krishna blushed and cleared his throat. Personally he thought that cow dung was no different from horse dung or the dung of any other grass eater, but to the Brahmin it was sacred, like the cow itself; to most of the people of Ravi it was a principal fuel.

Warren Bateman said wearily, 'As you can see, Krishna, my children are being raised by the Harz-Goldwasser method.'

'Sir?' he said puzzled.

'They're Austrian Jews who've invented a new way of raising children. You should read Saki's story *The Schartz-Metterklume Method*, where he satirizes that sort of thing beautifully.'

Joan Bateman said, 'That story's quite funny, but the idea

behind it is not. It's just narrow-minded. A lot of us think the old ways of raising children are barbaric and produce nothing but unhappiness later—perversions, impotence and worse ... class prejudice, colour prejudice, hate ... Oh, well hit!' She clapped enthusiastically and Krishna saw that Ralph Harris had hit a six. He watched a while longer and saw that Harris did not concentrate. He would not last long. Nor did he, clean bowled, to be succeeded by the young servant who had taken the trap away, Sam Marsh.

'They could do with *him* in the army,' Warren said.

Joan said, 'Mother needs him here. Besides, he doesn't believe in fighting. Ralph's told him not to volunteer, whatever pressure is put on him.'

Warren laughed, 'Well then, he won't go, will he? But we won't beat the Huns if we don't give our best.'

'The Huns?' Ralph Harris said. 'You mean the Germans? You never used to call them Huns, Warren.'

He shrugged and said, 'I've been reading the papers. About the sack of Louvain and Ypres. The killing of Belgian babies. They're acting like Attila.'

Joan Bateman said, 'You shouldn't believe all that you read, Warren. Don't you realize there are people trying to *make* us hate? Oh, God, I loathe this war.'

'Don't talk like that, Joan,' he said sharply. Then a shout from the field told them that Marsh had come to his doom, swinging energetically at a ball well out of reach, and been stumped. Warren walked out, bat in hand.

'That war turrible shot,' Marsh said, grinning, as he came in. 'Oi missed 'un by a moile.' He sat down, mopping his broad brow.

'Sam's father is the gamekeeper up at Pennel House,' Joan said, 'and he could follow in his footsteps if he wanted to, but he doesn't. Ralph's taught him how wrong it is to preserve game for the rich and privileged. So he helps Mother round the garden and stables.'

Young Marsh said, 'Taint what we preserve, loike, but what we change, as matters now, Ralph says.'

Krishna said, 'I see.' He had read a little about socialists, and Mr. Fleming had explained roughly what they believed in. He would have liked to ask Ralph Harris some questions, but now Ralph was talking to Joan Bateman, slowly and with much more concentration than he had shown when at bat. And Krishna felt a vague enmity towards the man. He obviously had a feeling of respect for Warren, but with it there was a latent hostility. What could the relation between them be? Or was it between Harris and Joan, Warren's wife? Whatever the truth was, neither Ralph nor Marsh, nor even Joan, were treating Warren Bateman the way he deserved. *He* was the salt of the earth—a stronger, braver Mr. Fleming, the sort of man Krishna so often wished his father had been.

The afternoon wore on at a pleasantly rural and unrhythmic pace. Krishna took his turn at umpiring and eventually, at 4.30, took the field, with Shrewford Pennel all out for 182. He fielded at cover point, made one catch, threw two men out at the crease, and with the light almost flat behind the church and the shadow of the elms that lined the road lying like giants across the pitch, he bowled the last Hangerton man out. Then the cows were let back into the field, and all twenty-two men climbed the stile, crossed the road, and flocked into the Green Man. The faces were sun-bronzed and happy. The voices were saying, ''Ee played nobly, zur, right nobly ... Them were the best late cuts Oi zeen zince Oi zaw Frank Woolley one day up to Lunnon.' The beer was heavy and bitter but he was thirsty and drank it down greedily. Joan Bateman had long since taken the dung-covered children, by then almost naked, back to the Old Vicarage. Warren Bateman drank one long whisky and soda before saying, 'Time we went home, Krishna. Are you ready, Ralph?'

They walked up the road together, silent, until Warren said, 'I suppose Joan's right about not hating the enemy ... but I don't know whether we can win if we don't. And we must win ... for this.' He gestured in the twilight, at the valley fading from sight, the tower of the church black against the dusk, the call of an owl from the graveyard copse.

'We will win,' Krishna said, 'for England.'

Ralph said sombrely, 'England isn't worth it. Not *this* England.'

'Shut up, Ralph!' Warren said angrily. 'If you have opinions like that, you've got to keep them to yourself in wartime.'

Krishna wanted to touch Warren's arm, or take his hand and press it, or even embrace him, as he would have done to his father or grandfather, to show how strongly he agreed with him; but that was not the way the English acted. They walked on in silence.

After dinner that night the whole family gathered round the piano, and old Mrs. Bateman played and sang with them, and when he went to bed Krishna thought he had never felt so great a peace, so warm a contentment.

A few minutes before eleven next morning the family walked through the stable gate, and crossed the churchyard to the church. This was Harvest Home, and the Vicar had come over from Hangerton to hold services in the old church. Krishna was introduced at the door to Sir Tristram Pennel, fat and sad, and his erect iron-faced wife ('They lost their only son in the Coldstream at Landrecies,' Mrs. Bateman whispered to him), and recognized several faces from yesterday's cricket match. In the church he was lost once more in recognition; for all this—the flowers and pumpkins and sheaves of corn, and the choir boys in white and red, the creaking of the old organ, the cold of the stone underfoot and the polished hardness of the wooden pews, the parson droning from the pulpit—all this he had read of, and all this Mr. Fleming had talked of, though more specifically of a school chapel rather than a village church. He sat between old Mrs. Bateman, whose musical contralto rang out unafraid in the hymns, and Diana, who sang out of tune, but not loudly.

Then it was roast beef and Yorkshire pudding and sherry trifle. Bees hummed in the flowers and a robin chirped on the sill of the open window. He thought he would find a comfortable chair in the sun, and doze.

Diana said, 'We ought to take a walk after eating all that. Warren?'

'Sorry, Di, I have accounts to go through with Mother.'

'Ralph?'

'You know I think exercise is for barbarians. Cricket hardly counts as exercise, does it?'

She looked at Krishna and he leaped to his feet. 'Certainly, Miss Bateman.'

She led off at a brisk pace down the road, the spaniel Fudge trotting at heel, his leash swinging unused in her hand.

'How did you like the church service?' she said.

'Oh, very nice,' he said. She walked with an athletic swing and a long stride, but she was not mannish. She wore a thin grey sweater with a single string of pearls, and a tweed skirt half way down her calves. Her hair glistened in the sun, for she wore no hat.

'I was engaged to the vicar, once,' she said.

'Oh,' he said, not knowing quite what tone to put into it.

'I thought Warrie must have told you. Years ago, when he was curate. Father was vicar here, you know ... This is the edge of Pennel land, the hedge here. Old Marsh is the Pennels' gamekeeper. Don't you think Sam should be in the army—Young Marsh?'

'Well ...'

'I think he's a slacker, but Warren says it's Ralph's fault. Ralph puts the ideas into his head, Warren thinks.'

'Oh.'

They walked up a long slope, thorn hedges thick on either side, the view slowly widening behind them. Thrushes sang in the hedges and larks climbed singing to the skies out of the short grass behind. At the top she turned and said, 'There it is. Pewsey Vale.'

Krishna gazed out over the green land. A small river wound between water meadows. The patchwork of the fields was dotted with copses and barns and farms. One or two roads showed white between the hedges. Five miles north the hills rose again.

'This'—she was pointing the other way—'is Salisbury Plain.'

In that direction the grass reached to an empty horizon doubly strange after the denseness of cultivation and habitation in the valley. The wind blew across the grass from a great distance, and there were no hedges, no cattle, no roads, only a few stark thorn trees, far apart.

She walked out on to the Plain where the lane and the hedges ended, saying, 'Come on! This is the best air in the world.'

For an hour they strode side by side southward into the teeth of the wind, before turning at an ancient milestone half buried in the grass and heading back to the brow of the escarpment. They had talked of cattle and cricket, of churches and gardens, of the regiment and the war. Standing at the edge of the Plain she said, sighing, 'Warrie's the best man in the world. We just don't see enough of him at home.'

'He's marvellous,' Krishna said fervently. She was marvellous herself, he thought: so open, looking you straight in the face, speaking directly without women's deceptions and circumventions. Such men as Warren Bateman had made the English rulers of the world, and women like Diana had supported them as no other women could have.

They started back down a shallow lane towards the valley. Diana broke a long silence when she said abruptly, 'Mother's upset because Ralph gave up the job she'd got for him in Edinburgh.'

'I think he said he was sacked—dismissed,' Krishna said.

'Oh, he did it on purpose, I'm sure ... Joan's pleased ... I wish Warren could get a job at the War Office or something.'

'He wouldn't take it!' Krishna said, shocked. 'Not with the regiment going on active service.'

'I know,' she said. 'But ... you like Warrie, don't you?'

'Of course,' he said.

'Well, Mother and I are worried because ...' She stopped, looking down the lane. A horseman was spurring up towards them, urging his horse. It was Young Marsh. As he rode up he leaned down from the saddle. 'There's a telegram calling 'ee and the major to France at once,' he said. 'The major said for 'ee to take the horse and ride back as fast as 'ee can, and the both of 'ee'll loikely catch the 5.26 from Woodborough.'

He swung down from the saddle and Krishna turned to Diana. 'I suppose I must ... Goodbye, Miss Bateman,' he said awkwardly, 'I can't tell you how much ...'

'Oh, call me Diana,' she said. She did not hold out her hand. Krishna swung up into the saddle.

'Good luck. Come back to see us again.'

He jabbed his heels into the gelding's side and at length urged it into an ungainly lurching gallop.

CLOUDS COVERED THE sky, but heat permeated the air with a heavy dampness that reminded Krishna of days late in the rains at home. The dust hung higher than the riders' heads and most of the men, riding slumped in the saddle, had covered their mouths with handkerchiefs or the ends of their turbans. Every now and then French refugee families would pass, squeezed into the ditch by the river of horsemen riding in the opposite direction.

Krishna turned in the saddle, as he did every fifteen minutes, and looked back down his squadron. There was his trumpeter at one quarter of his horse, Hanuman at the other and the two bodyguards behind them. Sweat ran down all their faces, making channels of mud in the caked dust. Behind them rode Rissaldar Shamsher Singh at the head of 1 Troop, and then the khaki column, black sweat staining all the heavy tunics. The lance points glittered back down the road—no red and white pennants now to relieve the cold glint of steel—and at the back two peaked caps, where young Ishar Lall, his own 2nd-in-command, was riding with the commander of the next squadron, Himat Singh.

All looked well, though the horses' heads were hanging and some of the sowars were tired. It was noon and the regiment had been on the move for forty-two hours, first marching from their camp outside Marseilles to a railhead twelve miles away, and then by train. Entraining had taken a considerable time because of a confusion over the loading of the wagons. Colonel Hanbury explained that the markings *Hommes 40, Chevaux 8* on the sides of the wagons meant forty Men, eight Horses. Soon the VCOs responsible for the actual loading came to complain that it was almost impossible. After investigation, Warren Bateman and a wildly gesticulating French movement control officer had to explain that the sign meant that *either* forty men *or* eight horses were to be fitted into each truck, not both. Krishna heard Warren's chuckling remark to Colonel Hanbury about it. 'Only the Indian Army would have tried to fit both in ... but you know, sir, they were actually getting it done!'

After nearly twenty hours the train stopped in the middle of the night, in a town which Krishna never did learn the name of, and found Brigadier-General Rogers, who told them they were under his command and would remain so until Divisional Headquarters arrived from Marseilles, in a couple of days. The Lahore infantry Brigade had already left and the Ravi Lancers were to follow as soon as possible. Ten minutes after its last squadron had detrained the Ravi Lancers were on the march. That was twelve hours ago.

Krishna's horse stopped and he realized he had almost ridden into the CO and Regimental Headquarters. Colonel Hanbury's long face was weary and he sat stiffly upright as though he knew that if he relaxed he would fall from the saddle.

In front of him the mass of the 1/12th Gurkhas blocked the road. Krishna said, 'Shall I go forward and see what's the trouble, sir?'

'Yes, please. We're two hours behind the timetable already ... Don't take all those men, Krishna, there's no room—just your trumpeter to send back a message, if you have to.'

Krishna trotted forward, his trumpeter at his heels, along the verge of the road, or in the ditch, sometimes pausing to ask the Gurkhas to ease out of his way. This move was nothing like moves he had made in India, during manoeuvres. A dozen times since dawn the regiment had been stopped by columns of troops crossing the line of march. Once it was a brigade of British infantry, which no one had told anyone else about, but they were in a hurry and their brigadier-general was a choleric man who disregarded Colonel Hanbury's protests, and marched his brigade firmly over the crossroad in column of route with sentries posted to prevent anyone breaking through their line of march.

This time Krishna found it was a battery of medium artillery, moving up the same road in the same direction. The teams of eight huge horses, straining at the harness, could move the 60-pounders at only three-quarters of the marching pace of infantry. General Rogers was there, arguing with the battery commander as Krishna rode up. He heard the gunner major say, 'You can put me under arrest, sir ... but I have the corps commander's written order to get this battery to St. Marc by 1800 at all costs.'

'Can't you turn off the road for half an hour to let my brigade pass?' the general said irritably.

'No, sir ... but may I suggest that your men could march—or ride—round and past us?'

Brigadier-General Rogers looked up and saw Krishna. He put his monocle in his eye and said, 'Your top button's undone, Major Krishna Ram. I won't tolerate slovenliness in officers.' The colonel of the Fusiliers was there. Behind him the road was blocked by columns of infantry. 'We can get the men past, sir,' the colonel said, 'but the GS wagons won't be able to follow.'

The brigadier-general chewed the end of his leather-covered swagger stick and then snapped. 'Very well.' He turned to his brigade major, 'Have the battalions march round the guns. GS wagons to rendezvous with us at St. Marc when they get there. Ravi Lancers to swing out wider and get ahead of the infantry on this same road.'

Krishna swung his horse and made his way back down the column. Twenty minutes later he was riding up out of the lane and trotting across the fields, his squadron following with a new sense of life as though leaving the overcrowded road had infused them with fresh energy.

An hour later it was all the same again ... This time a long column of transport carts moving against the flow of traffic. The regiment waited for half an hour while the carts were diverted into the fields; then on again. By now Krishna was swaying in the saddle, for they had had no proper rest, or food, for ten hours. Rissaldar Shamsher Singh rode up beside him, saluting. 'The horses need to be watered, lord.'

'I know,' he said. 'The colonel knows too, but there is no water.'

The column stopped again. An aeroplane flew out of the lowering clouds, the pilot very clear sitting on his bench amid the ethereal-looking struts. It passed low overhead, its engine back-firing, and several horses bolted into the fields. Krishna heard Jemadar Ganpat Singh roaring at the men as dolts, incapable of controlling their mounts, worse than foot soldiers. The aeroplane engine noise increased as it turned, sinking lower over the field towards the column. Then it was bumping along the tussocky grass, and after thirty yards, came to a stop. The pilot unstrapped himself, climbed down, and ran towards the column, leaving his aircraft's engine running and its propeller idling. He stopped at the edge of the road, and standing on top of the low bank, took off his flying helmet and goggles and cried aloud, 'Oh my God! Indians!'

Krishna said, 'I speak English.'

'Oh.' The pilot noticed the crown on Krishna's sleeve and saluted uncertainly. 'A message from the corps commander to Brigadier-General Rogers.' He held out an envelope.

'He's a little farther ahead,' Krishna said.

'I can't run and catch him. I've got to get back to my airfield and I'm short of petrol. Will you see that the message is delivered, sir? By the way, what is your name? I have to report who I gave the message to.'

'Major Krishna Ram, Ravi Lancers.'

The pilot saluted and hurried back to his plane. As Krishna took the message to Colonel Hanbury the aeroplane engine roared louder, the machine lurched across the hummocks and cow pats and after a few yards rose quickly into the air. Colonel Hanbury sent off a galloper with the message, and Krishna rode on at his side, wondering: what next in this chaotic day?

Twenty minutes later the brigade major came riding back down the road. To Colonel Hanbury he said, 'Orders have been changed, sir. The brigade is to go to La Chapelle St. Denis.' He proffered a folded map. 'Here, sir.'

The colonel bent over the map and said, 'That's twenty miles further than St. Marc. The men are exhausted, Temple. The horses need watering. We could just have reached St. Marc without a rest—but not another twenty miles.'

'I'm sorry, sir. The corps commander's orders give us no latitude.'

The column began to move again as the brigade major rode on down the road. Krishna turned off to watch his squadron go by. He spoke and made jokes to VCOs and sowars as they passed. When the tail came he walked along with Ishar Lall, telling him of the new orders.

Rissaldar Shamsher Singh joined them, 'We must water the animals at the next farm we come to,' he said.

'We will not!' Krishna said angrily. 'That is an order. *Hukm hai*, do you understand?'

'*Jee-han*, it is understood, prince,' the old rissaldar grumbled, 'but the horses will suffer.'

'This is war!' Krishna Ram exploded, but Ishar Lall said soothingly, 'Come, rissaldar-sahib, ride here at the back with me for a while and tell me how you won the kabaddi prize from the rajah's hands in 1884.' He winked at Krishna, for everyone knew that the old VCO was an indomitable bore.

Krishna smiled at the boy. He was only nineteen and showed no sign of fatigue. He and his twin had caused an unbelievable amount of trouble on the troopship, but now he was showing his worth. Krishna trotted forward, as Ishar Lall burst into a bawdy love song, a favourite among the loose women of the Hira Mandi in Lahore. The faces of the weary sowars lightened and one or two of them began to sing with the young 2nd Lieutenant.

Krishna settled into his place at the head of the squadron, noticing that the colonel, up ahead, was sitting straighter than ever, but swaying in the saddle, like an ill-balanced stick. The sun was setting behind them. They still had five miles to go to St. Marc and another twenty beyond that. Nearly seven hours, if they weren't delayed ... but they would be. The generals did not seem to be as good at moving troops here as they were on manoeuvres. He reproved himself. Real war was much harder; and there were the French refugees, spoiling all the plans.

Soon after dark it began to rain, rain with an edge of cold in it, harbinger of the northern winter. At first Krishna welcomed the rain, for it washed away the dust that was threatening to choke him, and cooled his hot, sweating face. But as it continued, and the weary horses and caped men kept plodding on into it through the darkness, it began to work through his uniform, chill his skin, and gnaw steadily in towards his bones.

Eight o'clock ... nine o'clock ... an enforced halt in a nameless village, the two-storey houses curling round the side of a hill, small lights behind drawn curtains, something like a slag heap above. He ate curry puffs from his saddlebag, drank a little from his waterbottle. Three horses lame, one with a severe girth gall. Nothing to be done.

On ... ten o'clock ... eleven o'clock, and a long stand in open country, nothing to be seen in any direction in the rain, no lights, the wind whistling through unseen trees somewhere to the right, to the left a scene of desolation, of dead crops and land unseeded, the breath of war. And then, for the first time, he heard a low grumbling rumble, that seemed to come through the earth, not on the wind.

He turned to ask the rissaldar what it was, but saw another shape, close. Peering, he recognized Warren Bateman, his dog Shikari on his saddle bow. He smiled through the cold and weariness, and said, 'What's that noise, sir? More thunder?'

'It might be,' the major said, 'but it isn't. It's the guns.'

'The guns!' Krishna muttered, half to himself. For the first time he was hearing the sound of the guns, the authentic voice of war. It was to this that he had devoted his life until fate should call him to the *gaddi* of his state. He expected a thrill, but an uncontrollable shiver shook his body.

'My burberry doesn't seem to keep out the rain. It's cold. I'm soaked through,' he said, feeling that the major must have sensed that shudder.

'Nothing will keep out rain that goes on this long,' Warren said. 'I'm on my way up to warn the colonel that we have about a dozen horses lame and unable to keep up. And we seem to have lost B Squadron.'

'Altogether?' Krishna said, amazed. 'How on earth ... ?'

'It's easy enough in the dark. Lose a little distance ... have a company of infantry or a gunner battery go through the column ... take the wrong road fork afterwards. They'll find us sooner or later.'

'When do you think we'll get to La Chapelle, sir?'

'Another four hours at this rate,' the major urged his horse into a trot and disappeared towards regimental headquarters. Krishna settled back into his saddle. The rain ran down his back in a cold trickle. The horses were very tired, and the dust in the road had congealed to mud. The pace had slowed from the regulation four and a half miles per hour of cavalry at the walk to less than three.

To forget his hunger and misery he thought of the weekend at Shrewford Pennel. The cricket had been everything he had dreamed of and Mr. Fleming had told him about. All those people had their stations in life, but for the match it was only their stations on the cricket field that mattered. The churches, and houses, and barns, even the fields and the woods rising up to the great empty sweep of the Plain, seemed to be rooted in and protected by the people, rather than the other way around ... Warren Bateman's wife was a strange lady. Seen walking at Ralph Harris's side in the vegetable garden she looked like an apparition from another age, another planet ... The old lady, Warren's mother, was rather like his own

116

grandmother as he remembered her before her death two years back; a strong woman, born to distinction and never losing it. But most she reminded him of Rissaldar-Major Baldev Singh. Both were calm, yet firm, both convinced that everyone else—like themselves—was doing, and would always do, the best of which he or she was capable, and always in honesty of purpose. What was it that worried her and Diana, which Diana had not had time to tell him about?

And Diana herself ... she was specially English—or was it perhaps European? Such girls did not exist among Indians, that was certain, not with her innocence, the direct way she looked at you, mud on her face and dirty strong hands secure on the reins. She seemed to be unaware of the fact that he was an Indian. She had not asked him one question about himself as an Indian, only as a person, and a man. It was a shame she had not married the curate, now vicar—that very one who gave the sermon which sent Warren to sleep—and had some children of her own. Though she didn't seem to miss all that, kept busy by the animals, helping her mother with the house and Joan with the children, when she was allowed to. No Indian parent would tolerate the way those children were being brought up, permitted, as they were, to do anything they chose, except when their wishes ran afoul of their grandmother's. He had been interested to notice that it was the old lady's company, with all its prohibitions and orders, that they sought before anyone else's, including their mother's.

The intermittent grumbling of the guns grew louder. At midnight by his watch he passed a battery of heavies in an orchard beside the road. One of the guns fired as the squadron rode by. An orange flash lit up the gleaming wet steel barrel, a man running, shells stacked beside a hayrick, four men crouched by the trail, other shining barrels, uptilted, beyond ... then it was dark again. It was lucky, he thought, that the horses were too tired to shy or there would have been broken ranks in the regiment; none had heard or seen so large an artillery piece firing before.

The guns fell back into the darkness. The Lancers trudged on, Krishna's horse rolling like a weary sleep-walker below him now. At last the adjutant, Lieutenant Dayal Ram, loomed out of the dark and the rain, and said, 'Bivouac here, sir. La Chapelle St. Denis is just ahead.' Hurricane lanterns swung, showing a mass of mounted figures in dripping capes. Now his VCOs were coming up for orders. The squadron moved into a dark field, formed squadron column, and dismounted. One man, unable to keep his feet after twenty-two hours in the saddle, simply rolled on over as his left foot joined his right, and lay like a corpse where he fell. Krishna's trumpeter held his horse, and he walked down the lines, trying to keep his eyes open and force his muscles to move one foot after the other. The ground underfoot was heavy and wet. Some of the horses had lain down. The men were tying their groundsheet-capes together to make bivouacs. Food ... where were the field kitchens that should have been rolling along at the back of the regiment? Why had the orders been changed? What had the heavy artillery been firing at? Did anyone know anything, or were they just keeping it a secret from the regiment? It was four a.m., and this place smelled of pig manure.

Hanuman appeared, mug in hand. 'Rum, lord. From the *Topkhana gora log*.'

Krishna took the mug, drank, and choked at the raw strength of the stuff burning down his throat. Trust British gunners to see that there was rum, even though there was no food or fodder. Warren Bateman appeared, flashing an electric torch, and said, 'There are two big animal water troughs in the corner of the field. Water in order of squadrons. We don't know when the rations will come up.'

'Yes, sir.'

'Orders at six a.m. Post lines-sentries and then get some sleep.'

The major rode away, and Krishna called up his VCOs. Ten minutes later Hanuman said, 'Your bivouac, lord. I've borrowed another groundsheet so that you won't be lying in the mud.'

He must have stolen it or told some sowar that the prince wanted it, Krishna thought. But he couldn't bother about that now. He crawled into the bivouac, put his cap under his head, and went out like a blown light.

An enormous explosion awoke him so violently that he was out of the bivouac, a scream only half suppressed, before he knew what he was doing. He stood trembling in the darkness, listening. He realized that all the men were out, huddled down the line of bivouacs. What had happened? He didn't know, but he knew the men must be reassured. 'Stand easy,' he said, as he walked down the ranks. 'Stay by your bivouacs.' At the end of the line he found the sentry, visibly shaking. He took the man's arm. 'What was it?'

'A shell, lord. A huge shell. It fell over there!'

Major Bateman appeared, on foot. A loud increasing whistle filled the air and a moment later there was another explosion. Mud hurled over him in a shower and someone nearby began to moan in pain.

'We're being shelled,' Warren Bateman said, 'heavy stuff. It seems to be burying itself in the mud before exploding or we'd be suffering more than we are.'

'Two horses killed in C Squadron, sahib,' someone said, running up to join the group.

'They can't know that we've arrived,' Warren said. 'My God, I know what it is! There's a pile of shell cases over beyond the water troughs. A battery must have been here before we moved in and the Huns think they are giving it harassing fire ... Dayal Ram, are you there?'

'Yes, sir.'

'Tell all squadron commanders to prepare to move. I'll speak to the CO and be back here in five minutes.'

'The CO's asleep, sir. I couldn't awaken him. Nor has the shelling.'

Krishna gave the necessary orders, thinking that with Colonel Hanbury too tired to wake up, Warren would probably order a move on his own initiative. They wouldn't have to go far. Meanwhile ... he walked up and down his lines in the eerie light. The men were standing at ease outside their dismantled bivouacs, facing the picketed horses. He felt their fear, for they had never been shelled before, but he knew they were not going to run away. They were afraid, but not nervous. These were his people, the men of Ravi, standing steady here in the darkness five thousand miles from their quiet fields on the slopes between the river and the eternal snows. 'Well done,' he said, 'stand firm. We will be moving soon ... Are you wounded, there?'

'No, lord. Only too stiff to stand.'

'Good ... good ...' Here he touched a shoulder, there a man dropped to one knee to lay his hand to Krishna's knee. Another shell shrieked over and exploded deep in the shaking earth.

Dayal Ram appeared and said, 'Squadrons on to the road and continue north—that's to the right—through the village, sir. Major Bateman is selecting a bivouac site the other side of La Chapelle.'

Krishna mounted, fell in his squadron, and moved off in slackening rain. Half an hour later he was again asleep on the ground rolled in his blanket. At five-thirty the lines-sentry awakened him.

He struggled out, shivering, to a scene of desolation that he would not have credited even twenty-four hours ago. The regiment lay like debris all over the two ploughed fields. Some horses stood and some lay, and the bivouacs were dotted everywhere, with no visible order. Everything was a dull browny black, and everything coated with mud. Rain dripped from the trees around the field and smoke curled up from the chimneys of La Chapelle, two hundred yards away. A column of GS wagons and field kitchens was moving into the field out of the road, led by Captain Sohan Singh, the quartermaster. That was a most welcome sight, Krishna thought, though how Sohan Singh had managed to come up so soon, and find the regiment after the night's chaos, was a mystery.

Dayal Ram arrived, saluting. He looked fit and cheerful in spite of everything, Krishna noted. He was a menace with the women and got himself and others into endless trouble over them—he remembered the camp at Kangrota, the afternoon the sowar ran amok and shot at Major Bateman—but he was a good officer, impossible to panic.

'Orders in the estaminet this end of the village, sir, as soon as the CO comes back from brigade. He was sent for at 5 a.m.'

'How is he?'

'Tired.' The adjutant made a very Indian gesture of sleeping, that contrasted comically with his clipped British moustache and cap.

Krishna walked stiffly across the field and into the village. The officers gathered in the estaminet, huddling into the small front room, which still showed traces of recent habitation by its rightful owners. Colonel Hanbury limped in and sat down heavily. His breathing was shallow and uneven, his skin was an unpleasant greenish colour in the grey light.

'We are to march at 0700 hours,' he said dully. 'The Lahore Brigade, with ourselves in the lead and under command, is moving up on the left of VIII Corps ready to exploit a breakthrough hourly expected ... I told the general we must have time to feed men and horses, and get more rest, but the general said we must march. It is our first chance.'

And the general's, Krishna thought: if all went well he might soon be Brigadier-General Rogers DSO, MVO.

'The horses are bad, tired,' Major Bholanath said. 'They were good before, even in Marseilles. But this—spoiling them quickly.'

'What about the men?' The colonel looked at the black doctor.

Captain Ramaswami spread his hands and said, 'They're tired. The squadron commanders can tell you. But they are young. They will be all right after a few hours' rest. All except you,' he added bluntly. 'You are not at all fit.'

The old colonel said, 'I did not ask your opinion on that, Captain Ramaswami.' He turned to the quartermaster, 'When and where are brigade opening a ration point, Sohan?'

'I have three days' food and fodder here, sah!' the fat little man said rubbing his hands like a bazaar salesman. Krishna looked at him in astonishment.

'Has the supply column come up, then?'

'No, sah. But . . . I am having rations! All for distribution now. With sahib's permission I going now tell quartermaster dafadars to draw at once . . . *Bahut mehrbhani*, sahib!' He ducked out of the room before the colonel could say yes or no. Krishna thought that he must have 'found' the rations in the night when everyone else was sleeping; and he didn't want to tell the CO any more.

'What is the situation at the front, sir?' Krishna asked.

'I don't know,' Colonel Hanbury said. 'As soon as I am told anything more, I shall pass it on.'

Krishna returned to find his squadron ravenously eating hot rice from the field kitchens, together with margarine from huge cans, jam, and chocolate, and the horses all had their noses deep into their feed bags. Then the sun began to dissolve the ground mist, the rain ended, and the trumpets were sounding *Mount*. A little later came the *Advance*. He led A Squadron on to the road, reflecting that B Squadron was still lost.

The mist was a shimmering fading carpet of white over rain-pearled grass. The fields began to take colour, pale green, dark brown, as the light strengthened. The river of lance points flowed on above the mist. The air shook to the boom and thud of gunfire, now right, now left, and always to the front. There was confusion, the same as the day before, but now everything and everybody moved in one direction, towards the light crack of the field guns ahead. Gradually, as they passed heavy batteries in action, they advanced under a rumble of shells flying over them towards the unseen enemy.

Near eleven in the morning, after a long advance, Krishna heard the distinctive rattle of small arms fire from close to the right front.

The regiment halted and the colonel rode forward. Half an hour later a brigade galloper dashed up and Major Bateman rode forward with him, his face stern. Twenty minutes after that the officers were called up for orders.

Major Bateman said, 'Gentlemen, I am very sorry to have to tell you that Colonel Hanbury died of a heart attack just now, at brigade orders. We will have a burial service for him here after the battle, if we can. Meantime, I am in command of the regiment until a new CO is appointed ... The enemy are holding that low rise of land in front there. VIII Corps is attacking now. The Lahore Brigade is to advance on their left, with ourselves on the left of the infantry. Our objective is the line of the road Echallon –Poucelle–Hazedon, which runs across the front behind the high ground. The 71st Punjabis will be on our right. Dividing line, inclusive to us, is the road Semur–Poucelle. Starting line is a farm track at the near edge of those woods there. Starting time is 1200, noon, that is ten minutes from now. We will move one squadron up, in the order C, RHQ, A, D. The Military Police are looking for B Squadron but I'm afraid they might be anywhere ... This will be our first action, gentlemen. I know I can rely on you to see that we acquit ourselves worthily. Good luck.' He saluted his officers as they wheeled their horses and trotted back to their posts.

A few minutes later C Squadron walked past, old Bholanath at its head. He saluted Krishna with his drawn sabre as he passed, and called in Hindi, 'We shall redden our swords for the Rajah today, highness. And in memory of the colonel-sahib.'

Krishna drew his heavy sabre and looked at it curiously. Would it really soon be red with blood ... European blood? What would it feel like to take a back cut at a German? What did they look like? He had seen pictures of men in spiked helmets, but where were these Germans? He had expected to see them drawn up on the hills, with guns somewhere behind, and perhaps standards flying.

The CO's trumpeter sounded *Walk-March* and the squadrons, in line of troop columns, moved out from the shelter of scattered copses, and on to the ploughed fields.

Looking to his right Krishna saw the khaki lines and the glittering bayonets of the 71st Punjabis. The rattle of machine gun fire increased in that direction, and he saw men fall. Then he heard the crack of bursting shells and the infantry lines began to waver.

122

The Punjabis were coming under increasing fire. He looked to his left. There should be nothing in that direction ... but there was. He pulled out his binoculars and stared. His horse's jogging mane made it hard to see, but he could clearly make out lance points ... and the men were wearing turbans. Indian cavalry? He spurred up beside Warren Bateman and pointed. Major Bateman looked, and said, 'B Squadron coming home to roost.'

Himat Singh cantered up, his squadron in column of route behind him, and began to gabble, 'B Squadron reporting, sir ... I don't know where we lost the regiment ... I heard that ... I'm very sorry ...'

Major Bateman said, 'We'll go into that later. Follow A Squadron, in line of troop columns. Krishna, tell him the orders.'

The sound of artillery fire increased and the Punjabis seemed to be halted. The Ravi Lancers rode on across the high expanse of Artois. Ten minutes later they reached their objective. The squadron commanders gathered at RHQ.

A brigade galloper arrived, clods of mud flying from his horse's hoofs and handed Warren Bateman a message. Warren read it, then turned to his officers. He said, 'We've been ordered to destroy the enemy guns that are holding up the Punjabis. I'm going to leave C and D Squadrons here while I tackle the guns with B and A ... The guns are on the hillside ... look, you can see one of them, there, about a mile from here. They are said to be protected by a platoon of infantry, but no machine guns. We'll take them from the rear, from behind that line of trees. B Squadron will lead. I'll follow with A. Both squadrons in line. Charge when we leave the trees.'

'Can A lead, sir? ... I'm afraid ... I'll do something wrong, and ...' Himat Singh began miserably.

'No, you won't,' Warren Bateman snapped, 'you'll lead, and you will do it well. Move out, now. We're right behind you.'

A moment later B Squadron trotted past and spread out into line. Krishna called, 'A Squadron—trot!' His charger's powerful muscles rippled into the rhythm and he posted easily in the saddle, his sabre blade on his shoulder. Glancing back he saw the line of lances coming steadily on. In front, Himat Singh's men rode in perfect line, covering a front of a hundred yards.

They were in the shelter of a fold in the ground. The land began to rise slowly. B Squadron rode into the line of trees, then suddenly they were all out of the sheltering wood, the trumpet was blaring *Charge!*, and there were the guns ... two ... three ... four of them! They were galloping hard, mud flying, bullets cracking about their ears as the German infantry realized their danger and began firing. Now the grey figures at the guns began to tug at the wheels and trails as the lance points swung down. A horse, three horses fell in B Squadron, and there was a man rolling like a shot rabbit. 'Hold your men tight, Krishna,' Warren Bateman shouted at him.

A gun flash caught his eye and a shell shrieked by, but there was no gap in the ranks of B Squadron; another, and he saw a man blasted from his horse, his head leaping one way and his torso another. Then B Squadron were over the infantry and into the gunners, lances thrusting and the gunners trying to shelter behind the shields and under the limbers. He saw a German officer with drawn pistol take a galloping sowar's lance in the chest, to be lifted four feet off the ground, and then fall as the sowar expertly swung up his lance butt and dropped the body off. The infantry were scattered, running, a few sowars galloping after them.

'They've done it!' Warren Bateman cried exultantly. 'Take your squadron to the top of the hill there, Krishna. Dismount there and hold it. I'll be up with you in a minute.'

Krishna swung his squadron out with a sweep of his arm, and cantered round the mêlée by the guns and up the hill. Bullets clattered by as the horses leaned into the slope, but they did not seem to be aimed at the squadron. Krishna saw, as he neared the crest, that they were behind the enemy lines, and the Germans down there were beginning to react to the threat from the engulfed battery. Then a machine gun opened up from close range to his left. The stream of bullets was clacking somewhere overhead, but any second now the gunners would correct their aim. Searching, he saw the gun in the open about two hundred yards to his left, near a ruined hayrick. The stream of bullets dropped lower. A man went down, two horses were struggling to rise. The squadron couldn't reach the crest of the hill, let alone hold it, while that machine gun was still in position. The bullets banged like hammers all round. Another man fell, clutching his shoulder and gasping in agony. Krishna began to sweat with anxiety. What should he do? Continue? Retreat? He gritted his teeth, shouted, 'Left front! Charge!'

He galloped down at the machine gun, his squadron in a ragged line behind him. The bullets all seemed to be aimed at him personally now, so that he felt he was riding into a steel hailstorm. Then the thick barrel was under him. He leaned far down, and cut fiercely at the machine gunner's neck. Blood spouted as high as Krishna's eyes, then he was past, the sabre again on his shoulder. There were no more bullets, only the overturned gun and seven still, grey bodies. Krishna wheeled his squadron back to the hill top. Almost at once Major Bateman cantered up. Sweat stained his tunic, his horse was flecked with foam, and he, too, had blood on his sabre. Field gun shells began to burst close to the hill top. Major Bateman said, 'We're pulling back.'

Krishna felt a wild exultation. He had charged and won! He cried, 'But, sir, we're behind them!'

Two more shells burst nearby, and Major Bateman said, 'I know, but the infantry attack failed and the Punjabis had to pull back, too. There's a two mile gap between them and us now. The Huns are getting ready to cut us off. Get mounted and withdraw at a trot, the way we came.'

Four shells burst among the squadron as they mounted, and four men fell. Machine gun fire began again, but from far off and inaccurate. Major Bateman said, 'Blow the trot, trumpeter! Get moving!'

Rissaldar Shamsher Singh cried, 'We must carry back our dead, sahib!'

'No!' Major Bateman shouted, 'the Germans are not Afridis to mutilate them. Leave them ... and any men too seriously wounded to ride. They will be well looked after!'

The rissaldar hesitated and then said something to a dafadar, which Krishna could not hear. As the troops began to trot away down the slope, Major Bateman already ahead of them, Krishna saw the dafadar hack a finger off each of the ten men dead on the hill. Then he stuffed the fingers into empty ammunition pouches and rode after the squadron. When Krishna saw that all his men had gone, several wounded being held in their saddles by comrades close on either side, he followed with Hanuman, his trumpeter, and his bodyguards.

The squadron trotted past the abandoned guns and the bodies huddled over trail and barrel, and soon caught up with B Squadron. On the original objective C and D fell in, and the regiment rode on towards the rear, each squadron in extended line, under desultory shell fire. Major Bateman called the squadron commanders to him. He said, 'Well done, all of you. Tell the sowars so, when you get a chance ... How many prisoners did you take, Himat?'

'Eight, sir. They're on their own horses.'

'Did you shoot the other horses, the gun team's?'

Himat Singh said, 'Sir ... I gave the orders ...'

'I didn't see any dead gun horses.'

'Sir, I ...'

'Look, Himat, when I give an order it's to be obeyed!'

'The men ... they couldn't seem to bring themselves to kill the horses, sir.'

'So the Huns will be able to use them again. My God, Himat Singh, this is war! ... See that those prisoners are sent back to Brigade Headquarters as soon as possible. They may have useful information. I'm going there now to report. Krishna, take the regiment back to where I gave orders this morning.'

He cantered off. Himat Singh said, 'The regiment will be different now, with him in command. Colonel Hanbury was a good man, but Major Bateman ... marvellous ... I never thought I could do it ... lead a charge. I wasn't afraid, I was just sure I would do it wrong ... charge the wrong enemy, something like that ... but with him ... you know, highness, I *felt* him there behind me, willing me to succeed ... and I did!'

'You certainly did. Major Bateman will probably put you in for a decoration.'

The two officers were returning to their own positions, at that moment riding past the flank of C Squadron where the eight German artillerymen, bare-headed and unarmed, were riding on five horses, escorted by three sowars. Suddenly the Germans turned, as one man, and headed back. The path of their flight took them straight at Krishna. He could not get out of the way, or draw his sabre, before he was knocked off his plunging horse. He lay on the ground, his hands over his head until the sound of hoofs faded. Then Hanuman was on the ground beside him and he heard heavy grunts and swearing in Hindi. He stood up and cleared the mud from his eyes just in time to see the last of the eight Germans, by then a hundred yards back, go down under a tremendous sabre slash from a C Squadron jemadar. Now all eight of them lay dead, crumpled, twisted, three headless, two armless, all impaled to the ground which the sowars were still thrusting into the inert lumps. His bodyguards were at his side, crying, 'Are you hurt, highness? Did they touch you?'

'No ... they were only trying to escape.'

'They rode at you, highness. They betrayed the trust we had in them. They are dead!'

'I see,' Krishna said climbing slowly back into his saddle. He heard Himat Singh say harshly, 'Shoot the Germans' horses. Go on!' The shots rang out. The squadrons rode on towards the rear.

Young Puran Lall rode up beside Krishna, and saluted elaborately with his sabre. 'A German's neck is no tougher than a Muslim's,' he said, grinning. He put away his sword and said, 'Is my brother all right, lord?'

'Yes. He didn't have much to do today.'

'May I talk to him? We have a bet on as to who would kill the most Germans in our first charge. I got three.'

'How much is the bet for?'

'Ten thousand rupees, highness.'

Krishna whistled and shook his head as the young man rode away. War was such a personal matter to these people, his people. He saw again the blind fury of the lancers at the Germans who they thought had made an attack on him, their prince and son of the Sun: the same men had shown no anger at the machine gunners and artillerymen who had killed and wounded so many men in A and B Squadrons. And here were the Terrible Twins turning a battle into a personal duel. He saw the German's neck where his sabre's edge had cut through, and the spouting blood. He saw Colonel Hanbury, a dead man in the saddle. He shook his head desperately but the visions would not go, and hovered ahead of him, his personal view of the day, as the regiment entered a lane and rode now in column of route, the lance points red in the afternoon sun.

December 1914

KRISHNA RAM, ONCE more second-in-command of the Ravi Lancers, paced slowly down C Squadron's stable lines with his great-uncle. The rissaldar-major and the salutri (veterinary jemadar) walked at their heels. The horses were picketed in a long line across the first fields out of St. Hubert-sur-Yevre. A hazy sun patterned the ground and the backs of the horses with the shadows of bare boughs.

'If they are to stay in the open, we ought to let them grow their coats,' Major Bholanath said in Hindi.

'Uncle,' Krishna said, 'how often must I remind you that it is forbidden for officers to speak Hindi among themselves?'

'I am sorry, highness,' the old man said in his halting English, 'but for me ... is not being easy.'

'I know, but you must try ... About the coats, I shall speak to the CO.'

'He is a wise man,' Bholanath said, 'but general-sahib may not liking.'

Krishna reached the end of the squadron's lines and Bholanath saluted. 'Very good,' Krishna said, 'except that a lot of your horses are overdue for shoeing. See to it, please.'

'*Jee-han* ... Very good, sah.'

Krishna walked along the edge of the wood to A Squadron, where Young Ishar Lall greeted him with a huge salute. He began the inspection, while Ishar Lall walked at his side. Opposite one horse Krishna stopped and said, 'This horse has been curry-combed.'

'Currycombed? You mean, he's put the currycomb direct on to the horse, sir?'

'Yes. Look.'

128

Krishna kept his face stern while the 2nd Lieutenant examined the horse thoroughly, the sowar standing stiffly at attention in stable dress—boots, puttees, breeches with braces hanging loose, and shirt sleeves—no spurs, tunic, or turban.

'I can't see any trace, sir.'

'Look at the brisket, nearside ... There.'

'You're right, sir. But how ... ?'

Krishna allowed himself a small smile. 'You forget that I commanded this squadron for some years. That sowar always uses a currycomb. He'd have been a lance-dafadar long since if he wasn't so lazy.' He turned sharply on the squadron rissaldar, Shamsher Singh. 'And you, sahib, you knew of that man's habits. It's your duty to tell the squadron commander all you know.'

'*Bahut achcha*, sahib,' the old man said; but his face showed that he had no intention of passing on to the young officer what it had taken him so many years to learn, and what was a major source of his power and influence.

Krishna moved on to B Squadron, whose stable lines were the other side of the village, with D's. Himat Singh wore a new authority these days, since the charge of the German guns at Poucelle. His squadron was fast beginning to show it and where the horses were once measurably less good than A's, and the men measurably less proud and smart than C's, now they were as good as both. Krishna congratulated the squadron commander, but he could tell that Himat Singh wished the CO had taken Stables in person. It was for Warren Bateman that Himat worked now, and it was admiration of and respect for Warren Bateman that had superseded his old nervousness and self-doubting. Only Warren Bateman's regard or disfavour mattered to him now.

Krishna walked over to D Squadron as B's trumpeter blew the *Stand Down*. Sher Singh was another admirer of Warren Bateman, but here Krishna did not feel so sure of the man. He was a handsome fellow, but ... He was intelligent, but ... The trouble was that Warren Bateman had never met someone like Sher Singh at such close quarters before, for British officers had few contacts with rich Indian merchants and their self-indulgent sons; and what they had would extend only to, 'Yes', or 'No', or 'How much?' A special problem with Sher Singh was that he preferred young boys to women, and that was an abnormality the British had an absolute horror of. Krishna wondered whether Major Bateman had any suspicion of it: probably, for he had an amazing peripheral vision, being able to notice things out of the corner of his eye while apparently looking only straight ahead.

Regimental Headquarters was composed of such oddments as the Signal Section, the Machine Gun Section, the Regimental Aid Post, clerks, farriers and orderlies, and Krishna could not summon up any real interest in it. The horses of the Signal Section were not in good shape and he told Lieutenant Flaherty so. The big man took the rebuke with a sullen frown and a clenching of his fists, but no more.

Krishna glanced at his watch and hurried the rest of the inspection. In twenty minutes he was due at the funeral of Dafadar Shiv Mall of A Squadron, killed by a motor lorry while he was crossing the village street without looking. He dismissed the salutes and walked away with the rissaldar-major.

'Well, sahib,' he asked, 'have you any points you wish to raise?'

The RM said, 'I want to move Rissaldar Ram Lall from B Squadron to the Machine Guns, and Chuni Ram from the Machine Guns to B.'

Krishna nodded. He understood, without the RM having to explain in detail, that Rissaldar Ram Lall had been a tower of strength in B while Himat Singh had yet to find his confidence; but now that he had, Ram Lall, who had been the real commander of the squadron, resented his loss of power. A young rissaldar would be best now in B, and a tough old one to run the machine gun section, which increased in importance with every day's experience of modern war.

'Anything else?'

'Major Bholanath is right about growing the coats, sahib ... And the sowars of A Squadron are not as well dressed as they should be. Boots not clean. Puttees ill-tied.'

Krishna nodded again. 'I will speak to the lieutenant,' he said. 'He is young yet. As to the other matters, I'll put them to Bateman-sahib.'

'Thank you, sahib ... We have set up the burning ghat by the stream, sahib. This way.'

Krishna Ram walked at the rissaldar-major's side towards the little stream that crossed the main road at the foot of the village. There, a hundred yards beyond the last house, a pyre of logs stood on the grass. It was eight feet long by four feet wide and four feet high. A few men were already squatted round it, smoking bidis through cupped hands. The Brahmin was there, a short cavalry greatcoat of coarse khaki over his *dhoti* and *kurta*, his feet bare on the cold grass. Other sowars of A Squadron were coming, their Stables over. They had put on tunics and turbans now and some wore their greatcoats as well. It was not as cold here as it would have been in most of Ravi on this date, but there the air was fresh and dry and a man could see far and breathe deep. Here there was a dampness in the air, a clutch at the throat, as of drowning, and the air itself often so thick that a man could not see the spire in the next village.

The Brahmin made *namasti* to Krishna, the rissaldar-major, and Ishar Lall, as they sat at the head of the pyre. Four sowars came from the house that was the Regimental Aid Post, where the dafadar's body had lain since the accident last night. It was wrapped in an army blanket, and under that, revealed as the bearers laid the body on the pyre, a white sheet, from which the bare feet stuck out at one end and the battered head at the other. The bearers removed and carefully folded the blanket.

The Brahmin began chanting the funeral hymn from the *Rigveda* as a couple of men beat on the little hand drums that Quartermaster Sohan Singh had managed to smuggle into the regimental baggage, together with half a hundred sets of ceremonial nautch clothes and costumes for the great Hindu festivals of Dussehra, Holi, and Dewali.

Him who has passed away along the mighty steps, and has spied out the path for many, him the son of Vivaswati, the assembler of people, Yama, the king, do thou present with oblation ...

Two bandsmen played softly on clarinets. The gathered sowars chanted the name of *Rama* and the sacred formula *Rama Naam Sat Hai.*

Unite with the fathers, unite with Yama, with the reward of thy sacrifices and good works in highest heaven! Leaving blemish behind go back to thy home, unite with the body, full of vigour!

Only the Brahmin wore his caste marks, Krishna noticed. He himself felt awkward, to be seated cross-legged at a burning without

131

the presiding Brahmin having pressed grains of rice on to his marked forehead, and murmured a word of blessing.

As the dead man had no son in the regiment or within reach, the youngest sowar in his troop acted as his son and performed a son's sacred duty of setting fire to his father's pyre. The sowar was barely seventeen, and looked unnaturally solemn as he took the lighted taper from the Brahmin's hand. The Brahmin and others poured melted *ghi* over the corpse and the piled wood. Then the young sowar thrust the taper deep into the pyre. Smoke began to curl out. The chanting grew louder.

Dust to dust, ashes to ashes, the Christians said. This was the same, but more literally. The flames were tinged with gold from the *ghi* now, and the smoke rose black. The sheet burned through, baring the dead dafadar's chest. His arms slowly rose. Then the fire began to burn with an intensity that scorched Krishna's face. The voices grew louder yet, the beat of the Himalayan drums more pronounced. A smell of burning incense and oil blew over him as the wind shifted, and in it, the smell of roasting flesh. He had always hated that before, when he went to a funeral, but this time ... it was not a sacrilege, nor a barbarism. It was his people's way. It *was*. He bowed his head and began to murmur the Sanskrit hymn with the Brahmin, while the flames towered higher on the bank of the Yevre.

He walked back to his billet, the flames still bright before his eyes, put on his belt and sabre and hurried to the school house at the other end of town, which had been taken over for the regimental offices. He was a few minutes later than the appointed hour and as he marched into the CO's office he said, 'I'm sorry I'm late sir. It was ...'

'I don't want to hear what it was,' Warren Bateman said sharply. 'Lateness is never excusable in the army.'

'I'm sorry, sir,' Krishna said formally.

Warren's voice softened and he half-smiled, 'Unless it's a matter of life or death.'

But a burning, the passing of a man's earthly cloak, *is* a matter of life and death, Krishna thought. Ah, that was the answer: life-*and*-death, not life-*or*-death. *That* did not matter so much, to a Hindu.

The rissaldar-major marched in, saluting and said, 'Prisoner and escort ready, sahib.'

Warren turned to Captain Himat Singh who was already there, standing beside his chair. 'This fellow Manraj. Is he a good man, otherwise?'

'Very good, sir. I saw him kill a German gunner at Poucelle just as the man was going to fire his gun into the troop.'

'All right. March him in.'

Krishna Ram stood at attention while the rissaldar-major had the escort march the prisoner in. He was a burly young man, fair skinned, eyes blue-green, face placid.

Warren Bateman read the charge in Hindi: 'Conduct prejudicial to good order and military discipline, that is, contracting venereal disease ... The Doctor-sahib says you have gonorrhoea. How did you get it?'

'A week ago, sahib, when I had a day's pass. I spent the day helping a man plough his land two miles down the road, for I saw he could not do it by himself. When we finished he fed me and then it was dark. Coming back through his village a woman came up to me and pulled my arm. I thought she needed help in some manner, for why else should an *Angrezi* woman ...'

'Not *Angrezi* [English],' Warren corrected him—'*Fransezi* [French]. There is a difference.'

'... a white Fransezi woman call upon a desi [native] man? But inside she pulled up her skirt and held out her hand and said, "*Ek rupaiya*" in our tongue. I knew then that she was a loose woman such as they have, it is said, in the Hira Mandi of Lahore, even *Angrezi* ...'

'Not *Angrezi*,' Warren said, 'half castes, perhaps.'

'Very good, sahib ... I am a man. It is a long time since I enjoyed my wife. I had a rupee in my pocket.'

He ended. Warren said, 'So you had intercourse with her?'

'Yes, sahib. Then, a week later ...'

'I know ... What does the doctor say, Himat Singh?'

'He's curing him with Vedic medicines, sir, at his request. He says he will be fit for duty in another week.'

Krishna looked at the sowar curiously. He had had carnal knowledge of a white woman—he, a peasant from the foothills—while he, himself, a Son of the Sun, could not imagine doing so.

Warren Bateman drummed his fingers on the table and finally said, 'You have done a disgraceful thing. You might have infected

133

your brothers in arms with this foulness. These women are destroyers of manhood, understand? If we were called to the front now, you would not be able to fight with your squadron. You would stay behind, like a woman or child.'

'Yes, sahib.'

'Do you plead guilty, or not guilty, to the charge?'

The man looked puzzled, 'Why, guilty, of course, sahib. I have just said ...'

'Twenty-eight days' rigorous imprisonment, to be served with his squadron as soon as he is fit. No confinement or special duties.' The RM barked orders, boots thumped, sabres glittered, spurs jingled and clashed. Krishna Ram said, 'Anything more for me, sir?' He felt warm and respectful towards the CO. He had expected him to give the man a heavier punishment; but the effect of the twenty-eight days' RI ordered was simply that the man would lose twenty-eight days' pay—there would be no humiliating imprisonment or extra punishment.

Major Bateman said, 'Yes. Sit down ... First, your appointment as acting second-in-command has been made permanent. Congratulations.'

Krishna said formally, 'Thank you, sir. I'll do my best to support you in whatever way you want me to.' Privately he thought, I wish they'd appoint another major and let me stay with A Squadron. Second-in-command was a hard job to handle, being always in the shadow of the CO, never expected or indeed able to give commands on your own—for you commanded nothing, not even a single sowar, except your orderlies and trumpeter.

Warren said, 'What do you think of the men's morale?'

'It's good, sir,' Krishna said without hesitation. 'The fatigues up the line are the worst thing. The men are getting barely one night in bed, and it's very exhausting work.'

'I know,' Warren said, 'but I don't know what we can do about it. The stuff has to be carried up the line somehow. We're no worse off than any other regiment.'

'Yes, sir ... There are some things they would like to have changed, I believe, but ...'

'Such as what?'

'Permission to wear caste marks when off duty would mean a lot to some of them ... As this Manraj case shows, I think they're going to miss women soon. In Basohli the bachelors used to go to brothels, but most of the men are married. They lived with their families in the city. They're not used to separation.'

'They'll have to *get* used to it, like the rest of us,' Major Bateman said grimly. 'I'd like to let them wear *tilaks*, myself, but neither General Glover nor General Rogers will permit it, as you know. About the women ... the problem is these damned French whores. Or loose women. Their husbands are away at the war and they make hay ...'

'I suppose some of them are short of money,' Krishna said.

'I suppose so,' Warren said grudgingly, 'but that doesn't help us. I've talked privately with some of the COs of Indian infantry battalions in the division, and we are all worried about it. It's not a good situation, but no one knows what to do, except restrict the men still more when they're out of the line, and that's not right.'

Krishna thought, no, it's not a good situation. In India where there were so few British, and they the rulers, it was as much as an Indian's life was worth to make the smallest advance to an English-woman. The lesson had been learned in the Mutiny, when the rape of a white woman, without other violence, would result in the slaughter of whole villages—men, women, and babies—and a wave of oppression that might last six months, with Indians forced to crawl on their stomachs past any English person. Then the English would agree to forget and all was smiles and offhand politeness again. But, then, surely someone in authority should have seen the danger of taking Indian soldiers to France, where there was noth-ing but white women, some of them naturally of a class that most sowars had never met and probably did not believe to exist. But now they *were* here, and they *did* need women, and willing women were obviously to be found, so ... He was about to make a sugges-tion but Major Bateman's manner discouraged him. He'd wait till he had had time to think it out more fully.

Major Bateman said, 'My wife's lost another relative. A cousin gone down in a destroyer. This war's hitting some of us very hard ... That's all, Krishna, except one thing.' He stood up, smiling. 'We're being inspected by the King-Emperor tomorrow.'

'King George?' Krishna gasped. 'Here?'

'Yes. I believe the Queen was going to come but she got influenza and His Majesty insisted on coming in her place. We'll have every-one in the BEF on our necks, from Sir John French down, so let's put on a good show. I'm going to work something out with the

135

adjutant and the RM now, and will issue orders here at four. Durbar at five.'

Krishna Ram saluted and went out. The King-Emperor! He never thought he would see him more closely than he had at the Delhi Durbar of 1911, when, as heir-presumptive to the *gaddi* of a rather small state, he had been one of the mass of young princes who had sat at the foot of the throne during the imperial coronation. The great Durbar had awed him, but his memories of it were less clear than of expeditions into the warrens of Delhi with a couple of other princes, considerably more profligate than himself, and of spending a great deal more money than he had been allotted. He remembered that his return to Basohli had felt unexpectedly like a first seeing, everything new and exciting, the air fresh, the trees extending bare arms along the river, the Himalayas a giant slash of white across the northern sky, wood-smoke, moving shapes in the dark temple, the sound of music from the city.

This time he would see the King differently, as the leader of his people, the figurehead and unifying soul for millions of every colour, religion, caste, and race. He called Hanuman and told him the news, adding, 'Tomorrow my boots and belt must shine more brightly than the sun.'

'Why not? It is the Son of the Sun who wears them,' the orderly replied matter-of-factly. 'The King-Emperor will be dazzled.'

The regimental durbar took place at the edge of the wood beyond A Squadron's horse lines, the CO and officers standing under the trees and the sowars squatting in a packed semicircle on the grass. When the men had settled themselves comfortably, Warren Bateman said, 'Lads, we will all stand for durbar ... It is a protection against those who would wish to hold our ears while our hair turns grey.'

The sowars laughed in appreciation as they stood. Krishna thought, it will be more efficient this way, but even so thoughtful an Englishman as Warren Bateman did not understand what it meant to these men to be able to talk to their rulers, for as long as they wanted.

The CO said, 'Durbar is open. Let any who wish speak without fear of what is in his heart ... You. Paraschand, is it not, C Squadron?'

'Yes, sahib ... Sahib, it is in my mind that these *Fransezi* cultivate their land in a manner different from ours. Yet their cattle are fatter than ours and give more milk. I milked some cows for a *Fransezi* the other day and as God hears me each cow gave six *seers* of milk, not watery or blue, but full of cream. The wheat is gathered for the year and the barns are full. It is hard to understand the *Fransezi* when they say how many *bighas* of land were ploughed and sown in order to gather in that wheat ... but the wheat itself is good, the kernels firm and large, the ears heavy and thick, and altogether good. It is in my mind that we could learn something from these *Fransezi* farmers that would benefit us at home. But how can it be done in a thorough manner? For we will not learn all that is necessary, nor will we understand much that we see, by merely milking a cow here or helping with a plough there ... as I hear that one of our brothers did last week ... to his sorrow, it is said.'

The sowars shouted and banged their thighs with laughter, for all had long since heard of Manraj's mishap with the woman in Longmont. Catching sight of Manraj's face among the crowd, Krishna saw that he was laughing with the rest.

Rissaldar-Major Baldev Singh said, 'Much could be learned by a man willing to spend his leave working for a *Fransezi* farmer, it being understood by the *Fransezi* that the wages of the man are not in money but in being taught. But I cannot arrange it, for I speak no *Fransezi*.'

'I will look into it,' Major Bateman said, 'but remember that we are here to fight, not to plough fields.'

Krishna Ram could see by the faces nearby him that to the sowars there was no distinction, or exclusion; the land was under foot, a part of you.

An old lance-dafadar said, 'With respect to all, I think we should be careful of what we learn from these *Fransezi*. The cows are fat, yes ... but the children are thin. On the edge of a town ten miles beyond Longmont there is a big house. Know you what they keep in that house? Orphans! As though they had done some crime, to be shut up, instead of cared for by every man and woman eager to please the gods ... for the lord Krishna was once a helpless babe.'

'Well spoken, well spoken,' a dozen voices murmured.

Warren said, 'Next ...'

A sowar of A Squadron spoke up: 'During the action at Poucelle, we left ten of our brothers dead on the field. From each a finger was taken that it might be properly burned, which was done, as I saw with these eyes. But ... it is in my mind that a man will not fight so bravely for the honour of our sovereign and our regiment if he feels that his body may be left for dogs and rats to feed upon. Or for the Germans, who do not know our rites, to bury under this distant earth. Or is it that the Germans have Brahmins also as we do, to perform the sacred duties?'

Major Bateman said, 'The Germans have no Brahmins, for they are Christians, like us *Angrezi* ... It is impossible in a real war to bring back the bodies of our dead unless they fall in our own place. And it is only necessary when we are fighting against such savages as the tribesmen of the Afghan frontier, who will mutilate the dead and shame the living. I was with the squadrons at Poucelle. It was I who ordered them back, and to leave our dead upon the field, for the enemy artillery was ranging on us, and we would have suffered much in men and horses.'

'Sahib, we are willing to suffer that our dead may pass to rest in the manner required.'

The CO said, 'I know ... but you have seen only a hundredth part of the power of weapons today. You should spend a week with the infantry, as I have. If we tried to bring back our dead after a big action, there would be no regiment left. So, except where an officer thinks the dead can be brought back with no loss to the living, it is forbidden. *Hukm hai*, it is an order,' he said with a snap, using the phrase that puts an end to discussion. After a pause he said, 'You may be learning the wisdom of this order soon. The infantry battalions go up the line in their turns. We spend our days and most of our nights on fatigues for them, because we are cavalry. I have asked the general to include us in the normal roster for spells in the front line. He was doubtful—because we have no bayonets, for instance—but he said he would think it over.'

The men stirred and whispered among themselves, and Warren Bateman said, 'Next ... You, Bahar Singh.'

The rations were short, the sowar said: 'Why?'

Sohan Singh the fat quartermaster blandly explained that no rations had come up for two days after the last move, and the men had nearly starved—was it not so? A chorus of yeses agreed. So, he said, he was building up a little reserve of food for another such emergency. It was forbidden by regulations, but the colonel-sahib had given his permission and until it was done, everyone would receive only three-quarters of his proper ration.

Caste marks again; and the CO again saying they were forbidden. He did not, Krishna noted, bring in General Glover to shoulder the blame for an unpopular move, but took it on himself. Yet the men would know who was responsible. They were simple, but they were shrewd.

The festival of Dewali was due in a week's time. Would there be proper nautches, feasts and prayers, as was customary?

Warren hesitated a moment before answering. The big Dussehra celebrations soon after the battle of Poucelle had gone off very well from one point of view, but they had emphasized the men's far origin and foreign faith, and brought crowds of British troops and French civilians to stare at the prayers and garlands and sacrificial ceremonies. It had made Warren feel, he said, that he was commanding a mob of circus freaks, or beings from another planet. His officers' carefully applied Englishness had temporarily evaporated, like a thin layer of wax burned away by the Brahmin's prayers; and he had had to demote a lance-dafadar to the ranks for wearing a caste mark in defiance of orders.

But, there was no help for it—not yet. Unless the regiment was sent up the line, he'd have to allow the men to celebrate Dewali in the usual way. He answered the question. 'Yes, if we are not in the line. I shall tell the Quartermaster-sahib he can spend 300 rupees out of the regimental fund. As you know, he has some costumes. There will be a great *tamasha*.'

The men clapped and cheered. Then, after a few more minor points, as full darkness fell, and rain began to drip from the beech boughs, Warren Bateman said, 'Anything more? Very well. Durbar is ended. The next durbar will be one month from now.'

He turned on his heel and left, as the officers saluted and the rissaldar-major bellowed, 'Ravi Lancers—'ten ... *shun*!'

Krishna walked slowly to his billet. An interesting durbar. Perhaps they should be held more often than once a month. In conditions as strange as these in France were to them, the men needed a safety valve.

An hour later he was still sitting in his billet, a bottle of *vin ordinaire* on the bare table and a candle guttering in the neck of another bottle. The house, part of a long row of brick houses which faced a similar row across the only street of the little hamlet, rumbled to the passage of guns towards the front. Other guns muttered and grumbled indistinctly, for the wind was in the north, and a chilling draught blew through the cracked windows and fluttered the worn curtains. The owners had fled, God knows where, and Krishna occupied one downstairs room among a welter of disregarded fragments of their lives. There was a picture of a solemn wedding couple on the mantelpiece, a crucifix and a large stain on one wall, and on another a discoloured patch where a picture had been taken away or stolen, and on the chest of drawers a basket containing the knicknacks of a woman's sewing. The bed he had had brought in from another house. He looked at his wristwatch— more and more officers were wearing them nowadays, but *he* had been the first. Still nearly an hour to dinner.

Hanuman came in saying, 'Captain Sher Singh, lord.'

'Come in,' Krishna called as his orderly went out. Sher Singh entered, his palms joined, the neck of a bottle sticking out of the pocket of his British warm. 'Don't make *namasti* to me,' Krishna said irritably. 'Salute, man.'

The captain saluted hastily, and straightened his back from the ritual half bow that had gone with the *namasti*. 'I found a bottle of vintage wine, and as I don't drink ...'

'Some of your men found it, you mean,' Krishna said, reaching out his hand. The dusty label hardly decipherable, read *Vosne Romanée 1904*. He didn't know anything about vintages beyond a few tips Warren Bateman had given him since he started to drink, but this was obviously too good to keep to himself. He'd take it to Warren's billet one evening and they'd demolish it over a chat. Sher Singh was hanging around, as though waiting to be invited in. Krishna did not like him, but felt suddenly lonely for company and said, '*Andar aiye, bhai* ... Come in. Sit down.'

The captain sat down with alacrity and, at Krishna's command, lit a cigarette. 'How does the CO think we're doing, sir?' he asked, leaning forward with a frank, open expression on his face.

'All right,' Krishna replied. 'Our march discipline used to be bad, but the night drills the CO has ordered, and being harder on the VCOs, has had a good effect. Of course we haven't seen any action since Poucelle.'

'He's a very good trainer,' Sher Singh said enthusiastically. 'My God, I think we are lucky to have a sahib like Major Bateman! It is fortunate, really, that Colonel Hanbury died.'

'I suppose so. He was an honest gentleman,' Krishna said, 'but ...' he shrugged.

'Too old,' Sher Singh finished for him. 'But Major Bateman is a very strong man, he rides like, like ... one of these half-horse men ... like our own Indra-ji! He is ...'

The orderly appeared again: 'Captain Doctor Sahib, lord.' Ramaswami's lantern-jawed black face appeared round the door under the battered and dirty military cap with the badge of the Indian Medical Service on awry. He did not salute but said, 'Major Krishna Ram, I would like to speak to you.'

'Come in. Sit down. Anything private?'

'No.' The doctor sat down waving away the wine Krishna offered him. 'I don't care who knows what I think. If they don't like it they can only send me back to Madras and my gynaecological research and there's nothing I would like more ... Something must be done about getting women and entertainment for the men here. It is not as though we were in the front line.'

'God knows whether we ever will be, unless the general lets us go up as infantry,' Krishna said. 'This doesn't seem to be a cavalry war. That charge at Poucelle succeeded because the front was fluid and because we took the Germans by surprise. Really I don't think horsemen stand a chance against machine guns, and the number of machine guns being used is increasing as fast as they can be manufactured. And more barbed wire, which is fatal to cavalry ... So you advise, what?'

'My medical advice is—start a regimental brothel somewhere close to the billet area.'

'We always used to have one on manoeuvres,' Sher Singh said. 'You know that, we'd take out a dozen girls from Basohli. In the old days, before the British, we took girls along, too, when we were fighting Kangra or Chamba.'

'That was a long time ago,' Krishna Ram said. 'Have you spoken to the CO about this?'

The doctor said, 'No. He wouldn't permit it, because the women would have to be white.'

'He's not like that,' Krishna said.

The doctor said, 'Perhaps he was not, once. But he is becoming so now.'

Krishna shook his head uneasily. This sort of talk among the Indian officers, behind the CO's back, was not quite cricket, though

141

not actually disloyal. Yet he ought to hear what the doctor had to say. He poured himself another glass of wine.

Ramaswami said, 'That's all. If something isn't done about it soon—in a month or so—you may have serious trouble of some kind. Don't say I didn't warn you.'

'If anyone can get the CO to agree, the prince can,' Sher Singh said sententiously.

The doctor rose. He had kept his hat on all the time, and now gave an ungainly salute. 'You have always taken alcohol?'

Krishna shook his head. The doctor said, 'You're drinking more than you should.'

'I like the taste of it,' Krishna said defensively, 'and it does make me feel good, just a couple of drinks.'

'You're taking much more than a couple of drinks,' the doctor said. 'Liquor also serves to help a man push out of his mind something that is worrying him.'

He saluted again and was gone. 'He has a nerve,' Sher Singh said, indignantly, 'speaking to you like that, highness! I mean—sir!'

Krishna drained his glass, 'Oh, what the bloody hell does it matter? He is only a black Madrassi *yoni* doctor, a peerer-up of cunts.' He poured himself another drink.

Next morning he awoke to a fuzzed head and a furred tongue, but after he had stripped and washed from head to toe in the ice cold water of a bucket, standing in the tiny back yard among derelict pea and tomato plants, he felt better. He dressed with care, praising Hanuman for the glasslike polish on his belt and riding boots and the chinstrap of his peaked cap. After examining his charger and its saddlery he went to the CO's office, where he had been bidden to meet the acting divisional commander an hour before the King was due to arrive. The CO was already there and a few minutes later Brigadier-General 'Rainbow' Rogers rode up accompanied by a General Staff officer.

When he had dismounted he said, 'Let's go into your office a moment, Bateman. There are some matters I'd like to discuss before the King arrives. You come too, Krishna Ram.' Warren Bateman led the way into his office. Warren said, 'Congratulations, sir.'

The general looked down at the double row of medal ribbons on his left breast. 'Oh, yes, it was in Divisional orders wasn't it, about the Cross of Serbia, 5th Class. Pretty ribbon, isn't it?'

'What are the rest, sir?' Warren Bateman asked, with every appearance of enthusiastic interest. 'I never had a chance to ask you on the *Nerbudda*.' Krishna looked at his CO with veiled suspicion. Major Bateman was buttering the general up; for on the ship he had said more than once that Rogers was the only man in the army who had managed to amass even one row of ribbons without including a single campaign medal or decoration. And now he had reached two full rows—ten medals, and still not one for battle!

'This is the MVO, of course,' the general said, craning his neck eagerly at his own ribbons. 'And this is the Légion d'Honneur. This is the Belgian Order of St. Leopold. This one's Russian. This is an Italian order. I was Military Attaché in Rome in 1907. This one . . .' —he went hurriedly on to the next, missing one—'This is the Order of Manoel. I had the honour of acting as Aide de Camp to His Majesty the King of Portugal when he came grouse shooting in Scotland in 1905.' He straightened his back where he sat on the edge of the CO's table, while the other two stood. 'Talking of medals, your fellow who led the charge against the German guns at Poucelle is getting a DSO. Can't remember these Indian names for the life of me.'

'Captain Himat Singh,' Major Bateman said. 'That's very good news, sir. Our first decoration.'

'That's the fellow. And some Indian medal for a few NCOs and troopers. The GSO has the names and details. His Majesty is going to present them this morning. I'm not getting anything, though the Corps Commander said in his dispatch that my plan was of great boldness . . . How are you getting on, turning these Indians into officers and gentlemen, Bateman?'

'Pretty well, I think, sir.'

'Good. Everyone know how to use a WC decently now?'

'Yes, sir.'

Krishna cut in, 'Though we have found that a good many of the French WCs are like the ones used in India.' Warren looked at him sharply, and he was silent. He had, after all, not been asked for his opinion.

'So they are,' the general said. 'Damned Frogs are as bad as Wogs! Ha ha . . . Got rather a tricky situation in Longmont. I wish I could leave it till General Glover gets back—he ought to be fit again in another week—but I can't. A couple of brothels have sprung up there, and we don't want the sepoys and sowars going to them and getting ideas. I've told the Gurkhas, who are nearest, to put strong regimental police patrols into the place. You'd better do the same.'

'Yes, sir,' Warren said.

'And the Fusiliers, sir?' Krishna asked. 'They're closer than either us or the Gurkhas.'

The general looked at him in astonishment. 'They're British,' he said. 'No reason they shouldn't patronize Frog whores. As long as we inspect the women regularly, which the RMO of the Fusiliers is doing ...' He looked at his watch. 'Half an hour to go. We'd better get ready.'

Major Bateman turned to Krishna as the general left, and snapped, 'Find out who's getting decorated. Have them lined up in front of the regiment, directly behind me, unless the GSO 1 orders it done some other way ... And if I want you to give your opinions to the general, I'll ask you to.' He strode out, his spurs clashing on the stone floor, before Krishna could speak.

For a moment he experienced an emotion new to him—a generalized anger which he could not point at any one person or thing. But, before it could build up, he was involved in the mounting splendour of an imperial review of a regiment of lancers. There was not the yellow and white of a parade at Basohli, nor the scarlet and blue and gold he had seen when the regulars marched past at Lahore, for the regiment was wearing khaki; but the leather belts and bandeliers winked in the winter sun, and the horses' coats shone and the heads tossed and the bits jingled while the band played the march, and His Majesty smiled at him. Soon the white and gold enamel cross of the Distinguished Service Order gleamed on Himat Singh's tunic, and Himat Singh stood a foot taller and rode like Arjun in the skies at the head of B Squadron; and Sowar Ajit Ram and Rissaldar Ram Lall wore the Indian Order of Merit, and half a dozen more the Indian Distinguished Service Medal.

To end the review, the regiment cantered past. From his post alone at the very back of them all, Krishna Ram saw the flanking guidons move past His Majesty standing in a big motor car, General Rogers at his side; then Warren riding to stand beside the car; then the leading squadron, his own old A under the young devil Ishar Lall, cantered past in a shaky line, to the music of *Bonny Dundee*. The ground shook to twenty-four hundred hoofs, the ends of six hundred turbans flew out in the wind, six hundred steel lance

144

points glittered in the wintry sun. The rear rank of D Squadron passed His Majesty. Krishna's trumpeter rode ahead on his right and Hanuman on his left. He raised the heavy sabre guard from his right thigh, brought it to his lips and, as he looked right, lowered the point out and down to the full extent of his right arm. He was looking straight into the eyes of the King, half hidden under the peak of his red-banded cap. A small man, he thought, but regal. The bearded lips parted in a half smile and one gloved hand touched the peak of the cap. Krishna snapped his eyes to the front, and brought his sabre back to attention. The point hovered in front of his right eye, moving slightly back and forth to the charger's powerful motion. King of England, he thought. Emperor of India.

Four days later the Hindustan Division moved up the line and into the First Battle of St. Rambert. They were mown down by machine guns, failed to take their objectives, were cut to pieces by German artillery, were then counter-attacked and destroyed by German infantry in overwhelming numbers. Major-General Glover returned from sick leave the day after the débâcle. Thirty-six hours later he sent for Warren Bateman and Krishna Ram. In the drawing room of the small château where his headquarters was established, the general said, 'Sit down, both of you ... Do you know how many casualties the Lahore Brigade had at St. Rambert? ... 515 killed and 1,300 wounded. The 8th Brahmins were the worst hit—247 killed, 408 wounded, that's 655 out of a total strength of 800. The other battalions have adequate reinforcement systems, but the Brahmins don't, and we can't post men to them from anywhere else. The brigade is due to go back up the line in three weeks or less, and it will be ready, except the Brahmins. There's been no task for divisional cavalry since the war of movement ended and we settled into the trenches. I foresee no suitable task in the immediate future, either. You know I'm an infantryman—40th Pathans—but that's the unfortunate fact ... I have received the Corps Commander's approval to pull the 8th Brahmins out of the Lahore Brigade and keep them in divisional reserve until they can be built up—if ever. You will replace them in the Lahore Brigade ... fighting as infantry. This is what you asked General Rogers for, isn't it, when he was acting for me?'

Krishna's first feeling was of dismay ... to lose their beautiful horses, to trudge in the mud instead of riding in splendour. But for some weeks now, as the ambulances came endlessly past from the front, he had felt uneasily aware that he was not doing what he had come to France to do. Also, the horses suffered horribly when exposed to modern explosives. He himself had volunteered for this war, but they had not.

Beside him, Warren Bateman said, 'Thank you, sir. It'll take a little time to teach the men bayonet drill. We'll need to be issued with infantry equipment. Otherwise I don't think there'll be any difficulties ... We'll miss our horses, of course, but if we have to give them up to get into the fighting, we're happy to do so.'

'Good man!' the general said heartily, 'I knew I could rely on you ... And you, Yuvraj, I hope you'll explain to your grandfather the necessity of this change.'

'I will, sir. How long do you think we will be infantry?'

The general hesitated, then said, 'It may be a long time. The Army Commander thinks that if the 8th Brahmins can't be properly reinforced, they had better be sent back to India. So count on a long haul.'

'That's the only way to tackle a change as big as this,' Warren said. 'Is that all, sir?'

'Yes. Brigadier-General Rogers is expecting you at his headquarters. Good luck.'

December 1914

WARREN BATEMAN SAT at the head of the table in the back room of the estaminet, methodically carving up the piece of meat on his plate. It was supposed to be hare, shot by the Terrible Twins on a recent shoot a few miles farther south, but it had not been hung long enough to be tender. Blankets covered the window. It was five o'clock in the afternoon, and dark; it was four days to Christmas. The officers, like the men, were eating dinner early, because the regiment was due to move up the line later that evening. A winter wind blew in under the warped door, and the stone flags chilled his feet even through the boots and thick socks he was wearing. Like the other officers he didn't wear field boots now, only hobnailed infantry marching boots, or fur-lined boots sent out by friends and relatives—in his case by his sister Diana— and thick woollen socks knitted by the same loving womenfolk. The sowars had no relatives in England and he had long ago asked his mother to arrange something, a request which resulted in a flood of mittens and socks, of which he had ordered that the first allotments should go to Ramaswami for use in the RAP.

The rumble of lorries passing down the street was continuous, punctuated now and then by the tramp of marching men and the squeal of bagpipes or the thud of a drum to give the step. Some of the infantry sang *Tipperary* as they passed, some went by in silence.

'It must be a very big attack,' someone said. 'The lorries have been going up all day.'

'And all last night,' another added.

'We're going to break through on the Longmont Canal,' Dayal Ram said with authority. 'The French are going to attack farther south and once the German reserves have moved down there, the

BEF will break through here. Then the cavalry will go through—and we've lost our horses.'

'How do you know all this,' Puran Lall scoffed, 'are you a personal friend of Sir John French?'

'I heard it in London,' Dayal Ram said. He was just back from a week's leave, and had dark circles under his eyes. 'Lady Harriet Symonds told me, and she heard it from her uncle, who's in the cabinet.' He turned his handsome head to Krishna Ram, a little down the table and said with a lazy smile, 'Lady Harriet is ... an exciting young lady, highness. I can't thank you enough for giving me her name. I found her in the telephone book, easily.'

Warren lifted his head, 'We do not discuss ladies in mess, Dayal.'

His adjutant turned to him with the same lazy smile, a smile subtly different from what it had been before he went on leave, as though he had learned something to Warren's detriment.

'But, sir ...' he began.

'No buts. We do not mention a woman's name in mess. Nor discuss politics. Nor religion. Nor shop.'

He bent again to his hare. He never used to think the old custom was very sensible. After all, what was left that should interest a man if you took out those four—in effect, his life and his work? But he had not been in command of a regiment in war then; and with his command resting on the whim of 'Rainbow' Rogers, for he was very junior to be promoted to lieutenant-colonel. If he displeased the general in any way, they could bring in someone of the right seniority to replace him. He sometimes wondered whether he would really mind. It was a hard business, and often unpleasant, to force such fundamentally nice people as these, with their different background and way of thought, to understand what was necessary to win wars and hold empires.

Now Dayal's talk of London and Harriet Symonds made him think of his own home, Shrewford Pennel under the Plain, and his wife and children. He missed them. Why couldn't they all, here at the table, talk about the people they loved, their homes so far away—for Shrewford Pennel was as far now as Basohli under the Himalayas, inaccessible both. Why not sit round showing each other photographs, talking of children, the first step, the first word?

He shook his head. That way led only to misery, regret, unhappiness, yearning for the impossible ... softness of mind and body.

148

'Oh, sahib, sir,' Sohan Singh the quartermaster said. 'Not wanting talking shop but any information on immediate future of regiment will be most welcome. Rations slow arriving and often going wrong place! Fodder often so bad *salutri* not allowing give to wagon horses, but where can I find other?'

Warren said, 'I told you all I know at orders this afternoon, Sohan. We're moving up tonight to Semur, where the brigade will wait in reserve to exploit success. How long we will have to wait, and what direction we will eventually advance in, will depend on the success of the leading waves.'

'They must be starting the barrage now,' Himat Singh said. 'Listen to the guns.'

The estaminet's walls trembled and the air in the room shuddered to a new sound that was also deeper than sound. Warren pulled back the blanket an inch to look out. Still the infantry tramped by, rifles slung reversed to protect the muzzles from the light sleet. Mud splashed the window as an officer cantered past on his charger. Warren dropped the blanket back into place. Inside no one spoke, all listening to the artillery. Then Ishar Lall leaned across the table to Mahadeo Singh, the ex-rissaldar, and said, 'I hope you enjoyed the meal, Mahadeo.'

'*Jee-ha*, sahib. Yes,' Mahadeo said, who could never get out of the habit of calling officers 'sahib' though he had been one himself for nearly three years now.

Ishar Lall said, 'I thought you would. But we must not tell the Brahmin. It was dog.'

Mahadeo pushed his chair back and stared at his plate with a look of horror, for he was devout in his observances. 'Dog, sahib?' he faltered. 'You said it was hare.'

'That's what we intended,' Ishar Lall said shaking his head, 'my brother and I, but alas ... we never saw a hare or a rabbit all day. We had promised the mess dafadar and the *khansamah* to bring back food. We had nothing. What could we do? We saw this plump dog, and ...'

Mahadeo put his hands over his mouth and rushed for the door. A moment later they heard him retching and vomiting at the door to the street.

'Is it really dog?' Bholanath said nervously.

'Some people think dog is a great delicacy,' Ishar Lall said. 'In China now, I have read ...'

'Of course it's not dog,' Himat Singh said firmly. He glanced at Warren with a smile. 'I suggest our young friend might be debagged, sir, don't you?'

'After dinner you can do what you like with him,' Warren said, smiling.

'I can defend myself, sir,' Ishar cried. 'I have my private army.'

There was a tremendous clatter at the door, the mess dafadar burst in backwards giggling like a girl, his hands over his mouth. In rode the other Twin, Puran Lall, astride a small donkey. He was carrying an aluminium basin like a shield and wielding a long loaf of French bread like a sword. The donkey kicked and farted and brayed deafeningly. Puran Lall cried, 'Who attacks my brother attacks me ... and Gokalji here!' He kicked the donkey's flanks.

Warren got up and said, 'Just leave enough of them for the Germans to finish off tomorrow.' He edged past the donkey's flank and went grinning to his office. At last, when they were just about to go into battle, the Ravi people were beginning to act and think like British officers—a boisterous family rather than feudal servants or a prince's cronies.

At eight the march began. The Gurkhas passed through, the Ravi Lancers uncoiled from the fields and yards where they had formed up, and moved out on to the road. Warren watched each squadron emerge and saw that the practices he had enforced, the shielded lights he had placed, the gallopers sent to the squadron ahead, the daylight reconnaissance, had paid dividends. The Ravi Lancers moved out now like Indian Army regulars, experienced regulars at that. He hurried up the flank of the column until he reached the head. Dayal Ram and Mahadeo made way for him and he settled down to the march, fastened the wrist bands of his burberry against the sleet, put on his gloves, adjusted the woollen ear muffs under his cap, and bent his head to keep the sleet out of his eyes. Shikari trotted at his side. St. Hubert-sur-Yevre, their home for over two months, fell back into the whistling dark.

It had felt good in the mess there when the subalterns began to show the boisterous energy that he remembered from his own regiment; but it had also emphasized his loneliness as the only Englishman. He had not had much to say to Hanbury while he was alive, but at least he'd been there. Now he was alone, and there was no one he could talk things over with. Sometimes he felt like taking

Flaherty into his confidence. At least he had been raised a Christian, and with English rather than Indian ideals. This was being unfair to Krishna, who was thoroughly loyal. Perhaps it was not so much the exchanging of words that he missed as a common feeling, a sense that the others *knew*, that they shared your thoughts and emotions, without words being necessary. With an Indian, you could not be sure what he felt until he told you ... and often not even then.

A voice called, 'Major Bateman?'

A horseman appeared. It was an officer from Brigade Headquarters. 'Change of orders, sir,' he said, riding alongside. 'The brigade's destination tonight is Triel, not Semur. That's about six miles east of Semur but no farther. We turn right off this road at a cross-roads a mile and a half ahead.'

'Are you posting route sentries there?' Warren asked.

'Yes, sir.'

'And I hope the Q people have been told, so that our rations don't finish up in Semur. Damn it, why can't we carry out a simple march without having the orders changed in the middle ... probably half a dozen times?'

'Sorry, sir,' the officer said, 'it's not our fault. Orders from Division.' He rode on down the column, while Warren turned to his officer-galloper, Mahadeo Singh, and told him to pass on the change of destination to the squadrons. Now he was awake and alert again, and noted the steady thud of the guns from the north-east. The heaviest of it seemed to come from the right, so the turn they were about to make would take them more directly towards the battle.

He watched the whole regiment make the turn at the cross-roads, not wanting to risk having another squadron go astray, as B had done in September, and ran back up to his place. The road began to be littered with the debris of recent shelling. He remembered that he had passed here a month ago when he had been taken on a tour of the front line. Now they were marching through a village where an infantry division HQ had been. He remembered it as a small friendly place, the windows like smiling eyes in the red brick walls. Now, dimly sensed in the darkness, it seemed to have subsided closer to the earth, to be lying there exhausted, beaten down. The houses spread in rubble half way across the street and the church was only a bigger lump, its ruin seen more clearly by the momentary flash of a nearby gun glaring through the empty windows.

They marched by a battery of heavy artillery in action, and Warren thought, that means we are now in range of the enemy's heavies, too. There was nothing he could do, no orders he could give, to lessen the danger. The regiment was in column of route, with other troops ahead and behind. If the move was to be completed, the risk would have to be taken.

An hour before dawn the brigade reached Triel. There the general formed the four battalions up in close column of companies in the empty plain, the right resting on a road and the 41st Field Battery on the flank. Once they were all in position, and at rest, Major Tommy Greville, the battery commander, strolled over to join Warren. Warren felt a warm delight to see him. 'Here,' he said, 'have a fill of tobacco.'

'Thanks, but I use these,' the gunner said. He opened his silver cigarette case and lit one. As the light strengthened they chatted desultorily. Then Greville said, 'Well, I'll be getting back. We've got a hot breakfast in the cooking.'

'Have breakfast with me,' Warren said, 'I don't know what we've got, but ...'

'Thanks, old man, but Bob and de Marquez are expecting me.' With a wave of his hand he strolled off. Warren watched him, wishing he had invited himself to join the gunners. Now he must eat his breakfast alone.

It began to snow. The rumble of the guns was muted by the thick air, though they were closer than before; and now, over the deep roar of the heavies and mediums the staccato bark of the field pieces was plain to hear.

Having eaten, Warren walked round the regiment. They were in good order, waiting patiently, huddled in little groups, rifles piled in neat rows, sentries at the ends of each squadron.

He reached the end of C Squadron's line, glanced north, and paused. A column of about a hundred grey-clad men was coming down the road, some marching in perfect rhythm, some stumbling and sliding in the snow, some bandaged, some supporting others. Here and there he saw spiked helmets, but mostly they showed cropped bare heads, seeming to have lost their helmets in the act of losing their liberty. Half a dozen British tommies with fixed bayonets escorted the prisoners. A moment later the corporal in charge gave an order and the column came to a straggling halt in the road opposite C Squadron.

The corporal said, 'Ten minutes 'alt, Jerry.' He lit a cigarette and strolled down the line with rifle slung, the bayonet sticking high in the air, snow a white mantle on his shoulders. Warren noticed with astonishment that several of the Germans near him wore the word GIBRALTAR embroidered in large letters high on the right sleeve of their tunics. He pointed with his pipe and said, 'Gibraltar? Why?' Scraping up what he could recall of the German he had learned in school, he said, '*Warum tragen Sie Gibraltar auf dem Frock?*'

The nearest German leaped up, clicked his heels, and said, 'We are the 14th Hanover, sir. The regiment served in the Great Siege of Gibraltar under Lord Eliott, when the King of England was also Elector of Hanover, and was awarded "Gibraltar" as a special battle honour, to be worn on the sleeve.'

'You speak English well,' Warren said.

'I should, sir. I spent fifteen years in Brighton playing in the orchestra at the Metropole.'

Warren nodded. A dozen sowars of C Squadron had come to the edge of the road to listen to the talk. Some pushed through the hedge now and, smiling, pulled out packets of *bidis* and pushed them towards the Germans in gestures of friendship.

'Never seen a cigarette like this before,' the German musician-soldier said, examining the *bidi* curiously.

Warren was about to explain that they were the miniature cigars of rolled green-leaf tobacco of India, very strong, foul smelling, and cheap; but he felt uneasily that he should not be so familiar. This was war, these men were the enemy, even though they had become prisoners. Suppose they overpowered the escort; it would take his men some time to realize that was happening, unpile the rifles ...

He heard a sowar saying to a prisoner with a bloodstained bandage round his head, '*Apka zakhm sakht hai, sahib?*' He was asking the German whether his wound was serious, but he was addressing the man, apparently a private, by the respectfully polite term 'sahib'. Warren felt perplexed and doubtful. The man was white, a European, therefore he *was* a sort of sahib ... but these were the enemy, men whom the sowars were supposed to kill, shoot, destroy.

He looked around, saw a jemadar nearby, and said to him curtly,

'Get the men back in the ranks, jemadar-sahib.'

'Understood, sahib!' The jemadar saluted and bustled down on the men in the road, shouting, 'Get back to your lines! Hurry up, now!'

Warren returned to his post, and settled down to wait, sometimes standing, sometimes sitting. The snow fell, the NCOs put the men through exercises to keep them warm. The guns shouted and roared to right and left, and a few enemy shells fell in the fields around the waiting brigade, but did no damage. Warren thought they were lucky that the scurrying impenetrable snow clouds prevented observation by enemy aircraft. A brigade of infantry drawn up in close column of companies, covering less than a quarter of a square mile of land, would make a very juicy artillery target.

At dusk the brigade-major came and told Warren they were to wait in position till further orders, but bivouacs could be made in the lines. The sowars unrolled their groundsheets, set up the little shelters, and crawled in. The rows of piled rifles stood like votive pyramids among the bivouacs. The hours passed in slow chill. The men ate the last of their rations. Towards the front star shells glowed in the white haze, and a change in the uncertain wind brought down the stammer of machine guns.

Warren dozed fitfully in his bivouac, awoke, walked the lines of his regiment, dozed again. The second dawn in the position came with continued snow, though still not heavy. An hour later a line of GS wagons rolled up the road from the south and in the fourth one Warren recognized the round, snow-draped figure of Sohan Singh the quartermaster. 'Rations coming, sah!' he cried, with a wide smile and a terrible salute somewhere behind his ear. Warren grinned back, out of his cold and hunger. Sohan Singh was no soldier but he was a gem. The quartermaster personally handed him a pair of tins, unlabelled, saying, 'That is only rations available, sah.' His voice sounded urgent and Warren looked up. The quartermaster was looking at him with a sort of dumb pleading.

It was on the tip of Warren's tongue to ask, 'What is it?' Then he realized. The tins in his hand were without doubt bully beef. Someone, somewhere, had taken off the labels, which usually showed a bull. None of the men had ever eaten beef so they would not know what this was. But was it fair to cheat them? The rissaldar-major would take it as a personal betrayal, if ...

The quartermaster said, 'Rissaldar-major sahib taking labels off

154

personally, sah. He and me, together. No one else knowing. No other food, nothing! I searching high, low, every place, upside, downside, inside out.'

Warren nodded. 'Very good.'

He opened one can of bully and ate slowly. Rissaldar-Major Baldev Singh was another gem, as unlike Sohan Singh as possible— but between them, invaluable.

Three more hours passed and he began to get irritated. His men had been kept in this bloody field for nearly twenty-eight hours now. He was striding off towards brigade headquarters when the brigade-major appeared from that direction, walking quickly through the churned snow. He said, 'We're going into billets here. Your regiment is allotted Triel village there, just up the road. It's in ruins, of course; Brigade Headquarters will be in a farmhouse about a mile back. All regiments are to be at two hours' notice to move.'

'All right,' Warren said, 'but what's happening? What's happened to the attack the infantry were making? We were supposed to be breaking through before now, weren't we?'

'We have heard nothing more than that there's been a change in plan.'

The BM rode off. A column of GS wagons came down the road, loaded with bandaged men lying under groundsheets. That was the cause—or the consequence—of the delay, Warren thought. He sent Dayal Ram to gather the officers for orders.

The next day he awoke in the second-least ruined house in Triel. The quartermaster had allotted the best to Captain Ramaswami for the Regimental Aid Post, as Warren's standing order instructed him to do. Warren shaved while a steady drip of water from melting snow fell through a hole in the battered roof on to his head. He decided that the men must be properly exercised. The ground was in a bad state, and they would be filthy, but there was no help for it. As soon as they had eaten, he sent the squadrons out to practise extended order drill, at the double. For two hours they ran around the fields and heaps of rubble, and came back splashed from head to foot.

When Regimental Headquarters dismissed from its exercise Krishna Ram came up to him and said, 'It's durbar day, sir. May I suggest we make it at three o'clock. It's dark later.'

Warren hesitated, then said, 'Do you think it's necessary to hold durbar in these conditions? I thought we might do without until we got back to a rest area.'

'The men will miss it, sir,' Krishna Ram said, his face troubled. Warren said, 'I'm not sure that durbars are really advisable here. Circumstances are very different from peace time in India.'

Krishna Ram said respectfully, 'I think that's why it's so important. When so much is strange to them durbar is something to hold on to.'

'Oh, very well then,' Warren said. 'Three o'clock.'

At three the men were gathered, except for the billet sentries and the quarter guard, all standing, snow again falling on their turbans and great coats. Warren glanced around and saw that all the officers and VCOs were present except the rissaldar-major. The senior rissaldar, Ram Lall, said, 'The rissaldar-major-sahib has gone back to visit two sowars in hospital, sir.'

Warren opened durbar. The first question was from a young sowar who wanted to know why there were so many changes of orders. 'It was not like this in Basohli,' he said seriously.

Warren answered, 'I fear the Germans do not obey our orders, lad. War is not run on a timetable, like the te-rains'; but privately, he would have liked to ask the general the same question.

Next, a sowar said, 'Yesterday the rations were of a strange food I have never seen in ten years of service. I ate, as we all did, for we were hungry and there was nothing else. But it is proper that a man know what he is eating. The rissaldar-major-sahib will perhaps tell us.'

Warren understood in a flash why the RM had taken himself off to the hospital. He had known that the meat was beef and had not eaten it; nor could he lie about it if asked a question. The sowars, on the other hand, who had not known, could not be held guilty of any serious sin.

The quartermaster raised his voice, 'The food was sheep, broken up and boiled with salt and a little spice. It is called bully mutton.'

Warren took the next question, thinking, Sohan Singh, being a good bazaar merchant, would have no hesitation in lying ... which was a good thing in the circumstances.

A lance dafadar said, 'Last week I bumped into Lieutenant Flaherty sahib by error. The lieutenant-sahib called me a black ape. It is not proper, I think, to speak so to a Dogra Rajput of the Kshatriya caste, especially ...'

Warren cut in quickly, for the man was clearly going to add, 'especially for one who is as black himself'. He said, 'Mr. Flaherty, did you use those words to the lance-dafadar?'

The big man shuffled his feet and said, 'I don't remember. He wasn't looking where he was going. I was tired, sir ... I may have.'

Warren said gently, 'Tell him now that you were tired, and meant no offence ... Go on, man!'

He tightened his lips. Flaherty's eyes dropped and he mumbled, 'I apologize. It was a bad thing to say. I ... I was tired.'

The NCO made *namasti* towards the lieutenant and there was a murmur from the six hundred men as though from a single throat. 'Well spoken, sahib!'

Warren said in English, 'You've done more for yourself by that little speech, Flaherty, than all your good work with the Signal Section.'

A youngish sowar whom Warren remembered as being in A Squadron—he thought he was trumpeter to No. 2 Troop—said, 'Sahib, I am an ignorant black man—' Warren almost smiled, thinking how typical it was for the sowars to call themselves 'only natives' or 'black men', but to object to anyone using the same words to them—'but it was said that this war was to save the Nazrani religion. Yet in every village we pass through, the church has been destroyed. It is said ... I have heard wise men in my village say it ... that the Nazranis do not believe it is right to kill. No man shall kill is an order of their god. It is also a command of their god, that if a man be hurt by another, then he who is hurt shall not smite him who hurts him, but turn the other cheek, to be again smitten. If this is truth, that I hear ... and as Vishnu knows, it may be no more than wind in the trees ... then my soul is troubled to know what this war is about. Why does one Nazrani kill another? Why do not the Fransezis and Germans each turn again to be smitten, rather than fight?'

Warren stared at the boy. Was he a barrack-room lawyer? Had some of those damned agitators got at him? He looked innocent enough, but that proved nothing. The question itself was impossible to answer, but he'd have to try. He wished he had a padre present to do it for him.

He said carefully, 'As to the churches ... we Nazranis do not believe that God resides in them. It is a pity that they have to be destroyed, but our God is not there, he is in our hearts ... As to the

157

other, it is true what you have heard, what is written in our Holy Book, but only certain holy men and saints can live by that word. For the rest of us, men and nations, when we are smitten, we smite back, only harder. Otherwise we would lose our honour, and our enemies would abuse our women before our eyes.'

The regiment murmured agreement, but the trumpeter's face remained troubled, and Warren noticed that Krishna Ram was gazing at him thoughtfully.

'Any more?' he said. 'Durbar is closed.' He strode away and to his billet.

He was awakened in the middle of the night by a hand on his shoulder and his adjutant's voice, 'Sir ... sir ... orders.'

Warren sat up in bed, swearing under his breath. 'What are they?'

'The brigade is to go into the front line tomorrow. The divisional commander is reinforcing all the machine gun sections. We're getting the 3rd Buffs machine gunners, under a sergeant ... We are to march at 0400 hours, sir.'

Warren sat with his stockinged feet on the cold floor, 'Any other news?'

'The galloper who brought the orders said he'd heard that the leading troops have been held up for days ... Would you like some tea, sir? I've told the mess dafadar to have it available in the mess from now on, and breakfast at three.'

'Good man ... I'll issue orders at two. Give the warning order right away. You get to the office. I'll tell Krishna Ram and Sher Singh. They're next door.'

'Very good, sir.'

Warren did not feel sleepy, for the news had set his mind to racing. They were going into the trenches, for the first time. The frantic training of the past two weeks, the issuing of infantry arms and equipment, was now to reach its target—war, on foot. He pulled on his breeches and boots, rolled his puttees, slipped into his British warm, took his flashlight and went out into the moonlit snow-covered road.

He found Krishna Ram already up and said, 'Come to the office with me ... Wait a minute. I said I'd awaken Sher Singh.'

He crossed the roofless hall, opened the door opposite and walked in, calling, 'Sher Singh? CO here. We ...'

The searching beam of his flashlight shone on a head in the bed, then another. Sher Singh sat up with a convulsive jerk, his uncomprehending eyes full of sleep. He was naked under the blankets. A naked young man lay beside him, his brown arm thrown across the captain's chest. He stirred in his sleep, as understanding came into Sher Singh's face, and murmured in Hindi, 'Oh, don't move, you lovely one.'

Warren felt Krishna Ram at his elbow. He said, 'Captain Sher Singh, you are under arrest. Major Krishna Ram, you are responsible for the prisoner. He is to accompany you until I give further orders. In uniform, without belt, sword, or revolver.'

'Yes, sir.' Warren could not tell from Krishna's voice, or from the wooden expression on his face, half seen at the edge of the flashlight beam, what he was thinking. He went back to his own billet and sat down on his bed.

'Is the sahib well?' Narayan Singh inquired anxiously. 'Is the presence sick?'

'No,' he said. 'Bring me tea from the mess. No, nothing to eat. I could not eat.'

His dog Shikari laid his head on his boots and Warren reached down to pat him, muttering, 'Good dog ... You're always with me, aren't you?' He had seen Sher Singh holding a sowar's hand at the very beginning but he'd never dreamed that the perversion would be thrust in his face like this. An officer of his regiment lying there with a sowar, male chest to male chest. It was disgusting, disgraceful ... un-English. But the fellow wasn't English. He was an Indian who'd been taught to use a knife and fork. How could they beat the Huns with animals like that? But what—was—he—to—do?

December 1914

WARREN BATEMAN STOOD in the bottom of the trench, his back to the forward wall, a copy of the orders in his hand. The officers of the Ravi Lancers crowded the trench on both sides of him. He had just finished giving out verbal orders for the attack due to take place at first light, 6.10 a.m., the next day. Beyond the officers, sowars filled the bottom of the trench, with every ten yards a sentry up on the firestep, his rifle beside him.

Warren said, 'Now, take a look through the periscope here, in turn. Remember to make sure you identify Hill 73, that's the low rise of land with a ruined barn on it, on the right of the field of view. Hill 73 is A Squadron's objective tomorrow. And on the left the remains of Lestelle Wood, which is C Squadron's objective. Then, right centre, about a hundred yards from here there is a wrecked German field gun. That is called Wrecked Gun, and is on the dividing line between A and C.' He stepped to one side and said to the gunner subaltern, 'You first, de Marquez.'

The gunner shook his head. 'I've seen it.'

Warren nodded at Krishna Ram, who stooped to put his eye to the eyepiece. After a pair of long minutes he stepped down, saying, 'There seem to be about three rows of barbed wire in front of the German trench.'

Warren said, 'That's what the Buffs' patrol last night reported. More wire cutters are coming up this evening with the supplies.'

One by one the other officers went to the periscope. When the last had looked Warren said, 'Any questions, then? The adjutant will send a correct watch round to all squadrons starting an hour before zero hour. Remember, the barrage begins at zero minus ten and at zero plus four lifts from the enemy front trench to his support trench. Our leading men *must* be at the enemy line when

the barrage lifts, or the Huns will have time to come up out of
their dugouts and man their machine guns.'

'We'll be there, sir,' young Ishar Lall said cheerfully.

'That's all then. Krishna ...' He beckoned his second-in-command. 'Here's Sergeant Durand, commanding the Buffs' machine
gun section. I'm going to put you in overall charge of the machine
guns, Krishna.' He turned to the sergeant, a deep-tanned, hard-
bitten, unmistakable regular. He said, 'Have you ever served in
India, sergeant?'

'That I 'ave, sir. Twelve years. An' I can speak the *bat*.'

Warren smiled. 'That will help. Our machine gun rissaldar, Ram
Lall, has no English. Krishna, I want all the guns in position on
the left of our line here. Do some ranging, but only one gun at a
time.'

Sergeant Durand said, 'Jerry won't guess what's up, sir. We
would fire a burst now and then all day, when we was in the line
'ere, to show the Jerries we was awake, and make 'em keep their
'eads down.'

He tapped his rifle sling in salute and went off. Warren said,
'We're going to rely a lot on you and those machine guns tomorrow,
Krishna. Not in the attack so much, but if the Germans counter-
attack.'

'*When* they do, sir,' Krishna said. 'I understand that they always
do.'

Now was the time, Warren thought, to settle the other business.
He said, 'I'd like to have your opinion on what is the best course
to follow about Sher Singh. You understand that the responsibility
is entirely mine,' he added quickly, in case the prince should
imagine he was trying to shirk his duty.

Krishna Ram said evenly, 'Of course, sir ... The trouble is that
what he and Sowar Janak were doing is not a crime in our State.'

'But it's ... disgraceful, unnatural!'

'*I* think so, sir,' Krishna said, 'because I was taught so by Mr.
Fleming and by what I have read in English ... Though Mr.
Fleming did say once that many people much admired in history
were sodomites, such as King Richard the Lion Heart and ...'

'Nonsense!' Warren exclaimed.

'Perhaps, sir ... but although you and I think it is disgusting,
I am afraid that my grandfather does not. Nor does Major Bholanath.
Nor the sowars. Not many of them are sodomites, but it is hard

161

to tell because, as I say, it has not been a crime. If no one complains, no one bothers.'

'That's all very well in Basohli,' Warren snapped, 'but when you offered the regiment to the King-Emperor it was embodied into the Indian Army and subjected to the Indian Army Act and the Indian Penal Code.'

Krishna Ram said, 'Yes, sir.'

Warren looked at him. What was he thinking? Did he want the whole thing hushed up for the sake of the State? For the sake of the regiment even, for surely there would be snickering in the rest of the brigade if it came out? Could it be that he was a bit like that himself? He had certainly gone out of his way to avoid the ladies in England ... but that was because they were white, and English.

He said, 'What would happen if this had occurred in Ravi State?'

Krishna Ram said, 'If there had been no complaint—nothing. If the CO thought it was bad for any reason, he could dismiss the officer, or the sowar, or both. There is no code of military law in Ravi, sir. An officer can do what he likes. He can award any punishment he wishes, except death, without trial. But if what he has done does not please the Rajah in durbar, he himself can be similarly punished ... except, of course, that the Rajah can order execution.'

Warren thought, it is completely feudal. An officer of the Indian Army had great power compared to one in the British service; but it was nothing compared to this. He said, 'So, as I am the CO, and I don't think it is right, I can punish both of them in any way I think fit?'

'In Ravi, yes,' Krishna Ram said. 'Here ... I think Captain Sher Singh is the sort of man who might demand to be tried by court-martial, because he knows that he now has that right.'

'Well, what would *you* do?' Warren asked, exasperated.

'I think I would order the holding of a *panchayat*, sir,' Krishna Ram said. 'It is our way of settling such matters.'

'But it has no powers,' Warren said.

'No, sir. But you have the power to accept the *panchayat*'s recommendation ... I would suggest a *panchayat* of three officers, the rissaldar-major, and the Brahmin.'

'Do you realize what will happen to me if the general gets to hear of this, and that I put it in the hands of a *panchayat*?' Warren said.

Krishna Ram said, 'Yes, sir. But in this case I think it's the best solution.'

Warren said, 'I'll think about it. Meantime, continue Sher Singh's arrest until an hour before zero hour. Then send him to his squadron. I'm damned if I'm going to have him escape the attack by being a sodomite.'

He acknowledged Krishna Ram's salute and strode off down the communication trench. A *panchayat* for a military crime ... committing a civil offence, that is to say, sodomy: conduct unbecoming an officer and a gentleman ... they didn't seem to think so ... God, he must get Sher Singh out of his mind, at least until the attack was over. The men looked strange in the trench, for they were still wearing cavalry breeches and downward-rolled puttees. You felt that they were only here on a visit, had left their lances round the corner, because tomorrow they'd be on horseback again. Well, perhaps they would. This trench warfare, a grappling of moles in ever deeper mud, could not go on forever. It was only a matter of gritting the teeth, facing the casualties, and breaking through this belt of trench and barbed wire and dugout and pillbox into the open fields and low hills of Artois gleaming white under snow there.

'*Sab thik hai, jawan?*' he asked a crouching sowar.

The man leaped to his feet. '*Jee-han, huzoor.*'

'*Ration ab thik hai?*'

'*Jee-han, huzoor. Bahut achcha!*'

He walked on, speaking to one man in four. They all looked cold and seemed to have shrunk, as though trying to make themselves small and warm inside the short cavalry greatcoats. But they were fit enough, and there had been a hot meal this morning and another was ready in the hay boxes. In his pocket he had a letter from Joan; she wished the two sides would come to their senses and end the war before Christmas. By God, he wished it himself sometimes, but only with victory. Over by Christmas, they'd thought once. Here it was December 23 and no sign of a break. Well, tomorrow might alter that. By God, tomorrow *would* alter that. His jaw set. Tomorrow the sowars would learn what real war was like. They'd defeat the Germans too, or he'd know the reason why ...

An hour before dawn the stars, which had been dimly visible all night, slid behind low clouds and the wind dropped. Warren stood with his adjutant in the middle of the front line trench where C and A Squadrons joined. The men had already fixed bayonets, and a heavy silence pervaded the trenches.

'Zero minus eleven,' Lieutenant Dayal Ram murmured. Warren put his eyes to the periscope and waited. Soon he heard the crack and rumble of artillery from far behind and simultaneously shells began to shriek overhead, to burst in thunder along the dimly darker line of the German trench and wire, barely two hundred and fifty yards away.

'On target!' the gunner subaltern cried, and Warren said, 'I should hope so.'

Heavy guns, medium, and field guns were all firing, howitzer shells whined down in lazy arcs, shells from 60- and 18-pounder guns cracked low overhead. The shell bursts laid a glaring curtain of orange and yellow flame all along the German front. The Lahore Brigade made their final preparations to go over the top, the Oxford Fusiliers and the Ravi Lancers in the lead.

'Zero minus seven,' Dayal Ram said.

Warren wondered why he did not feel more afraid. A few bursts of machine gun fire clattered overhead, as though the Germans were sweeping the ground in case the attack had already started. It would be unpleasant when the time came to get up there. But all he could think of was Joan ... Sher Singh ... Krishna Ram ...

'Zero minus two, sir.'

Warren knocked out his pipe against the heel of his boot, and looked right and left along the trench.

'Zero!'

Whistles blew, and the men, already on the firestep, clambered up and out. The light was a faint greenish tinge on the snow to the right, an infinitesimal warming of the darkness to the left. Warren climbed up on to the firestep and watched the dim figures walk away towards the enemy. He looked round, searching for the commanders of the two reserve companies—'Himat Singh? Sher Singh?'

'Here, sir.'

'I just wanted to make sure you were here. Are your men on the way?'

'Moving up, sir. They'll be here in three minutes.'

Warren nodded, and put his binoculars to his eyes. Now he could just make out the ruined houses on Hill 73 and the shatttered stumps of Lestelle Wood, but not Wrecked Gun, for that was in the denser darkness of a hollow.

'Zero plus five, sir.'

The guns didn't sound any different and Warren shouted, 'The barrage is supposed to have lifted!'

'It has, sir,' Lieutenant de Marquez said. 'It just sounds the same. It only lifted two hundred yards, you know.'

Warren watched anxiously. The leading squadron commanders were supposed to send back gallopers with reports of progress as soon as they reached the enemy trench; and fire two green Very lights into the air, as a success signal. His own machine guns were firing from the flank, and he thought he heard the sound of bursting grenades and the intermittent crack and rattle of rifle fire from ahead. The light was strengthening by jerks and starts. Two green lights towered into the pale sky from Hill 73.

'A Squadron's there!' Dayal Ram cried triumphantly.

Two greens arched up from Lestelle Wood. 'And Bholanath! *Shahbash, shahbash!*' Dayal Ram cried.

'RHQ advance!' Warren shouted. 'And you just hold this trench tight, Himat Singh. D's under your command. Don't move unless you get a direct order from me. And watch the flanks.'

'Yes, sir.' The red and blue ribbon of the DSO was a little bar of colour on Himat Singh's breast and his voice was steady. 'Good luck, sir.'

Warren stepped out across No Man's Land, Shikari at his heels, followed by his orderly and trumpeter, the adjutant, Flaherty the signals officer, Mahadeo Singh the officer-galloper and three sowar-gallopers, as they were still called, though they all had to do their message carrying on their own feet now. Warren glanced back and saw a pale face in the trench. He was the intelligence officer. He stopped and called, 'Come along, Pahlwan!'

'Oh, s-s—sir ...' the lieutenant stuttered.

Warren saw that the man was in a blue funk. He was a dark and dwarfish fellow, physically ugly at the best of times. Now, with his jaw hanging, his eyes rotating and his body pressed back against the parados, he looked like a panic-stricken ape.

Warren said, 'If you're not out of there in five seconds, I'm going to shoot you.' He drew the heavy .45 Webley from his holster. Pahlwan Ram scrambled up and forward, and Warren said, 'Now you walk here beside me.' Pahlwan's legs were buckling and

Warren put an arm under his elbow, 'Stand up, man! We'll be in cover soon.'

A few shells were bursting around them, and desultory machine gun fire that seemed to be going high. They found the German wire had been cut in many places by the artillery bombardment, and more passages through it were now being systematically cut by men of A and C Squadrons. Some shattered bodies lay in shell holes, all wearing the grey-green of Germany. A sowar of the regiment lay dead under the wire, on his back, blood trickling from his mouth. Then Warren jumped down into the captured trench. To Pahlwan Ram he said, 'Go to A and C. Tell them we're here. Get reports.' Then he scribbled a note on a message pad on his knee, reporting that the Ravi Lancers were in possession of Hill 73 and Lestelle Wood, and sent it back to brigade by a galloper. Noting that the gunner telephone wire had come forward, and de Marquez was already talking to his gun position, he crawled up on the reverse lip of the trench and settled down to examine the country beyond.

The next German trench was two hundred yards away, protected by three double aprons of barbed wire, with more behind, as though they expected to be attacked from the rear. He could see no movement there, and no signs of pillboxes, but two or three machine guns were sweeping the pock-marked snow between the two trench lines. The zigzag of a German communication trench started some twenty yards to his right. He called down, 'Mahadeo ... there's a communication trench going back ... on, towards the Germans ... twenty yards right of here. Tell A Squadron to send a fighting patrol down it as far as they can get, and to hold it at least a hundred yards in.'

A shell landed close, showering him with mud and dirty snow.

'Sahib,' an agitated voice called up, in Hindi, 'our artillery are firing at us.'

'No,' he said, sliding down into the trench, 'it's the Germans, ranging.'

A C Squadron galloper came running along the trench from the left. 'Major Bholanath says all is well, sahib. We have had five men killed and twelve wounded.'

Pahlwan Ram came from the other direction. His voice was under better control as he reported. 'Ishar Lall is badly wounded, sir. I saw him ... his shoulder's smashed, half his chest. Oh, my God, he looks awful ...'

166

'The report!' Warren grated.

'Three killed and sixteen wounded, sir. Rissaldar Shamsher Singh says the enemy are massing on his front and fire is very severe. No one can put his head up.'

Warren stared at the officer, unseeing. One of the Terrible Twins badly hit, probably a goner. What a damned shame that the best should go so soon, and so young. Shamsher Singh was an old woman. How could he know that the enemy were massing if no one could put his head up? And what would they see if they could?

He said, 'Send a galloper back to B Squadron and tell them to send 2nd Lieutenant Puran Lall up to take command of A, at once. I'm going to talk to Rissaldar Shamsher Singh. RHQ will stay here.'

He began working along the trench, followed by his orderly and trumpeter. Here were German bodies, two here, one there, here a German wounded, lying against the back wall, pale as clay, here was the debris of war, coats, rifles, ammunition, mess tins, half-eaten food in the dirty snow. He passed half a dozen sowars, all bandaged with the khaki field dressings, as they were climbing out of the trench and starting back across No Man's Land to the British lines. A group of laden stretcher bearers under the band dafadar followed. He spoke to the men on the stretchers: 'Well done—You'll be all right—Home to Basohli for you—*Shahbash!*'

Round a traverse he found Rissaldar Shamsher Singh and, lying in the bottom of the trench, 2nd Lieutenant Ishar Lall. The boy was very pale, only his face showing above and his boots below a German greatcoat that had been spread over him.

'Hullo, sir,' he said feebly. 'We took it.'

'Yes. Well done ... Where are you hit?'

'Right shoulder gone, sir. Such a mess I didn't want the jawans to see it, but ...' The voice trailed away, the brown eyes closed.

The rissaldar said, 'Half his chest is gone too, sahib. He is not long for this world.'

'Have you given him morphia yet? Well, do it now. You were taught last month how to do it ... There ... You'll be all right soon, Ishar. We'll have you back to hospital in a jiffy.'

'Don't send me back, sir ... I shall not live long. I'd rather stay with my squadron.'

'You've got to go back,' Warren said, 'the doctors can save you.

Lie still. Rest ... Come down the trench with me, rissaldar-sahib ... Now, where are these enemy massing?'

'There is movement. A sentry reported it.'

'And where's the severe fire?'

'It was heavy, sahib. It has stopped now.'

Warren said, 'I'm sending 2nd Lieutenant Puran Lall up to take over command.'

'Thanks be to God,' the rissaldar murmured.

'But until he arrives, you are in command. Have you blocked and guarded all German communication trenches? Why aren't half your men digging out a firestep on that side? They can't fire towards the Germans until they do.'

'We have only ten entrenching tools, sahib.'

'My God, I know that! But dead Germans have them. There are picks and shovels in these dugouts. I'll be back in an hour and your sector must be in perfect shape to repel a counterattack by then.'

He turned back. Ishar Lall's eyes were closed and his breathing fast and shallow. No use to wake him, even if it were possible. He hurried back to RHQ and found a message from brigade that the 71st Punjabis were going to move through in an hour to capture the German second and third lines, 'taking advantage of German demoralization and disorganization'.

He climbed up on to the parados again, and crouched awkwardly under the lip. He could detect no demoralization or disorganization. There weren't enough German bodies in this trench to account for the men who must originally have been manning it. They had left only a few men in it, with orders to pull back in face of any serious attack. Why?

The answer came in a whistling scream that pierced his head and then a gigantic explosion fifty yards behind him. Eight more big shells burst simultaneously up and down the line of the trench. There was lighter field artillery bursting all over the ground that had once been No Man's Land. Warren slid down into the trench. There was no barbed wire towards the enemy. The Punjabis would be passing through later—perhaps—but the crisis would come before that. This bombardment was so intense that it could not go on for long. There must be at least eight heavy and medium batteries and four field batteries engaging just this short sector of trench. He noticed that most of the fire was landing on A Squadron to the right. At that moment a flying figure landed head first into the trench beside him. It was Puran Lall, scrambling to his feet, scraping mud off his face.

'You came through that?' Warren shouted.

'Yes, sir. How's my brother?'

'Bad, I'm afraid. Get him back as soon as this bombardment lifts. I don't know whether there's any hope, but we've got to try.'

'Yes, sir.' Puran Lall's jaw was set and his face seemed thinner and older than when Warren had last seen him barely an hour ago, waiting with B Squadron.

The young man hurried off along the trench. Now Warren saw that the sowars in the trench were all crouched against the forward wall, like terrified animals. The whites of their eyes were staring, they looked from one to another, seeming to ask, what is this, what is this diabolical blasting of steel? How can human beings create such a sound, such horror? He saw that they were nervous. It was their first time under heavy bombardment. He must do something to steady them. There was Pahlwan, his eyes closed, trembling: no help there. Dayal Ram was writing out a message. Flaherty was on the parados, peering out. He called up, 'Come along with me, Flaherty. We must steady the sowars. You smoke cigarettes, don't you? Well, light one ... Come on, then. Come on, Shikari.'

He set off along the trench towards C Squadron. There was no doubt the men were jumpy. They lay against the shaking wall of mud and earth, tree roots sticking out, and here and there bricks and stones, unable to see the enemy who was pounding them thus. In places the walls of the trench were collapsing under the bombardment. A man got a shell splinter in the side as they passed, and began to shriek with uncontrollable pain.

'Well done, lad,' Warren said. 'Well done. Keep close to the forward wall. Stand up, lad! Where's your rifle? Well done. Where's the sentry here? Get up, lad. You can't see the Germans from down there. Dafadar, see that your sentries keep their posts. Are you hurt, lad? Ah, that's just a scratch. You can show that to the girls in Basohli and say a German bit you ... Hullo, Bholanath.'

The old major hurried round a traverse, and Warren saw that he was on the same errand as himself, steadying the men under the bombardment. 'How is it?' Warren asked in a low voice.

'All right, sahib,' Bholanath said, 'as long as it doesn't go on too long.' His white moustaches swept up as fiercely as ever.

'I don't think it will,' Warren said.

'I was going to see Ishar Lall. I heard he was wounded.'

'He is. But get back to your squadron. I think the Germans will attack soon.'

'I ought to see him,' the old man said doubtfully.

'Get back to your squadron!' Warren snapped. 'And hold tight!'

He hurried back towards RHQ. As he passed behind one of the sentries on the parados he heard the man gasp, *'Dushman a-rahe!'*

He scrambled up and saw a dense grey-green mass advancing from the north. The enemy artillery fire had lifted and was now falling on the original British front trench, behind him. He dropped down, blew his whistle and shouted, 'Enemy coming! Fire! Fire!'

Then as the sowars jumped into position and a sporadic rifle fire broke out he ran with all his might to reach RHQ. The guns ought to be firing their defensive tasks ... even as he thought it, the whistling crack of the 18-pounders burst overhead, quickly increasing in volume. He reached RHQ and ran up to the little firestep they had dug out while he was away. The Germans were still coming, and now barely a hundred yards off.

From the left fire from four machine guns raked the Germans and men began to fall.

Warren exulted as the German mass wavered, began to break up, eddied to and fro, a fury of British artillery shells bursting among them. The Germans disappeared into holes and craters and trenches. A few minutes later their artillery opened up again, as heavy as before on the front line, and with a couple of extra batteries of mediums searching the left flank for the machine guns which had held up their assault. The smoke and lyddite fumes made him choke. A direct hit on the trench to his right hurled half a dozen broken bodies of A Squadron twenty feet into the air. The shelling grew insanely furious. At his feet Shikari began to whine and fidget. Crouched on the firestep, looking towards the enemy, Warren caught movement from the corner of his eye. Turning his head he saw a handful of men—sowars of the regiment—appear on the rear edge of A Squadron's trench and begin running to the rear. One threw away his rifle as an encumbrance in his flight even as Warren watched. A moment later a huge shell burst, hiding the runners from sight. When the smoke cleared there was only one man running.

'Bloody fools,' Warren muttered. 'They're safer in the trench.'

He jumped down, drew his revolver and called to Flaherty, 'Come with me! Use your revolver if you have to.'

'Very good, sir,' the big lieutenant said, drawing his revolver. The German shelling stopped suddenly. Most of the men of A Squadron were huddled in the bottom of the trench, wide-eyed and dumb. 'Up on the firestep,' Warren shouted, 'up, up!' Behind him he heard Flaherty's curt, 'Get up, you,' and the thud of kicks. The sowars began to shake their heads like men recovering from a nightmare. Some got up on to the step.

Round a traverse he came upon half a dozen men climbing out in the other direction, among them Rissaldar Shamsher Singh.

'Stop, rissaldar-sahib!' he yelled. The old rissaldar looked at him with blank eyes and continued trying to get out of the trench and away. Warren thrust his revolver forward, shouting again, 'Stop!' The bloody old fool was not really scared, just numbed, shocked. He changed the grip on his pistol, meaning to knock the man out, but Flaherty stepped close, and his revolver was up. 'Don't . . .' Warren cried, but it was too late. The Webley exploded heavily by his ear. Rissaldar Shamsher Singh's face broke up, blood spurting from the eye and the mouth and the jaw falling to pieces. He fell, rolling back into the trench. But more men were scrambling out of the trench behind Warren, and more in front. To the left, he saw that C Squadron were out too, and streaming to the rear like a football crowd at the end of a match. Krishna Ram's machine guns which had begun to fire again, had had to stop for fear of hitting the fleeing men.

Now he saw Dayal Ram and the RHQ start back, for their lives, followed by de Marquez and his gunner signal group. He was alone in the once-captured trench with his orderly, his trumpeter, Lieutenant Flaherty, and Shikari. The Germans were advancing again.

'We'd better get back, sir,' Flaherty said, 'our Indans have run and left us.'

The four men scrambled out and ran, the dog racing away ahead as though he knew the danger as clearly as they. Bullets whistled and cracked about them. Once Warren glanced over his shoulder and saw that the Germans were not stopping at their old trench but were still coming on, at a steady walk, bayonets glistening under the cloud wrack. The artillery on both sides had lifted their fire off the immediate battlefield, though gouts of earth and the continuous thunder of explosions showed that they were firing on the flanks and rear areas to prevent the movement of reserves.

Now, Warren thought, it all depends on Himat Singh and B and D Squadrons. He dropped into the trench which he had left nearly three hours earlier. At once a withering fire broke out all along the line. Himat Singh was there, but gave no more than a word. 'All right, sir? ... Fire, B Squadron, fire!' He and his rissaldar ran up and down the trench like sheep dogs, calling, 'Fire! ... Aim and fire as fast as you can! They shall not come! *Ahne mat do!*'

The Germans were wavering once more, the mass stopping, the men lying down. The four machine guns opened fire from the left again. A little to his right Warren saw Captain Himat Singh emerge from the trench, drawn sabre waving, at the head of a dozen men with fixed bayonets. They charged, firing and throwing jampot bombs as they went and attacked a group of Germans in a shell hole barely twenty yards from the trench. Three minutes later they returned, bayonets and sabre dripping red.

De Marquez got a message through to his 18-pounders and the whipcrack of the light shells bursting in No Man's Land finished the job. The remaining Germans started back for their own trenches. Almost at once the German heavies opened on the British lines and a few minutes later the scene was almost as it had been before zero hour—heavy shelling, the Ravi Lancers in this trench, the Germans in that. But it was not the same. Nothing ever would be again, Warren knew. The Ravi Lancers had faced war, and been found out.

He turned to the adjutant and snapped, 'Tell Bholanath to re-form and take over the left section of the front line, where they were this morning. D Squadron into reserve when it's done.'

'You're wounded, sir. In the head.'

Warren touched his head and felt a sharp stab of pain. There was blood on his hand. 'It's nothing ... a splinter. I suppose ... Send for Mr. Puran Lall.'

'Yes, sir ... Rissaldar Ram Lall here reports that Major Krishna Ram is missing.'

Warren said, 'Speak, rissaldar-sahib.'

The rissaldar's uniform was torn and covered in mud. He said, 'We were firing while the enemy was shelling, sahib. But the prince said we would not be able to fire on the enemy properly if they

172

advanced past their old front line. He went alone, with his trumpeter, to look for a better place. Then there was heavy shelling upon us. He did not come back. Just as I started to go and look for him, the enemy attacked, and the squadrons began to retreat.'

'To run away, you should say,' Warren snapped.

'We had to save our machine guns, sahib. I stayed till the Germans were so close I was throwing bombs at them.'

'So the major's out there, somewhere near where the machine guns were, and you don't know whether he's dead or alive? ... Dayal Ram, tell Major Bholanath to send out a strong patrol as soon as it's dark, to look for the major or his body.'

'Yes, sir.'

Warren sat down wearily on an ammunition box. Lieutenant Flaherty handed him a tin mug, saying, 'Here, sir. Tea. The gunners have been brewing it ...' and, as Warren took the tea, 'I'm sorry about Rissaldar Shamsher Singh, sir. I thought you meant me to shoot ...'

'I did,' Warren said, 'but when I saw the numb look in the old man's eyes, I realized ... It doesn't matter. You were right. We can't afford any softness in this kind of war. You did well, Flaherty.'

'Thank you, sir.' The lieutenant flushed with pleasure.

Warren sipped wearily. What a débâcle. He needed more British officers. Even more Flahertys. Flaherty was a good deal senior to Puran Lall. Perhaps he would resent Puran being given A Squadron. He said, 'I know you're fit to command a squadron, but for the moment I'd rather keep you near me in RHQ. Besides you understand signals better than anyone else could.'

'I understand, sir,' Flaherty said; but did he, Warren wondered? He leaned down and patted Shikari's head. 'You didn't like it out there, did you?' he said, fondling the dog's ears. 'Well, no more did I, but we have to do our job, don't we?'

Warren drank again, thirsty now. Krishna Ram gone ... There had been times recently when he had almost wished for something like this, for the young man seemed to be wilfully opposing him. If there was any discontent and intrigue among the officers, he'd be the focus of it, with his rank and royal blood he could hardly help that ... and now he was gone, and in truth the odds were five to one against ever seeing him again. He felt saddened, as sad as the memory of Ishar Lall lying shattered in the bottom of

the trench. Krishna was a good young man ... Indian, more Indian
than he perhaps realized, but good, and brave. He did not have to
risk his life; and now he was gone.

What was he to do about the disaster of the battle? His men
had run away. Even Bholanath had been unable to prevent it.
They had acted illogically, running when the artillery fire made it
suicidal, running when they could have held the Germans, as B
Squadron had shown. They were Indians, that was the answer—
their minds didn't work the same way, even yet. But, what sort of
an answer was that, when he knew that in the old days the Rajputs
had gone out en masse to die in hopeless battle against the Moguls;
and while the battle raged, the Rajput woman had burned themselves to death on vast funeral pyres inside the beleaguered fortress?
Was the failure due to something in the conditions of this particular war? He remembered the words of the Commissioner in
Lahore ... 'the gods of Europe do not speak Hindi ...'

Dayal Ram said, 'Sir, the Punjabis' attack has been cancelled.
The brigade commander wants to see you at his HQ.'

Warren nodded, too weary to speak.

Brigadier-General Rogers was angry. 'The attack failed,' he
snapped, 'when I had promised General Glover that it would succeed. Why? What am I going to tell him?'

'It was not difficult to take the German front line,' Warren said.
'I think they moved most of their men from it as soon as our
preliminary bombardment began. But unless the second and third
lines are also taken in the same assault the Germans are ready
there for a counterattack. The trenches that have just been captured face the wrong way and there's no barbed wire to hold up a
counterattack.'

'Your men ran away, I am told,' the general said coldly.

'Yes, sir. The bombardment up there was very heavy. I was in
it.'

'The Fusiliers held on your right.'

'Yes, sir,' Warren said.

British troops were more used to noises, blasts, and machines,
he thought. Besides, they were British. But, then, his men were
Rajputs.

'What do you propose to do to raise the morale of your regiment?'

'I haven't worked it out yet, sir,' Warren said. 'I think probably the answer is to institute aggressive patrolling. I must prove to the sowars that they are as good men as the Germans, which they are.'

That would help them stand up under the impersonal rain of steel. They had not lost their pride, from what he had seen, as British troops would have done, knowing they had disgraced themselves. They had been assailed by something no Indian had ever known, that there was nothing in his blood or experience to prepare him for, and now they were considering.

'They'll be all right, sir,' Warren said. 'We need a little more infantry training.'

'I thought you were clamouring for action on foot,' the general snapped. 'You told me when you were converted that the men felt ashamed of seeing no fighting while the infantry were suffering so heavily.' The monocle gleamed angrily in his eye.

Warren said, 'Yes, sir. But when we actually lost our horses the world was turned upside down for the men. I didn't realize quite how lost they would feel. This attack came before they were mentally sure again ... sure of who they are.'

'They'd better learn.'

'Yes, sir ... I would like to have another British officer posted to me.'

'You've lost the Yuvraj fellow, haven't you?'

'He's missing. I'm sending patrols out to look for him.'

'He seemed a good chap, for one of these fat rajah's sons. Full of opium all the time, I suppose, like the rest of them.'

'I don't think so, sir. He was a very good cricketer.'

'Well, about another BO ... You realize he'd have to be your second-in-command? Can't have natives ordering British officers about, especially not States Forces fellows.'

'No, sir,' Warren said. Personally he wouldn't have minded a junior officer. A young man would learn a lot serving under such as Bholanath and even Krishna Ram ... if he came back. But the general was probably right from the point of view of the army as a whole.

The general said, 'Well, I'll try, but officers trained to serve with Indian troops don't grow on trees, you know. And we've lost half a dozen in this attack already.'

Warren saluted and started trudging back up the line. Brigade headquarters was two miles in rear of his own rear area. They couldn't have seen anything of what was going on in the attack from back there, and no one had come forward to see for himself. No one had come forward since the attack ended, either. His orderly, at his heels, said, 'The sahib should go to RAP now.'

Warren said, 'What for?'

'To have his wound properly dressed.'

'Oh, that.' Warren had forgotten about it and as the dried cut was under his hat the general had not seen it. 'But I must visit the wounded.'

He turned off the shell-pocked muddy road just before the trench lines began, and found the RAP in the ruins of a cowshed, the vanished roof replaced by tarpaulins and a large red cross painted on the front wall, facing the Germans.

The smells of formaldehyde and carbolic were overpowering, and the colour was red ... red stained earth and red stained khaki bandages, the soldiers' brown faces reddened by the hurricane lanterns placed on benches and empty shell boxes down the muddy floor. Captain Ramaswami was operating in the corner on a man sitting on a table, holding out his hand. The doctor was digging a sliver of steel out of the hand. The man's face was wet with sweat and he had the end of his turban clenched between his teeth. The doctor finished, expertly bandaged the wound and said, 'All right. You can go now.'

Warren said, 'Didn't you give him an anaesthetic?'

'Don't have enough to spare. Besides, he didn't want to be sent back to the CCS. He just wanted to be returned to his squadron.'

'Which is that?'

'A.'

Warren thought, that's the squadron that started the débâcle. And this man wanted to get back up the line rather than rest in safety for a few days.

'How's Ishar Lall,' he asked.

'Dead,' the doctor said coldly, as though Warren had killed him himself.

Warren frowned at the black face, and was about to make a sharp retort; but Ishar Lall was dead. 'I'm sorry,' he said. 'He was one of the best.'

The doctor's surly expression softened a little and he said, 'He had no business coming to this war and dying this way ...'

176

'How many men have you treated here,' Warren interrupted.

'Forty-eight. Sent twenty back to CCS and ten back to their squadrons. I can hold the rest. Three died here of wounds, including 2nd Lieutenant Ishar Lall.'

'You've done well,' Warren said.

'Well? Patching these men up so that they can get back into this murderous war? I would be doing a thousand times better saving one woman in Madras.'

Warren lost his temper and shouted, 'If you want to get out of the fighting, Ramaswami, put in an official request and I'll see that it is forwarded to brigade. Or go and see the ADMS.'

He walked out, his orderly muttering, 'Your wound, sahib.'

He snapped, 'Quiet, son! Say no more.'

He trudged up the communication trenches towards the front. He must put Himat Singh in for another DSO. And speak to Puran Lall about A Squadron. Of course, the poor fellow had hardly been in command ten minutes when it happened. With his twin brother dying beside him. And there was the *panchayat* on Sher Singh which he had decided to hold. The general would have a fit if he knew. The general was going to lose one medal because of the failure of the attack—Warren could sense it—and if the truth about this affair ever reached him ... Still, he must go through with it.

He reached RHQ and said, 'Send for Major Bholanath.'

The major came soon and Warren said, 'I have decided that the matter of Captain Sher Singh's behaviour should be judged by a *panchayat*. It shall consist of yourself, as a prince of the blood and representative of the rajah, your brother. Captain Ramaswami. Lieutenant Dayal Ram. Rissaldar-Major Baldev Singh. And the Pandit-ji.'

'It is understood, sahib,' the old major said in Hindi.

'Hold it here, as soon as you can. Give no decision to the prisoner, but advise me before midnight what you recommend.'

'It is understood, sahib.'

'Make proper arrangements to be recalled to your squadrons in case of alarm.'

'It is understood, sahib ... I was going to go out with the patrol to look for my great-nephew, the Yuvraj.'

'You're too senior for that. Send your rissaldar.'

'The Yuvraj is of my blood, sahib.'

'*Hukm hai!*' Warren snapped. 'You have plenty of work in your squadron, to see that it does not run away again.'

'They have blackened my face,' the old man said seriously. 'They know it. They will not do it again. It was the noise, sahib, and the sight of A Squadron running ... It is said that Lieutenant Flaherty killed Rissaldar Shamsher Singh.'

'Yes. On my order. He wasn't dead when we had to leave, but he couldn't have lived for long.'

'Was it not possible to bring him back, sahib?'

Warren glared at the major, 'No, it wasn't. And I wouldn't have done it if I could. He would only have faced a court martial, lost his rank, and perhaps been shot. Now, we'll say nothing and his widow will get a pension.'

'It is understood, sahib,' the major insisted quietly, 'but if he could have been brought back we would know why he ran away. Perhaps he would have seen how foolish he had been, and done better next time. He was a good officer.'

'Was, is right,' Warren said grimly. 'You may go.'

Alone again he thought, it didn't need much cogitation to know what had caused Shamsher Singh to behave so badly. He was disoriented, the noise and concussion having disconnected the nerve channels leaving him unable to respond to the normal commands and logic of the brain, but only to primeval messages from the solar plexus, as a drowning man will yet try to strangle his rescuer.

He waited, after eating a light supper in the RHQ mess dugout, until Major Bholanath came to him near eleven o'clock. The air was cold, and the sky overcast, with a wind that presaged more snow. Christmas Eve in the trenches, he thought: he thought of Christmas in England. His mother would have holly round the door of the Old Vicarage and mistletoe hanging from the lamp in the hall. There'd be children's parties and charades and Louise would dress up in her mother's cloak and teeter about in high-heeled shoes four sizes too big for her ...

The major saluted and said, 'Is there permission to speak in Hindi, sahib?'

'I suppose so. Yes.'

'This Captain Sher Singh has no father, sahib. I know his family. His mother is a noble woman, strong to lift the burden of raising the family of six girls and this Sher Singh, who was the youngest. He says he was always afraid of women. They betrothed him to a

178

girl of good family when he was six and it was to be consummated on his fifteenth birthday. But he failed. Again and again he failed to do what a man should. The girl left the house in shame and his mother hid her head, for she had borne a eunuch. Sher Singh says he was drawn to the love of man by an elder man, whom he named, and whom we of Ravi all know as a lover of boys.'

'What do you recommend?' Warren said.

The old major continued unhurriedly, 'This sowar Janak with whom he was in bed was originally of C Squadron. During Holi celebrations two years ago, Sher Singh discovered that he was of the same persuasion. As Sher Singh was of D Squadron all was well.'

'Why?'

'Because it is our custom that no sin or fault shall lie if the lovers are of different squadrons, if they be of different ranks. If they be of the same rank, then they may be of the same squadron. But six months ago, Sher Singh, being infatuated, arranged for the sowar to be transferred to his own squadron, that he might see more of him.'

'Why didn't anyone stop it? The RM? You? You all knew, didn't you?'

'None knew but the previous rissaldar-major. Why he did not prevent the transfer, we do not know, nor did we ask. But it is said that Sher Singh, who is very rich, granted the RM some land of his at a very low price.'

'Well?'

'We recommend that Sowar Janak be posted back to C Squadron.'

Warren waited. After a time he said, 'And that is all?'

'We have spoken to Captain Sher Singh. We have spoken severely. He was weeping when we finished, and has sworn never to break our customs in this matter again.'

Warren thought, and that'll be the end of it. No one will say another word. How could a regiment function, led by sodomites? 'Did the rissaldar-major agree to this?' he asked.

'Yes, sahib.'

Warren said, 'All right. See that the sowar is transferred.'

The major left. Warren sat alone at the table. He wished he could talk this matter over with Krishna Ram, a bottle of whisky between them. But Krishna was gone. And what would have been the use anyway, for no amount of talk would make either of them really accept the way the other's mind worked? The true answer was the opposite of futile talk over a bottle ... simply an unyielding front. For victory there must be no compromise with Hindu gods, or superstitions, from now on. At his feet, deep in a dream, Shikari growled. 'That's it!' Warren said. 'No compromise!'

December 1914

K RISHNA RAM STARED forward, motionless. He wanted to turn his head, but it would not move. Nor would his eyes alone, however hard he tried to swivel them so that he could see what lay to right and left of what he was looking at. There was earth close in front of him, and presumably under him, and earth or mud in his mouth, and on his lips, which would not move, either. He lay on his stomach, his head twisted to the left. He could see farther with his left eye than his right, which was almost in the mud. There was snow in all the area he saw, and, about three feet away, the clear imprint of army boot nails in the snow, but becoming blurred as the snow continued to fall. It must be early.

Or perhaps it was late. There was no way of telling. The light came and went, without reason, and seemingly very quickly. Either time had slowed or he was becoming conscious and then again unconscious, so it was impossible to tell whether the darknesses were outside himself, such as night, or inside, such as unconsciousness.

The boot marks meant that someone had passed close since the snow began to fall; but when was that? He had been with the machine guns at the side of an old communication trench now in No Man's Land. Something had gone wrong, and he had crawled off to put it right. Then there was very heavy shelling and ... it was dark.

Light came slowly. Snow, mud, the boot print ... ah, unchanged, though it was still snowing! So he had not been unconscious for more than a few minutes. Where was he? Crawling along the fallen-in trench looking for something or someone. A place? Warren Bateman? The god Brahma? Arjun the mighty warrior? Brahma seemed very close, but would not speak. There was music in this place. Strange music. Singing.

Then something had hit him on the side of the head, was it? Or the back? He could feel no pain, no pleasure. But something had hit him out of an enormous brightness, orange and yellow. It could not have been a shell fragment or he wouldn't be looking at the boot print in the snow. He'd be dead and there would be blood in the snow.

Suppose he was dead. The boot was someone looking for him. Major Bateman, perhaps. He'd have to ... darkness.

Ah, a longer time this time, the boot print so blurred by the new snow it was hard to count the hobnails. He must have snow on his head now, or perhaps there was earth on top of that, too. On top of his body. Earth everywhere with him under and the snow on top. Was it possible that he had been buried? And the music he heard was a choir in the sky? Was it perhaps the voice of Brahma? No living human had heard Brahma speak, so who could say for certain that his voice was not like a choir? But would it come from two places, for surely there was a singing ahead, the way his eyes were looking, and also a singing from behind, somewhere behind his feet, where he could not look? The darkness advanced again, but like a fearful company, slowing, leaving a half light on the snow and the mud, then retreating ... again Krishna knew that he saw, and saw clearly, and was not dead.

He was lying out in No Man's Land, covered by earth. If he had been in a shell hole, perhaps they would have found him, but in the open, the earth hiding him was just another hummock among a thousand, and there were bodies everywhere. He could see none, but there must be, for he remembered seeing them, before the shell burst.

A voice said, 'Merry Christmas!'

Merry Christmas? Merry Christmas?

From nearby another answered, '*Fröhliche Weihnachten!*'

He did not know what language that was. The voice of Brahma when he was not a choir? He saw khaki puttees here, and a little way off, but still close, at the top end of his field of view, black jackboots.

'Here,' an upper-class English voice said. 'Have some of this pipe tobacco.'

Others answered unintelligibly. More boots appeared. Oh, God, if he could only lift his head and see what was happening above the boots. The English were offering the others cigarettes, cap badges, a watch, even. The voices were all educated, the voices of officers. The others must surely be Germans. It was not French they were speaking, and anyway there were no French soldiers within fifteen miles of this part of the Western Front.

It was Christmas Day, so the choir he had heard was not the voice of Brahma but people singing carols, as Mr. Fleming had told him about. And once he had been in Lahore over Christmas and had himself heard carols sung. But now English and Germans were out in No Man's Land giving each other gifts and speaking gently—Merry Christmas, *Fröhliche Weihnachten* ... messages of love.

The war was over! They had decided that it was impossible for Christians to behave in this way, as the young sowar had pointed out in durbar. The fighting had been no more than a temporary madness. England, the England of cricket, of green lawns and quiet churches, had come back to its senses.

Again the light wavered, but the voices remained strong and clear. More were coming now, for he heard men speaking behind him, again Merry Christmas, again *Fröhliche Weihnachten*. He felt sudden fear as he remembered again the inhuman cataclysm of the shelling, both British and German, sweeping over him as he lay paralysed in No Man's Land. He had felt no fear at Poucelle, why was he afraid now, hours or days after the shelling?

The darkness snapped away as though an electric light had been switched on six inches in front of his face. He was lying in No Man's Land and these people talking all round him thought he was dead. Or could not see him. The war was over, and if he were left out here he would die of cold and hunger. Perhaps he would die anyway, for he must be badly wounded somewhere to be lying here unable to move even his eyes.

He made a tremendous effort to move his head. Nothing happened—he stared at the same patch of mud and snow, the same boots. He chose his left leg, and willed it to move with all his might and main ... If it did, no one saw. Then his arm, the left arm thrown out in front of him there, half buried under the mud. That he could see ... Nothing. His eyes again. Perhaps someone would notice the rolling of his eyes. Nothing.

He said, 'Merry Christmas.' The nearest boots moved suddenly and a voice said, 'Good God, did you hear that?'

'Yes. What was it?'

His voice must be working. He said again, 'Merry Christmas.'

He saw knees now, where the boots had been, and hands scraping, mud and snow flying. 'There's a man here, he must be alive ... a major ... I saw his hand all the time but thought he must be dead.' He was being lifted. 'Easy now.' Two faces close in front of him, one wearing a British cap and one a German. 'How are you?'

'All right ... Thank God the war's over.'

'The war's not over, old chap ... sir. It's just, we started singing carols in the trenches.'

'I heard.'

'Then some of us came out. It's sort of a truce.'

Krishna Ram sighed and closed his eyes. He felt miserable and full of doubt again. He was wounded and would die. The voice said, 'He's a major of the Ravi Lancers. That's why he's an Indian.'

'They're on our right. Better call for stretcher bearers right away. Heaven knows how long he's been lying out here.'

'Cover him with a greatcoat till they come. He must be freezing to death.'

Krishna thought, yes, I suppose I am, but I can't feel it, or anything else. He saw the greatcoat spreading over his body, where he half lay, supported by a German's arm. He said, 'Thank you. I am sorry. About the war.'

'Traces of frostbite in the fingers and toes,' a voice said, 'but they'll be all right if he recovers.'

The voice was muttering and Krishna opened his eyes. Ah, he could do that. And close them. Before, he could not.

He was looking at Captain Ramaswami, the doctor, very close. The doctor was stooping over him with a stethoscope hung round his neck, apparently talking to himself.

'Hullo, doctor,' Krishna said.

The doctor turned, 'Oh ... you can move your head? Good.'

'What's wrong with me?'

'Concussion. Partial paralysis, but I can't find any wound. Bad bruise on the head. What hit you?'

'I don't know ... Another man's head, perhaps? Blown off his shoulders?'

The doctor looked at him sharply. 'It was nothing sharp-edged, or

184

you'd be dead, that is certain. How do you feel?'

'Something. I didn't before. My feet hurt. My head a little, too.'

The doctor nodded, loosening up. 'It'll get worse as you get better.'

'What casualties did we have in the attack?'

'2nd Lieutenant Ishar Lall died of wounds. Some others. They're burning Ishar Lall now, in the rear area. I've sent a message to tell Major Bholanath and the CO that you've been brought in.'

'Ishar Lall?' Krishna said. 'Oh, that is a shame ... a tragedy.'

'He did not have to lose his life in French mud for the British Empire,' the doctor said, 'nor do you have to risk yours. I'll get you some tea.'

He went out. Krishna saw that he was in a curtained-off part of the RAP. There was a hole in the tarpaulin roof. Water dripped steadily through it on to the muddy floor. The snow must be melting. A voice said in Hindi, 'I am so glad that you are with us again, Highness.'

He turned his head to a sharp jab of pain, which he received nevertheless with joy, and saw Lieutenant Mahadeo Singh on a bench the other side of the room. 'I was hit in the wrist,' the old lieutenant said apologetically. 'I asked the doctor sahib not to send me back as there is no one else to be the CO's officer-galloper.'

'How was the attack? I think ... didn't I see A Squadron running away?'

'Yes, Highness. And C.'

Krishna Ram focused his eyes with another, smaller pang. The lieutenant was sitting up on the bench, fully dressed and wearing his greatcoat. His left arm was in a sling. He said, 'The general-sahib is angry, because some of the men ran away, but he was not there! I cannot understand what happened. It was said that the German machine guns had been destroyed, but they had not. And their artillery ... Your Highness was there.'

Krishna Ram thought, this man served twenty-one years in the regulars. To him the Raj had been all-powerful, faultless, divine in its wisdom. Now he sounded not only afraid, but as though doubting the earth under his feet.

The doctor came back, followed by an orderly carrying a mug of tea. He said, 'I'm going to keep you here overnight, Yuvraj. Then, unless some wound or disability appears, I'm going to have you

185

sent to England for convalescent leave. You are suffering from exposure and general weakness, but as far as I can find out, nothing more. With rest and good food you'll be all right in a week or two. Ready to be put into the mincing machine again.'

Krishna Ram thought, I should reprimand him for speaking like that in front of the orderly and the lieutenant. As he hesitated, pain stabbed into his head, and that brought back the searing yellow flame bursting all round him, and the mud and snow. He closed his eyes against them, and the world shivered. The flame was replaced at once by a vision of grinding steel. The thing that he had seen out there was not human, let alone civilized. Nor yet was it superhuman, or divine. The shells that burst invisibly, killing and maiming, were nothing like the thunderbolts of Indra, but instruments created directly by evil. He shuddered, and heard the doctor say, 'Take these with the tea. You'll sleep and feel better when you wake up.'

As Krishna was taking the pills he saw Mahadeo Singh stand up and salute with his good hand. Then Colonel Bateman came forward, his hand out, 'Krishna, I'm glad to see you ... How is he, doctor?'

'All right,' Ramaswami said, with a brief explanation.

Bateman said, 'I had patrols out all last night, looking for you. Two officer's patrols, two dafadar's patrols. No one could find a trace. I'd made up my mind we'd lost you. That's why I'm so glad to see you back ... Did you say you were recommending convalescent leave in England, doc?'

'Yes.'

'Spend it at Shrewford Pennel, Krishna. I know my mother will be delighted to see you again. Though there'll be no cricket now.' He looked tired, Krishna thought, and grim.

'Thank you very much, sir,' Krishna Ram said, 'I can't think of anything better.'

'Send a telegram as soon as you reach England. Tell them I'm sending you.'

'The patient should rest now,' the doctor said. 'He's just taken some sleeping pills.'

Major Bateman said, 'Well, I'll see you again in the morning. Lie back now.'

Krishna Ram lay back, closing his eyes. He hurt all over now, and felt as feeble as a sick rat. He heard Warren Bateman say, 'Go

186

outside a minute, Mahadeo, please.' And, a moment later, 'What's wrong with the rissaldar-major, doctor? By God, I can't afford to lose him even for a day.'

'Nothing but starvation. When he agreed to let the quartermaster take those bully beef labels off the tins, he couldn't eat the food himself, because he did know what was inside. For him it would have been a mortal sin. He also decided he must not eat even proper food for another four days, as penance for the deception he had practised. Then there was the attack and you know what he did. It was he who led the stretcher party that carried Ishar Lall back through the German bombardment. This morning, he fainted.'

'From hunger?'

'And horror. He's not a man to show it, but that makes what he feels worse.'

'I'll go and see him. Where is he?'

'In his own dugout. His orderly's looking after him. He ought to be all right tomorrow. He's eating again.'

The voices faded. Darkness came over Krishna, with ideas, half formed visions: horror ... machines. Gradually his hurts ceased.

He dozed in the train to Boulogne, slept on the cross-channel steamer and all the way up to London, went to bed at once in the officers' hostelry and, the next morning, dozed most of the way from Paddington to Woodborough—all this in spite of himself, for London had been just as majestic, the countryside just as gentle, doubly so after the trenches in Artois, but he was weak, and could not help himself. He awoke to a hand on his knee and a voice saying, 'I think this is your station, major.' The man opposite was old and polite. Krishna thanked him and stood up to lift his suitcase down from the luggage rack. The train glided to a standstill and he got out.

On the platform the station master touched his gold-braided cap to him. Behind, Diana Bateman, smiling, came towards him with her long firm strides. Kishna's heart warmed. She looked so healthy, so fair, her gaze so direct. He fumbled to take off his glove, make his hand ready for her hand. She was wearing a long black dress, and a long grey coat, fur lined, and a grey hat with a touch of fur round it.

'You look pale,' she said. 'Where were you wounded?' She picked up his suitcase before he could protest and said, 'Come on now.

You'll catch cold standing out here on the platform.'

The engine whistled and chuffed off westward. A minute later, snug under a carriage rug beside Diana Bateman on the driver's seat of the trap, Krishna rolled out towards Shrewford Pennel.

The snow had stopped somewhere in mid-channel, yesterday. In the setting sun, under scattered clouds, the cliffs of England had glowed gold like the battlements of the city of God. The land lay under a blanket of pure white, so bright that it hurt the eyes to look at it for long. Here, now, the hedges along the roadside were hung with white bands and wreaths of snow, and red berries gleamed in the white-draped holly trees. Smoke curled up from cottages nestled low in the snow. Rooks wheeled against the blue sky above the etched fingers of the elms. A group of boys outside a farm cottage were gathering snow and throwing snowballs after two girls. The girls ran away down the lane, their faces bright and laughing. Dogs barked and ran in a field, and by the Old Vicarage a dozen young people were riding toboggans down the slope below the churchyard wall. An old man, passing with a saw over his shoulder, touched his cap with a smile and a cheerful, 'Afternoon, miss!'

Krishna sighed in tired contentment. This was England, seen in winter as he had imagined it from reading Dickens and from Mr. Fleming's descriptions. He felt better every moment. There could be nothing seriously wrong with a country, a people, so warm, so so sensible, so stable. The trap turned into the driveway of the Old Vicarage, the horses' hoofs silent in the snow, and drew up in front of the door. Old Mrs. Bateman, Warren's mother, came out and Krishna stepped down carefully, aware of the weakness in his legs.

'Come in, Krishna,' she said. She looked at him. 'Take him straight to his room, Diana.'

He felt a hand under his arm. 'Here, lean on me. There now.'

Five minutes later he was undressed and asleep.

When he awoke and peered at his watch he saw it was four o'clock. He had slept nearly five hours, but he felt more than refreshed, as though the blasting, the paralysis, the exhaustion and horror of the Battle of Hill 73 were parts of a dream long gone. He dressed and went downstairs to find the family gathered in the drawing room eating buttered crumpets. Warren's wife, Joan, greeted him pleasantly. She was wearing a bright red blouse of what looked like sandbag material, and a sheepskin skirt not half way down her calf. The children, stuffing their mouths with crumpets and dripping butter on to the carpet, also wore sheepskin trousers, both the boy and the girl. Outside, the daylight had faded, and a lamp in the window of a cottage across the valley glowed like a big star. Ralph Harris stood by the fire, his gaze turned inward, his eyes unfocused.

Diana examined Krishna critically. 'You look much better now. Quite different. But I don't think ...' She looked at her sister-in-law.

'Oh, ask him,' Joan Bateman said impatiently. 'I will lend him a sheepskin coat and he will come to no harm.'

Krishna looked inquiringly at Diana, his tea cup poised, a crumpet in the other hand. She said, 'We're going carol singing this evening—a little group we call the Pennel Carollers—and I was going to invite you to come along with us. It's awfully good fun, really. But when I saw how tired you were ...'

Joan Bateman interrupted, 'You go, Krishna. But you'll wear a skin coat, of course.'

'Er, yes, of course,' Krishna said cautiously. Joan was lying on her stomach on the floor with the children now, seemingly oblivious of the fact that her skirt had ridden above her knees, exposing the backs of her thighs. He averted his eyes and gazed at her face, turned towards him.

'You know what the Swami Draupananda writes?' Joan said. 'About the skins of the innocent filtering out evil? Sheep are innocent, aren't they?'

'Er, yes, I think so.'

'Come on, then,' Diana said breezily, 'put on extra thick socks, and the sheepskin coat.'

'I bought it for Warren,' Joan said, 'but he didn't want it. I'll go and get it.' She rose from her ungainly position with a grace Krishna would not have believed possible and floated out of the room.

Old Mrs. Bateman said, 'Swami Draupananda is Joan's latest find. I suppose he's very famous in India?'

Krishna said, 'I'm afraid I have never heard of him.' He caught Diana's eye and they both suddenly smiled. Diana said, 'The waistcoat won't do you any *harm* at least ... but, oh dear, I'd like to smack those children sometimes. But Mother's the only one who can do that ... Now wrap up well, because it's cold as long as we're outside.'

Half an hour later Krishna stood at one end of a little half moon of bundled-up carol singers outside the doctor's house at the other end of Shrewford Pennel, Diana next to him. A lamp by the front door over the doctor's night bell turned the falling snow into golden spears. They started with *Good King Wenceslas*, because, as he had apologetically explained to Diana, that and *A Partridge in a Pear Tree* were the only carols he knew, both taught him by Mr. Fleming. 'The "Partridge" carol was the favourite of Mr. Fuller, when he used to come out with the Pennel Carollers,' Diana said.

Krishna remembered the name and said, 'Didn't he play cricket, too?'

'Yes, but in the past few years he's become a, what do you call it, recluse, hermit. He's supposed to have done something ... I don't know what.'

Krishna remembered more then—that this Mr. Fuller was suspected of having the same sexual tastes as Captain Sher Singh. But here the perversion was not spoken of, and Diana Bateman obviously had no idea what Mr. Fuller was accused of. And if he told her, she would be no wiser. That was a sort of innocence. Every Indian woman of her age, or of many years younger, would know, however virtuous she was. Here it was hard to separate virtue, or innocence, from ignorance.

> *On the feast of Stephen,*
> *When the snow lay round about,*
> *Deep and crisp and even ...*

The doctor came out with his wife and when they had finished singing invited them in for a glass of ginger wine. The wine was sweet and peppery on the tongue and Krishna loved it. He smiled warmly at Diana, glass in hand. She said, 'You sing very well.'

'Only those two songs.'

'We'll have to sing others later. You can just hum.'

From the doctor's they went to a farm under the rise of the Plain, and more ginger wine. From there to Pennel House, and sad Sir Tristram and his big stern Lady and on the grand piano the picture of the boy killed with the Coldstream Guards, in his full dress, and this time ginger wine for the ladies and for the men a whisky-mac—the same with a large tot of whisky poured into the wine glass on top of the ginger wine.

Lady Pennel swept up to Krishna where he was drinking at Diana's side and said, 'It is nice to see our gallant Indian fellow subjects fighting at our side for their Emperor ... and our king.'

'Yes, Lady Pennel,' Krishna muttered. He thought, she's like an image of a goddess such as we carry in procession in Basohli—five times life size.

'Civilization is at stake. No sacrifice is too great. I think you know we have already given our only son, and the heir to the title.'

'I'm sorry,' Krishna mumbled.

Lady Pennel turned on Diana. 'I hear your mother still has Young Marsh working for her, Diana.'

'Yes. Two or three hours a day.'

'If no one would employ that young man, he'd be forced to do his duty, and volunteer for the army,' Lady Pennel said. 'His poor father is dying of shame.'

'He says he thinks war is immoral,' Diana said.

'He's a slacker,' Lady Pennel said sharply, 'or a coward. I don't know which is worse. And, of course, it's Ralph Harris who puts these ridiculous ideas into his head. There's another young man who ought to be in the trenches. I'm surprised your mother doesn't make him go.'

'No one can make Ralph do what he doesn't want to,' Diana said with a touch of weariness.

'I heard your mother had got him a position in Manchester.'

'He didn't want to accept it.'

'A very difficult young man,' Lady Pennel said, majestically. 'I understand, of course, but ... Give your mother my regards, please.' She sailed away, nodding, and a few minutes later they were out in the snow again. 'Only one more house and then we finish back at the Old Vicarage,' Diana said.

The new snow lay two inches deep on top of the old now. The clouds were low but not thick and a silver moonlight diffused through them so that everything was clear but without depth, for there were no shadows. Snow mantled the singers' shoulders and lay in white coronets on top of caps and bonnets. They walked together down the lane, a dozen talking, all but he and Diana in the broad soft slur of the Wiltshire dialect, back past the crested gates at the entry to the Pennel House drive, and the gatehouse where Old Marsh lived, now doubling as gatekeeper and gamekeeper, too, because a younger man had volunteered for the Navy.

Outside the Old Vicarage, as soon as they began to sing, the curtains were pulled back in the drawing room and they looked in, singing to the two children standing on the window seat, dressed in pyjamas and quilted dressing gowns, with their grandmother standing behind them, an arm round each slight shoulder, and Joan by the fire, a book in her hands, and Ralph Harris beside her, looking not at the carollers but at her.

It's beautiful, Krishna said to himself. He glanced at Diana as he sang, and she turned to look at him at the same time, and again, as once before but for a different reason, his heart missed a beat. If she had been an Indian, perhaps even a Frenchwoman, it would have been impossible to doubt that she was offering him herself, her body. But with Diana it was impossible to doubt just the opposite. That look was a direct communication, undistorted by the fact that they were of different sexes, with all that that carried, for most, of threat and promise, danger and excitement.

Then she turned her head away, still singing, and soon they were inside, drinking more ginger wine. Diana was pouring whisky into his glass with a generous hand. 'Warrie loves whisky-macs at Christmas time,' she said.

Krishna Ram drank, and had another after the rest of the carol singers had gone, with a touching of forelocks from the men, and bobbed half-curtsies from the rose-cheeked women. The whisky and wine ran warm through all his blood now, and when once or twice a memory of Hill 73 came to his mind, the whisky itself seemed to rush to the attack and drive it out. He was warm and well. Lines were softening, blurring. Diana was talking, and so was he, but what they talked about, he did not know. They served him food, but what it was, did not matter. More wine! There was a Christmas pudding covered with a brandy sauce, and holly stuck into it. Before that Mrs. Bateman asked him if he would like to carve the meat as he was the only gentleman present, but he begged to be excused. He knew nothing of carving meat. What sort of meat was it? Probably beef, for the English ate little else. What did it matter? And then, after dinner, trying to get up from a deep chair by the fire, and stumbling back into it ...

'You're still weak,' Diana said. 'You should go to bed, really, Krishna.'

Really, yes, he thought; and the whisky was helping as well as the fatigue. He said good nights and went slowly up the stairs, and in a moment, only half undressed, was asleep.

Krishna steadied the log with his left hand and with his right

rhythmically worked the long cross-cut saw backwards and for-
wards. It was damp in the carriage house, for the doors were open,
a cold rain was falling outside and visibility was down to a hundred
yards. Water dripped from the trees on to the dirty remains of the
snow, and the drive was a channel of mud between the pleached
hedges. It was January 5, 1915, the last day of his convalescent
leave. In truth he had felt fully recovered a couple of days before,
with a corresponding sense of guilt that he had not returned at once
to the regiment; but there was the doc's direct order not to return
before his full week was up, however he felt; and there was the
quiet grace of life here; and there was Diana. For seven days he had
shared her life—grooming the spaniel, exercising the horses, taking
the trap to Devizes for the week's shopping, a ten-mile drive each
way across the downs, past mysterious white horses carved into
the chalk—becoming visible again as the rain washed the snow off
the slope. He had offered to help old Mrs. Bateman but there was
no work for a man at this time of year, until now. Yesterday they'd
bought a tree at the back of the Pennel estate, and Young Marsh
had felled it, sawed it into pieces small enough for loading into the
borrowed farm cart, and brought them to the Old Vicarage. Now
the huge logs had to be sawed and then split into pieces that could
be used in the kitchen range and the fireplaces in the drawing room
and the bedrooms.

Ralph Harris was at the other end of the two-handed saw. He
was stripped to his shirt sleeves, a pair of old corduroy trousers
loose round his waist, the braces hanging down, inappropriately
thin shoes heavily splashed with the greyish mud of the vale. They
had been working for half an hour, saying almost nothing, but
there was no sign of sweat on Ralph's pale, narrow face, while
Krishna was sweating heavily under his khaki shirt and tunic—but
he was glad of it. In the trenches he had felt a lack of physical
condition. A foot soldier's life, digging, carrying, bending, was very
different from that of a mounted lancer.

Ralph Harris said, 'So you're going back to France tomorrow.'

Krishna said, 'I'm afraid so. I shall be sorry to go ... I could live
here forever.'

'Yes,' the other said. 'It's a good life for people with money, and
class. It's different for the others ... the ordinary people.'

Krishna did not speak, not knowing quite what Harris meant.
Harris continued, 'The rich have the poor by the short hairs here,

193

but most of them are too stupid to realize it. Except people like Young Marsh, who are willing to see what's really quite obvious.'

Krishna said, 'I don't see anything bad here. Nothing like it is in India at any rate, even in my grandfather's state. Or in Germany and Poland and Russia, from what I have read.'

'You wouldn't know ... because you can't see, I suppose ... George Jenkins and his wife were kicked out of their cottage last week, just before Christmas, because he wouldn't work any more for one of the Pennel tenants—Isaiah Tate at Hill Farm. Tate was paying George only fifteen shillings a week, though George is a good and experienced man. He asked for more, so Tate kicked him out. George went to Pennel House to tell Pennel he had nowhere else to go, but Pennel said he had to get out. It was a tied cottage.'

'What's that?'

'The cottage goes with the job. If a farm labourer doesn't like what the farmer pays him, or how he's treated, or gets sacked for any reason, he's thrown out of the cottage, too.'

Krishna said, 'I can see how it could be unfair ... but surely if a farmer's to get any labourers, he must have cottages nearby for them?'

'Yes, but the result is that the farmer has the power to make a man work any hours, for any wage ... But in spite of everything there's very little crime here, except what the gentry call poaching. And if anything is reported, the policeman just goes out and arrests some labourer. The magistrates are all gentry. They don't care what a working man's life is like, only about protecting their property. *Their* pheasants!'

He sawed away with an angry energy, so that Krishna had to work harder to keep pace.

'And now they're trying to starve Young Marsh because he won't go to this war. All kinds of people are telling Mother she must stop employing him. But he's not going. They'll never make him ... even if Mother has to give in. And I don't think she will.'

They sawed on. Krishna thought, it may be true, what he says, but he does not realize how much better off they were here than in India. Yet an Indian peasant would not be looking for the same freedoms, or expecting the same rewards. He'd have his own hopes, and they would be different.

Joan Bateman came out, a man's old hat on her head. She ran

in under the shelter of the carriage house crying, 'Goodness, you've sawn a lot, Ralph.'

Harris said, 'With His Highness here.'

'Mother sent me out to tell you it's lunch time.' She took his coat off the hook where he had hung it and held it out for him. 'Here, put this on, Ralph, or you'll catch cold.'

Harris eased into the coat saying, 'I was telling Krishna how the gentry oppress the working people here.'

'Oh, yes,' Joan said, 'but that's almost not the worst of it, though it is *really* . . . They're such appalling *bores*, talking and thinking nothing but horses and pheasants and foxes. Not one of them has read a book since he left school, or knows the difference between Velasquez and Brahms. If it weren't for Ralph here I would have died of sheer boredom long since. I didn't think anyone could be more boneheaded than officers of Indian cavalry, but at least they've seen another world, another way of life.'

Krishna put on his tunic and turned to Ralph, a little nettled because all these denigrations could be taken to include Warren. He said, 'You hate the upper classes, don't you, Ralph?'

Ralph's face creased into a sardonic smile. 'Why not? I'm a byblow of one of them . . . old Henry Bateman, seducing my mother when she was a cowman's daughter and he the vicar here. Mrs. Bateman's done her best, bringing me up the way she brought up her own children, after my mother died . . . but from where I stand everything looks different . . . different, and bad.'

Joan Bateman laid a hand on his arm and said, 'Ralph dear, don't talk about it. It doesn't matter to me . . . to Mother . . . to anyone who *matters* . . . Come in for lunch.'

They walked away together, across the yard and into the house, looking at each other, not speaking, Krishna forgotten. He felt a cold chill of certainty that they were lovers.

That afternoon Diana said, 'What a shame it's such a miserable day. I wanted to ride up on the Plain this afternoon, as it's your last day.'

'Let's go,' Krishna said, 'but walking. From what I've seen of defence systems in France, cavalry will never be used again. I'd better get used to walking.'

They put on raincoats and Diana wore a sou'wester over her hair, and Mrs. Bateman gave Krishna a blackthorn stick from the umbrella stand in the hall and they strode off side by side down the drive, along the lane, left at the Upavon Road and so up on to the Plain. The rain stung Krishna's face as they headed south-west. He hardly spoke, for what he had guessed deeply troubled him. Surely it was the war, in some way, causing it, for surely Warren would have been different back in India a year ago, at the training camp, at the cricket, if Joan was already turning away from him then. But gradually the awareness of Diana striding along at his side drove his apprehensions deeper into his consciousness, and finally out of sight. She was more than herself, a young woman, Warren's sister; she was England, England walking through the rain, her spaniel hunting the dulled scent of rabbits, lonely trees like distant ghosts across the short grass.

Soon after they returned to the Old Vicarage half a dozen children came for a party with Rodney and Louise and after they had all eaten cakes and drunk tea, and pulled crackers, and the maid had cleared away the mess, everyone, grown-ups included, divided into two teams to play Charades. Krishna had never played before —in turns each side acted out a word, syllable by syllable, while the other side had to guess what the word was. He loved it, and loved the bright-eyed eagerness of the children, the whole-hearted way they flung themselves into their parts, how they loved to dress up in the finery Mrs. Bateman brought down from the attic.

'That's the best part of Charades for them,' she said, smiling. 'Dressing up. We never throw away old clothes, but keep them just for this.'

'We should give more to the poor people, Mother,' Ralph Harris said.

'If they are working clothes, we do,' the old lady replied equably, 'but that silk ball gown there which Caroline Gill is wearing ... I wore that to the Hunt Balls in—let me see, Sir George was Master—1877 and '78. That would not be much use to a poor woman.'

'How do you know, Mother?' Joan Bateman said. 'It's up to them to decide how they use it, not us.'

'Yes, dear,' Mrs. Bateman said. 'It's your side's turn to go out now. And we shall have to make this the last one. It's nearly seven o'clock.'

The maid awakened Krishna at six next morning. It was still

raining. The fields disappeared green-grey into the thick air, and if any gods existed they were shivering damply in the formless clouds that filled the sky. Krishna washed slowly, dressed, and took out his cigarette case. He looked at the cigarette between his fingers and said aloud, 'No.' No more. There was an unpleasant taste of old tobacco smoke in his mouth and in the room, but that was not what led him to empty the case into the wastepaper basket. It was time to give up, to abstain, not to acquire. Warren would not understand. He felt the oppression of sadness again. He would have liked to talk to Diana about Warren and Joan, but that was impossible, now. Another time, perhaps, if he survived. And Warren.

He was going back to the trenches. Back to Warren, his friend and teacher. He felt an uneasy malaise as though he were to face some severe test and did not know how he would pass it. Ralph Harris's words weighed heavily on him. Those sodden fields and thatched cottages held sorrows, lusts, and angers as bitter as any in India. Cricket would not assuage them. Nor destroying the Hun. Something was breaking here, even as he had seen administration break down on the Western Front. Was the war causing it? Or only exposing it?

He had drunk too much last night—again. But perhaps his malaise came from the fact that he was going to say goodbye to Diana Bateman, and might never see her again. He began to shave, noting how very brown his face looked here, in this pale light.

March 1915

KRISHNA RAM DUCKED under the low door and settled himself quickly at the back of the small crowd. It was another roofless house (were there any with roofs in France?) in St. Hubert, this one allotted for use as a Hindu temple. A tattered tarpaulin suspended from the ends of beams sticking out of the walls covered most but not all of it. A sowar in C Squadron had carved a *lingam* out of another beam, that must have been there for five hundred years, and the Brahmin had set it up in the centre of the tiled floor. A few primroses and snowdrops lay scattered at the base of the *lingam,* a garland of small fresh daisies hung round it, and the top was scattered with turmeric.

It was March 20, the second and most important day of the great Hindu spring festival of Holi. The Brahmin, squatting in front of the *lingam,* rocked back and forth in white robes, palms joined, eyes closed, chanting endless Sanskrit verses of prayer to the Fire God. A dozen sowars seemed to fill the room, some chanting holy names, some praying silently with hands joined and heads bowed. They were all wearing their grey army socks, for the tiles were cold and damp, though the boots were left outside.

> O Fire, you are immortal among mortals,
> You protect us as a friend does,
> In front and at the back and at higher
> levels and lower levels.
> Destroy the strength and might of the demons!

The letter burned like a live coal in the pocket of Krishna's tunic. Her writing was almost unformed, and certainly the wording was banal enough: 'It rained hard yesterday and we had to get

198

Young Marsh to come and clear the ditch ... Fudge is getting fat
with not enough exercise now that I work for the Women's Volunteer League every afternoon ... Mother asks what size socks you
wear as she is going to knit you a pair of heavy woollen ones ...'

> *O beloved we are celebrating the festival*
> *of Holi today in Brij*
> *Two ladies of fair complexion and two of*
> *dark have come out of their homes to play*
> *Holi*

But it was the first letter she'd written him, and it arrived the
day the regiment came out of the line a week ago, after a fortnight
in the trenches, again opposite Lestelle Wood and Hill 73. That
was the first half of March, two weeks of sleet and rain and snow,
and raw cold, men going down with pneumonia and influenza and
Major Bateman insisting on an even more rigorous discipline, even
more aggressive patrolling. Now, in the rear area, he was trying
to stop the men from washing themselves every morning by strip-
ping naked, except for the loin cloth, and washing the whole body
at a pump or in a bucket. That was the only form of ceremonial
cleanliness for a Hindu, but Major Bateman said it was causing
pneumonia, from which the regiment was losing 500 man-days a
month, and he wanted to forbid it. 'Why can't they wash like everyone else does in this climate?' he demanded of Krishna. 'A bit at
a time, keeping the rest of their clothes on?'

> *My beloved, the red powder is flying in the air,*
> *And the clouds are red in the sky.*
> *I am drenched in saffron coloured water,*
> *And the people are playing various musical*
> *instruments—*
> *Mridang, Jhanj, Dhup, Majera!*

Krishna bowed ceremonially, made a last silent prayer, went out,
and sat on the step tying his boot laces. It was good to see, at the
edge of the wood, the fifty horses which had been brought up for
the celebrations.

In this hour before the beginning of the long northern twilight,
there was an appropriate breath of spring in the air. Music—

Indian music—sounded from the left and Krishna followed it down a narrow alley to its source in a big barn. The regimental band was playing, squatted in a half circle on earth and straw. Half a dozen sowars in the full costume of the Ravi hills danced in the centre of the circle. Two men astride makeshift hobby horses danced after beckoning, escaping girls. The barn was jammed with sowars. There must have been over two hundred of them and from the crests on turbans, and the brass shoulder titles, Krishna saw that many men from the division's regular infantry battalions— Punjabis, Gurkhas, Dogras, Mahrattas—had come to join in the celebration. A pair of Gurkhas had made huge phalluses out of wood for themselves, and fastened them round their waists and, obviously full of cheap brandy, danced after the men in women's clothing, to the applause and laughter of the crowd.

Krishna noticed some French villagers at the edge of the crowd and smiled to himself. They would never have seen a celebration of Holi before, or even heard of it; but they would recognize what it was about easily enough. After all, there were spring festivals in every religion, Mr. Fleming had said. Even Easter was a spring festival, timed to replace the old Saturnalias.

The band played more loudly. The dancers spread out from the barn on to the twilit field. A couple of young soldiers ran down from the street and began to hurl red and blue powder. Louder the music, more heavy the beat ...

One of the phallus-armed Gurkhas jerked his hips in front of the French women at the edge of the crowd. The women giggled, turned away, looked again, moved their legs comfortably. Their eyes enlarged, focused on the stiffly upthrust phallus jerking there so close against their skirts.

There'd be a lot of men going down the road to Longmont tonight, Krishna thought. Holi was the Rite of Spring. The men had not seen their wives and lovers for over six months now. They were drinking, too, passing round brandy and wine.

He went back into the village. The doors were open, the men inside drinking and singing lascivious songs. Other men ran down the street hurling the red powder, symbol of women's blood. From behind half drawn curtains French villagers watched, wondering.

At Major Bateman's billet the orderly sat in the doorway polishing the major's boots. Through the window, Krishna saw Warren writing by the light of a hurricane lantern set on the table beside him. Krishna stopped. He should go and talk to him. He was the only Christian of the regiment, the only Englishman. He must feel specially alone on an evening like this, when everyone about him was involved in something he could not share. Warren's family had taken him, Krishna, to the Christian church in Shrewford Pennel. Surely he should do something for Warren now?

But it was different. Warren despised Holi as an obscene heathen spectacle, typifying the worst of India. He had not tried to stop the celebrations, but had told Krishna that he himself would take no part in them. If there was any religious ceremony involved, as in the blessing of weapons at Dussehra, Krishna was to represent him. He was not willing to take whatever the Hindu faith, or the Brahmin, or this gaudy rite of Holi could give him; as Krishna had been willing to take what the little church in Shrewford Pennel held out to him. So he sat there, isolated, working, Shikari at his feet. Krishna thought, is he writing to Joan? Has she told him something, to bring that frown to his face? Perhaps yes, perhaps no, but the frown was becoming almost permanent now, together with a jerky, nervy irritability quite foreign to the Warren whom Krishna had known in India. Overwork ... the war ... Joan, perhaps ...

He moved on, among men now dancing in the street in the dusk, and powder bursting like bombs against doors and windows, and the sound of the band a spring wind in the air, full of longing.

'Sowar Alam Singh, Ravi Lancers, you are charged under Section 40 of the Indian Army Act with desertion in the face of the enemy, in that ...'

The voice of the British lieutenant-colonel of the 1/12th Gurkhas droned on with the details of the charge in fluent Hindustani. At the end he said, 'How do you plead, guilty or not guilty?'

'Guilty, sahib,' the prisoner replied promptly.

The colonel said, 'Since the charge is liable to the death penalty, your plea must be recorded as Not Guilty. The trial will proceed on that basis.'

Krishna Ram settled more comfortably in his chair behind the two blanket-covered tables. The General Court Martial was being held in Divisional HQ at Pont des Moines, five miles farther back than St. Hubert. The other members of the court were Krishna, Captain Sher Singh, Captain Longmire of the 71st Punjabis, and 2nd Lieutenant Puran Lall.

The evidence was plain. Sowar Alam Singh had run away during the débâcle at Hill 73, and had disappeared. The rest of his squadron had stopped when they reached B Squadron standing steady in the old front line; but Alam Singh had kept on, not running now but walking, all the way past the reserve regiments, past the gun lines until he reached an Indian AT company. He'd spent the night there, the next day got into a cattle truck on a train and stayed in it till it stopped, six hours later. Then he'd walked across a couple of fields, knocked at the door of an isolated farm, and by gestures asked for food. It was a lonely farm, the men away at the war, and two women, an old one and a young one, had looked after him. They kept pigs and chickens and had no man to do the heavy work. Alam Singh became their farm labourer.

'What did you do while at the farm?' the defending officer asked in his examination-in-chief.

'Worked, sahib. I worked hard. Those Fransezi women showed me much that I did not know about pigs. Their pigs were bigger than any I have seen. Their chickens laid more and bigger eggs.'

'Did you intend to return to the regiment?'

'No, sahib,' the man said. 'I was tired of the war. I wanted to leave a month before, and return to my farm at home, but the major-sahib—Bholanath—would not permit it. I had then served the Rajah five years, as I promised when I joined.'

Krishna thought, he's one of the old type, brave, tenacious, simple, totally honest. Since he had missed the rigorous training that Warren had given the regiment since the débâcle at Hill 73 he had not, like the rest of the men, become harder, tougher, more sophisticated, and, to tell the truth, less likable. Such a man as Alam Singh still was could not survive in the new regiment. It would be better for him, and the Rajah, and the regiment, if he were allowed to go back to farming.

The defending officer tried hard to get the sowar to say that he had intended to return to the regiment some day—for the intention never to return is the essence of the crime of desertion; but Alam Singh remained adamant that he intended to give up soldiering forever. The prosecuting officer, Dayal Ram, hardly had to prove any of the points that he needed to substantiate the charge, for they had all been proven for him. The evidence completed, Major Bholanath gave witness of the man's excellent character, and—until the time of his absence—reliability. The prosecution did not rebut that, and the court retired to consider their verdict.

The colonel turned to the junior officer, as was the order of a court martial, and asked him for his opinion. Puran Lall glanced covertly at Krishna, looking for a lead as to what the prince thought; but the colonel said irritably, 'Don't look at Major Krishna Ram, man! What do *you* think?'

'I think, guilty,' Puran Lall said, 'but ...'

'That's all I'm asking you now,' the colonel snapped. 'Longmire?'

'Guilty.'

One by one the other officers followed suit, all saying, 'Guilty.'

The colonel said, 'Now, the punishment. As you know, the Indian Army Act says that this crime shall be punished by "death or such less punishment as the court shall decide". In other words we have complete latitude to award any punishment whatsoever, and as we are a General Court Martial, we have the power to award the death penalty ... I consider this man's crime as serious as it could be. He ran away in the face of the enemy. He found a safe place a hundred miles in the rear and simply stayed there, betraying his oath, his comrades, and his military duty. He lived with these two French women and God knows what he didn't ... well, that's not in the charge, and the women said he'd been a model labourer and had done nothing against them or anyone else. But they'd say that anyway ... The general thinks that desertions will increase disastrously if we don't jump hard on the ones we catch. So ... Mr. Puran Lall?'

Again Puran Lall sought Krishna Ram's eyes. Krishna imperceptibly shook his head. He had suddenly decided that the man must not be shot. He was an Indian farmer. No one but other farmers, other Indians, other men from Ravi, could really understand what he had done and why.

Puran Lall understood, and said, 'Not death, sir. Some years imprisonment. I do not know how many.'

The colonel said impatiently, 'If that's what you say we'd better vote first for or against the death penalty. Then we can settle the number of years if we have to. You are against the death penalty in this case?'

'Yes, sir.'

'Longmire?'

'Death, sir.'

'Sher Singh?'

'Not death, sir.'

'Major Krishna Ram?'

'I am against the death penalty, sir.'

The colonel shuffled his papers angrily. 'I am of the opinion—strongly—that the man deserves death. But we are three to two against, and I so record it. Now, what do you suggest as the appropriate punishment for this ... the most serious crime a soldier can commit? Two extra guards, perhaps, Major Krishna Ram?'

Krishna thought, this procedure was all very well for the British, and for them it worked well; but for Indians it was better to discuss, for everyone to have his say and for everyone to be aware of what the others thought, the decision would not then be the result of a hard mathematical count—so many yes, so many no—but a consensus, a compromise commonly arrived at. By attacking with this sarcastic question the colonel had given him the chance he needed.

He said, 'I think Alam Singh should serve the army for the same period he failed to, and then he should be dismissed to go back to Ravi. He believed he had done all that he undertook to do when he enlisted five years ago, and according to our thoughts, that is true. I would recommend that he be given four months rigorous imprisonment, to be served in the ranks of the regiment, and then to be discharged.'

The two other Indians spoke up at once, 'I agree, sir. Four months rigorous imprisonment.'

The colonel turned to the young British captain and said, 'It looks as though we are outnumbered, Longmire ... Well, he's your man, Major Krishna Ram. If this is the sort of discipline you keep in the Ravi Lancers I'm not surprised your people run away. Call the court back into session.'

When it was all over Krishna walked slowly back up the road, noticing with another part of his mind that there was more traffic than usual, loaded carts going forward, empties coming back. He stopped half an hour at the Regimental Aid Post to visit the sick and talk to Ramaswami. When he got back to the regiment there was a message for him to report at once to Major Bateman.

Warren's nose was pinched, the broad face closed. 'Colonel Lovat's been by. He told me about the proceedings of the court. I don't understand how you could press for this ... ridiculous punishment in a case of desertion. If you have any explanation, I'd like to hear it.'

Krishna Ram said, 'Sir ...' He stopped. Warren did not understand. Warren would never understand. Perhaps he might have, back in India, but not here, not in the tightening grip of the war. He said, 'I believe I understand what Alam Singh thought, what he felt. We changed his obligation when we embodied the regiment into the Indian Army. In Ravi a man can leave whenever he wants to, after his agreed term of service is up.'

'Always? In war?' Warren snapped.

'Yes, sir. But a man left in war would have his action judged. I mean, the people would decide whether he was leaving for cowardice, or from some proper reason. To till the fields is always a proper reason. The ground must be seeded and grow its fruit, the Brahmins say.'

Warren said, 'I am dissatisfied with your reasoning and with your action. Also with the *panchayat* proceedings on Sher Singh. I suppose I ought to have known that *he'd* do whatever you wanted, though. That's all.'

Krishna Ram saluted and went out. Poor Warren ... but he was a good man, too, and the hell of a soldier. He had never told Warren about the letter Diana had written him. He wondered why. It still warmed his tunic pocket. He reached his billet and took it out to read it once more.

The following afternoon was the last day of the Holi celebrations. The celebration of fertility was over, and there remained only a morning of prayer outside the temple, the regiment squatting on the grass while the Brahmin read extracts from the holy books and the rissaldar-major gave a short speech; then, in the afternoon, gymkhana sports. A long awning was set up on one side of the biggest field, under it chairs and benches and stools and boxes of every kind set in rows to make seats and tables for the officers and VCOs. In the centre a large sofa, most of its springs showing, held the CO and the rissaldar-major. Brandy appeared, and bottles of wine, while Captain Sohan Singh cheerfully rubbed his fat hands. When Warren Bateman said, 'Good God, man, where on earth did you get all this?' he bowed and grinned and said, 'On information received, sah!' Krishna sipped brandy and water and watched the *kabaddi*. The players' oiled bodies began to glisten as the game progressed, changing from shivering goose-pimples at the beginning to a full sweat at the end. Then came wrestling, and Krishna's old squadron, A, emerged as champion, though no one could beat that fat Dafadar Bural Ram in B, who was rumoured to have been a professional somewhere down country before coming to Basohli ... to escape a criminal charge in British India, it was also said. Then came foot races, then hurdle racing on horses borrowed from a cavalry regiment, the riders seated backwards, and bareback.

Puran Lall was sitting a little to Krishna's right. Krishna leaned across and said, 'The squadron's doing well, Puran.'

The young man was staring straight ahead, apparently watching the sowars setting up the hurdles that had been knocked over in the first heat.

'Puran!' Krishna said, more loudly.

The young man started and turned his head. 'Sir?'

'I said, A Squadron's doing well.'

'Yes, sir. I was thinking of my brother. My father wrote, you know. He said I must kill many Germans to revenge Ishar.'

Krishna Ram said, 'We have to kill them, but I don't think we should feel revenge.'

Puran Lall said, 'I don't know ... On the court martial yesterday one part of me wanted to sentence Alam Singh to death because he had escaped to live while my brother died and because he had let us all down, so that they'—he lowered his voice—'the sahibs—can make jokes about us ... Another part of me was thinking, if he does not want to fight at my side, I don't want him. It is difficult to know what is right.'

'It is,' Krishna Ram said. Then, 'Have a drink. You'll forget more easily.'

'I don't want to forget,' Puran Lall said grimly.

The last item began. Sowars under the woordie-major ran out and placed a line of tent pegs across the field. Bareback, their feet and legs bare below the military breeches, the competing riders took position at the far end, each carrying one of the lances that had been borrowed with the horses. Then they started down, one by one. Beginning at a canter they passed the awning at full gallop, lance point lowered, and tried to impale a tent peg on the point. As they galloped away the lance point swung up behind them, and the crowd gave a triumphant yell or a loud hiss according as to whether the peg was seen on the point or not.

A dozen villagers were watching the spectacle from the other side of the field, among them the woman who owned Lieutenant Dayal

Ram's billet. She clapped and called out encouragement in French every time it came to Dayal's turn. As he got through the preliminary heats, never failing to spear the tent peg, her excitement increased. She was, of course, Dayal's mistress, Krishna thought; she never attempted to hide it, rather flaunting the fact that the handsome Indian was her lover. Dayal Ram took as little trouble to conceal the liaison, though he never flaunted it in front of the CO. Now, as his lance point swept down for the last time, he needing only this peg to win the championship, the woman stood out in front of the other villagers, her hands clasped and her body tensed. The bay mare stretched into the gallop. Dayal leaned forward, the steel point eased down down down ... He yelled *Yeh hai!* at the top of his voice, the tent peg whirling up on the point behind him. As the sowars jumped up, applauding, he reined in and slipped to the ground, all in one movement, and the French woman ran into his arms. He laughed, hugging her, while all the sowars laughed to see her simple joy. Krishna, glancing along the line of officers, saw that they were all standing, except the CO. Warren Bateman's face was set in an expression of deliberately trying but failing, to be neutral. Then he stood up, scowling, and said to the RM, 'I'll award the prizes right away, sahib, and then I'll hold durbar, here.'

The regiment stood close packed on the field where a few minutes ago Dayal Ram had been hugging the French woman. Warren Bateman said in his well pronounced but almost uninflected Hindi, 'Durbar is open ... First, step forward, all men of the draft ... Face the rest of your comrades. Lads, here are the men who have to join us, to replace those we have lost.'

He introduced the four new VCOs one by one, giving their names, homes, and the regiments from which they had been drafted. The draft had arrived a couple of days earlier, and were all from regular Indian Army cavalry regiments in India. As this process went on, of replacing losses with men from the regulars, or with recruits trained at regular depots, the Ravi Lancers would gradually lose its character as the private army of an Indian prince. Other changes were taking place in the character of the regiment, more subtle than anything in its organization or composition. At the gymkhana Krishna had seen a sowar brutally cuff some French children out of his way with a curse. That would never have happened a year ago ... not because they were French but because they

207

were children. Men charged with petty military crime were beginning to make excuses instead of admitting their guilt. It was perhaps
inevitable, like young Ishar Lall's death ... but he did not like it.

The introductions ended, Warren said, 'Let him who wishes to
speak in durbar, speak ... You, dafadar-ji.'

'Sahib, it is in my mind that we will be serving in this France
for many months or years to come.'

'Don't say that, dafadar-ji,' Warren snapped. 'We will win the
war before the end of the year.'

'As the presence says ... even for a month, three months perchance, it is in my mind that some of us, one man in each troop
perchance, should be able to speak a little French. In the front
line, it is not needed, but as soon as we go to the rear, it is needed,
for ...'

'It is understood,' Warren said cutting in impatiently. 'The
adjutant will see what can be done. The difficulty will be to find
those understanding Hindi, to teach us. Among the regiment I think
that I alone do ... and it is not proposed, I hope, that I shall
become a schoolmaster-*babu*.'

The regiment laughed, a little louder, a little more sycophantic-
ally than was necessary, Krishna Ram thought.

Warren said, 'Next ... you ...'

An oldish sowar with a sharp dark face said, 'Sahib, may the
presence know that I have served eleven years. Never have I failed
to do what was ordered. I am the senior sowar of the squadron.'

'Which?'

'B, sahib ... It is my right, by ancient custom, to be storeman
of ...'

'Silence!' Warren Bateman snapped. 'Did I not say at the last
durbar that no matters of discipline were to be brought up in
durbar?'

'But, sahib ... ?'

'Hold your tongue!' a jemadar roared, drowning the rissaldar-
major's quieter admonition to the same effect.

'*Hukm hai!*' Warren said. 'I have said it before, and I say it again,
for the last time: it is forbidden to discuss orders, promotions, or
anything military in durbar.'

'*Jo hukm*,' the man said, his face closed.

Krishna saw a sowar, his arm raised. It was the same young man who had asked the difficult questions about Christianity and the war in the durbar before Christmas. Warren Bateman's eye swept the crowd. He must have seen the young man, but he was ignoring him.

'Durbar is ended. Stay. I have some announcements to make ... There is not enough desire to kill Germans among you. Your hearts are not filled with a consuming hatred. You must be as Duryodhan, implacable ... The Germans are not men but beasts. They slaughter women and children. They take their own parents and, seeing they are too old to fight, put them in ovens and broil them down so that they can use the fat to make munitions. Prisoners they torture in despite of the rules of war and the laws of chivalry among soldiers. Let it be clear—there can be no chivalry, neither English nor Rajput towards them. They are rats, to be exterminated. Fill your hearts with hatred ... Tomorrow a British sergeant, expert in this matter, will give a lecture and demonstration to all officers, VCOs and NCOs of the regiment. Major Krishna Ram will translate.'

He glanced at Krishna. Krishna said, 'Yes, sir,' wondering why he had not heard of this before.

Warren Bateman said, 'Next, we are due to move up the line on March 25, four days from now. All short leave is therefore cancelled ... One last matter. During Holi it was permitted, as a special case, that men should wear caste marks. I remind all ranks that this will not be permitted again while the regiment serves directly under the King-Emperor. Many of your uniforms were spoiled or stained by the powder thrown during Holi. This is a shameful mark to put upon the King-Emperor's uniform. Let it be known now, that there be no misunderstanding later—it is forbidden to throw powder during Holi or on any other occasion! *Hukm hai!*'

'*Jo hukm!*' the regiment cried.

Warren turned to Krishna, 'That's all.' He nodded and strode off as Krishna called, 'Ravi Lancers, shun! ... Ravi Lancers, dismiss!'

Krishna walked slowly back to his billet, full of a nostalgic melancholy. This Holi and durbar marked the end of an era. Now, finally, they were not Ravi cavalry but Imperial infantry. It seemed a hundred years ago that there had been *panchayats* round a *hookah*, long discussions under a tree in the warm twilight, Himalayan snows afire along the horizon. Now they took rapped-out orders, one by one: this has been decided, that will be done! *Jo hukm!*

The sergeant's name was Mackintosh and he was from the Gordon Highlanders. He was black-avised and lantern-jawed, tiny eyes glittering in a sunburned slab of face. He stood six feet two inches and must have weighed sixteen stone, all as solid as so much elephant bone. The rifle with fixed bayonet was no more than a swagger stick in his huge calloused hands. A standing dummy had been set up for him on the gymkhana field, and two or three lying dummies, sacks stuffed with straw, lay ready nearby.

The sergeant quickly began his demonstration. Long point. Short point. Jab. Butt stroke, kick, and kill. The ribbons fluttered out behind the red and white checkered Glengarry. Krishna Ram thought, we've seen all this before, and our NCOs teach it just as well.

The sergeant turned, and said, 'That's how you've been taught the bayonet, I dare say, sorr.' His Scots accent was strong.

'Yes, sergeant,' Warren Bateman said.

The sergeant swelled up like a turkey cock, 'Sorr, that's not the bayonet ... that's a tea party for old ladies. The bayonet is to *kill*!' The last word came out as a shriek.

Krishna translated quickly for the VCOs and NCOs, while the sergeant signalled to a British private soldier who had come with him. The private opened a large box on the back of the sergeant's car and dragged out a dummy made to look not like a sack but like a man, a man in German uniform. The private threw the dummy down, as one throwing meat before a hungry tiger, and the sergeant leaped at it screaming, 'Die, you Hun bastard!' He jabbed his bayonet clear through the dummy, which spouted blood, to gasps of horror from the assembled men. 'Die, die, you baby-eating swine!' the sergeant shrieked, lifting the dummy on the point of his bayonet, throwing it down, jumping on it with both feet, stabbing the bayonet through the face. 'Die! die!'

He whipped round, the bayonet red to the rifle muzzle, and snarled, '*This* is bayonet fighting ...'

'*Yeh bayonet ka larai hai,*' Krishna said, but the sergeant's storm of words overwhelmed him and he fell silent. It was no use trying to translate; everyone was hypnotized by the sergeant, and in any case no translation was needed.

The sergeant whipped off his Glengarry, showing a shaven bullet head. 'Shave your heads,' he snarled, 'so the Hun can't grab a hair. Keeps the lice out, too ... You're not sticking your bayonet into a dummy but into a swine, a rat ...' (he leaped at the German and stabbed it again) 'rat!' (he kicked it in the balls and thrust his bayonet into its stomach), 'the man who raped your wife ... stuck his dirty syphilitic prick right into her cunt before your eyes' (he was sobbing, tears coming down his cheeks as he systematically ripped the German to ribbons) ... 'she's shrieking "Save me, save me!"' (stab stab) ... 'but you can't ... because you're a dirty sissy, a pansy ...' (a savage butt stroke, the rifle whistling round reversed, took the battered dummy's head clear off). 'This bastard took your job ... bashed your baby's head in before your eyes ... strangled your mother ... yes, your mother, she died right here, this fucker's hands round her throat and she trying to scream help, help and *you* ...' He wheeled round, the bayonet thrusting towards the audience—'And you can't do a thing because you're fucking sissies ... pansies ... nancy boys ... bed-wetting mothers' darlings. You're not men!' He whirled up and down the ranks, ranting, glaring. Krishna saw that the sowars were convinced they had a madman in front of them. But for the presence of Warren Bateman standing steady there, who presumably understood what the sergeant was saying and doing, they would have run away.

The sergeant hurled the rifle at a dafadar, and yelled, 'There, sergeant, you do it ... Go on!'

The dafadar looked helplessly at Krishna who said, '*Bayonet practice karo, issi mwafik.*'

The dafadar, a mild-mannered quiet man, an excellent rider and disciplinarian who never had to raise his voice to get what he wanted done, tentatively stabbed at the upright dummy. 'Not that one, the German,' the sergeant yelled, 'Go on ... you sissy, you useless fancy man ... Kill, kill!' He ran beside the dafadar, shrieking in his ear. Krishna Ram thought, the epithets would be more effective on an Englishman, who would understand what was being said. The dafadar knew that the sergeant was abusing him, but not the exact terms. Krishna could hardly understand, himself, because of the sergeant's frenetic rage and strong Glasgow accent.

After a couple of minutes the sergeant grabbed his rifle back and again fell on the dummy, growling and snarling like a blood-maddened tiger. Straw and sacking and bits of rubber flew, the

German disintegrated, blood spattered the spectators. Suddenly Krishna Ram had an almost uncontrollable desire to burst out laughing. This was grotesque. It was the funniest thing he'd ever seen. He tried to catch Warren Bateman's eye, but the CO was watching intently, wholly absorbed.

The sergeant suddenly stood upright, slammed the rifle on to his left shoulder and slapped the butt in a correct salute. His chest bulged and he was looking at a point a couple of inches above Warren Bateman's head, as per regulations. 'Bayonet demonstration ended, sorr!'

'Well done, sergeant ... that was magnificent. Will you let the RM give you a drink?'

'I'm due at the Gurkhas in ten minutes, sorr. Permission to dismiss, please.'

'Very well, sergeant. Dismiss. Thank you again.'

The sergeant turned smartly to the right, slapped the rifle butt again, and said to his private, 'Pick up that dummy and see the next one's ready, Johnson.' A minute later their car puttered away down the road.

Warren Bateman turned to the assembled men. 'You have seen how bayonet fighting should be done. In future that is how it will be done in this regiment. It is a demonstration of what I said yesterday at durbar. You must hate. Every man in the regiment will have one hour a day of bayonet drill from now until we move up the line, Dayal.'

'Yes, sir.'

'Dismiss, please.' He beckoned to Krishna Ram to follow him to his office. 'That sergeant's a genius,' Warren said thoughtfully.

Krishna said nothing; he thought that Sergeant Mackintosh was a madman. The CO said, 'He instilled the offensive spirit even though no one but a few officers understood a word he was saying.'

It was more than that, Krishna thought: there was a lack of communication on deeper levels. Indians could hate all right, and become mad in battle ... but to order? Pretending that the enemy had raped your wife when he had not? It turned reality into make-believe.

They were inside the CO's office, and Warren carefully closed the ramshackle door leading to the adjutant's office next door. He sat down, indicating a chair for Krishna. He said, 'What I am going to tell you is still secret. I have the general's order to tell you

212

though, so that preparations would not be held up if anything were to happen to me ... What I told the men about a routine relief up the line was not true. General French is going to make a major attack. The whole of First Army will be involved, with our Hindustan Division in army reserve. Second Army are making heavy diversionary attacks, starting tonight, to draw the enemy reserves farther south. As soon as the movements of German reserves are confirmed, the First Army attack will begin. They will break through on the second day. The day after that we pass through them to the high ground beyond the Longmont Canal. Here.' He stood up and pointed out the names on the map of the Western Front pinned on the wall behind him.

Krishna said, 'Yes, sir ... How is it proposed to get the leading troops through the enemy wire this time? There can't be a long bombardment, or the Germans would guess what was going to happen.'

'No, there will be no long bombardment,' Warren said. 'The assaulting troops will cut the wire with Bangalore torpedoes, and break into the forward German trench line under cover of smoke shells.'

'Yes, sir,' Krishna said, 'but ... you saw the German defences at Lestelle Wood and Hill 73, sir. There were belts of wire extending back as far as we could see. And more men in reserve than in the front line. That was in December. The Germans have had three months to improve the defences that we couldn't get through then. You remember how much improved they were even in February when we were patrolling in that sector.'

'First Army will break through,' Warren said. After a pause he said, 'They must.' He spoke as though willing himself to believe something that in his heart he didn't.

Krishna, emboldened, said, 'I don't see how the attack can succeed. I was talking to a sapper captain last month, when I went down to Abbeville about the stores. He said that the railway systems on both sides of the Western Front can move defensive reserves along the front quicker than the attacking troops can overcome the defences. I think he ...'

'Our RFC machines can spot the slightest movement as soon as it begins,' Warren Bateman said sharply. 'By dropping bombs and firing their guns—they have machine guns now, you know—they can stop or delay all movement.'

'But, sir ...' Krishna remembered the bespectacled captain with the long nose and the cynical twisted half smile: 'My dear major, they can put twenty thousand troops on trains behind, say, Sedan, after dark today, when our aircraft can see nothing—and before dawn have them detraining ten miles behind the front lines opposite you.'

'What?' Warren said.

Krishna summoned his courage and determination. He said, 'I don't think the attack has a hope of success unless something new and different is done. I am afraid that First Army will fail, and then we will be sent to the same place where they failed, with the situation not better but worse than it was for them. We shall lose many men and officers, for nothing.'

'What do you think we should do?' Warren said, his voice cold.

'I think we should protest, sir. Or suggest a different plan of our own.'

'Such as ...?'

'I don't know ... Perhaps there is none. But at least if we stay where we are, the Germans cannot get through us any more than we can get through them, and then, after a time ... people will realize there is no solution here, and think of a way out.'

'That is a defeatist attitude,' Warren said, 'and I will not tolerate it. We are going to attack, on the Commander-in-Chief's plan—and I hope you will agree that he knows a little more about what he is doing than you do—and we are going to succeed. You will obey orders not only in the letter but also in the spirit. Is that clear?'

'Yes, sir,' Krishna said. He felt weak and dispirited. Perhaps he was no good for war after all. Warren Bateman's strong face was hewn of steel and leather. He was one of those who had come in little boats five thousand miles from home and conquered millions —millions who had thought, before they came, that they were warriors, proud and invincible. Warren was right. He himself was an Indian weakling. No more argument.

'Yes, sir,' he said.

'One more thing,' Warren Bateman said, 'I am discontinuing the special privileges allowed you as grandson and heir of the Rajah. You will no longer permit VCOs or men to touch your knees, but will only accept military salutes. Your two bodyguards will be absorbed into a squadron. This is a regiment of Indian cavalry, not a Rajah's toy.'

'Yes, sir,' Krishna said. He saluted, wheeled, and started out. As he passed the end of the CO's table the little fox-terrier Shikari snarled at him and moved as though to bite his feet. Krishna stared at the dog in amazement, then, as he went out, his eyes began to fill with tears.

March 1915

KRISHNA RAM WALKED slowly down the ride, his hand deep thrust into the pockets of his British warm. It was ten o'clock in the morning, after a long night march which had brought the regiment up to its position in reserve, five miles behind the front line. The march had gone well. The men were hard and fit, the weather had improved, and brigade and division staffs were learning more about their business and there were no refugees to block the road and make shambles of the staff tables.

They had arrived a few minutes before first light, spread out in the wood here, set up their bivouacs, and promptly gone to sleep —again, a mark of the trained professional soldier. Krishna Ram had made the march half drunk, for he had shared a bottle of brandy with Sher Singh and Pahlwan Ram before starting out, and there had been extra nips from a bottle carried by Hanuman along the way, until the early hours. Now unpleasant fumes filled his head, which ached steadily. He would have liked to go to sleep, but he was on duty as Field Officer of the week and must wait till he had had the morning reports.

The wood was thin. Most of the trees had been shattered by heavy artillery during fighting here in November and December. The Ravi Lancers, having arrived in darkness, could not be seen by enemy observers on the high ground the other side of the valley, a good seven miles away. Nor could such observers see the other battalions of the brigade, though they were bivouacked more in the open behind and to the left rear of the Ravi Lancers. The other brigades of the division were in bivouac close behind in echelon right, also scattered in copses, woods, and farm buildings.

Krishna decided he'd have another drink. The bottle in Hanuman's pack was only half empty; and there was another full one in his valise. Sohan Singh would get him more, somehow—as much as he wanted, any time. Sohan Singh was a marvel. A real bazaar babu. He licked his lips. He remembered the look Warren Bateman had given him when he went to RHQ at the end of the march to report the tail in, no stragglers. The CO had smelled the brandy on his breath, with a look of disgust, a look saying, the fellow's running true to type, the educated native, drinking himself out of his funk.

He looked at the men asleep in the bivouacs, their boots sticking out; at the sentries standing guard over the rows of piled arms. They didn't have any brandy to ... a low droning noise caught his wandering attention and he looked round, puzzled. No lorry could come into the quiet aisles of the ride, cut for the landowner's pheasant shooting, for there was no motorable road into the wood. The noise increased and now he placed it. It came from the air. An aeroplane, of course! They had been becoming more and more common on the front since the winter weather began to break. There it was now, two wings like moths, an enclosed body—ah, that must be a new type, for in the old ones you could clearly see the pilot and the observer sitting one behind the other in a sort of open cage. This one had a machine gun mounted on a ring, and the propeller whirling away in front to pull the machine through the air.

The biplane turned, banking steeply, and he saw the mark on the wing—a large black Maltese cross. German!

He broke into a run, tugging at the whistle on its lanyard round his neck. He yelled at the nearest sentry, '*Dushman! Dushman! Fire!*' Reaching the man, he grabbed the rifle from his hand, took aim, and fired. Between shots he blew a series of short blasts on the whistle.

The German aeroplane flew low over the wood, turned and headed south. Krishna Ram fired at it again and again. A scattering of other shots came out of the woods as other sentries realized what was happening, and opened fire. The sleepy sowars were tumbling out of the bivouacs and grabbing their rifles from the piles. Krishna could clearly see the aircraft, now half a mile away, circling low over the bivouac areas of the rest of the brigade, and then of the rest of the division.

He gave the rifle back to the sentry, and started towards RHQ to report, when he remembered that Warren had gone to Brigade HQ for orders, taking the adjutant with him. He turned to the woordie-major, running down the aisle of the trees with his revolver drawn, and said, 'Stand down, jemadar-sahib. Everyone back to sleep.'

Captain Himat Singh came up. 'Do you think we got it, sir?'

He shook his head, wincing from the sudden motion. 'No, though I think I put one pretty close to the pilot.' He added in Hindi, 'Now our attack will have even less chance of success.'

Himat Singh said stiffly, 'How is that, sir?'

Krishna said, 'That aeroplane was not here for a little jaunt, you know. It was reconnoitring, and the observer must have seen us ... all of us. A whole division, newly arrived behind a section of the front where nothing is supposed to be in prospect.'

Himat Singh said, 'We will beat them anyway!'

Krishna Ram thought, the two DSOs have made him a different man altogether from the one who left Basohli, and it was Warren Bateman who had brought out the qualities that enabled him to win them. He said, 'I hope so. But it isn't going to be easy.'

'The CO will not let us be put to anything we cannot achieve,' Himat Singh said now, almost sternly. 'And if he says we can do it, we can.'

'Yes, Himat,' Krishna said wearily. 'You're right. You're right.'

The guns opened up an hour before dusk for the First Army attack, and an hour after dusk the Lahore Brigade started to move forward to occupy the trenches vacated by the forward movement of the attacking troops. It was a clear night, the stars only now and then hidden by drifting clouds, and a first quarter crescent moon dipping into the misty haze above the spring earth. At first the march was up a road shell-pocked but not badly damaged, and through villages that housed the bivouacs of the medium and heavy gunners. The guns were still firing as the regiment passed and Krishna wondered what they were firing at, what was happening up there in the darkness ahead. The breeze blew slow and heavy out of the south, burdened with the scent of primroses and new grass and the burgeoning buds on the surviving trees.

The regiment marched silently and easily. The bayonets hung familiarly on each man's hip now, and on his back the heavy infantry pack. The gospel of Sergeant Mackintosh had been passed down to the youngest sowars, and Krishna had never seen such facial contortions, or heard such screaming and cursing and maniacal abuse as during the bayonet practice that seemed to fill every spare hour of those last days in rear billets. He wondered how much of it was real and how much put on to please Bateman-sahib ... but after all, was that really any different from the good sergeant, who could switch his hate on and off like an electric light?

Where he marched at the head of the regiment—Warren was again at Brigade HQ getting orders—they came upon a wagon, broken and left in the road, one horse dead in the trace and one still struggling, wounded. Krishna opened his mouth to say, 'Get them out of the way,' when it was already happening. A rifle exploded, the woordie-major's voice was sharp—'Cut the reins. Push the cart into the ditch. And the horses ... Get more men, then. Bring up the leading troop.' Men doubled past him where he stood, there was a chorus of grunts and low cries, then the woordie-major trotted back saluting, 'Rasta saf hai, sahib.' The delay had been barely four minutes.

Krishna marched on, thinking. Three months ago they would have stood around wondering how they could move the wagon without further damaging it—it was Government property, well made and valuable; how they could save the wounded horse—perhaps it wasn't badly hurt, it was a good horse. A working horse represented not only property but crops, seeds, the fruit of the holy earth. Now they went at obstacles like wolves ... and the obstacles vanished, destroyed without compunction.

The regiment swung on into the darkness, rifles slung on the shoulder. The road ended in a huge shell-hole beside a battery of field guns, firing away into the night, the orange flashes momentarily lighting up the scene, the layers crouched behind the shield, the loaders pushing in fresh shells, sergeants kneeling by the trails. Enemy shells were bursting not far to the right. A military police-man holding a shaded lantern peered at him, then at a piece of paper in his hand. 'Ravi Lancers, sir? Here's your guide.' A corporal of British infantry materialized out of the blackness behind the yellow glow and saluted. 'Follow me, sir ... Jerry's 'aving a bit of an 'ate on the communication trenches, so keep your 'ead down.'

He led into a trench that began just beyond the gun positions. The walls of the trench were well revetted, lined with pit props, and it was fairly wide, but the pace at once slowed. Soon the men were shuffling forward five paces, then stopping five minutes, then forward again. Shells burst louder and closer, and the sharp reek of lyddite was continuously in Krishna's nostrils. Now traffic began coming the other way down the trench and progress was slowed still more. Wounded men came, walking, hopping, supporting themselves on their rifles, or a comrade's shoulder; men carrying tools and rolled wire; more wounded; someone scrambling like a madman back along the trench, up the sides, anyhow he could move faster, shouting hoarsely, 'Division runner, division runner, make way, make way!' Krishna wondered idly whether he really was a messenger, or whether he was a man like Sowar Alam Singh, a soldier who'd decided he'd had enough and out of his fear and need somehow finding the right words to clear his path.

A huge flash and roar just behind him threw him against the wall of the trench. Earth rammed into his face and his shoulder hurt. He was on his knees, his head singing. Hanuman was over him. 'Are you all right, Highness? Are you hurt? ... Let me take you back.'

He crawled to his feet. He was wet ... there was water running down his cheek, water on his tunic, more on his arm. Something solid fell on his shoulder. He felt it and realized he was holding a hand. It was Captain Himat Singh's. 'Are you all right, sir? That was a direct hit in the trench just behind us. Four of my men killed and two vanished, as far as I can make out.'

Krishna realized that the wet on him was blood, blood blasted out of the men killed behind him, blood of the two others 'vanished' —what did that mean but smashed to pieces, separated into their component parts, especially blood?

'Move on, sir?' Himat Singh said.

'Yes,' Krishna muttered. 'Yes.' His legs began to move again. He was not hurt. The shelling grew louder, heavier. The guide shouted, 'We're close now.' Krishna peered at the luminous dial of his watch: 3.30 a.m. They were an hour behind time. He began to tremble, his body shaking with a rapid slight motion that he could not control. A figure loomed out of the dark and took his arm—'Who's there? Krishna Ram? ... Why, you're trembling.' It was Warren Bateman.

'Yes, sir.' He had heard the surprise and then the contempt, or perhaps it was triumph, in the CO's voice. How could he explain? He had charged without fear at Poucelle. He had stood to the machine guns at Hill 73 without fear. No qualm had crossed his mind while he lay helpless after being blown unconscious and half buried in No Man's Land; but something had happened since—a slow realization that it was not men fighting this war, but machines. The enemy which had annihilated those six men of B Squadron was a machine, a machine with a mind and purpose of its own— destruction; and it fed on youth, beauty, and love. Only the cowardly, the ugly, and the old would escape.

Warren Bateman let go of Krishna's arm. He said, 'The Devons and the HLI are in front of us. They've been held up in the enemy's second line trenches and can't advance. We are going through them at dawn.'

Krishna's trembling ceased as suddenly as it had begun. Warren, at least, was not an impersonal machine but a man, an obstinate man determined to do or die. He was not afraid of that. He thought that Warren was waiting for him to say, I told you so, but he said nothing and Warren said, 'Dayal Ram has guides here to lead the squadrons to their places. I want all officers, also the RM and woordie-major, for orders here at 4.15 ack emma.'

They were huddled in a fire bay off the trench, the adjutant playing a flashlight on the map in Warren Bateman's hands. It was still dark, the wind had died away leaving a motionless stink of turned earth, mud, and picric acid. A few enemy shells still burst occasionally around them. Machine gun fire rattled haphazardly across the front, interspersed with the crump of grenades and mortars.

Warren Bateman said, 'The brigade's objective is the St. Rambert Ridge, one mile from here and nearly 800 yards ahead of the positions reached during the early stages of the attack. We're on the left, Fusiliers on the right, 71st Punjabis and 1/12th Gurkhas in reserve. Dividing line, all inclusive to us, is the point of junction here in this trench, to the ruins of St. Rambert church, which you will see very clearly on the skyline as soon as it's light. Sapper squads, two men each, are going with each leading squadron. Each squad has six Bangalore torpedoes, but squadrons have to provide men to carry them. The torpedoes are to be placed as the sappers direct, under the enemy wire. Then the sappers will fire them. We move off from this line at 0500 and are due to pass through the Devons at 0520. First light is at 0515...'

He started to give details of administrative matters, routes of evacuation for the wounded, and communication lines. A group of men of the Royal Corps of Signals passed laying telephone cable along the edge of the trench. Krishna Ram thought, we are to blow holes in wire we may encounter? But why didn't someone *know* whether there was wire or not, and where it was? Perhaps the Devons knew, who had been preparing for this attack for days, and still could not succeed. How was it expected that the Ravi Lancers and the Fusiliers could?

'The barrage starts forward from the Devons at 5.20 ack emma,' Warren said, 'and, I repeat, you *must* keep the men close up behind it, *really* close. Any questions?'

The officers were silent. It was a simple plan, Krishna thought, and Warren had explained it clearly. What questions could there be, except, how many will survive?

Warren said, 'One last thing. I want you to know that General Rogers planned to put the Gurkhas into the front wave, keeping us in reserve. After what happened at Hill 73 he felt that he could not trust us to do our best. I persuaded him to give us this chance to retrieve our name. He was good enough to agree. That's all, gentlemen. Good luck.'

Krishna Ram walked away along the trench. The trembling returned. They did not have a chance, these brown-skinned men who trusted him because he was a Son of the Sun. He could smell the familiar tang of the coriander that they sucked, and the oil they put on their hair, and even could imagine in his nostrils the leather and sweat of those horses which had been their pride—but there were no horses here, and the men were but fodder, to be fed into a mechanized slaughterhouse and ground to mincemeat by unseen European gods, whose praise was death.

'No, no!' he cried aloud.

'What, prince?' It was Lieutenant Pahlwan Ram, black, squat, ugly, fearful. They were alone in a fire bay, the dark trench empty. 'Why do you say no?'

'Because it is slaughter, the machines of death,' Krishna said in a low voice.

'Yes, highness. There will be terrible slaughter, for nothing ... Let us only pretend to attack but really stay in the trench ...'

Krishna Ram said, 'We must do our duty. Go to your place, man. If you fail ... if you do what you suggested ... I shall shoot you.'

He found the machine gun section and, feeling that he was talking in his sleep, gave them their orders. Warren Bateman came along and said, 'Ten minutes to go. Now, you're quite clear what you're to do, Krishna?'

'Yes, sir.'

'Tell me then.'

'Follow to the first objective, with A and B Squadron and the machine guns. Then, on your signal, given by galloper or telephone, take them both through to the final objective. Once that is taken, report success by red over green Very lights.'

'Right.' A light shone briefly in his face and the CO's voice was cheerful—'You look as though you've seen a ghost. Cheer up, man. We're going to make Ravi history today.'

'Yes, sir.'

Warren disappeared and Krishna waited again. Time passed under a blanket of meaningless sound—distant explosions, rattling clack of machine guns, crack of single rifle shots. Then whistles blew and he climbed on to the firestep to watch the regiment going over the top. D Squadron was on the left, C on the right. Between and behind them, as they stepped off into the eastern dawn, he saw the CO amid a scattered group of gallopers, trumpeters, orderlies, and HQ officers, with the gunner subaltern and his signallers.

Then it was time for him to move and he climbed out into the open. At once the trembling stopped. A and B Squadrons strode steadily forward. The machine gunners—the section had four Vickers now—bent under the weight of guns, tripods, and ammunition boxes, tried to keep up with them. They reached the Devons' line with no casualties and dropped in among them. They were small men, wan and mud-covered, sitting along the trench, with many wounded lying among them, and many dead, their faces covered by a handkerchief or a bloodspattered cap. Other dead had been shoved up on parapet and parados. Krishna hardly noticed them as he stared through his binoculars at the still advancing lines of the leading squadrons. Their bayonets were catching the light now. Here and there he saw a man falling. The line beginning to run. Faint he heard a cheer, but could not make out the words. Surely it would be, *'A-gye Krishna-ka choral'*—'the sons of Krishna are upon you'—the war cry of Ravi, heard once upon a score of battlefields in the land of the Five Rivers. They vanished into the enemy's reserve trench. They had done what he had believed to be impossible: they had reached their objective.

Two minutes later the field telephone beside him buzzed and the signaller said, 'For you, lord.'

Warren Bateman's voice was metallic and distorted, but exultant. 'We've done it! Move at once, Krishna, in quick time, and keep moving right through us on to your objective. I'll speak to you as you come through.'

'Yes, sir.'

He blew his whistle and the men climbed out all along the trench. Young Puran Lall was there near him, his face cold and set, the revolver drawn in his hand; and the new rissaldar of the squadron, Chaman Lall; and Rissaldar Ram Lall urging on the men staggering under the Vickers guns, and over to the left Himat Singh and B Squadron. After five minutes under light artillery fire Krishna dropped into the newly captured trench almost on top of Warren Bateman. The CO seized his elbow and cried, 'They're on the run, Krishna. Go! I'll come myself to take over as soon as you're in position.'

Krishna Ram climbed out of the back of the trench and saw that all his men were continuing the advance. The next three hundred yards up to the church, so plain there on the ridge, the stump of the tower barely twelve feet high, would be murderous. He saw wire ahead, and his stomach felt empty. But the sappers were running forward, beckoning, and a sowar carrying a Bangalore torpedo ran up, thrust it in under the wire. Sappers and sowars flung themselves down. A sharp explosion cracked at his eardrums, and a twelve-foot stretch of the wire was gone. To right and left more explosions showed where other holes had been blasted. The squadrons filed through, running, spread out again, and slowed to a walk. Machine gun fire began to cut in on the right and half a dozen men of A Squadron fell, mown down like hay by the unseen blades. White smoke began to creep along the ridge ahead, obliterating first the church tower, then the outline of the ridge itself. The machine gun fire stopped. Puran Lall shouted, 'They're giving us smoke, sir ... We'll make it now!'

Krishna blew madly on his whistle, shouting, 'Charge, charge!'

The sowars lowered their rifles from the 'high port' to the 'on guard', the bayonets levelled, and broke into a run. They began to mouth curses, their faces became distorted with hate and blind blood lust. Screaming the high unearthly scream of mountain leopards they drove into the smoke. The British artillery stopped firing. A German loomed up on Krishna's left, and a sowar leaped at him with a scream of 'Swine!' and thrust his bayonet clear through his neck and out a foot the other side. Puran Lall fired his revolver twice, then threw it at another German's face, whirled his sabre and took his head off. The figures, all half seen in the smoke, loomed like warriors from the apocalyptic last fight of the Mahabharata, and Krishna thought, at any moment Arjun will ride down from the clouds, and Duryodhan claw at him through the smoke.

As the visibility increased he saw more clearly with what grim efficiency the squadron was setting about its work of slaughter. It had been perhaps a German headquarters of some kind, for among the dead he saw many wearing the collar badges of officers. They lay all round the church, and in the cemetery among the shattered gravestones. The sowars still worked in a frenzy of killing, the rifles rising and falling. Here a wounded man tried to struggle to his feet, there another to crawl to safety, but there was no safety, no refuge, no quarter. The forward men reached the front edge of the trees—now only stumps—guarding the cemetery towards the north and Krishna shouted to Puran Lall, 'Stop there. Dig in! Hanuman, run and tell B Squadron the same ... Rissaldar-sahib, put the machine guns at the corner of the churchyard. Not too close to the tower. Put down wire in front of them, any wire, as much as you can get!' He found the Very pistol in his haversack, and fired first a red then a green light into the sky, as the signal of success.

For the next ten minutes he hurried from one end of the position to the other, supervising its consolidation. The Oxford Fusiliers, who had not been able to advance at first, were moving forward now on the right, freed of the fire from the church that had held them up. To the left the ground was open, but lines of bursting shells showed that British fire to prevent any enemy movement round that flank was in force and effective. The machine gun crews were dragging up wire they'd found in the church crypt, and pegging it down forty yards in front of their position, outside hand grenade range. The local German command did not seem to realize what had happened. No survivors had escaped from the church ridge to tell them, and Krishna thought they believed they still held it. British heavy artillery was systematically pounding the areas where they might be expected to be forming up for a counterattack, hiding the green land under fountains of black earth that rose slowly out of the ground, hung in the air a long while and then slowly fell.

Warren Bateman appeared at his side, with Lieutenant de Marquez of the artillery. 'Well done, Krishna! We did it, you see! Well done, Puran Lall ... Ah, Himat, you're on the left, are you? Good, refuse your flank so no one can get in behind us on that side.'

Suddenly shells began to burst among them. Krishna dropped flat, head pressed into the earth. Splinters of metal whined and whistled through the tattered shrubs. The distinctive patter of shrapnel bursting overhead and raining down its steel balls filled the air. The sowars lay among the gravestones or crouched close behind the cemetery wall. Warren Bateman was on his feet, binoculars to his eyes. Reluctantly, Krishna stood up beside him. He saw a line of Germans rise out of the ground two hundred yards down the far side of the St. Rambert Ridge. The view extended in that direction for miles. What a position they had lost here. They would not count the cost to get it back.

The German line came on, but de Marquez was barking orders into the artillery telephone which had come up with him, and a hail of 18-pounder shells burst among the advancing Germans. A second later the four machine guns opened up with a hammering rattle. For a moment the Germans kept coming, but their lines were melting away, the ground becoming pimpled with molehill humps, that had been men, and twisted shapes, fallen weapons. At last they turned and went back, only a handful, and those beginning to run as the relentless machine guns scythed them down to the very edge of the fold of ground whence they had emerged.

'They'll never turn us out of here now,' Warren said energetically, 'but start your men digging. Dig! Two out of every three men, dig—the other on watch. I'm sending back for more wire, urgently. They'll attack again tonight and we must be ready for them.'

He bent to write on the message pad on his knee. A shell burst against the wall of the church behind him, and he fell forward with a gasp and a cry, quickly cut off by clenched teeth. Blood was pouring from his left leg. Krishna quickly knelt and tried to undo the puttee but could make no headway until the CO's orderly drew his bayonet, which had been sharpened like a razor and carefully cut the material through. White bone sticking out through broken

226

and bleeding skin showed where the shell splinter had broken Warren Bateman's leg. He was white and sweating as Krishna poured iodine into the wound, and applied the first field dressing.

'Stretcher bearers!' he called.

'No!' Warren Bateman said, 'I'm staying here.' But even as he spoke his eyes closed and he fell back into the arms of his orderly.

Krishna finished the message, calling for wire, which Warren had been writing when he was hit. Stretcher bearers came up, running crouched, as German shell fire steadily battered the ridge. All around earth flew as the sowars dug, and with the earth the skulls and bones of the men, women and children who had lain in peace for two or six centuries in the churchyard of St. Rambert.

The stretcher bearers started back down the reverse side of the ridge. Krishna watched until he saw them disappear safely into the old front line trench. Captain Himat Singh came, crawling along behind the cemetery wall, to his side. 'I heard the CO's been hit? How bad is he?'

'Broken left leg, below the knee.'

'He won't die?'

'Not unless he gets gangrene. The stretcher bearers gave him an anti-tetanus injection.'

'He mustn't die ... he must come back,' Himat Singh muttered. 'He must, he must!'

Yes, he must come back, Krishna thought, for there was a great matter to be settled between them, which they had as yet only begun to face. To the captain he said, 'Himat, I don't know when the wire I've asked for will come up. We've got to put more out, at once. Send a working party down to try to bring up the wire that the Germans laid down on our side of this ridge. Down there. With enough wire, we can hold this place.'

'We can hold it without wire,' Himat Singh said fiercely. He hurried off. At the back of the church tower a flight of steps led down into the crypt. Krishna went there now, sat down, and wished he had a cigarette. Hanuman was smoking a *bidi*. He was on the point of breaking down and asking his orderly to give him one when Hanuman said, 'Would the presence like a drink?'

By God yes, Krishna thought, that's what I need! Hanuman thrust the bottle into his hand, he put the neck to his lips, and drank. He choked and coughed for it was pure brandy; and wiped his eyes and drank again. For the moment he was Commanding

Officer of the Ravi Lancers. They had cut through the Germans like Arjun through the ranks of the Kurus. They had overcome machine guns, barbed wire, mud, artillery. They had overcome everything that he, Yuvraj Krishna Ram, had said they could not overcome. They had perfectly upheld Warren Bateman's faith in them; and shown that he, their prince and future lord, Son of the Sun, knew nothing and had no stomach for a fight into the bargain.

'*Brigadier-general sahib a-raha,*' Hanuman said quietly, taking the brandy bottle from Krishna's hand and slipping it into his pack.

Rainbow Rogers here? Krishna thought. No one had ever seen him even as far forward as a reserve trench, but here he was in an unconsolidated position taken from the enemy at bayonet point barely an hour since!

'Major Krishna Ram? Ah, there you are ...' The general's long face was pale but determined. His monocle dangled loose on the end of its cord. 'You have done magnificently. I shall see that your action is properly recognized ... General Glover directs that this ridge be held at all costs ... *at all costs*, do you understand? ... now that it has been captured.'

'Yes, sir ... We need barbed wire and more machine guns. And more artillery on the tasks.'

'I'll see that you get them, never fear ... Poor Bateman's in a good deal of pain, I passed him on my way up.' The general was perspiring with fear, Krishna noticed. But he was here. Well, different bullocks needed different goads.

'We must hold it,' General Rogers repeated. 'General Glover told me that if we did, I ... well, for all our sakes, we must.'

'We will,' Krishna said. Not for the general's CMG, he thought, but for Bateman-sahib, and this new god Mars, the European god of war, whom they were just learning to worship with the proper human sacrifices.

April 1915

THE CHESTNUT TREE over Krishna's head dropped blossoms on him in a white shower, filling the air with a heavy
almond-flavoured smell of human seed. Along the edge of the
wood wild cherries in full blossom dripped red and white petals
on the khaki turbans of the sowars gathered close around the place
where he stood. The afternoon sun slanting low over the river
painted the brick houses of Longmont an antique red, dulled and
gentle, touched with golden spots where windows reflected the
sun.

The officers and VCOs stood to his right and left, and immediately behind him those who by the custom of his kingdom had the
right to stand closest—Hanuman, his orderly, his trumpeter, and
—reappeared, with no word spoken, from the anonymous depths of
the squadrons where they had been posted—his two bodyguards.
Also by custom, the rissaldar-major stood closest at his right hand
and the latest joined recruit at his left.

He said, 'Be seated...' After the briefest of hesitations the six
hundred men lowered themselves to squat on their hunkers.
Krishna thought, they know I am disobeying the wishes of the
commanding-sahib—but a durbar was a very personal thing, and
for this moment it was he, not Warren Bateman, who was the
centre of it. There would be longer speeches, longer questions,
more discussions—but he welcomed it. And, like any Indian prince,
when his patience ran out there was nothing to stop him saying,
Enough, and stalking out. No one would think any the worse of
him for it. They would not expect him to act like an Englishman
because they did not expect him to think like one, in spite of his
peaked cap.

'Durbar is open,' he said. 'Let who will, speak.'

A dafadar asked if anything could be done to lessen the number of fatigues. The men were not getting the rest they were surely entitled to when out of the line. One particular fatigue, of carrying heavy water cans up to the reserve trenches, was *bhisti*'s work, and took up scores of men's time every night.

Krishna said, 'The colonel-sahib spoke to the general some time ago about this. Then, nothing could be done. I will look into it again.'

Privately he thought, at least part of the heavy work load was due to stupidity on the part of the higher command. The ground sloped generally downward for a mile or two from the rear towards the trenches, and only three days ago he had suggested that semi-permanent piping might be installed to carry water forward ... to be told that when the army wanted the advice of a plumber they would ask one.

'Next—you,' he said.

A young sowar wanted to go home.

'But you have only just come, with the latest draft,' an older man spoke up from the middle of the crowd.

'I had a letter from my village,' the young man said. 'My brother was killed by a leopard, at the well.'

'What village is that?' a lance-dafadar asked from under the cherry trees.

'Budhgaon, Tehsil Kangra.'

'I know it,' a rissaldar said. 'There was a leopard there when I was a boy—a *shaitan* that killed many cows and took a baby.'

'Its son or grandson is there now,' the young man said. 'My brother is dead, and the fields will lie untilled.'

'I have seen the letter,' the head clerk said. 'The postmark is of Jogindar Nagar, veritably.'

Krishna Ram said, 'You may go. The head clerk will make out the proper papers ... You!'

A man asked whether they could not revert to the customary method of washing their whole bodies, as he was feeling unclean.

A chorus of voices spoke out on the subject. A jemadar of C Squadron recited a hundred lines of the Ramayana in support of cleanliness, listened to with rapt attention by the gathered men. The Brahmin capped him with a hundred and fifty lines from an obscure Tantric hymn pouring curses on uncleanness of body. A pockmarked sowar from the Signal Section pointed out that

230

though no one could call the weather hot, it was certainly much less cold than it had been two months ago when the order was made. A lance-dafadar said that no one in his squadron—B—had had influenza or feverish cold or pneumonia for over a month.

Krishna Ram said, 'Let all wash as they wish, whether piece by piece, or stripped to the loin cloth at the well or tap or bucket, as customary. But let any man who goes to hospital of a cold, beware.'

A lance-dafadar of the Machine Gun Section said, 'Lord, when we came out of the battle of St. Rambert, bringing with us as many of our dead as we could find, they were buried in a common grave behind the trenches. It is our right and custom that the dead shall be burned. It is understood that the ashes cannot be scattered on a stream that will take them to Holy Ganga, but certainly the bodies should be burned, not buried, to hold the spirit under this foreign soil instead of releasing it to the air, that circles the whole earth, and might perhaps carry our dust to fall on Holy Ganga's waters.'

The quartermaster said, 'Lord, I indented for wood, but was refused. The DAQMG sahib said there was a grave shortage of wood, and what he had was needed for revetting the trenches.'

'I know,' Krishna said. 'I have written to the brigadier-general about this matter, and will speak also when I see him tomorrow. Meantime, the quartermaster, who can collect and hide many things in his store without the knowledge of anyone—even his commanding officer—may perhaps collect some wood.'

'Yes, lord,' Sohan Singh said, 'I can do that. But it is not easy to transport, if we are moved to another part of the front.'

'Do what you can ... Next.'

A grizzled sowar said, 'We have talked of death. I talk of life ... We are men far from our homes. It is proper that we should have the service of women from time to time. There are none, except some of the public sort even here in this village, as anyone can see who watches the *gora log* going to the houses at the end of the street in the afternoons and evenings. But it is forbidden to us of the *rissalas* and *paltans* to enter those places. What is to be done, before perchance some man deprived too long of what is his right, shall commit a crime against an honourable and proper woman of this country, while she is working in the fields perhaps, or taking a child home at night? Who then will be guilty of the crime, for surely it will not be he who assaults the woman, needing what a woman gives?'

A man said, 'Surely the public women of this place should be opened to such as us, for ...'

Krishna recognized him as a clerk from RHQ, a slight middle-aged man who had come to Ravi from British India a dozen years ago, and had been heard to talk of Swaraj and other dangerous subjects. The previous RM had threatened to have his ears cut off if he fomented any sedition in the regiment, and, as far as was known he had not. It was thought that he, like the wrestler, was in flight from the British, and did not dare to make trouble for fear he would be handed back to them.

Krishna cut in, saying, 'Enough! This will be considered by me. Let there be no more discussion until I have spoken ... Next.'

The regiment talked, comfortably squatted. A young sowar asked how to cure homesickness and an old one asked what he should do with some money he had taken off a German corpse.

Sunset was the customary time to end durbar, and a man spoke hurriedly: 'It is in my mind that after our time in the front line, and after the great victory of your highness at St. Rambert Ridge, it would be meet to hold a *tamasha* ... We have eaten what was given us, for we are soldiers, but it was not our food and many are always hungry. Can we not fill great tuns of rice, and make mountains of *pakka* chupattis, full of *ghi*, and goats let there be ...

'Ai, ai, yes!' the men murmured.

'And music, and dance, and a play that we may watch ...'

Krishna Ram said, 'It shall be so. As soon as it can be arranged.'

The men clapped and a loud shout of approval rose. Krishna said, 'Durbar is ended.'

Major Bholanath barked, 'Attention!' His palms joined, Krishna bowed to the men and they to him. He walked quickly away across the field, through the dusk to his billet, his suite following respectfully ten paces behind him.

An hour later he was sitting in the one comfortable armchair in his billet room, drinking, two hurricane lanterns burning, one on the table and one on the window. Hanuman announced the adjutant and quartermaster, Dayal Ram and Sohan Singh. Dayal Ram saluted as he came in, Sohan Singh made a low obeisance, touching his hands quickly to Krishna Ram's feet and then to his own forehead. Krishna said, 'Wait a minute.' He was sitting in his stockinged feet, riding breeches and shirt, a British warm thrown loosely over his shoulders. Now he stepped up on to the bed and squatted there, his feet tucked under him. 'Be seated,' he said. Sohan Singh squatted on the floor, and Dayal Ram took the armchair. Going back to type, Warren Bateman would say, if he could see them now, Krishna mused; but he was really more comfortable this way; he had only told himself the chairs were more comfortable under the influence of Mr. Fleming, and his desire to become English.

Hanuman brought tidbits on a metal *tali* and set the bottle of brandy close to Krishna's hand on the bedside table. Krishna poured a glass for Dayal Ram, but Sohan Singh refused, making a *namasti* and shaking his head. Business began, all conducted in Hindi.

'Highness,' Sohan Singh said, 'if I may take a thousand rupees out of the imprest account, I can arrange a place where public women can be made available to our men. There are enough women here who need the money ... or the men.'

'That is beyond doubt,' Dayal Ram said with a lazy, half-satisfied smile. 'Plenty would *give* money.'

'Ah, to a young bull like you, perhaps,' the quartermaster said, 'but, on demand, our men will have to pay.'

'What do you need the thousand rupees for?' Krishna asked.

'To prepare a house or two—or perhaps a barn or cowshed. To buy some medicines ... your highness knows that some of these Fransezi women suffer from the sickness ... To pay any Military Policeman who might come across what we are doing.'

'And there will be nothing in your accounts?'

'Nothing, lord. In a month or two there will be a profit, perhaps five hundred rupees a month.'

'What would you do with that?'

'Buy necessities that are not in the ration ... More money for *tamashas* when we are out of the line. There will be more bribes.'

Dayal Ram said, 'Have you spoken to the doctor? These whores will have to be inspected, or we will start getting a number of venereal cases, and the general will ask questions.'

Sohan Singh popped a sweetmeat into his mouth and chewed appreciatively. 'Ai, your highness will make me fatter than ever. The Doctor-sahib will inspect the women as often as necessary—

twice a week, he said—and he will see that no case of venereal disease is reported in the sick states. He will treat them in the RAP.'

Krishna Ram considered a moment, while the two staff officers talked of other matters in low voices. This was all against rules and regulations. It would involve several officers in lying, and the falsification of books and accounts, for he'd have to invent some reason for drawing the thousand rupees out of the imprest. It was indefensible ... but it seemed to be necessary. The men—not all, but many—badly needed women. The army was doing nothing, because of British puritanism and because of their feelings against allowing Indian troops to couple with white women. But why should Indians suffer for the guilts and fears of Europe? Why should they not seek solace from the bloody battlefield in European *yonis*?

Dayal Ram said, 'The men need it ... It's only been their discipline that's kept them out of trouble so far. And a lot of these women throw themselves at your head. Not as much as the English ladies, though.' He drank and smacked his lips. Krishna took another drink of his brandy. 'Tell me,' he said on an impulse, 'what happened on that leave of yours?'

Dayal's handsome face lit up eagerly. He leaned forward. 'Highness, the English are different from what they pretend to be. The women certainly ... and, I think, the men, too. The women present a front so cold, so stiff, and formal ... but only approach them and they are as hot under their skirts as the loosest women in Basohli. As soon as I reached London, I found out how to work the telephone and then rang Lady Harriet Symonds. I asked her if she would do me the honour of dining with me ... at the Savoy. You know my father is giving me a very big allowance and I can afford it. She suggested instead that I go to her house, to see what I looked like, I suppose. After two drinks she became, well, affectionate ... you know, sitting close to me on the sofa, looking at me with her eyes big and her eyelashes fluttering. We were in the drawing-room, with butlers and servants about. Then she suggested we go for a drive. I can't drive, of course, but she did. It was a Rolls Royce. She drove me up to a park, Hampstead or something, and stopped. It was dark. She just turned, lay on my shoulder and put her hand ... right on my prick!'

'Ai, ai!' Sohan Singh crowed. '*I* would have to wrap a twenty-

234

rupee note round it before a woman would lay her hand to it.'

Dayal's rapid Hindi continued. 'For a time I couldn't believe what was happening. A peer's daughter. A noblewoman. An Englishwoman ... But by then my prick was as stiff as a pole and she undid the buttons and then crawled on to me. She was pulling at her skirts and petticoats. They wear more than our women do, prince—*you* know—but nothing delays them getting their slit bared when they want to ... She lowered herself greedily on to me and I thrust up into her. She was as hot and wet as a Basohli whore in Holi. I was so excited I came at once. Then we stayed quite a time and I made love twice more ... And every day of my leave. And she introduced me to two other young ladies, and they, too, both came to me ... Englishwomen are—pfft!'—he made a gesture of dismissal—'no different from whores.'

'Not all,' Krishna said, a touch of stiffness in his voice.

Hanuman was setting up a hookah on the floor. He handed the mouthpiece to Krishna as the adjutant said, 'By God, English men know how to make themselves comfortable, but they can't satisfy their women. Perhaps they don't try. I think I'm going to live in London after this ... if I survive.'

Krishna drew on the hookah pipe. Hanuman put more charcoal in the bowl. Yes, Krishna thought, one side of London would attract Dayal Ram, and vice versa ... with his unearthly good looks, and no coward behind it. The class of women he had met— the ones seeking sensation in a specially European way—would seize him as harpies seized sailors, or as the gods took what they needed from earth. He happened to be rich, but women like Lady Harriet would keep him anyway, either directly, or by having their fathers or husbands give him jobs. And now he had enjoyed the sexual favours of European women. Why should he be alone in that position?

He turned to the quartermaster and said, 'Very well, Sohan. You may proceed with your plan.'

'Thank you, lord. I am sure Your Highness is making a wise decision.'

The quartermaster began to talk about accounts, and Krishna Ram thought, all that he tells me will be the truth, for I am a prince of the blood; but it will not be the whole truth. He will do what he says he will do, for the regiment, but there will be an extra hundred or so rupees a week for himself; and with that he will start a business buying grain at Amiens and selling it to the government or the dealers for twice what he paid for it, and the profits will go to London to buy shares in arms companies, steel works, banks ...

The two left, as they had come, and a few minutes later Hanuman announced Captain Pahlwan Ram and Lieutenant Puran Lall. Krishna took another drink of brandy. He had eaten a number of parathas and sweetmeats, and now would eat some more with the new visitors. There would be no formal dinner in the mess tonight, as there was when Warren Bateman was present. This was how they used to live in Basohli before they were embodied into the Sirkar's army, and it came more easily to them. But it did not allow for horseplay and games in the mess.

He looked down at Puran Lall, squatting beside the bed, and said, 'Are you going to eat in mess tonight?'

The young man shook his head, 'No, highness. I am having some food sent to my billet.'

Krishna said, 'You should go out more. It is unhealthy for a young man like you to sit in your room like an old hermit on the mountain.'

'There is nothing to live for, now that Ishar is gone,' he said.

'Not even to kill Germans?' Krishna Ram said.

'A little, highness. I tried at St. Rambert to hate ... like the Scottish sergeant told us ... but it was not the Germans that I hated.'

'The English?' Pahlwan Ram suggested softly.

'A little ... not Bateman-sahib, of course ... some of the sort one meets in the base areas, yes. But there is something else wrong with me, too, and I do not know what. Perhaps it is myself that I hate, because I am alive and Ishar dead.'

He sat, his face closed, neither eating nor drinking, occasionally taking a puff at the hookah for another fifteen minutes—then he left.

Krishna Ram looked at his watch, to indicate to Pahlwan Ram that he was outstaying his welcome. But the brutish lieutenant said, 'When will Bateman-sahib be well again?'

'I don't know,' Krishna Ram said. 'I had a letter from him in hospital two days ago. He was making a good recovery and said he'd be going to Shrewford Pennel, that's his home, in a week or so, and hoped to rejoin in another month after that.'

236

Pahlwan said, 'And he will come back to us ... or to a regular regiment?'

'I don't know. To us, I hope.' As he said it he wondered whether he meant it. Pahlwan Ram detected the doubt and said, 'The regiment would wish that he did not return...' He went on quickly, before Krishna Ram could tell him to be quiet: 'He is English, lord, and though he shares our tongue he does not share our hearts. *You* are our lord and prince ... All trust Bateman-sahib with their money, their food, their clothes—but what do these matter to a Rajput? They would trust you with their souls ... This war is going to destroy us, highness.'

'You take good care it won't destroy you, I notice,' Krishna said. He recognized that his own voice was blurred.

'This war is nothing to do with us,' the lieutenant insisted. 'It is turning the sowars into Christians with brown skins, instead of what they would be, Hindus, servants of the Sun. It is only you who can save us, and Bateman-sahib knows it. He will kill you, highness ... if you don't see that he dies first.'

'Don't be stupid,' Krishna snapped. 'He does not want to kill me.'

'Not you, as prince, but what you mean, what you *are* ... for until that is killed, or conquered, he will never...'

Krishna said, 'Enough! I wish to be alone.'

Pahlwan Ram rose quickly. 'As the prince pleases.' He bowed out.

Krishna sat moodily, cross-legged, on the bed. The CO had been gone barely three weeks, and the regiment was already full of intrigue, backbiting, slander, defalcations of money, cheating with accounts. Yet ... yet ... He poured another drink, recognizing in the blurred outline of the door and the swing and dip of the lights that he was quite drunk. What *was* the evil in Warren Bateman, then? There was something but he could not see exactly what through the pleasant fumes of the brandy.

I thrust up into her. She was as hot and wet as a Basohli whore in Holi.

He swayed forward, Dayal Ram's words slithering lasciviously through his mind. His penis began to stiffen. By God, he wanted a woman. An image of a woman with white skin kept trying to form in his mind, but before the face took shape he dismissed it with violent shakes of his head and a physical gesture with his hand, as though brushing something away and out of the room. Images of woman, unfaced now, returned more strongly, the triangle between the legs, two swelling breasts, the velvet feel of the skin on the thighs. His loins hurt with a piercing pain.

He called thickly, 'Hanuman!'

'Huzoor?'

'Tell the Captain Sohan Singh to bring me a woman here. At once. And more brandy.'

'*Jee-han, huzoor.*'

The orderly withdrew and Krishna leaned back against the wall at the head of the bed and closed his eyes, waiting, thinking.

He thought he must have been asleep when the knock came on the door. He half heard it, then waited, dozing, refusing to open his eyes until it came again. When it did he raised his head off the pillow and saw that the door was open, a woman standing in the opening, Hanuman's face visible over her shoulder. It was Hanuman's hand knocking at the door.

'*Ane do. Darwaza band karo,*' he said thickly. Hanuman pushed the woman into the room and closed the door behind her. The key had long since disappeared, but Krishna knew his orderly would be squatted down outside, blocking all entrance.

The woman was short and sturdy, with an open face lined by work in the fields and browned by the sun. Her eyes were blue and set wide apart, her hair thick, brown, and straight. She must be about thirty or perhaps thirty-five, he thought. She waited against the door, her hands folded in front of her plain dark blue skirt. She wore a thick grey cotton blouse, with a wool kerchief thrown over her shoulders, cotton stockings and bedroom slippers. All the local people wore bedroom slippers, and then slipped their feet into wooden clogs to work in the fields, or to go down the street if it was muddy.

She said timidly, 'You sending me, monsieur?'

He said, 'Yes ... Take off your clothes.'

'Ees ten shillin',' she said, 'for visit. Five shillin' my 'ouse but ten shillin' visit.'

He swung his legs off the bed, felt in the pocket of his tunic, found his wallet and held out a ten-shilling note to her. She took it with a murmured '*Merci, monsieur,*' and tucked it away into a pocket hidden in her skirt.

Then she began to slip out of the white cotton drawers that

238

extended to just above her knees. The drawers off and neatly folded over the back of the chair by the fire, she sat down on the bed and made to lift her legs up on to it. Krishna Ram said, 'All clothes off!'

She opened her mouth to speak but he was already holding out another ten-shilling note. After she had tucked that away with the first she began to undress fully. Krishna sat on the edge of the bed, watching, his lust slowly fading. She had thick tufts of brown hair, darker than the hair of her head, sticking out under her armpits. Indian women shaved or plucked such hair. He wondered suddenly if Diana Bateman shaved or plucked, and if not, what colour the hair would be. He thrust the thought from him.

'What's your name?' he said.

'Marthe, monsieur,' she said, when her head emerged from the blouse she had been pulling over her head. Her breasts were full, round, and heavy. The nipples stood up dark and strong out of big dark areolas. Then she stepped out of her petticoat and stood a moment, naked but for the stockings and bedroom slippers, looking at him. Her belly was well rounded, curving down to a big strong bush of curly brown hair set between the round white thighs. Again, Indian women pluck that off, he thought. It must be very insanitary in hot weather ... but of course they didn't have hot weather in Europe. But it must be insanitary at any time, really, since they poured urine and sweat into that crotch where the hair would retain it. It would not be so odd if Europeans were not always lifting their noses at the insanitariness of Indians ... they, who bathed in still water, so that they wallowed in their own dirt, and allowed women to enter public swimming baths on every day of the month!

His flagging penis stiffened convulsively as she crossed her legs and began to unroll the stockings. The tuft of her bush stuck out dense and rough from under her crossed thighs. He began to undo his fly buttons. When he had got his trousers off she was not quite ready and he took a swig of the brandy, direct from the bottle.

At last she gave him a half smile, lay back on the bed, and held out her arms with a little gesture—'Come.'

She was all that he had read or been told or imagined of the European peasant of the middle ages, something that had once existed here, but had never been seen in India. She was plump and round and strong. The hands still held up to him were rough and chapped, the soles of her feet thickened and split, her skin dead white to her neck, brown and red above that. She opened her legs and pink lips gaped in the depths of the brown thicket. His penis again lost its errant stiffness and he threw himself on top of her with an exclamation of anger. She wrapped her arms about his neck, murmured in French, raised her legs and locked her feet over his back. But his erection was going faster than he could thrust it at the slippery gulf felt and seen in the depths of the bush. For a moment he pushed despairingly at her, but it was no good . . . it was gone . . . gone . . . He stood up, tense as a bowstring about to snap. Her white skin mocked the wrinkled brown of his penis, of the malehood which a minute before had stood like a staff ready to enter the fleshy arch in triumph. She was murmuring, ''Ees all righ', 'ees all righ',' and trying to pull him down on her again. She reached out her hand and began to fondle his limpness.

He seized his swagger stick and struck out at her. 'Wait!' she cried, and turned over, thrusting her big buttocks up into the air. He struck out, again and again, slashing the cane across and across. She groaned and moaned and shrieked, but not loudly. Red weals began to spring up across the white flesh, and as they appeared the power returned to Krishna Ram's penis. It rose in jerks and spasms and in a minute thrust up proud, the knob dark and bulging. He dropped the swagger stick, seized the woman by the waist where she half lay, half knelt on the bed and pushed his phallus between her thighs into the depths of the protruding bush. The hairs parted and before he could begin to thrust, he was into her. She was whimpering, 'You 'urt too much. . .' but he pulled her buttocks viciously back against his belly and rammed harder into the wet depths below. In a few seconds he felt the ecstasy rising, and screamed aloud, 'Bitch, white English bitch!' Then he was coming, squirting, sobbing, doubled over her bare back, his head on her shoulders, his face in her streaming hair.

After a time he let her go, and sank on to the bed.

''Urting too much,' she said reproachfully, sitting on the bed beside him. '*Aussi*, 'ees ten shillin' more for beat.'

He motioned to his wallet on the table. 'Take what you want . . . I am sorry.'

She took out a note, held it up for him to see, and put it away in her skirt over the chair. Then she sat down again and said,

' 'Ees all right. Many mans no come up wizout beat.'

'Not me,' he said. 'I don't know why it was ... this time. I've been drinking.'

She said, 'Too moch whisky make soft cock, eh? But I teenk no one beat drunk unless 'ee want beat sober, no?' The blue eyes on him were shrewd and, as Krishna realized for the first time, sympathetic. ' 'Ees first time fucking white woman?'

He nodded.

'And you major? But servant of English ... no?'

'Yes. No,' he said. 'I am heir to the Rajah of Ravi.' He saw the puzzled look on her face and said, 'I am a prince of India.'

'Ah ... but still servant of English? Thees my 'ouse once ... my 'usband killed first week of war. Now I living weeth sister, we both 'ores ... Was good fuck?'

He nodded. 'Very good.' He wanted to tell her to get her clothes on, covering the tufts under her armpits and the now wet bush gleaming between her parted thighs. But she said, 'I understand ... you like beat me again? 'Ere!' She took the swagger stick and gave it to him and knelt on the bed. 'Go on ... I no charging no more money.'

The criss-crossed welts stood up scarlet now, and already beginning to tinge dark blue at the ends. Krishna Ram felt another stirring of desire, the stick twitched involuntarily in his hands and his penis jerked half upright. But suddenly it was not Marthe the French whore but *her* ... her buttocks, her bush sticking out between the thighs, her parted lips half hiding, half beckoning. Would he want to slash at *her*? For the same reasons? He threw the cane down and said, 'Get dressed. No more.'

She dressed methodically. When she was ready she said formally, '*Merci, monsieur* ... When you wanting, sending servant, yes?'

'No,' Krishna cried. 'No! Go now. Please!'

He threw himself back on the bed and tried to shut out the visions streaming steadily through his mind, like pictures across the screen of a bioscope, but they came steadily on, an endless succession of views of *her*, from in front, from behind, from the side, as she washed, stood, brushed her hair, urinated, ran, ate, petted her dog. She was always naked, white, and marked with those three thick stigmata of hair, one under each arm and one in the crotch.

A week later he sent Hanuman with a message to Captain Rama-swami, asking him to come over. When the black captain arrived, with an ungainly salute, Krishna Ram said, 'I think I've got VD.'

The doctor said, 'Take down your trousers. Let's have a look.' A minute later: 'Yes. A dose of gonorrhoea.'

Krishna began to button himself up again. 'Sohan Singh got me a woman a week ... exactly seven days ago. It was the whore Marthe. She and her sister practise at the end of the village, she said.'

He stood, feeling unclean, thinking that the discharge from his penis was visible to all the world, staining his trousers and his body.

'You should have waited till Sohan had had time to get his brothel for our men going. Yes, it's in operation now. He got two girls from a long way off. They are set up in an old cowshed about half-mile along the road to Boulouris. I inspect them both every other day, but there's better protection than that—Sohan Singh keeps a guard on them day and night, and no one but our men gets anywhere near them.'

'Have none of our men got VD?'

The doctor said, 'Oh, there are a few hereditary syphilitics, and one or two men caught gonorrhoea by slipping into Amiens or Abbeville on short leave, but we know who they are and they've all been cured ... Come over to the RAP and I'll start treating that. The first thing I have to do is stop the inflammation. And then I'll give you the hockey sticks.'

'What's that?' Krishna asked, pulling on his trousers.

'Silver sticks of gradually increasing size, which we have to work down the urethra once a day to make sure that scar tissue from the inflammation that is causing that discharge doesn't grow on to the opposite wall of the urethra, and so block it. By the way, no more alcohol until you're cured. It prevents healing of the inflammation.'

Krishna said, 'I'm giving it up anyway. What happened that night ... what I was feeling and thinking ... has made me realize that we ... I ... have enough problems without drinking.'

'Good,' the doctor said. 'You were hitting the bottle much too hard. Whatever they are, *you* can stand up to them without it.'

Half an hour later, in the RAP, when Captain Ramaswami had bathed and anointed his penis and he had just finished dressing, the RAP orderly rushed in with a hissed message. *'Brigadier-general sahib ane wala hai!'*

The doctor frowned, 'What does that idiot want here?'

Rainbow Rogers burst into the RAP on the heels of the orderly. 'Ah, there you are, Krishna ... and you, Captain, what's your name, I keep forgetting?'

'Ramaswami,' the doctor said briefly.

'Ramaswami, of course ... Well, this is a great day for all of us.'

'Yes, sir,' Krishna said. His penis felt sore and again the thought obsessed him that the discharge was staining the front of his breeches. 'Why, sir?'

The brigadier-general touched his medal ribbons, glancing down. 'I have been given an immediate award of the CMG. Here's the ribbon. See!' His finger rested on a new blue-red ribbon at the head of all the others on his left breast. 'It was awarded for the action at St. Rambert Ridge,' he said. His hand dropped and he raised his head. 'It was won by all the gallant soldiers of my brigade, and in their names I shall wear it proudly.'

'Yes, sir,' Krishna Ram said.

'I have put you in for a decoration, too, Krishna Ram, but as yet we have heard nothing about it. I most sincerely hope you get it ... Now I must dash back to my headquarters. The Russian General Podgorov is coming for dinner and I must be there to do the honours. I may be showing him round one of the regiments tomorrow, but the Brigade Major will telephone ahead.'

'Yes, sir.'

'Anything you want? ... Oh, we've heard from Division that there's no hope of getting another British officer for you. Oh, you didn't know Major Bateman had asked for one? Well, he had ... Do you have any idea when he's returning to duty?'

'About a month, he thinks, sir,' Krishna said.

'Good, good. We need him ... though you're doing very well, yes, very well.'

He strode out, an almost ethereal light of happiness lighting up his thin face.

Ramaswami said, 'Brigadier-general Roland Vernon Rogers, CMG, MVO! What a goal to live for ... I must get back to work.'

'Don't forget that the big *tamasha*'s due to start in an hour.'

'I know,' the doctor said, 'but I promised myself I'd try to read up on all the gynaecological work that's been published since I left India. I have a friend at St. Mary's in London who's been sending it over to me.'

'Oh, come on,' Krishna said. 'There's going to be a nautch. We're going to light big fires, and wear every bit of costume we brought with us, and more that Sohan Singh has had made up somewhere. There won't be an Englishman there. You'll think you're back in India—not a white face to be seen!'

'That couldn't be India,' the doctor said grimly.

'Yes it could—in Basohli.'

The doctor grinned suddenly, the smile transforming his big harsh face and said, 'Very well, Rajah sahib. I hear and I obey. Who am I, a mere black man, to counter the prince's command?' He made a mock *namasti*.

May 1915

WARREN DOZED FITFULLY in a corner seat of a first-class compartment as the leave train bumped slowly towards St. Omer. His leg ached slightly, as it still did when he had to hold it in any one position for too long, but otherwise he was again fit, and fully recovered from his wound. Three days ago he had walked twenty miles with Diana, from the house to Netheravon on the Plain and back, as a final test. They had lunched on bread and cheese at a pub by Stonehenge. It was quite like old times. Diana was a good scout, but even she had changed in some ways. She was not quite so open and transparent, seeming now to hide emotions where before she would show them. But it was Joan who had changed the most. He found himself frowning and tried to keep his face impassive. It was that damned Ralph ... the poor chap couldn't help his background and birth, but why did that have to turn him into a raving socialist and pacifist? And why did Joan have to swallow the whole thing hook, line, and sinker? Mother still kept trying to get him a job but he wouldn't go. The two of them were having a bad effect on the children, too, teaching them to sit around in fuggy rooms, painting or drawing when they ought to have been out of doors with a dog and a gun ... well, they were a little small for the gun yet, but that was the right idea.

The train ground to a stop and the major in the opposite corner of the crowded compartment peered through the window. 'Arnay-le-Poste,' he said. 'Where's that?'

'About half way, sir,' a lieutenant in the middle said, stifling a yawn.

'What are we stopped for now?' someone asked.

'God knows. To get a cow off the line, probably.'

245

The station building was tall and silent, lit by a faint lamp over the name inscribed in red tiles high on the side. With a rumble and a hiss-hiss-hiss a train pulled up on the other line. Dimly Warren could make out cattle trucks full of soldiers. Not British, he thought—French, or perhaps Belgian. Where were they going? They were mostly asleep, the doors of the cattle trucks open to the May night air, here and there a man standing in the door or sitting on the step, his legs dangling dangerously. The troop train hissed out of the station and still the leave train waited. Half an hour passed, then another train drew up on the other line, this one coming from behind. It stopped and Warren saw that it was a long goods train loaded with stores—mainly artillery ammunition from the shapes of the objects under the dimly gleaming tarpaulins. He peered at his watch and saw that it was 4.20 a.m.

The ammunition train pulled out northward and half an hour later the leave train followed. The first light spread a pinkish haze over the flat fields of Artois and Warren felt a momentary shiver of recollection: thus came the dawn the morning of the attack at St. Rambert. He closed his eyes against the memory, and the sight of the captain opposite snoring, his mouth open, stubble dark on his lean jaw.

Yes, his leg had recovered and the broken bone healed, but now there was a hurt in his mind. It was not only Joan who had changed. England itself wasn't the same as it used to be, even as it had been when he and Krishna spent a few days there in September last, and played cricket ... Everything was going to the bad. He thought of the girls he had seen in London on his way through. Respectable girls, you would have said—you would have *known*, once, from their accents. Now they were selling themselves on the Strand and down the Haymarket. Giving themselves away, more accurately, for the money they asked went to war charities, they proclaimed. One had accosted him and she was a lady. That was bad enough, but when he told Joan about it she had actually defended the girl: she had a right to do what she liked with her own body, Joan said. Prostitution was only wrong if it was exploiting women for economic reasons, Joan said. Thank God the children were too young to understand what she was saying, or thinking. He'd have to put a stop to that kind of talk before they grew much older ... And take Ralph and Young Marsh and their talk of social injustice and pacifism! Joan's arty friends

246

laughed at his standards, but in times of difficulty they were what helped you win through. In hard times you didn't relax standards, but tightened them. He remembered meeting Fuller in the lane one dusk—Fuller, the man who'd made an indecent advance to a boy three or four years ago. At the time—himself home on furlough—he'd been among those who favoured taking no action, overt or covert. Live and let live, he'd said, and he remembered telling Sir Tristram Pennel that India was full of buggers, and none the worse for it.

But running into the fellow in the lane just last week was an awkward business, for Fuller had come forward with hand outstretched crying, 'Major Bateman! I heard you were back. I do hope your wound is not serious.' Warren had taken the hand, because his mind hadn't worked quickly enough, and the fellow had practically popped out of the hedge at him. But then he'd thought, this man's a sodomite, like Sher Singh. He's as bad as Young Marsh refusing to volunteer, as bad as the girls giving themselves away on Piccadilly. They were all in their way undermining the foundations of society. So he'd said stiffly, 'Yes, my leg is almost healed now. Good evening,' and strode on, as Fuller quickly stepped aside for him. He'd just caught the expression on Fuller's face ... like a child slapped without warning. He'd believed that Warren was his friend, and now he'd been snubbed. Warren gritted his teeth: he wasn't any bugger's friend, or any loose woman's, or any traitor's.

That was a bad evening, for he'd arrived home, his face grim, thinking of Fuller, and been met at the door by Joan, white, the light behind her, a telegram in her hand. 'Tim's dead,' she said, 'shot down over the German lines.'

Tim was her second brother, recently transferred from the Green Howards to the Royal Flying Corps. Warren could think of nothing to say except, 'He was doing his duty.'

Then Joan did the extraordinary thing. She lifted her hand with the telegram in it and dashed it across his face as he stood there in the hall, crying, 'To hell with duty! Don't you see it's destroying what it's supposed to defend? And turning you all into animals. Worse—into machines!'

She ran upstairs sobbing, her long hair trailing down her back. For a moment Warren thought he'd go up after her, and try to comfort her, but decided that in her present mood she would not accept his comforting.

'I say, are you all right, sir?'

It was the lieutenant opposite, looking at him with concern. He said shortly, 'Yes, why?'

'You cried out ... in your sleep.'

'I wasn't asleep,' he said gruffly. 'Are we nearly there?'

It was full dawn now, and the rising sun shone on rumpled fields, shattered buildings, and a huge barbed-wire enclosure holding thousands of tons of ammunition, and millions of boxes and crates, all geometrically divided by duckboarded walks and gravelled roads. Here and there tall lorries were being loaded by working parties. The train drew into St. Omer station. He was back at the war. He stood up with a sense of grim exhilaration. During these weeks lying in bed with his leg in traction, staring at the ceiling, thinking; during those days walking the lanes alone or with Diana —he had digested all that he had seen, at the front and in England. He had worked out what was right and what was wrong. He knew what he had to do.

At the RTO's office he found a message directing him to report to the Divisional commander before returning to his regiment, which was at Mennecy. An hour later he was with Major-General Glover, eating a breakfast served by khaki-clad waiters. The general said, 'Had a good leave, I hope, Bateman.'

'Yes, sir. Of course I was in bed the first part, which wasn't much fun.'

'It gave you time to think, though, eh?'

'Yes, sir.'

'The reason I sent for you is that the 8th Brahmins are now nearly back to strength. They're fit to take their place in the Lahore Brigade.'

Warren said, 'And we'd become the Divisional Cavalry again?'

The general said, 'No. A regiment of cavalry is absolutely useless to me in trench warfare, whereas I have found the Brahmins invaluable as an extra battalion in my hand, even in the state they've been in.'

Warren thought, as divisional troops his regiment would spend most of its time guarding headquarters, or on fatigue duty, only occasionally being used in action. That was just what the Ravi

Lancers did not need—to become semi-ceremonial dogsbodies and odd job men.

He said, 'I'd much rather we stayed in the Lahore Brigade, sir.'

The general nodded. 'I thought you'd say that. After your excellent showing at St. Rambert, General Rogers wouldn't want to lose you, either. So we'll leave it the way it is—you remain in the Lahore Brigade and the 8th Brahmins remain as divisional troops.'

'Yes, sir. Thank you, sir.'

The general began to talk of ibex shooting beyond the Karakorams.

Warren arrived at Mennecy in the twilight, riding on top of a London bus, the inside full of Fusiliers returning from leave. He stepped down with his belongings, and the bus went on to the Fusiliers' billets a mile farther south. It was eight o'clock and he asked the first sower he saw where the officers' mess was. The man peered at him and said, '*Arfisar mess?*' He had not saluted and from the tone of his voice Warren realized that he thought it was a private of the Fusiliers who had accosted him. He was in shirt sleeves and wearing a Vaishnavi caste mark on his forehead. Warren said coldly, 'What is your name, and squadron? I am the commanding officer.'

The man straightened into salute. 'I am sorry, sahib. I came with a draft only a month ago.'

'Name and squadron,' Warren insisted.

'Gokal Ram, B Squadron, huzoor.'

'Who gave you permission to wear a caste mark?'

'It is permitted without special asking, sahib, every day after the last parade and the evening meal. It was much discussed at the last durbar—just after my draft came.'

Warren said, 'Show me the officers' mess now.'

The sower led him up the street and pointed out a building at the far end. Like the previous mess, it had been an estaminet. He dismissed the man with an order to remove his caste mark at once, and entered the mess. In the big room the table was not laid, and no mess orderly answered his call, '*Koi hai!*'

After waiting a few minutes in the dusk he went out the back. The mess dafadar was sitting on a bench in the yard, surrounded by the mess orderlies. They were playing cards by the light of a hurricane lantern set on the end of the bench.

Warren called, 'Dafadar! Here!'

The dafadar nearly fell off the bench in his surprise and alarm. He grabbed up his turban, set it on his head, dusted off his tunic and came running. 'What does the presence want?'

'What time is dinner?' Warren snapped.

'Eight o'clock, sahib, but...'

'It is past eight now. Why is it not served? Where are the officers?'

'Sahib!' The dafadar said nothing more, standing stiffly at attention.

Warren said, 'The officers do not eat in mess, is that it?'

'Yes, sahib,' the dafadar muttered.

Warren said, 'Send the orderlies to bring the officers here, all of them, at once. Tell the khansamah to cook a meal and serve it at eight-thirty, that's in twenty-five minutes from now. Bring me a whisky and soda.'

'Yes, sahib. Very good, sahib,' the dafadar stammered.

Warren turned on his heel and stalked into the building. He sat down, picked up the paper—a copy of the *Times of India* a month old—and began to read. The mess dafadar and a couple of orderlies scurried around lighting lamps, drawing curtains, dusting off the table, setting a cloth, laying the places, putting out glasses. A uniformed orderly brought him his drink. He eyed the man thoroughly, checking every detail of his dress, before accepting it. One by one the officers came, and each said, 'Good evening, sir,' as he entered, sometimes with a muttered word that they were glad to see him back. He noticed that they were all wearing turbans, which they took off and put on the little side table before they sat down. Then they waited, sitting, in silence. At half past eight Warren glanced at his watch, looked up, and said to Krishna Ram, 'Is everyone here?'

'Everyone except the doctor,' Krishna said, 'he has a man very sick he thinks he ought to stay near.'

'Tell him from me to come here at once,' Warren said.

Krishna Ram went out. He's the one responsible, Warren thought. A pleasant young man, but weak. And being a prince of the blood, the natural ruler of these people, had made it more difficult for him. How could you expect backbone in someone who's been given all he wanted, without his having to raise his finger, and practically worshipped as a god, since the cradle?

Ten minutes later the doctor appeared, looking grim, followed by Krishna Ram. Warren stood up and said, 'When I give an order, Captain Ramaswami, in future you will obey it without delay or question ... Dafadar, serve dinner.'

They ate dinner in complete silence. Warren could feel the nervous tension building up, in the taut faces, the concentration on their food, the way first one and then another would drop his knife or fork on to his plate or knock over a glass.

When the pudding plates had been cleared away and coffee served, Warren said, 'Dafadar, leave the room. Allow no one to enter.' He waited until the NCO had gone, then said, 'Gentlemen, may I have your attention, please? I would not normally raise disciplinary matters in the mess, since it is our home, but because some of these matters concern the mess itself, I will do so ...' He stared slowly from man to man round the table. 'I have been gone just seven weeks. When I left you were eating in the mess like the officers and gentlemen you are supposed to be. Today I find you eating in your own rooms, like ... *babus*. What is the rule about dining in mess? ... You, Pahlwan Ram.'

The dark-skinned lieutenant started and knocked over his coffee cup. 'I taught you on the troopship,' Warren said. 'Speak up.'

Pahlwan Ram mumbled, 'Bachelor officers and officers who do not have their wives present in the station will eat all meals in mess, except in action, when they may eat with their squadrons.'

'Note the word *will*,' Warren ground. 'It does not say they may eat meals in mess, it says *will*. You have been commanding in my absence, Major Krishna Ram. What is your explanation of this state of affairs?'

'Sir ...' Krishna began. Warren waited, his hands clenched on the table top. He'd give the young man such a wound that he'd carry it to his grave.

'I have no excuse, sir,' Krishna Ram said. 'I permitted the officers to eat as and where they wished. It is not their fault but mine.'

'We shall discuss this later,' Warren said. 'Another matter. Who gave the officers permission to wear turbans?'

'I did, sir,' Krishna said, 'the caps make them conspicuous in action. And the turban is our normal headgear.'

'Brigadier-General Rogers specifically ordered all officers to wear caps,' Warren grated. 'Has he rescinded that order?'

'No, sir. But he's seen us in turbans. He hasn't said anything.'

'Who gave the men permission to wear caste marks?'

Krishna Ram said promptly, 'I did, sir. It was discussed at...'

'I know it was discussed at durbar,' Warren said. 'By God, this is not a woman's social club but a regiment, a REGIMENT OF INDIAN CAVALRY!' His voice rose and rasped. 'What is to be done is not decided by everyone sitting round under a banyan tree like a lot of bloody Bengali villagers, but by the commanding officer!'

'I was the commanding officer, sir,' Krishna Ram said quietly.

'You're not now. Adjutant, rescind those orders tomorrow morning.'

'Yes, sir,' Dayal Ram said.

Warren again circled the room with his glare. Only old Bholanath and young Krishna Ram met and held his eyes.

He said, 'Gentlemen, we are at war. This is already the bloodiest war in history and it has not yet begun to make its real demands on us. Last month the Germans used poisonous gas. Who knows what will come next? We must be prepared to face *anything*, endure *anything*! We are going to face death and mutilation not by the scores but by the hundreds, by the thousands. The Germans master themselves by brutal discipline and determination ... and we must match them. The greater the dangers, the more severe the obstacles at which we are going to put our spirit, the more we must train and discipline that spirit. Discipline is not to be slackened because we are at war ... but tightened. Men are not to be punished less severely for crimes, because life is hard— but more severely. We are fighting for our countries and our homes —but the last man shall die, the last village burn, the last blade of grass wither, before we admit defeat. We shall win, at any cost ... I shall inspect the regiment tomorrow, by squadrons, starting at five-thirty a.m. with A squadron. Field Service marching order. Men first, then billets, then stores.'

He stood up and all the officers stood with him. He went out, as Krishna Ram barked, 'Officers—salute!' and told the mess dafadar to show him to his billet.

But Warren found his orderly Narayan Singh waiting outside, holding Shikari by the collar. Narayan Singh saluted, smiling, and Shikari broke free and jumped up into Warren's arms, whining

and licking his face. 'There, there,' Warren said, 'I'm back ...
Good dog. *You* haven't changed, have you? ... Down, now! Is
this my billet? Good. Give the rissaldar-major-sahib my salaams.'
'*Jee-han, huzoor.*'

Next day Warren finished his inspection at four o'clock in the
afternoon having been at it all day, except for a two-hour break
for lunch and to deal with paper work. When he started he was
already wearing on his sleeves the woven crown and star, for before he went to bed the adjutant had come with the news, supposed
to have been given him at once but driven out of Dayal's head by
Warren's reprimands, that he was gazetted a temporary lieutenant-
colonel while in command of the Ravi Lancers; and Narayan had
at once taken his tunic to the *darzi*.

The inspection over, Warren went to the room at the back of the
school where his office was set up, and summoned the second-in-
command and the rissaldar-major. Then he began to put his notes
on the inspection in order. The details—the number of rifles cord-
worn or corroded; the state of the men's boots and clothes; the
condition of the webbing equipment and accoutrements—all these
he had pointed out to the squadron commanders at the time,
and Dayal Ram had made notes so that the deficiencies and defects
could be pursued. Now he wanted to get clear in his own mind
how he found the regiment. He had barely finished when the
orderly announced Krishna Ram and the RM.

They sat down—Krishna under a portrait of his grandfather in
his robes as a Knight Commander of the Star of India that was
always carried with the office files and records—and Warren began
to speak, in Hindi for the benefit of the RM. 'The general state of
the regiment is good,' he said. 'B Squadron has more corroded
rifles than any other—nearly double. Captain Himat Singh has
been told to take as much care over that as he does over the
discipline and training of his men. Dress and drill are good. Billets
are generally clean though some men have not been using the
latrines. I am issuing orders that any man found urinating or
defecating anywhere but in the proper latrine will receive twenty-
eight days Field Punishment No. 1. As you know, that means being
tied to the wheel of a cart.'

'That will be a great shame, sahib,' the rissaldar-major said.

'It will,' Warren said grimly. 'So, to avoid such shame, let the men learn to go to the latrine, whatever the weather or the time of day. This is not Bustiepore ... What I find lacking in the regiment is the offensive spirit. The bayonet practices I ordered in A and D Squadrons were weak-kneed and feeble. Those men wouldn't have frightened a French housemaid, and they're supposed to strike terror into the hearts of German infantry. Get back to what Sergeant Mackintosh taught us, which seems to have been forgotten since we proved it worked at St. Rambert ... In general, all standards must be tightened. Let no man get away with the slightest slackness in dress or deportment. Officers and VCOs will be saluted, at whatever distance they are seen, day and night. No excuse will be accepted. Any officer who does not take a man's name for failing to salute him will be severely disciplined himself. You were from the Guides, sahib—we must make this regiment as uncompromising as the Guides.'

'*Jee-han, huzoor*,' the RM said stolidly.

Warren turned to Krishna. 'I want you to see that all *desi* customs and habits are purged, particularly among the officers ... Now, I am issuing certain specific orders with the aim of tightening morale, and making the regiment a better fighting machine. First, I am forbidding the doctor to practise or talk about Vedic medicine. I should never have allowed it in the first place. It is nothing but superstitious mumbo-jumbo and it will no longer be tolerated. Second, I am trebling regimental police patrols, day and night, as long as we are in the rear area, to see that none of our men visit houses of prostitution in Longmont and elsewhere. No man is to be allowed out of the billet area without a signed chit from his squadron commander, authorizing him to go to a specific place for a specific purpose, and return by the shortest route. Venereal disease is very low ... only three in the whole regiment ... but that's too many. Those three men, incidentally, are being transferred to the Service Corps. I will not have our men having any dealing with French women ... Finally, I am abolishing durbars for the duration of our stay in France. They are well suited to conditions of service in India but not to a great war in Europe. They breed dissension and allow the men to think that military orders can be discussed and changed to suit their conveniences or prejudices ... Any questions?'

Krishna Ram said, 'I think the men will miss the durbars very much, sir. They bring us all together.'

'Yes,' Warren snapped, 'for the purpose of rumour-mongering and gossip! I know it's an old Indian Army custom. I believe the regular regiments are still holding them ... but this regiment is different. Give an inch and they take an ell, because they don't have the same hard core of discipline as regiments with British officers. That's all, rissaldar-major-sahib. Krishna Ram, will you stay, please.'

When he was alone with the prince he said, 'Last night I meant to reprimand you very severely, and perhaps send you back to India for what I considered gross slackness in allowing the officers to behave like *desi babus* ... but the fact is that you were the commanding officer. You were within your rights to run the regiment the way you thought best. I am only very sorry that you seem to have learned so little of what I have been trying to teach you for the last nine months.'

'I have been learning,' Krishna Ram said.

'Not much, apparently,' Warren said. 'I am going to make one change in the officers. Flaherty will become adjutant and Dayal Ram go to the Signal Section.'

Krishna's eyes flickered at that, and he said, 'Has Dayal been unsatisfactory, sir?'

'No,' Warren said grimly, 'I just think this will work better.'

He meant that he would trust even a Eurasian to enforce his will upon the regiment, rather than any Indian, even Dayal, even Krishna ... especially Krishna; and he saw in Krishna's face that the prince understood.

Krishna Ram got up, saluted punctiliously and went out, closing the door carefully behind him.

Warren Bateman watched him go with pursed lips. He looked about ten years older than when he had last seen him. He was not surly or sullen over his reprimand—far from it, it was almost as though he felt sorry for Warren. And also as though his mind were some distance off, groping, thinking ... about what?

Krishna, too, was changing. Everyone was changing. But was the changing for good reason or bad? Were the changes themselves desirable or not? That was the heart of the argument he'd had with Joan his last night at home. He had hoped for some warmth in her, especially in love-making, which seemed to have become more and more distasteful to her, but at his approach she'd talked about the girls offering their bodies in the Strand, and said, 'Wouldn't you rather have one of them? They're patriotic, too. *I* think women should accept love *only* from pacifists.'

'From slackers like Ralph,' he had said angrily.

'You keep him out of this,' she had flared up, suddenly fierce as a hawk. 'He's ... how could you understand?'

He had said, 'I understand that if we loosen our morals, we can't win this war—and we don't deserve to, because we shall have lost what we are fighting for.'

She said, 'Warren, you're becoming more brutal, more narrow-minded and obstinate every day.'

'I am not changing!' he said vehemently then. 'It is you who have changed ... you and people like you! You wouldn't have tolerated Fuller a year ago. Now you upbraid me because I snubbed him in the lane. A year ago you wouldn't have had a good word to say for well-bred girls who act like cheap harlots—now you say they have a perfect right to. A year ago so-called ladies didn't wear trousers everywhere, puff cigarettes in public, and ...'

She said wearily, 'It's the war, Warren. The longer the war goes on, the more changes there will be. Some for the better. Why shouldn't a woman smoke in public? What's disgraceful about it? Some for the worse ... like the state of mind you and all the patriots are getting into, here and in France, and Germany and Russia, of course. Everywhere! You were a gentleman once. A gentle man. Now you're an officer. It took this war to show that the two don't really go together.'

'That's an insult,' he had said, 'and a damned lie!'

A damned lie, a damned lie, a damned lie ... the words kept repeating themselves in his mind. Was that what was on Krishna Ram's mind, too? Was that what troubled Diana's brow?

Dayal Ram took his transfer to the Signals with a hurt stiffness that Warren tried to assuage with praise for the work done. Then Flaherty came in, and Warren said, bluntly, 'I am making you my adjutant, Flaherty, because I need another Englishman close to me.'

The big Anglo-Indian flushed with pleasure and there was a wetness in the corner of his eye as he said, 'You can count on me, sir.' He added, 'I didn't want to wear a turban but the Yuvraj said we must all dress alike, like the men.'

'Well, you're *not* one of the men,' Warren said. 'You're the adjutant, my right arm, and my eyes, too, seeing that my intentions are carried out in the letter and in the spirit. Our officers are individually excellent fellows—most of them—but there is a spirit, something about them taken together, that is devious ... Indian. I am unable to be everywhere at once. I am going to rely on you to cover my back.'

The lieutenant said, startled, 'Literally, sir? You mean that you think someone might try to murder you? By God, if ...'

'I don't think so ... yet,' Warren said. 'I meant it figuratively— I want you to see that when my back is turned all that I have ordered is not ignored.'

'You can count on me, sir,' Flaherty said again.

'Now,' Warren said, 'I am going to attack a problem which I previously shirked, because it seemed to me to be doing no harm. I have realized that that was simply my weakness. Listen...' He leaned forward and spoke in a low voice.

A little less than forty-eight hours later, near midnight, Warren awoke to a hand gently, insistently pushing at his shoulder. He recognized the new adjutant's singsong in the whispered words, 'It iss me, Flaherty, sir. It iss in the back of the other estaminet, sir, the one that iss not the mess. I have seen two go in.'

'But are they actually doing it now?'

'Oah yes, sir! I can smell it ... I know the smell.'

I bet you do, Warren thought; you don't grow up in Basohli without learning about opium.

'Shall I light the lantern, sir?'

'No,' Warren said, 'I know where my clothes are.' He dressed quickly, found his torch and made sure it worked properly. He said to Flaherty, 'You have a torch, too? Test it here, pointing down ... Good. We must have no mistake over who or what we see. Come on.' Then he went with Flaherty at his side to Krishna Ram's billet. The ape-like orderly Hanuman was asleep outside the door and two other sowars at the end of the hallway. Warren frowned to see them—they were obviously the personal bodyguards he had ordered to be discontinued; but he could deal with that later, after this night's work had shown them all that he meant business. Flaherty stirred the orderly with his toe and growled, 'Wake up, you. Tell the major that the colonel-sahib is here.'

Krishna Ram came out rubbing his eyes in the dim light thrown by Warren's torch. 'What is it, sir?'

'Get dressed,' Warren said. 'No lights or noise.'

Five minutes later, in the empty street, Warren said, 'Come close ... I have received information that opium is being smoked in a room at the back of the building that was the other estaminet here. We will go there now to catch the smokers redhanded. When I throw open the door you will be at my shoulders. The adjutant and I will shine our flashlights. All three of us are to note carefully what we see, as we will have to give evidence at the courts-martial that will follow. Is that clear?'

After a brief hesitation Krishna Ram said, 'You will catch Major Bholanath, sir. He smokes opium nearly every night with one or two others ... older men.'

'VCOs?' Warren said.

'Some. And sowars. They have been doing it all their lives.'

'And you knew, and did nothing about it, knowing that the taking of any form of dope is forbidden?'

'I didn't think it was ... I *knew* it wasn't doing any harm,' Krishna Ram said. 'Not to these men. It's our custom.'

'It's going to end, now, with Bholanath's being cashiered and sent to prison.'

'He'll kill himself with his own sword rather than go to prison, sir,' Krishna said.

'We'll see. Follow me.'

Warren started up the street, the others beside him. When they were very close to the estaminet he paused as he heard running feet. The booted feet, approaching from the direction of the school at the south end, came close and loud. It was a sowar of the regiment, dressed, belted, and armed. Warren held out his hand and whispered, 'Who are you looking for?'

'You, colonel-sahib,' the sowar barked.

Warren swore under his breath and said, 'Quiet! What is it?'

There might yet be a chance, he thought. The runner's boots had clashed sharp and loud on the cobbles, but men absorbed in smoking opium would not have heard—or cared.

At the end of the village a trumpet sounded the regimental call, followed by the 'Stand-to'.

The runner said, 'The Duty-sahib says the regiment is to move up the line at once. There is a message from brigade.'

By now the trumpet's incessant repetitions were awakening the village. Lanterns glowed, torches flashed, half-dressed sowars tumbled out into the street pulling on boots or breeches. Another trumpet began to repeat the call.

Warren stood in the middle of the street. They were to go up the line at once. No chance to hold a court-martial even if he did catch them, and get the evidence on them. He made up his mind and turned to the other officers. 'We'll have to put this off to another time. I rely on your words of honour that you will say nothing to anyone about what we were going to do. Flaherty, orders in my office in thirty minutes. Meantime, all officers to prepare their squadrons to move up the line.'

He went to the office, then. The duty officer was Himat Singh. He saluted as Warren came in, his face bright and alert. He handed Warren a message pad. 'This was a telephone message from the Brigade Major, sir. It came at 0011—nine minutes ago.'

'Did you order the "Stand-to" blown?'

'Yes, sir. I thought it would save time.'

'Quite right.' Warren read the message: GERMANS HAVE ATTACKED AREA TRESIGNY–ORIVAL WITH POISONED GAS AAA HINDUSTAN DIV IS OCCUPYING SECTOR BEAUMONT 4587 RIVEDOUX 3809 IMMEDIATELY LAHORE BDE RIGHT JHANSI BDE LEFT. LAHORE BDE SECTOR BEAUMONT TO ROSIERS 4267 71ST PUNJABIS RIGHT RAVI L LEFT MEETING PT BEAUMONT CHURCH AAA 1/12 GR AND R OXF FUS IN RESERVE ONE MILE SOUTH OF BEAUMONT BRIG GEN WILL GIVE ORDERS BEAUMONT CHURCH 1000 HRS MAY 19 MARCH ORDERS ADMIN INTERCOMN FOLLOW ACKNOWLEDGE.

'Here's the map, sir,' Himat Singh said. 'Beaumont's twenty-eight miles by the most direct road.'

The field telephone buzzed and the signal orderly on it said, 'For you, sahib.'

Himat Singh picked it up and listened. After a moment he said, 'It's march orders, sir.'

'Take them down.'

Warren thought, we'll have about nine hours to cover twenty-eight miles. But first the men must be issued with rations and get some hot tea. To Himat Singh, writing busily on a message pad, he said, 'Send the adjutant to the mess when he arrives. All other officers to wait here until I return.'

He walked quickly down the street, now full of men hurrying this way and that, and the tramp of boots and the crunch of wheels as the GS wagons were brought out and the draught horses harnessed. In the mess he told the dafadar to make him *andar rumble-tumble* at once, with bread and butter, jam and tea, and to prepare breakfast for all the officers immediately after that. Then he sat, thinking. The Germans were attacking, without any warning. They seemed to have caught First Army with its pants down, as usual. And using poisonous gas. Why hadn't we thought of it first?

Poisonous gas ... drifting across the green fields and flower-speckled hedges; poisoning the song birds in their nests and the cattle in the stream and the women hoeing the potatoes.

He shook his head determinedly. It was a weapon of war, no more. When inspecting the regiment the day after his return he had seen for the first time the peculiar masks that had been issued only a few days earlier. The mask appeared to be a piece of de-composed fish in a black net bag. When facing chlorine—for that was the gas the Germans had used for the first time three weeks ago—the men were to moisten the bag with ammonia by urinating on it and then fasten it over the mouth and nose. Not only was it a disgusting device, but it seemed highly unlikely that it would work. Still, it was the only protection anyone had been able to devise so far.

He must tell Krishna Ram to bring the regiment up as fast as he could. Fix a rendezvous on the line of march where he could send Mahadeo Singh to guide the regiment to its appointed sector. Extra ammunition in the GS wagons, at least 100 rounds a man and twenty-four belts per gun for the machine guns; more en-trenching tools and wire ...

'*Hazri tayyar hai, sahib,*' the dafadar announced respectfully, indicating the plate of scrambled eggs, the steaming mug of tea, the pot of jam and the pile of sliced bread and butter.

Flaherty came in and Warren said, 'You and I and Mahadeo are going to eat now, and ride like hell for Beaumont as soon as I've given orders. Just our orderlies, two trumpeters and two gallop-ers with us ... We'll deal with that other matter, that was interrup-ted, some other time.'

'Yes, sir.'

May 1915

KRISHNA RAM WALKED across the field and through the straggly wood for what seemed the twentieth time, Hanuman and his trumpeter at his heels. The men were digging in little groups and clumps, under a hot sun. The village of Beaumont was almost intact, for the earlier advances and retreats had passed it by. Villagers were struggling out even now, herding cows across the fields, for the roads were forbidden to them so that they could be used by the flood of ambulance vehicles going forward to pick up the wounded.

It was two o'clock in the afternoon. The regiment had marched the twenty-eight miles in from its rest area in ten hours, starting at one-thirty a.m. Now the cookers had arrived, but Colonel Bateman had ordered that no one should eat until all the new trenches were at least three feet deep. So the men sweated and dug, dug and sweated, leaning dizzily on picks and shovels, their brown faces lined with fatigue and thick with dust. All about, artillery rumbled like approaching thunder.

Warren Bateman strode up as Krishna reached the left end of the line, where C Squadron linked with the Sherwood Foresters of the flanking brigade, at a brick-lined well beyond the copse.

'Everything all right?' Warren asked.

'Yes, sir,' Krishna said. 'The men are tired, of course, but they're not dead beat yet.'

'Keep them at it,' Warren said briefly. 'I'm going back to brigade personally, to get more barbed wire. Or have the BM's liver on a plate ... Stay at RHQ, please, until I get back.'

Krishna watched the CO walk briskly away. The man was only back a couple of days from a severe wound and a long convalescence, but he seemed to be tireless. What kept him going? Was it pride in the regiment? Determination to beat the Germans? Lust to get at them again, for more killing?

He set out for RHQ which was behind a hayrick half a mile west of Beaumont. The guns were getting louder, and 41st Field Battery, now in position a mile back, was beginning to range in. Now that he had experienced heavy and medium artillery fire, Krishna realized how relatively ineffectual the 18-pounders were. They would be great for a war of movement, supporting infantry against enemy in the open, or tribesmen or lightly armed irregulars; against entrenched Germans they were of little more use than peashooters.

So we need bigger guns, he thought moodily, and more of them. More barbed wire, more machine guns, some sort of light machine gun that a man could carry unaided, more lorries. Everything automatic, mechanical. The amount of ammunition being used was too much for flesh and blood to move. It had to be brought up by machines. The shells for some guns were so heavy that machines had to be used to lift them and ram them into the breech. The war was not being fought by men but by machines. Machines had no feelings, and no ability to think, so how would they know when to stop, when to make peace, even when to change the direction of the fighting?

At RHQ he sat down with his back to the haystack, watching a squad from the Signal Section digging weapon pits and putting out a single apron of barbed wire. Hanuman said, 'Sleep, lord. I'll wake you if the Colonel-sahib comes.'

Krishna nodded. No reason why he shouldn't sleep. 'Wake me in half an hour,' he said.

He closed his eyes. Sleep, come, he murmured. But instead he was at the table in the estaminet in Mennecy, Warren Bateman cold and white and bitter at the head, and sweat in his own palms. The words were like lashes across his face. But had he done wrong to try to lead the regiment back to the wellspring of its spirit? And afterwards, only Ramaswami and Pahlwan Ram still there, everyone else slunk off like beaten dogs, Indian pi-dogs cringing before their master. Ramaswami said, 'He doesn't seem to realize what he's saying ... "We must fight for our land, our women, our civilization." What have France or England or Germany got to do with our land, our women, our civilization?'

And Pahlwan Ram, always ready with the word that would

separate, 'Yes, and practically calling us savages to our faces . . .'

Then Krishna had got up and said curtly, 'That's enough of that. I'm going to bed.'

Bed . . . dreams . . . thoughts . . . dreams . . . Marthe's white thighs and brown bush. Or *was* it Marthe's? He remembered the silken flesh petals of the servant girl someone—his father? his mother?—had sent him on his fourteenth birthday, to teach him the grace of women. She was twenty, experienced and delicate, a ruby set in her nostril, her brown skin cool under his hand, patchouli scenting her sleek dark hair.

'Colonel-sahib ane-wala hai!'

He sat up with a start and looked automatically at his wrist watch. Four o'clock. He'd slept nearly two hours. He could smell cooking *dal*, and noticed the wind was blowing from the south-west. The trenches at RHQ were four feet deep. Some men were still at work, digging communication trenches and machine gun emplacements, the rest were eating or sleeping where they had sat down to rest. He felt a pang of hunger himself, and stood up. Warren Bateman arrived and said, 'Four GS wagons full of wire are right behind me. See that one goes to each squadron. Then eat. Then go and take command of the Rear Echelon. See that the RAP has good covered exits to the rear. See that the RM has the reserve ammunition well sandbagged.'

'Yes, sir,' Krishna said. The CO was beginning to look tired now, but still the orders came out crisp and sharp. His brain was running like a machine that would not stop. Surely, if this great strain continued, it would run off the rails?

Half an hour later, full of chupattis and dal, he started towards the rear. A heavy retching from somewhere close by made him halt. Hanuman said, 'There he is, lord . . . In the ditch. A *gora*.'

Krishna stooped and saw, under the blackthorn blossoms, a pair of ammunition boots, the nails bright and shiny. They were turning this way and that as the English soldier, lying on his back, tried to vomit. His open tunic was thick with greeny slime and his face was the same colour. He pulled feebly at his throat as he retched and retched, and the boots jerked and drummed under the white flowers, and a blackbird flew trilling down the hedge.

Krishna Ram felt a heaving sickness in his own stomach. This was the poisonous gas. Either the man had lost his gas mask, or it had not worked. He stopped, made to hold the man in his arms, then recoiled from the filth drenching his chest and belly—then again stooped, and took him, and gently lifted him. 'Give him water,' he said to Hanuman.

Hanuman held his waterbottle to the man's lips but he could not drink. Krishna thought he did not even know the bottle was there. His head lolled and still that dreadful, straining retching shook his body and contorted his face, still the sweat ran down the cold skin, and the head jerked and the boots drummed in the dust. Suddenly a mass of green and red slime poured up over Krishna's arms. For a moment the flood continued, spongey and clotted grey-yellow matter, streaked with blood. Then as the soldier coughed, the vomit became dark pure blood. The body in Krishna's arms went limp, the head fell back on to his shoulder.

Krishna Ram stood up, slowly. Here was another soldier, in soiled khaki swaying down the lane, from one side to the other ... Another ... a wagon load full, a horse pulling it, five men sprawled in the back, vomit and dissolved lungs drenching the floor boards, a dead man lying head down over the back, no driver, the horse plodding steadily on. More ... platoons, companies. He thought he was seeing the disdain of Vishnu, all the diseases of earth, worse than the cholera he had seen once by the river at Basohli, the year of the great Fair. This was not war, but pestilence, in the mind of man. This was Europe, the work of Europe's gods, the pride of its civilization!

Warren Bateman was at his side, muttering, 'My God, the men mustn't see this. Flaherty!'

'Sir?'

'Get our empty GS wagons here at the trot, load these men—the ones who can't walk—on to them and evacuate them to the CCS ... past our rear line, anyway. Then the wagons are to return to rear HQ.'

'Yes, sir.'

The trail of gassed men kept passing. 'Manchesters,' Warren muttered; 'Gunners. HLI. Sappers. Rifle Brigade. KOSB. Seaforths ... They must have wiped out a division ... Here, corporal, were you wearing your masks when the gas came?'

The stocky corporal coughed and moaned: 'Yes, sir. They helped some of us. But ... on a hot day ... like this ... can't keep them wet enough...' He tramped on.

Krishna Ram felt the ground swaying. His eyes blurred and his forehead was as cold and wet as the man's who had coughed out his lungs in his arms. Those lungs, that blood and mucus, were drying on his tunic now. He must wash ... cleanse ... purify. No, he must keep them for ever, as a warning, a message from Vishnu.

Warren Bateman said, 'We'll just have to do our best ... Do you know if the gas affects animals?'

Flaherty's brow wrinkled. 'I don't remember reading anything about that in the intelligence reports, sir ... Were you thinking of the GS wagon horses?'

'No,' Warren said, 'I was thinking of Shikari ... Well, he'll have to take his chances like the rest of us.'

Krishna said, 'Will he make *pashap* on his own mask or will someone have to do it for him?'

Warren Bateman looked at him strangely as he staggered off to the rear. In Krishna's reeling mind he thought he heard the gods laughing, a scornful laugh. He felt himself swaying, and then, when he thought he must fall, Hanuman's strong arm was under his elbow. 'Sit down, lord ... by the ditch here.'

The sun was low, near six o'clock, when Warren Bateman came on the field telephone to Rear HQ. 'Krishna?' the voice was taut.

'Yes, sir?'

'Is any of this enemy shelling falling in the rear areas?'

'No, sir.'

'We're getting a lot. De Marquez has been killed. Very few other casualties so far, though. I think they're going to attack if the wind changes.'

Krishna Ram stared puzzled at the line of the hedgerow on the skyline to the east. 'Why if the wind changes?' he asked.

'Now it's blowing from us to them, or nearly so,' Warren's voice was impatient. 'They release this poisonous gas from cylinders in their front line, so they can only do it when the wind is towards us ... Put out a gas sentry, to keep note of the wind. As soon as it changes—it's veering slowly now—tell the RM to call a stand-to in the rear echelon. When you've done that go to the machine guns. Make sure they have fixed lines arranged and night aiming lights out so that they can fire across our front.'

Krishna gave the handset back to the signaller and sent for the rissaldar-major. While he waited he climbed out of the trench, stretched, and looked around. It was a scene of entrancing beauty, slowly being desecrated by the action of the two sides' artillery, as though two boys with sharp pencils had been let loose on an old oil painting. The even fields were becoming dotted with shell holes. Loads of soil gouged out of the earth and flung all about, were pockmarking the green grass. The late spring foliage was being blasted off the trees. Even the sky, a huge arch of primrose slashed with crimson, was dotted with puffs of dark smoke as German anti-aircraft guns followed an invisible British areoplane down the horizon. The scent of the blackthorn was sweet in his nostrils, and the blackbirds still trilled in the hedges.

Then Rissaldar-Major Baldev Singh came, and five minutes later Krishna set off for the machine gun position. When he had done what he had to do there, he curled up and went to sleep, fully dressed, behind one of the guns.

Rissaldar Ram Lall awakened him at five a.m. A chilly dawn mist hung low over the land, and his skin was wet and cold with dew. The rissaldar said quietly, '*Huzoor*, the wind is in the north-east.'

He started up and felt the slight breeze blowing in his face from the direction of the German lines. He said, 'Stand-to!' and felt for his binoculars. Shells suddenly began to shriek and explode all around. The shelling increased, mostly from 5.9s. The trench was deep and narrow, the machine guns were mounted on a wide fire-step, each protected by a separate traverse. All four guns were in position, ready to fire on their fixed lines, but only one sowar was up as sentry. The rest, as ordered by Warren Bateman, were in dugouts cut into the forward wall of the trench, protected from the shelling but ready to come out when the sentry called them.

Krishna Ram leaned against the parapet with the rissaldar, staring into the east. The morning mist writhed like snakes, like dragons flattened out by some colossal pressure to be wider than they were long, and barely four feet high, with no legs visible. Yet there were eyes to the dragons—eyes everywhere as flashes of bursting shells sparkled in the vapour, then for a moment glowed evil red, then died down, to flash into wakefulness again somewhere else.

The field telephone buzzed and the rissaldar took it. He listened, spoke a few words and put it down. He called up to Krishna Ram, 'It was the colonel-sahib. He said you are to go to D Squadron. He thinks the Germans are attacking there. He can't get through on the telephone to them.'

266

Krishna Ram peered into the noisy fog, loud with the crash of unseen shells and his heart sank. If only there were live dragons out here, serpents of flesh and blood, instead of this impersonal, mechanical death ... D Squadron was in the centre of the line, between Beaumont and the Well, and set back in echelon. He clambered out of the trench, a sowar pulled aside the heavy chevaux-de-frise in the barbed wire to allow him to get through it, and he set off at a jog trot through the bombardment, his orderly and trumpeter on either side.

As he reached D's position several bullets smacked close by and he shouted, 'Don't fire, idiots!' Then Indian faces loomed out of the mist behind the aimed rifles and a jemadar was shouting, 'Stop! It's the Yuvraj!'

He jumped down into the trench and at once felt a stinging sensation in his eyes. For a second he thought someone had thrown pepper at him, then he saw the men around him beginning to cough, and understood. Shouting, 'Gas!' he found his mask, undid his fly buttons, and tried to urinate on it, while holding his breath. Up and down the trench the sowars did the same. The gas cloud was a pale yellow and the fitful wind was breaking it into narrow streamers creeping down upon them mingled in the mist; but the mist was rising as the sun rose, and some of the gas was rising with it, to pass over the top of the trench. But some gas was coming in, and some men were unable to dampen their masks in time. Krishna saw that one man in every five was falling back from the firestep, doubled up, coughing or retching through his mask.

Captain Sher Singh ran down the trench shouting, 'Gas! Gas! ... Rissaldar-sahib where are you?' His voice sounded strangled behind the mask, but his words could be understood. He peered at Krishna Ram, recognized him, and cried, 'Prince, what are we to do? The masks give no protection!'

'Yes, they do!' Krishna Ram shouted, and added in Hindi, 'Stand up, man! Control yourself. For our name!'

'But ... Oh, by the bones of Kali, we are dead men! Here they come!'

Rifle fire spat and crackled along the trench. Krishna looked out, and gasped in horror, a horror as intense as when the British tommy had coughed up his lungs over his arm. The things coming out of the mist were not men but animals, monkey gods of legend, flat-faced demons on two legs ... With trembling hand he sighted

267

along the barrel of his revolver and fired. A monster twenty yards away spun round, his hands to his chest, and fell. They were mortal then! The sowar on his left had fallen or run, and Krishna grabbed his rifle and began rapid fire. More demons towered out of the yellow-streaked fog. One by one and two by two they fell. Only one masked demon reached the trench, to be bayoneted by Hanuman as he leaped down on top of Krishna Ram.

'We are alone, here, lord,' Hanuman said then.

Krishna looked to right and left and saw no one close by, except the dead, some writhing wounded, and a few men vomiting on the parados.

'What happened?' he said.

'Captain Sher Singh said there was no hope, and gave the order each man for himself.'

Krishna swore and said, 'We'd better go, then.'

But should he? What was the point? This horror would pursue him now until it choked him. Better to stay here and die now before it got worse. He began to collect ammunition clips from dead and wounded sowars, cramming them into his own pockets; then he again jumped up on to the firestep. By the ripping crackle of bullets ahead he knew the Ravi machine guns were firing. That meant the Germans were also attacking Beaumont.

But British shells were bursting close, too, and he thought he heard a faint cheering from the rear. Some Germans who had got into the trench farther to the right began to work towards him. He and Hanuman took position behind a traverse and shot each masked man as he came round the corner, until four dead bodies blocked the way. Then a potato-masher bomb came whirling over the parapet, and Krishna caught it and threw it back in one motion. The explosion behind the traverse was followed by a confusion of screams and groans. After a long wait, while Hanuman continued to guard the traverse, Krishna climbed up on to the firestep to see what was happening. He saw Germans close by scrambling out of the trench and hurrying away, to join others already retreating across No Man's Land under a storm of fire; and a line of cheering khaki figures appearing out of the mist from the opposite direction. Coming directly at him he recognized the distinctive shapes of Warren Bateman and Himat Singh, with drawn revolvers, and at their side, Captain Sher Singh. The line of masked sowars stretched away on both sides, all with fixed bayonets gleaming. Krishna Ram stood up waving his rifle, yelling, 'Don't fire!'

Warren recognized him and jumped across the trench to him. Sher Singh leaped down into the trench and stayed there crouched in the bottom. Warren said, 'Get up, Sher Singh. Up here. Stand beside us. There. Don't move an inch or I'll shoot you.' To Krishna he said, 'What happened?'

Krishna told him, as accurately as he could, which was not very. The action, like every other one he had seen so far, had started with a plan as clear as a geometrical drawing, and ended in a meaningless struggle among sweating terrified individuals.

Warren said, 'I thought it was something like that. When D Squadron came back, in a rabble, I told B to retake the trench and came along with them ... God, I wish this bugger Sher Singh here had got a bullet through his head. This is what your softness at that *panchayat* has led to.' He glared at Sher Singh, a yard away and barely able to stand he was trembling so much. 'Mahadeo Singh is reorganizing D in the rear area, and then they'll take over B's old trenches ... Here, let's have a look at this.' He stooped, and took the mask off a German corpse at his feet. 'H'm ... a sort of mask, like ours. They don't seem to have had to piss on them. Probably some chemical inside.'

He put the mask on and peered at Krishna through gauze veiled eyepieces. Krishna restrained an impulse to cry out, 'Don't!' for the mask converted Warren Bateman, too, into a demon, an inhuman monster from legend, an evil monkey feeding on the offal of the civilization it has destroyed.

The CO took off the mask and sniffed the air. 'It's blown away. We can take our masks off, for the time being ... When the Germans first used gas a month ago they must have already worked out how to protect their own men against it. So it's safe to assume that their masks are better than ours. Himat, have these collected off every dead and wounded German in the area. Send them to our machine gunners ... Where's the telephone here, Krishna? Call A and get a situation report.'

Krishna slid down, hurried fifty yards along the trench and found the telephone intact in the old squadron headquarter's position. Soon Puran Lall came on the line.

'The CO wants a report.'

The young officer's voice was hard and impersonal—'They attacked about half an hour ago. The machine guns stopped them on my front.'

'Did they use gas?'

'Yes. But most of it blew over above us. I have three killed and eight wounded, all by shelling.'

'Any German dead within reach of your trenches?'

'About forty.'

'Send men out to get their gas masks. Keep twenty and send the rest back to RHQ for distribution.'

'I won't wear one,' Puran Lall said. 'Have you seen what a man looks like in it?'

'Yes. I understand.'

He hung up. Now the CO would want him to get a similar report from C Squadron at the Well. He told the signaller to get through.

Suddenly the German artillery opened heavy fire again, several field and medium batteries firing what was obviously concentrations, just as they had before the attack. The new gunner subaltern, 2nd Lieutenant Bruington, came up at a run, his signallers unwinding his telephone wire behind him. He tumbled into the trench, saw Krishna and said, 'Looks as if the Hun is going to come again, sir ... Gun positions? 41st Field Battery, DF 43, fire!'

The wind was still veering, and now blew across the line of trenches from south-east to north-west. The Germans would not be able to use gas under these conditions, Krishna thought, unless they carried the cylinders to the south end of the British trenches, even behind them, and released the gas from there.

'My God, look at the CO.' The voice beside him was reverent and proud. It was Captain Himat Singh speaking, the ribbon and silver rosette of the DSO and bar bright on his stained tunic. Shells burst like dry geysers in the friable earth all along the line. The mist had risen and was no more than a haze across the low sun and somewhere, unbelievably, birds were singing. Out in the open, arms linked, Warren Bateman and Sher Singh were strolling along the front of the trench system.

2nd Lieutenant Bruington muttered, 'Good heavens, he'll get himself killed for certain, sir!'

'He has a purpose,' Himat Singh said briefly. Krishna Ram thought, you can't say a word against Warren in front of Himat Singh now.

The strolling figures came closer, Warren's crown and star linked with Sher Singh's three stars. The fox terrier Shikari walked at Warren Bateman's heels, but he was nervous, cowering at the explosions and twice trying to run away into the trenches, to be recalled by Warren's sharp order, 'Heel!' Every few paces they all stopped and Warren looked down into the trench, smiled, and said a few words to the men in it. Machine gun bullets began to clack overhead from a German gun firing at long range from the left.

They came close and Krishna saw that it was only the CO's arm which was holding Sher Singh up. The captain's face was greasy pale under the brown pigmentation, as though all blood had drained out of it, and not even Warren Bateman's strong arm could hide the knocking of his knees.

They stopped above the telephone and Warren said, 'Hullo, what's your name?'

'Bruington, sir.'

'Glad to see you.'

'Thank you, sir ... We've been alloted three medium and three field batteries for DF on your front, sir.'

'Good. And well done, Krishna, we'd have had a hard time retaking this trench without you. *Eh jawan, ab sab thik hai?*' He chattered on in Hindi with a sowar peering over the parapet behind his rifle. Then, as he moved on, rifles began to fire all along the line. 'Here they come again,' Krishna shouted. 'Get down, sir!'

Warren looked round, and pushing Sher Singh in front of him, slid down into the trench. His face was pale and strained, his eyes glaring. Himat Singh, on the firestep a little to the right, said, 'Sir ...' Then he gasped, jerked, and fell backwards into the bottom of the trench three feet below. Warren Bateman bent over him quickly: 'Are you hit, old man?'

'Chest somewhere, sir ... I'll be all right.'

Warren said, 'We'll have you back as soon as we beat off the Hun. Just lie there ... Sher Singh, take command of B Squadron here. You've got another chance. If you fail this time it'll be a court martial on a capital charge. So make up your mind to die bravely here, or disgracefully in front of a firing squad.'

Sher Singh staggered off down the trench, still trembling. Warren Bateman said to Krishna, 'Stay here and see that he holds firm. Shoot him if he doesn't. Make him show himself to the troops. When I can I'm going to A Squadron in Beaumont. I'm sure that's where the heaviest Hun attacks will come. Meantime I'll get a bite to eat.'

He climbed up on the parapet, laid his revolver down on a sandbag beside him and opened his haversack. He began to eat a sandwich, every now and then raising his head to watch the progress of the Germans' attack. Krishna shook himself into realization that he had work to do. It was hard to believe, looking at Warren Bateman, that the Germans were actually attacking this very position. Figures in grey-green, no longer masked, were coming across the fields, disappearing into shell holes, reappearing. Bullets ripped overhead in a continual stream. Himat Singh, lying on the rear step, his cap off, a greatcoat under his head and red-stained field dressing on his bare chest, gaped with glazed worshipping eyes at Warren Bateman on the forward side of the same trench. The sowars stood like supple willows in their positions, not a man looking back, each picking up the clips of ammunition set on the parapet beside him, ramming them into the magazine, working the bolts with an easy flick of the right wrist, aiming, firing, the shoulders jarring to the explosions but the heads steady as boulders set into the earth.

By ten o'clock the second German attack had been beaten back. The CO left, stretcher bearers carried Himat Singh and the other wounded to the rear. Krishna spent an hour with Sher Singh, whose nerves were settling down as the danger receded; also perhaps with the realization that as he had survived the terrible fifteen minutes in the open at the CO's side, nothing worse could happen to him.

The signaller at the telephone said, 'CO for you, sir.'

Warren Bateman's voice was crackling taut. 'We have been given a report that one of our aeroplanes reports enemy massing in front of Beaumont. It looks like another attack. How's Sher Singh doing?'

'All right, sir.'

'G-good. No-now we have A right B-B centre, C left, D in reserve under Mahadeo S-ssingh.' Bateman was stammering, halting over the words. Then, with an effort obvious even at the end of the field telephone line he steadied his voice. 'Any other officer casualties?'

'No, sir.'

'I'm going along the line and then back to D, where I'll stay.

You come here to A. As soon as it's dark we must start linking the squadron trench systems.'

'Yes, sir.'

Krishna began to collect himself. There was his pack, with his two days reserve rations, on the back step beside the signaller. There was the rifle he'd taken from the dead sowar. It was a much better weapon than a revolver, and also made him less conspicuous as an officer. He'd keep it. He wondered whether Warren would approve. According to his code, an officer ought to make himself conspicuous, so that the men could always see he was there, and unafraid. But this war, that turned men into monkeys and horses into automobiles, was forcing new rules ... not good ones. He slung the rifle on his shoulder and signalled to Hanuman and his trumpeter to follow him.

It had turned into a gusty day and he realized almost as soon as he left the shelter of B Squadron's trenches and started across the pitted fields behind the tattered hedgerows that the wind had backed into the north-east. He felt for his mask, made sure it was in his haversack, and hastened his pace to a fast walk. Beaumont, the steeple sharp against the sky, was a quarter of a mile to his right front. There were no troops covering the gaps between the squadrons, only scattered aprons of barbed wire and fire from the machine guns by the Well on the left, behind C Squadron.

Shelling began to fall heavily on Beaumont and for a moment he quailed, stopping to watch. He had to go into that ... that holocaust of flying bricks and crumbling mortar and shattering trees. The steeple of Beaumont Church lost part of one side even as he watched. He forced his legs to run. Suddenly he was in the middle of an immense, impersonal clatter. Hanuman was down, bowled over at full run like a hare, but sitting up. The trumpeter was going down, his knees sagging, his turban off, a round blue hole in the centre of his forehead. A yellow cloud came down on the wind, creeping along the earth out of the eye of the storm of bullets. Krishna threw himself flat. He had run into machine gun and rifle fire at close range. Beaumont was still there to the right. This was coming from directly in front, from Germans outflanking Beaumont. The bullets still whistled and clacked low all around, dollops of earth flew, dust kicked into his eyes. If they kept firing it was only a question of time before they got him. He pushed his rifle forward, searched the ground in front, thought he

273

saw a helmet gleam, took aim, and fired. Then he began to choke. His head swam. He dropped the rifle, fumbled for the mask, found it, and held it over his mouth and nostrils. The pad was dry. His eyes smarted, and he could see nothing. He could breathe, just, but his eyes ... He lay face down, pressing desperately closer to the breasts of earth.

A voice above him cried, '*Raus!* ... *Himmel, es ist ein Major!*' A hand grabbed him and cried, '*Auf, auf!* ... *Laufen!*'

Someone had taken his revolver from its holster. The rifle was gone. They were pushing and pulling him along at a stumbling trot, the voices now guttural, now sibilant in his ear. He could see a few blurred yards when he opened his eyes, but it hurt so much that he shut them again.

Only one man was with him now, something hard occasionally pressed into his side, muttering fiercely but unintelligibly. The stumbling passage did not go on long. After a time among bursting shells and a time under machine gun fire passing overhead, the man cried, '*Still gestanden!*' An arm held him still. Another voice spoke in German, the first answered, then the new voice said in excellent English, 'You are a prisoner. What is your name and regiment?'

'Major Krishna Ram,' he got out before an attack of retching overcame him.

'It will go soon, unless you had a big dose.' Then there were words in German and a soft wet cloth was carefully wiped across Krishna's eyes.

The voice said, 'Ravi Lancers, I see. We were told that is a second-line regiment, not regulars. But you have been fighting very well. Allow me to congratulate you ... Now if you will just rest there, I will evacuate you to the rear as soon as I can spare an escort ... and as soon as the British stop shelling our support line. Our trenches here are very simple, or do not exist at all, because of the rapidity of our advance.'

Krishna staggered off, and vomited. Then he sat with his back to a wall, and waited. His eyes gradually cleared but he still had a pain every time he breathed. The sun climbed past the zenith and began to sink. German soldiers brought him water and food and he began to take an interest in them and what he was experiencing. The Germans looked and smelled like British troops, and the French people he had seen in the villages ... mostly a little more

274

blue of eye, but not enough to counteract the effect of the similarities
—the way they moved, ate, handled their weapons, stood or
crouched together to talk. It seemed to be the headquarters of an
infantry company that he had been brought to. The commander's
name, a soldier told him, was Hauptmann von Gerhard. The hauptmann was tall, not very good looking, with a wide intelligent forehead and a ready smile for his men, though he was obviously
very tired and had been wounded in his left hand.

Near two in the afternoon he came to Krishna and said, 'I regret to say our attack failed again. It was your machine guns that
did it, even though I saw the clouds of gas go right into their
position ... I do not know how they survived to fire their guns,
but they did.'

Krishna thought, Warren's union with the gods of this war was
very close; the German masks had got to their destination just in
time.

The hauptmann said, 'We are going to retreat at dusk, as this
position is dangerously isolated. The British could easily cut us off
if they attacked quickly ... but they will not.'

'How do you know?' Krishna asked.

The hauptmann sat down beside him, fitted a cigarette into a
long silver holder, and offered Krishna another. He shook his head
with a murmured, 'No, thanks.'

The hauptmann said, 'Because when the British propose to attack, they start with a barrage of one, six, or more hours' duration.
That enables us to know what is coming and make the necessary
preparations. Then the heavies lift to the rear and the communication trenches and the fire on our front is only from 13- or 18-
pounders and 4.5 inch howitzers, which as you know are useless
against entrenched troops. So, then our men get up on the firestep
once more, with their machine guns, and when the field artillery
fire lifts, we know we shall see the infantry advancing in straight
lines—admirably straight lines—with bayonets fixed, and rifles like
this.' He imitated the position.

'The high port,' Krishna said. What the hauptmann said was
quite true. That was war, British style.

The hauptmann said, 'I don't understand why you are fighting
for the English. What cause do you have to love them?'

Krishna suppressed another pang of queasiness and said, 'The
king is Emperor of India.'

'You want to support him in that role? Perpetuate the yoke?'

'It will be either his ... or yours,' Krishna said.

The hauptmann shrugged. 'That is true. So why lose thousands of your best men to change from one yoke to another? And ours might be lighter ... This is a European war, major. We Germans are fighting because we are surrounded by enemies. The French mean to destroy us utterly, in revenge for our victory in 1870. They have been planning this war ever since. Waiting for *La Revanche*, as they call it. England is jealous because Germany has surpassed her in industrial power and population. So, when we asked for just a little strength at sea, they made up their minds to strangle us ... But we shall win, major! Whatever it costs, for we have our heritage to protect. We shall spill every last drop of our blood if necessary.'

Krishna said, 'Then what will be left?'

'Germany,' the hauptmann said with a little impatient bark. 'Deutschland! Our culture ... but you are a Hindu, how can you understand? That is why I repeat, this is not your war. Europe is not your country. Our gods ...'

'The gods you share with the French and British,' Krishna said.

'... are not your gods. Go home, major. You should have stayed there. You and all your men. But it is too late now—for you, at least. Now if you'll excuse me, I must write some messages.'

The hauptmann turned away with a salute and a click of his jack-booted heels. Krishna Ram noticed that he wore a sword hanging from a wide belt outside his grey frock coat. The number on the front of his cloth-covered spiked helmet was '143'. Then he heard a shot and a cry in German from close to his right. The hauptmann swung round, his hand dropping to the automatic in its holster at his right side. A storm of firing swept up from behind the wall. The hauptmann's Mauser jerked out of his hand as a bullet hit it. He drew his sword and ran forward shouting, *'Mit mir! Vorwärts!'*

Then Rissaldar-Major Baldev Singh dropped over the wall almost on to Krishna Ram's feet and ran at the hauptmann with his sabre raised. He feinted once, parried the hauptmann's blow with the heavy blade and then leaped in, the sabre whistling. The hauptmann's head sprang off and fell to the ground ten feet back, to roll away under the apple blossom. More sowars were coming over the wall, firing rifles from the hip as they came. Krishna recognized the two men who had originally been his bodyguards, and a dafadar from A Squadron, and a sowar who had been his orderly before Hanuman. All wore, tied round their right wrists, the tied kerchief announcing a man committed to marriage or death ... marriage to death.

The bodyguards, huge men, were raising him with murmurs: 'Lord! Prince! Are you all right?' One lifted him over the wall, the other caught him. Then they started back, the three of them, back towards Beaumont's crumpled steeple.

'Stop!' Krishna cried. 'Wait for the rissaldar-major-sahib, and the others.'

'They will return when you are safe,' the bodyguards said, 'not before.' Shells began to shriek overhead to burst on the German position where he had just been. He turned, in spite of the tugging of the bodyguards, and watched, kneeling by a shell-shattered pear tree, its broken branches in full bloom. Men were running out of the smoke of the orchard which had been the hauptmann's headquarters. He saw the rissaldar-major, his sabre waving, men to right and left of him...

'Twelve ... thirteen,' the bodyguards counted. 'We have lost only four.'

'To rescue me?' Krishna said. 'It was wrong.'

'It was our honour, lord!' one of the bodyguards said. 'The colonel-sahib wanted to give us artillery preparation but the rissaldar-major-sahib said it was better that we should just go, in the old way, for we were all committed to take death as a bride if we did not bring you back.' He touched the handkerchief.

'Volunteers, all?' Krishna Ram asked. He was up again, walking the last few feet to the front line trench outside Beaumont. He could see Puran Lall kneeling on the parapet, beckoning him to hurry.

'No,' the bodyguard said. 'The rissaldar-major-sahib said we were all shamed until you were recovered. He named who would have the honour of wearing the yellow cord ... for of course, lord, as you know, that is what we should be wearing, but there are none except what the quartermaster has, far to the rear, so we wore these handkerchiefs instead.'

Krishna Ram dropped wearily into the trench. The rissaldar-major followed, knelt at his feet, and said, 'Prince, forgive us...'

'For what?'

'That we permitted the Son of the Sun to fall into the hands of the enemy.'

'Of course ... Thank you, sahib. Thank everyone, from me.'

He began to retch again and sank back against the trench wall. From an immense distance he heard Puran Lall saying, 'Yes, sir ... They got him. Safe. No, sir ... But I think he's been gassed ... I'll send him back with the bodyguards and a stretcher crew. He shouldn't walk. He looks very ill...'

He slipped slowly into cold, pain, and darkness.

June 1915

KRISHNA RAM BEGAN again on his run, flung up his left arm, and bowled. The batsman came a step out of his crease and killed it neatly. He tapped the ball back up the net. Richardson, at Krishna's side, growled, 'Keep a length, now, that's all—just keep a length.'

Krishna stepped off his run. That last ball had been about three inches over length. If *he* had been at the crease he'd have taken an extra half step down the pitch and driven it straight. Still, it was wonderful to be playing cricket again, the smell of linseed oil heavy on the summer air ... and at the Oval, after Lord's the most famous cricket ground in the world.

He bowled again, exactly of a length. 'That's reet,' Richardson muttered, and to the batsman, 'Get tha' head reet over t' ball, lad!'

Krishna walked back, ball in hand. Glancing up, he could see his room in the little convalescent home. From that window, as soon as he came here a month ago, at first sitting, then leaning on the sill, he had watched the daily net practice of the Surrey team. He had recognized the classic style of Jack Hobbs even though the nets were too far away for him to recognize his features: there was only one man in the world who stepped down the pitch with that flowing grace, whose bat flashed as decisively off the front foot as off the back. He had bought a pair of binoculars so that he could watch more closely, and as soon as he was allowed out he had gone to the club house and asked if he could help in any way with the practice. Now, after three weeks of throwing at the slip cradle, picking up balls at the back of the nets, hitting balls to the deep for fielders, or throwing them back for bowlers in the nets, occasionally donning pads and gloves and keeping wicket for a

279

bowler being tutored by Richardson, he was sometimes being allowed to take a turn at bat himself.

He bowled another couple of overs, then the familiar slight figure with the long sharp nose came out of the pavilion and walked over to the nets. He stood a while, his hands in the pockets of his blazer, the Surrey cap set straight on his head. Then he walked up and down behind the nets, now and then throwing a word to the batsmen in them.

Richardson said, 'All reet, sir, that's enough bowling. Put on the pads. I'll send down a few to 'ee.'

Krishna knelt quickly to put on the pads and gloves of the out-coming batsman, ducking his head to hide his embarrassed delight. To be bowled at by Richardson with Jack Hobbs watching! He took middle and leg, adjusted his batting gloves, and faced the bowler.

Richardson was still the fastest man in England when he chose, but he started off bowling a little over half pace, the length immaculate. Krishna took five balls dead centre on his bat, leaning far over to smother the bounce. The sixth, the same speed, came six inches long, and he took a quick half step and drove it scorching the grass past Richardson's foot. From behind he heard a quiet, 'Good shot, sir,' from Hobbs.

Richardson stepped up his pace a good two yards. Krishna blocked three balls, late-cut a rising short one, and was comprehensively yorked by the next. 'Ah, got thee!' Richardson crowed. 'Keep tha' eye on t' ruddy ball, man, *all* the time!'

Krishna thought, I haven't really had enough practice ... well, the only way to overcome that was concentration, absolute and unwavering. He stared at the ball as though it were a bomb about to blow up, and thought of nothing else. Richardson's speed had been a little knot of anxiety in the back of his mind at first. A man could get badly hurt by one of those blinding inswingers, particularly if Richardson got angry and bumped one; but now Krishna forgot the danger, forgot that the greatest batsman in the world was watching from six feet behind him, forgot the window of his room, forgot everything except the ball ... yorkers, flashing outswingers an inch outside his off stump, inviting him to nick them, inswingers whipping at his legs from a perfect length, a couple of balls that stood up and begged, two bumpers at his head, even a leg-cutter bowled with no variation of Richardson's action and only a little off his speed. He was clean bowled once more, and would have been caught once if there had been any fielders, because he had changed his mind at the last moment and snicked one into the slips, as Richardson shouted, 'Going fishing, lad? Hit, or doan't hit, but doan't hang t' ruddy bat out to dry!'

'That's enough,' Richardson said at last, and, as Krishna took off his pads, 'Tha' has some bonny strokes, lad.' He called down the net, 'What do 'ee think, Jack?'

Hobbs said, 'Very good, Tom. Well worth a try.'

Richardson said, 'Like to play for us next Saturday, lad? It's A Surrey XI—not t' County, y'know—against London District?'

'I know. I was going to watch,' Krishna said.

'Well, what about playing? Mr. Wilkinson's t' captain, and Jack's playing.'

Krishna Ram said, 'You mean it? Why, I'd love to ... Oh, I suppose I'll have to ask the doctor, but I am sure he'll let me. I don't know how to thank you.'

He said thank you again, and thank you to Hobbs, picked up his coat and ran back to the convalescent home. So deeply and happily had the cricket absorbed him that it was not until midnight that he remembered he must sooner or later go back to France, and Warren Bateman. Most days that thought never left him for more than a half an hour at a time.

That was a Monday. The next day he had promised to take Diana Bateman out to dinner. She was working in a factory in Woolwich now, and he was to meet her at the factory gate at five o'clock. Woolwich was ten miles away, and he decided to walk, for it was a beautiful day of mid-June, only a few days short of midsummer. He set out at two, wearing uniform with khaki slacks and walking shoes. He bore two gold wound stripes on his sleeve above the embroidered crown, and on his left breast, ahead of the Order of the Sun, the white-purple-white ribbon of the Military Cross, which he had at last been awarded for his part in the Battle of St. Rambert Ridge. He stepped out with a will, swinging his swagger cane, for the sun shone, his lungs did not hurt any more and the specialist had said he could play in the match, though warning him he would feel tired at the end of it, especially if he had to spend a long time in the field. The specialist, a visitor from the London Chest and Lung Hospital, who had treated him while he was there, told him there was some permanent damage to the left lung, but very slight. The rest had healed. Unless he took up mountaineering, or long-distance swimming he should not suffer any more. 'But,' the specialist had ended, wagging a plump forefinger, 'don't get caught in any more gas attacks.'

'I'm afraid that's hardly for me to choose,' Krishna had answered, not smiling. The memory of the gas itself was less terrible to him than the memory of the Germans in their masks and —worst of all—the look of his own people, thus deformed into monkeys.

He realized that a voice was calling, 'Nigger, nigger!' and glanced around, to see three urchins running behind him, darting back and forth and cocking snooks at his back. He was walking down a long row of soot-stained brick houses, offal and dirt in the gutters, women sitting on the steps. The urchins were barefoot, their feet black, their clothes ragged. A workman in corduroy trousers and heavy flannel shirt, walking the same way, turned on the boys. 'Garn, he ain't a nigger. 'Es an Indian. *Thik hai,* mate?'

Krishna Ram said, '*Thik hai.*'

The man stared more closely and said, 'Gawd, a major! ... No, wot they called a Subadar-Major-Sab, eh?'

'No,' Krishna said, 'I am a major. I am from an Indian State —Ravi.'

'Never was there, sir, just seven years in Patna and Bareilly. Gawd, what 'oles.' Then, to the urchins, 'Now cut along, you little bastards. Leave the gent alone.'

He turned down a side alley with a touch of his cap and Krishna walked on. Nigger ... they were only nine or ten years old, of course, but where had they learned such scorn? They were lower class, but that made it worse, in a way. They, who were not masters of anything, but mere instruments of the aristocracy, felt the same scorn for his brown skin. Why not? He himself had thought white was superior, once. In some ways it still was. He remembered his grandfather showing him where a hundred white British soldiers had stormed Basohli Fort in the face of a thousand ... drunk perhaps, debased, brutal, as ignorant as these urchins, but sure of their superiority.

The streets became dirtier, narrower, more full of humanity. The bricks were blackened, windows broken, dirt-stained flowers trying to grow in home-made window boxes, a dead puppy in the

282

gutter, five boys swinging a cat round and round by its tail then hurling it against a wall. He went on, past tall factory gates, walls ten feet high of yellow brick, topped with broken glass, revolving spikes, endless buildings, six storeys high, with grimed window panes, from inside the grind and roar and clack of huge machines. Girls walked towards him their young faces drawn, rings under the eyes, mouths tight, stockings holed, shuffling, shuffling. Soot in his hair, ash under his tongue, the smell of privies in the sunless heat, urine in every corner, dog shit slimy on the pavement under the bare feet of the girls playing hopscotch, wafts of stale beer, like the blast from some dank engine room at every pub, men face down in the gutter, vomit on their clothes, their faces in grey-green pools. He walked faster. Where was escape? It was the gas attack again, but here the poison was everywhere, in the air men breathed, in the sky that covered them, in the water they drank—this noisome silent canal beside him, a dead rat bloated in it, another swimming, another eating something the far side, the water sheened with oil, full of metal refuse, dense with the perpetual rain of soot falling on it from above, foul bubbles breaking the thick surface. He wanted to run, but dared not for fear that all the drawn white faces listlessly watching him would recognize his panic and break away from the walls and windows and corners and come after him, grey rats, snarling, teeth bared...

He reached Diana's factory nearly an hour early and found a grimy bench by the river and sat down. Slowly, as his panic subsided, giving place to a terrible pessimism, he thought that he had been looking into the fundament of the war being waged and to be waged in France and Flanders. There was no romance there, only the desolation of machines fighting machines and grinding man to pieces in the process. Those machines were made in this sulphurous blight—which they had created. Without this, there would be no such war. Without the war, perhaps, this could not exist.

When she came out he was waiting at the tall gates, wondering how working in this place would have changed her. She was wearing her hair done up tight in a dark blue bandanna and looked tired, like those girls he had seen on the nightmare walk, and like them she had dark circles under her eyes. She stopped when she saw him and said, 'Oh, Krishna—you look tired!'

'Me, too?' he exclaimed, then, 'I walked,' knowing that was not the reason for his appearance and expression.

'You shouldn't have,' she said; then, 'See, I've had to give up my hair.' She took off the bandanna and shook her head. Her hair was cut short, not much longer than a boy's.

'The war demands women's hair now?' Krishna said.

She linked her arm in his. 'No, silly. If we don't keep it short it won't fit inside the bandannas, and then it might get caught in the machinery.'

She was guiding him down the street. Her manner had become more familiar since he last saw her in Shrewford Pennel; not that she was anything like the women who had shouted to him from their doorsteps, the blowzy girl hiccuping endearments at him from outside a pub, her skirt half way up her plump, dirty thighs—she was just no longer a parson's daughter from Wiltshire.

'More bloody drunks,' she muttered, dodging a man careening from side to side of the pavement. 'Oh dear, I do apologize. You wouldn't believe the language the other girls use—most of them. I didn't know half the words existed, let alone what they meant.'

He wondered whether she wished she still didn't. This Diana, who had come with her mother to see him in hospital the day after he arrived from France, was not the Shrewford Pennel girl. She was losing not exactly innocence but a country placidity, something rooted in the heavy Wiltshire earth.

'Here we are,' she said. 'I'm ravenous. I hope you are, too, because really, the food's not very good.'

It was the dining-room of an old-fashioned pub on the river front, and as they ate Diana gradually reverted to her old manner, as though slowly sloughing off the influence of the factory. Contrary to what he expected, as she drank sherry and then beer, she became calmer and less talkative. He told her of his selection to play for A Surrey XI, and she cried, 'Oh, how marvellous, Krishna! Can I come and watch, and then we'll catch the late train down, as we were planning to?'

'Of course,' he said, 'I'll get you a good ticket. Do you want to bring anyone with you?'

'Who?' she said. 'I don't have any men friends and I certainly don't think I'd like having one of the factory girls with me when I was watching *you* ... You'll make a century!'

'I doubt it,' he said, smiling at her. Her eyes were warm and for a moment they looked at each other without saying a word. Then she took up her beer and said, 'Look at me drinking beer!

I'd never done that until I came here.'

'You're changing,' he said, and knew that he meant not only her, or Warren Bateman her brother, but all England, all Europe. He wished suddenly that he could talk to Prince Ranjitsinhji and ask him whether he, who had known England well through cricket for twenty years, had noticed any change in the people's character and outlook since the war started.

'Some of the girls rush to a pub as soon as the hooter blows, and have a port and lemon,' Diana said. 'Can you imagine! And others take neat gin. Do you know what they call it? Mothers' Ruin!' She smiled, the shyness of the smile belying the pertness of the words. She said, 'The person who really ought to be seeing you play is Warrie.'

'Yes,' Krishna said cautiously.

'He'd be so proud of you.' Her face clouded. 'I wish he could come back ... for good.'

Krishna said quietly, 'Why?'

'Oh,' she said, her hands knotting together. She looked up at him then down at the table. 'It's Joan.'

'What about her?' he insisted. He thought he knew what she was trying to say and was trying to help her say it.

'She's ... growing away from him,' Diana said.

'I saw that last time I was over,' he said. 'It seems to be caused by the war. They have different ideas about it. Is there anything else?'

'No, no,' she said suddenly breezy. 'Let's not talk about her, but about you. Tell me about the trenches, the battles, about Warrie...'

He sighed. She could not bring herself to share the truth with him. Not yet, at least. He tried to switch to her new mood and after a time began to succeed. The horror of the afternoon's walk faded. It did not leave him. It would never leave him, he knew— but it stepped back and down, into some deep, hidden part of him, where it would always remain, to stain certain emotions, thoughts and ideas with a sense of debasement and squalor. But for now, the immediacy of his fear was gone, and this Englishwoman with her openness, her slow smile, her new and transparent urban veneer, had done it. When he took her to the door of the dingy house where she lodged, she said, 'You're looking much better now, Krishna. Perhaps you hadn't eaten enough for lunch.' She went inside with a wave of her hand. In the train back to Charing Cross, and the bus to the convalescent home, Krishna realized that he was hovering on the edge of falling in love.

Falling in love, he thought, with a shock of surprise. That meant marriage ... making love. And he had contracted a vile disease with a French whore. Was he really cured? It was somehow impossible to associate sex with Diana, and yet whenever lustful thoughts came to him the un-faced female body that he used—he had to admit it openly to himself now—was hers.

Saturday was a grey day of low clouds and a hint of rain in the air. Mr. Wilkinson, the captain, said before they went out to field, 'Keep a sharp eye on the ball today. It'll be easy to lose it against the gas works or the crowd.' The ground was almost full, but Krishna felt no nervousness as he walked out with the rest of the side, only pride that he was playing cricket at the Oval. How proud Mr. Fleming would be of him now, if he could see him; and Diana was there, watching. The match had two faces, obverse and reverse of the same medal. On one side were the white flannels, the red ball, the golden-varnished stumps, the shaved turf, the easy gait of the famous professionals, the umpires in their long white smocks, like the ritual robes of Brahmins; and on the other the gas works hunched in appalling ugliness over the ground, the close-packed crowd, smoke rising from a thousand chimneys all round; but the latter was necessary to pay for the former.

The London Military District side contained several names he recognized from his study of Wisden. 'Put in cushy jobs back 'ome to keep 'em from being sent to France,' one wizened old pro muttered as he read the other side's batting order. They played well and declared two hours after lunch with a score of 208 for 6. Krishna took one easy catch at mid-on, but did not bowl. Back in the pavilion the Surrey captain said, 'We can make it if we don't try to hurry. There are nearly four hours of play left. Any special things we should look for, Hobbs?'

Hobbs said, 'Just watch that Kendrick, sir. He's a foot quicker off the pitch than he looks to be.' Then he and Sandham went out to open the innings, as they had done a hundred times before for Surrey; but now, in the batting order below them were only two or three names that anyone had ever heard of, the rest in Flanders, above or below ground, or in warships on or under the North Sea.

It wasn't Kendrick who got Hobbs, but an unknown club player who bowled him an unintentional yorker before he'd got his eye in, and the scorers had to put down one of the very few Os ever to follow Hobbs's name on a score sheet. Kendrick then bowled two men in quick succession, and a little later had another caught in the slips. Four for 37 when Krishna went in to bat, a very different kettle of fish from 209 to make and all wickets in hand. And, as the last man out muttered with an oath, the pitch was crumbling at the gasworks end. Hobbs touched Krishna's arm as he went out and said, 'Concentrate, sir ... concentrate, and you'll do all right.'

He walked out on to the green turf, his bat under his arm. Diana was sitting there near the steps. He knew that if he didn't see her now he would be thinking of her when he was at the crease, and that would ruin his concentration. He searched for her in the crowd as he walked down, and at last she shyly waved her gloved hand. He smiled at her, touching his free hand to the peak of his yellow and white Ravi cap.

He took guard and faced the last two balls of Kendrick's over. The second lifted viciously and for a fraction of a second, the vital one, he lost sight of it. It struck him hard on the ribs and the bowler was already spinning round shrieking 'Huzzat?' But the umpire turned his head away with a look of immense disdain, and Krishna had survived.

He watched the old professional, Nash, stonewall an over from a cunning slow left-hander at the other end, then again faced Kendrick. Kendrick bowled exactly the same ball that had hit Krishna last time, but now he was sunk in the utter concentration he had known at the nets, and with the same sense that Hobbs was watching not his play, but looking inside his head, gauging his concentration. The ball floated up seeming as big as a football, but slower. He hooked it over the square leg boundary for 6. For a moment he heard the clapping before his concentration again closed in, this time never to relax, so that he heard nothing, saw nothing, felt nothing, but the ball. He straight drove the next three in succession for 4 each then ran a sharp single past cover. When he faced the slow bowler he scored 19 off him in an over, and the man was taken off. Kendrick again, by now getting angry and trying to bump him. Twice he cut him for 4, and once, down on one knee, swept him over the leg boundary for 6. Then, seeing that

Kendrick was recovering his guile in proportion as he was losing the aggressiveness of the attacking fast bowler, and realizing that the time for shock action was over, Krishna batted very carefully, scoring only 21 runs in an hour. By then the back of the bowling was broken, and though the pitch was rapidly deteriorating—so rapidly that three wickets were lost by easy catches to balls that stood up in the air—the Surrey XI had no difficulty in passing the 208 half an hour before stumps were due to be drawn, Krishna walking back with 103 not out on the big board against his number. The pavilion rose to him as he came in, an unknown young pro at his side. He raised his cap silently, again looking for Diana. She was there, clapping like a madwoman, then holding her hands pressed to her chest, gazing at him. He went inside the pavilion, her worshipping face a vision steady before his eyes.

While he was in the dressing room a messenger came to him. The Secretary of the Surrey County Cricket Club would like to speak to him in his office, if he could spare a moment.

The Secretary was a sharp-nosed accountant-looking sort of man, about fifty years of age. 'Sit down, Mr. Ram,' he said genially. 'That was a remarkable innings you played ... quite remarkable! Jack Hobbs had told me before that you were capable of it, but I must say ... Well, I wondered if we could have a little talk about your future.'

Krishna looked at his watch. 'Certainly, sir. But I have a friend waiting.'

'I won't be long ... You are from ... what part of India, if I may ask?'

'Ravi State,' Krishna said, 'it's in the north of the Punjab.'

'Quite. I fear I do not know as much as I should about the geography of our great Indian Empire. You are currently with a regiment in France, I am told.'

'Yes. On convalescent leave. I was gassed.'

'How dreadful! Though you appear to have made a remarkable recovery ... Do you know Prince Ranjitsinhji?'

'Not personally, although he is distantly related to my family.'

'Really? Indeed?' The little man's sharp nose quivered and he took off his pince-nez. 'Does that mean that you are a prince, too?'

Krishna said, 'Yes, of a sort. My grandfather is the rajah. I suppose I shall inherit in due course, if I am not killed first.'

'That would be appalling,' the little man said energetically, 'a needless waste, your highness, when there are so many others the world can well afford to lose ... This merely doubles the force of what I was going to propose to you. I spoke to Mr. Wilkinson and our senior professionals while you were batting. They all agreed that you should be asked to turn out regularly for the county side. We are not playing a full schedule of course because of this wretched war, but there are enough matches and charity games to keep the players' eyes in for when the war is over and we can get back to real cricket. Will you accept?'

'I can't think of anything I'd like more,' Krishna said slowly. 'It's been my dream, my ambition all my life. Of course I used to imagine myself playing for Sussex ... like Ranjit ... but I'm going down to Wiltshire now to finish my convalescence, and then I have to go...'

'But you have done your bit!' Mr. Holmes said eagerly. 'Already wounded and gassed! We are in a position, through our contacts in the government—I may say that a member of our committee is in the Cabinet—to give you a posting here in England—in London District, in fact—which would enable you to play cricket nearly every day. Indeed, playing cricket would be part of your duties.'

Krishna looked out of the window. The great sweep of turf was empty except for the heavy roller going over the centre pitch, the horses plodding on padded hoofs, and a band of men clearing paper off the benches. A strong smell of coal gas wafted through the window from the gasworks. He said, 'It is my grandfather's regiment that I am serving with. How can I leave it?'

Mr. Holmes cried, 'He would not want his grandson and heir to die in a muddy French ditch, when he could be gracing the playing fields of England ... And you would have a considerable effect on our club's finances, your highness. We need money to attract the best young professional prospects, and we'd like to pay a little more to those we already have. We want to put in some improvements here at the Oval, and we are starting a scouting scheme to find good players around the county ... Your name, Prince Krishna Ram, would draw the crowds. That's my business...'

Krishna Ram thought sadly, the smell of poisonous gas, coal gas, is drifting across the striped turf, and a layer of soot is steadily falling on it. It was going on when he was out there, soiling the white flannels and the peaked caps and the sunburned forearms and the graceful bats, overlaying the smell of linseed oil with a layer of chemical filth, even as this sharp-nosed little man was burying the beauty of the game under commercial pollution. In that moment he knew that even cricket, his first and greatest love, would never be the same for him again. Damn them all! What was going to be left to live with, and live for?

He rose to his feet. 'I appreciate your offer,' he said. 'I must go back to France.'

He had started to say it was his duty, but the word sounded pompous, and indeed was false, for what was sending him back to France was not duty but something more complex, which he could not yet properly define or explain to himself, except that it was to do with Warren Bateman.

'After the war, then?' Mr. Holmes said, coming round the desk.

'I shall be returning to India,' Krishna said.

Mr. Holmes dropped his hand in despair. 'Well, your highness, may I please have your promise that you won't sign up with any other county, then?'

Krishna Ram said, 'Yes, I'll give you that. Good-bye.'

Diana was waiting at the pavilion exit when he came out, carrying his suitcase. Some men at a pub across the road were catcalling and whistling at her. He frowned at them, but she came running to him, her eyes shining. 'Oh, Krishna, I'm so proud of you! After Jack Hobbs making a duck, too! Here, let me help you carry that suitcase. It looks as though it weighs a ton.'

'It does,' he said, 'but I'm fit again. I can carry it.' But she had grabbed the handle, her hand behind his, and so they went down the Kennington Road together until Krishna saw a motor taxi-cab approaching and hailed it. 'It'll be terribly expensive, all the way to Paddington,' Diana said. 'I thought we were going to the tube station.'

He smiled at her almost masterfully. 'I've had nothing else to spend my money on while I've been in France. We could take a taxi all the way to Shrewford Pennel if we wanted to.'

'Oh, no!' she said.

Then they were in the high cab and the driver was turning it skilfully in the street and they were off. The clouds had lifted and the sky was a dusty grey damask, alive with swallows and martins swooping about the silhouetted chimney pots, and golden points of light piercing the twilight to unimaginable depths. The growing dusk hid the squalor of the streets and lights made the river a luminescent carpet under Westminster Bridge. The trees were heavy in the parks, and the people walking under them pale smudges of movement on the new-cut sweet-smelling grass.

For a time the presence of London, as Krishna had first sensed it in September '14, came back to him, and behind it the bearing strength of England, the ancientness of her foundations—the Abbey towers a darker bulk against the sky—then the walk to Woolwich slithered up from its deep resting place, and the smells of gas and vomit overcame him. The awe subsided. This was a foreign city, of which he knew much—perhaps too much; and this a foreign land, which had forced its tongue on him; off a foreign continent, its monuments not his, its gods no more ancient, only different, and now showing themselves to be disgusting and dangerous.

It was the woman at his side who awed him now, in the taxi, in the clamour of Paddington. They were early, and having taken their places, strolled up the platform. The green and copper engine hissed at the head of the immaculate train and signal lights gleamed like red stars on the road bridge at the end of the platforms. There was a mixed smell of steam, coal smoke and burning anthracite, but it was not unpleasant. She linked her arm again in his, unbidden, and he caught a few curious stares, but he did not care. Let them stare. His thoughts were beyond their ken, for they were not Indians. Then they took their places, full darkness fell, and with a long whistle the train glided out through the lamplit slums towards the country.

Sunday morning, the bells ringing for church, and the Bateman women pulling on their gloves in the hall. 'I don't know why I go,' Joan Bateman said. 'Not many people in this country are behaving in a Christian manner ... and certainly none of the parishioners here.'

'Now, Joan,' old Mrs. Bateman said equably, 'while you're in this house, you'll go to church, like the rest of us. It would be very impolite to Mr. Wyatt if we didn't.'

'Oh, Mother,' Joan said impatiently, 'politeness doesn't matter compared with honesty.'

'One can be too honest for one's own good,' Mrs. Bateman said. She looked at Krishna, who opened the door, and offered her his arm. From behind them Joan, her arm on Ralph Harris's, said, 'And charity is another thing that's missing here. You wait till the trial tomorrow and see how much charity there'll be for Sam, on account of six miserable pheasants. Six! It isn't charity that'll help him, but the lawyer I've got from London.'

Diana said plaintively, 'Please don't let's talk about it any more, Joan. You'll spoil Krishna's holiday.'

Then they were in the church, and the sexton was tolling the sharp hurry-up bells, and the service began. In London it had been the chemical filth and the terrifying power of the machines that came between Krishna and an acceptance of so much that was beautiful and good in Europe. Here it was the contrast between what the Christian church taught and what Christians did. The church believed in poverty—but many here were far from poor, certainly the vicar with his fat smooth face; and it believed in charity—but as Joan said, who was being charitable towards Young Marsh? And it taught 'Thou shalt not kill'—but the parson was preaching a sermon of hate against the Huns, as the despoilers of Christianity. What he said was not true, Krishna thought, listening: it was not the Germans who were destroying Christianity, but Christendom bent on destroying itself, and with the very qualities that had made it what it was and sent it out to dominate the world.

After lunch Diana said, 'Can I walk the puppies for you today, Joan?'

'Yes, please,' Joan said moodily. 'I'm going to give them back to the Master soon. Not a soul in the hunt has a spark of generosity in him. Why should I help them with hounds?'

Diana said, 'Come on, Krishna, a good walk will do us good.' She collected the three gangling fox-hound puppies from the stables, took a whip, and set off down the lane towards the north. 'Last season's puppies have to be walked every day, to get them fit, and they have to be taught to obey the voice and the whip—the sound of it,' she said. 'You never actually hit them except to whip them off the kill or a false scent or if they chase a cat or something awful like that.' She cracked the whip over the puppies' heads with a bloodcurdling shriek, 'Coo-o-me back there, Hector, Ajax! Coooome back! ... There are usually about six couple of new hounds to be walked every summer. We agreed to walk one and a half couple for the dog pack, and then I went to work in Woolwich. I felt dreadful, asking Joan to walk them for me, and now she doesn't want to. Oh dear.'

She strode on, her grey skirt a clear foot above her ankles, her short hair free in the unmoving air. Cows dozed somnolently under the oaks in the big fields, bees hummed and butterflies flitted among the flower banks. Along the banks of the Avon the pups barked at trout clear in the water and Diana cracked her whip and called them fool and idiot. The tower of Woodborough church fell back on their left and they began the gentle climb to the Canal. Then they strode out along the towpath towards Wilcot, the vale of Pewsey spread like a chequerboard below. A long train, green and copper, chocolate and cream, drew a plume of white steam down the vale as it raced through oak copses and elm rows, past long barns and the gleam of ponds. On the far hill a white horse, cut into the chalk by a Saxon king 800 years before, stood out like a prehistoric talisman against the bare green of the slope.

In the distance, down a long stretch of the grass-grown towpath, a walker approached. He was swinging a cane, a man walking alone, without a dog. When still a quarter of a mile away it seemed to Krishna that he hesitated and looked to right and left for a way to escape; but the canal ran here on an embankment and there was a thick hedge at the foot of the steep slope.

Krishna thought, the man's walk is familiar, I have seen him before. Then Diana cracked her whip and shouted, 'Coooome back, Apollo! Heel, heel!' as the hounds bounded forward to meet the oncoming walker, and Krishna recognized him. His heart too leaped and, like the hounds, he bounded forward, wondering for a moment whether the whip would crack over him, too. As the big puppies bayed, he cried, 'Mr. Fleming!'

Diana said, 'Down, Ajax! ... It's Mr. Fuller.'

Krishna said, 'It's Mr. Fleming ... How are you, sir?' His hand was out, the other had taken it, and Krishna pumped eagerly. This was his old tutor, there was no mistaking the sandy hair, long thin face, pale eyes and full lips, the look at once bookish and athletic. It was ten years since he had left Basohli and so he must be about forty-five now. He looked a little older.

'It is Mr. Fuller, isn't it?' Diana said.

'Yes, Miss Bateman,' the man said. He hesitated and then said to Krishna, 'And Mr. Fleming, too. But I suggest you forget that ... that you ever knew me.'

'How can I forget?' Krishna cried. 'You taught me everything I know about England ... manners ... cricket ...'

'Today's *Observer* has quite a long account of your innings yes-

293

terday,' Mr. Fleming said with a half-smile. 'Congratulations.'

'Thank you, sir ... I had no idea you lived near here. You must come to the Old Vicarage, and...'

The other man said, 'I don't think that would be welcomed.'

'Then I will come and see you. There is so much to talk about. My father died ... my mother and I were so worried when you didn't write.'

The man said again, supplicating, 'Krishna, I beg of you, forget that I ever existed.'

'I can't,' he said, realizing that Diana had taken herself a little way off under pretence of controlling the hounds. 'I'm staying a week more, then I have to go back to France.'

'I know,' the man said. 'And I watched you play for the village last summer ... from a long way off.'

'When can I come and see you?'

The man hesitated a long time, then said, 'I suppose it'll be best ... Will tea on Wednesday do? My cottage is off the Pewsey road, two doors past the post office. It's called Hill Cottage and it has begonias growing in the front garden. Four o'clock then. Goodbye, Miss Bateman.' He replaced the tweed cap, which he had taken off when Diana first spoke his name, and strode quickly away along the towpath.

Krishna and Diana walked on in the opposite direction. 'What an extraordinary thing,' Krishna said slowly, 'he was my tutor for five years in Basohli, and his name was Fleming.'

'He calls himself Fuller here,' Diana said, and then, 'They say he's a ... pansy, the girls at the factory call them.' She was blushing. 'He was in everything here—shooting, cricket, carol singing—until something happened, something to do with a boy on holiday from Eton. I don't know how serious it was, but...'

Krishna remembered the talk at the cricket match in September. And Warren Bateman telling him one afternoon—they'd been discussing Sher Singh—that he'd met the man Fuller in the lane on his leave and snubbed him. Fuller was his dear Mr. Fleming. He realized now, knowing what he knew and having seen what he had seen, that he accepted without question that Mr. Fleming was a homosexual. Perhaps he had always guessed it although he had made no sexual advance during his five years as Krishna's tutor.

But this man *was* his Mr. Fleming. He had not become a drunkard, taken to dope, or changed in some other way. He was the same man he had always been. This village—and people like Warren—were rejecting him because of his suspected homosexuality. This in the name of charity? How differently they, Indians, had dealt with Sher Singh!

The puppies bounded on and Diana cracked her whip and shouted. She was getting a little hoarse, he noted. She at any rate was real, and generous.

The train steamed away, Londonward, the barrister leaning out and waving. Diana said briskly, 'Well, there's nothing more we can do. If we hurry we won't keep Mother waiting long for lunch.'

She took the driver's seat of the trap, with Krishna beside her and Ralph Harris and Joan Bateman in the back. She shook the whip and cried, 'Hup, Mr. Harcourt!' They trotted down the station approach and set off on the drive to Shrewford Pennel.

No one spoke for a while, until Ralph said bitterly, 'There's English justice for you today! Those magistrates had no right to make that offer they made Sam.'

'It's quite common, nowadays,' Diana said defensively. 'After all, men are wanted in France.'

Joan said, 'Yes, but to offer a man—a self-confessed pacifist—the choice of three months in jail or volunteering for the army, is a disgrace. For Sam it isn't a choice at all. It's like fining him a hundred pounds or sending him to jail. He doesn't have a hundred pounds.' Her scarf flew out in the breeze. Her face was made up white with pale mauve lips and huge kohl-ringed eyes. Her long skirt was of yellow and mauve silk, and both her arms were covered in bangles and hanging charms.

'What do you think, Krishna?' she said suddenly. 'Would you allow a thing like that in India?'

'Not exactly the same,' he said cautiously, turning round to speak to her. He reflected that his grandfather might have ordered Young Marsh's hand cut off, or set him free, but he wouldn't have made it a choice; and pacifists were not going to make good soldiers.

Diana said, 'Poaching has got to be punished. Especially taking birds out of season.'

Ralph said, 'I don't agree. As Sam said in court, the rich have no right to preserve wild birds for their own use. He only poached ... took ... those six birds to give to the poor in London.'

'Someone must have betrayed him,' Diana said thoughtfully. 'The policeman arriving and knowing where to look was too much for a coincidence.'

'It was his father,' Ralph said. 'Old Marsh. Old Marsh would do anything for Sir Tristram.'

'Well, the Pennels have employed him for over sixty years,' Diana said.

'That doesn't matter any more,' Joan said. 'There are more important things than loyalty to feudal overlords ... Can't you see? Can't you feel? The wrongness was always there, but what's happening in France is making everyone see it.'

'I wish the war was over,' Diana said, glancing at Krishna.

'I used to pray for that,' Joan said, 'when I thought of my father. Harry. Tim. Young Tristram Pennel. Dick Sturgess. Jim Hall. Tommy Cutler. People I'd grown up with ... Now, I don't. I want the war to go on until it destroys everything we've believed in. Then we can start again.'

There was a long silence. The horse's hoofs clopped on. A light summer shower drifted over, cloud shadows momentarily dark above the white horse carved on the hill. Diana said, 'I'm glad we were allowed to give notice of appeal, and keep Young Marsh out on bail ... but where's the money coming from? Mr. Woodhouse must be very expensive.'

'Mother said she'd pay as much as she could,' Ralph said shortly. 'I told Mr. Woodhouse and he agreed to mark his brief accordingly.'

'For Mother's sake,' Diana said pointedly.

'Yes,' Ralph said. 'Certainly not for mine. Or Sam's. Mr Woodhouse thinks he's a danger to society. I saw it in his face. And a coward...'

'So does Mother, sometimes,' Diana said.

'I know, but Mother ... she's different. She's the only person in the world I care about hurting. Or losing the respect of.'

Like the rissaldar-major, Krishna thought suddenly. There was something very similar about Margaret Bateman and Baldev Singh —serenity, courage, opinions held decidedly but with a tenderness to the opinions of others, firmness with gentleness.

Diana glanced at him again. 'I wish you didn't have to go back to France,' she said.

'So do I,' he said. 'But I must.'

*   *   *

Hill Cottage was small, square and ugly, built of brick about 1880 to house a farm labourer's family in the minimum acceptable conditions. Mr. Fleming greeted him in the tiny parlour into which the front door opened. The tea kettle was on a black range in the back of the room, a silver teapot warming, and a Coalport tea set arranged on a small table. Mr. Fleming seemed to hurry him into the house, with nervous gestures, but once he was inside his manner gradually relaxed. While he poured tea, offered Krishna buttered toast and Gentleman's Relish, he demanded and listened to a stroke by stroke description of Saturday's innings at the Oval. Outside the begonias made splashes of dark green and scarlet behind the lace curtains. Now and then a farm cart plodded down the lane, or they heard the sharp clip-clop of a delivery cart, and once the put-put of a motor car.

At last Mr. Fleming sat back and said, 'I suppose you want to know why I call myself Fuller now.'

'No,' Krishna said quickly. 'I don't. I don't care. You're just the man who was so good to me when I was a boy.'

'Thank you, Krishna ... You were always something quite out of the ordinary. So much sensitivity. You know, Indians don't have as much sensitivity as the world gives them credit for. I mean, they don't necessarily feel *with* another person. It's usually that they can read *what* the other person is feeling quicker than Europeans. Krishna, I ... I ...'

Krishna thought desperately, Oh God, *Parmeshwar, Brahma,* how can I get him out of this? And then he prayed that the tutor would not belie or lessen the truth, but would trust him to have grown up in soul as much as he had grown in body.

Mr. Fleming said, 'I have a compulsion towards the vice for which Oscar Wilde was sent to gaol.'

'If it is a vice,' Krishna said quietly.

The tutor shot him a quick, wondering look. 'Yes ... Only God knows that. *I* know it is a burden, a cross to bear.'

'Only here,' Krishna said.

'Ah, these small villages! I suppose in London, I could disappear ... or no one would care.'

'I meant, in England. In Christendom,' Krishna said. 'Not in India. Afghanistan. Turkey. Arabia.'

'Oh.' The tutor was silent, sipping his tea. 'I am more afraid of women than I am fond of ... men,' he said. 'There is something about women that, when we get close—in spirit, I mean, when they begin to show affection—that is like what hearing a barrage approaching must be to you. I feel I am going to be destroyed.' He laughed, pleased at his little simile.

Krishna Ram said, 'Worse. The barrages will end some day.'

'But not womankind, eh? ... It is not as bad here as you might imagine. The lower classes generally do not bother me one way or another. I get respectful service at the butcher's and baker's. It is only the people of my own class and education...'

'I know,' Krishna said.

The tutor said, 'After leaving Basohli ... with a very generous gift from your grandfather, a *very* generous gift, indeed, I may say ... I obtained an appointment as an assistant master at Uppingham. That lasted four years, and I was very happy until ... I could not control myself. The boy was partly to blame. He was of our persuasion. Still is. Quite a famous actor now ... Then I came here, under a different name. I thought the shock of being dismissed from Uppingham had cured me. It had not. There was an Eton boy, seeming to beg my affection. I was wrong ... Warren Bateman snubbed me brutally, not long ago. I had thought him different from the others.'

'I know,' Krishna said, 'but that's not the real him, sir. He's under a terrible strain. I can't explain ... Mr. Fleming, come back to Basohli. I will pay your fare. I will see that my grandfather employs you—*you*, as you are, not as what some others think you ought to be. You are welcome in India. You know it.'

'I *do* know it!' the tutor cried unhappily. 'I have even thought of writing to you ... but I am not Indian! I am English. I believe in English standards, and try, try, to live up to them. It is these people, these villagers of Wiltshire, gentlemen such as Warren Bateman, ladies such as his mother and Lady Pennel, whom I need the acceptance of. I am of *them*, and cannot live among others, however kind.'

'Please remember what I have said, though,' Krishna said. 'You may change your mind. My address is Ravi Lancers, Field Post Office No. 46, B.E.F.'

He stood up. The tutor stood, his hand out. 'Thank you, Krishna. And I can't tell you how deeply I am moved by seeing you in our uniform, risking your life a score of times a day, for my country, for those things that I think I taught you to value.'

Krishna shook the proffered hand warmly, but his thoughts were grey. Him, too? When it came to the crisis, would Mr. Fleming be on Warren's side, just because they shared the same colour of skin? Or because they had both, with their mother's milk, absorbed the spirit of the West, been cradled in the laps of the West's gods?

Half an hour later he was back at the Old Vicarage, walking up and down the emerald green of the lawn, thinking, thinking, thinking, and finding no exit from the closed wall of his thoughts.

Saturday, a week after the great day at the Oval, was his last full day of leave. In the morning he walked the puppies for an hour, afterwards helped prepare the Old Vicarage display at the flower show. In the afternoon he wandered round the show with Diana, watching old Mrs. Bateman, who was a judge, and drinking in the scents and colours of the flowers and basking for the last time in the peace, however shallow, of the day. Young Marsh, big and strong and curly-haired, was helping Mrs. Bateman, and Ralph Harris was walking with Joan; and many were the knowing looks that Krishna intercepted, sent at their backs as they strolled among the marquees set up on the lawns of Pennel House—the tall willowy shape of Joan arrayed now like Ariadne, her hair down her back held at the nape of the neck with a plain gold clasp, her children dressed in Greek togas—Ralph Harris, as close and carelessly possessive as it might be her husband or acknowledged lover, instead of her husband's bastard half-brother.

The long afternoon wore slowly on and as the sun set in red flame down the vale Krishna bathed and then dressed for the ball at Manningford Bohun. He was going to wear uniform, but after he had put on his khaki shirt and trousers, he stopped. In the suitcase he had a set of the formal dress of his kingdom—white jodhpur trousers, tightly wrinkled from ankle to knee, fuller above that, and a long gold-silk *achkan*, like a frock coat, buttoning to the stand-up collar, cuffs and collar heavily embroidered with silver metal thread. With these there were ornate white and gold slippers, a necklace of worked-gold chain, sapphire studded, and the diamond and ruby star of the Royal Order of the Sun of Ravi. He only hesitated a second before quickly taking off his uniform and dressing again as the Yuvraj of Ravi.

Diana was passing across the hall, a shimmer of white organdie and blue ribbon, as he came down the stairs. She stopped, stared, put her hand to her mouth and gasped, 'Krishna ... Oh, Krishna! You look *marvellous*! I feel we ought to have outriders and an escort of cavalry ... The trap's ready.'

Then old Mrs. Bateman came down, exclaimed over Krishna, and made sure they were well wrapped; and Joan came and said, 'Well ... enjoy yourselves. It may be the last time.'

'Joan,' her mother-in-law said reprovingly.

'I didn't mean the war,' she said. 'I meant, the last time anyone will be holding balls like this. Anyway, I really mean, have a good time.' She pecked Diana on the cheek.

The ball was being held, in a house three miles away, in honour of the heir to the estate's twenty-first birthday. He was home on a week's leave from his regiment, the Rifle Brigade, and greeted them at the door with a grin and a wave. He said, 'Major Krishna Ram, isn't it? And a century for Surrey.' He was wearing tails and Krishna Ram thought he was already slightly drunk. Then he took off his overcoat and led Diana into the decorated drawing-room, to an audible gasp from the young men and women already gathered there.

The dinner was excellent; he did not eat the roast beef, but managed to make do with soup, roast potatoes, vegetables and dessert. Nor did he touch the wine, again managing to avoid the attentions of the butler without causing comment from anyone. When the dancing began he felt light and almost as though again at the wicket, entirely concentrated now on Diana Bateman. Her body was firm and close in his arms in the waltz, her eyes level, close to his, and, he thought, questioning, waiting. She looked as she had looked in court in Pewsey, while waiting for the magistrates' decision on Young Marsh. The hostess introduced him to other young women, and he danced with them, but always returned to Diana. The heady sweetness of night-scented stock wafted in through open windows, with the smell of cut grass, and a soughing in the huge trees at the far edge of the lawn. He floated, knowing he was floating, and when the end came, floated through the farewells, through the good wishes to the twenty-one-year-old, who by now was absolutely drunk. Like Krishna, his leave was at an end. In a few more hours, they would both be back in France. But for Krishna, floating without wine, there was no tomorrow, no yesterday, only this day, this hour.

He shook the reins and the horse trotted down the white road between the tall hedges. The moon rose over the downs and a nightingale sang along the wall of the Old Vicarage. He unharnessed the horse and walked at Diana's side into the moonlight in front of the house, where the nightingale was singing.

They stood together, listening to the soaring song. When it stopped he took her in his arms. Her head sank on to his shoulder and he kissed her. Her mouth was soft, and slowly opened to him, as for the first time, doing something strange but natural. Her body moved a little but not with any strain or lust, only content and fulfilment. She turned her head up and whispered, 'I love you . . . I love you.'

He stooped again to kiss her, suddenly aware. Down in the fold of her body, under the organdie pressed against him, were the visions that had come to him, night and day. His phallus stiffened against her, thrusting at the organdie like a blind animal. For a time she did not move, neither towards nor away; then she sighed and pressed against him, parting her thighs so that the rod of his maleness pushed into the hidden divide of her thighs.

'No!' he cried, and realized that he had said it aloud. He broke away from her and ran into the house.

July 1915

KRISHNA RAM WAS inspecting the trenches. As he left one bay and turned into the next the lance-dafadar in command greeted him with a rigid salute. By the light of the candle guttering on top of an ammunition box at the back of the trench Krishna began to count the bombs laid out ready on the firestep. Twenty-four. 'How many men in the bay?' he asked the NCO.

'Six, lord.'

Krishna nodded. Four bombs a man was correct. Carefully he examined one bomb. The detonator was in position. The NCO drew back a groundsheet to display two boxes of small arms ammunition. Krishna pulled out a few clips at random and checked that they were properly loaded, one up, one down. He checked that each man was in possession of the new type of gas mask, a flannel helmet with mica eyepieces. Then he examined the sandbag walls of the trench, the revetments, firestep, parapet, and parados. The sentry was on the firestep, his orders on a board hanging from a nail in a revetting post behind him. Krishna climbed up, checked the man's periscope, which was not used at night, and joined him on the actual firestep. He asked him questions about his orders, and, receiving the right answers, peered out to see what he could see. It was a dark night, clouds low and the air heavy with promised thunder, the enemy quiet in their trenches beyond the waste of torn earth called No Man's Land; he saw nothing.

He dropped down, congratulated the lance-dafadar on his bay, and went on, Hanuman limping at his heels and the new trumpeter behind. Passing a traverse he entered the next bay and began the process again. Here the NCO had forgotten to put out the sticks or bayonets which, thrust into the earth, fixed some sort of right and left limits for night firing. He reprimanded the man, reflecting that at night, really, only the Vickers on their fixed tripods could fire accurately without being able to see their target.

After a look at his watch and a long silent spell on the firestep, listening, he went on. It was a few minutes before midnight. The CO had sent out a strong fighting patrol under Lieutenant Mahadeo Singh to bring back at least two prisoners for identification. They had gone out from the right end of the Ravi Lancers' trenches at half past eleven. Nothing was to be expected from them for a little while yet.

The next bay had only four men in it. The acting lance-dafadar said that two had gone sick that afternoon, one with bad feet and one with a fever. There were too many sick, Krishna thought. That was making Warren Bateman stricter than ever. The regiment was harder, tougher, and more efficient than he had ever imagined possible with these amiable and uneducated peasants from the slopes of the Himalayas. The systems and techniques of trench warfare had much improved since the early days along this front, when the war first congealed. Then, generals and senior officers knew nothing of static warfare, and treated it only as an unpleasant interlude to be suffered through until once again the trumpets would sound and the armies sweep across hill and dale, the cavalry out in front. Gradually, Krishna saw, the war had ground the idea of motion into the soil, and with it the idea of fresh air, of change, of hope. First it had stopped the moving, then the breathing, so that men went underground like corpses, to be held down by barbed wire, mud, sandbags, steel, ruins. In this motionless subterranean struggle the Ravi Lancers were now proficient. The sandbag walls were faultless, and sloped at just the ordered angle to the vertical. The firesteps were at the right height, Very lights and gas alarm bells where they ought to be. The floors of the trenches muddy—that was inevitable—but clear of debris.

He moved on. Sentry with no string to the bay commander's wrist. Sandbag holed and leaking. Machine gun in C Squadron sector, night aiming light gone out. Dafadar with fever, must be sent back, no other NCO in bay. All the time, listening, watching, looking out over No Man's Land, wondering how Mahadeo Singh's patrol was faring. Warren sent out a reconnaissance patrol nearly every night, and a fighting patrol at least twice a week. 'We've got to dominate the Hun,' he said. 'He's got to be afraid of us, never knowing when or where we'll be coming. No Man's Land must belong to us, not to him.'

Last week a fighting patrol had lain out, all night, four nights in succession, waiting to catch German reconnaissance patrols suspected of being sent out to make maps of the British wire. The fourth night they'd got it—a feldwebel and three men creeping through the dank weeds towards the centre of the line, in a heavy July rain. The Ravi patrol, a troop of twenty men under Jemadar Sunder Singh, killed them all, and brought in the bodies. Two nights later the Germans tried to retaliate, but were caught by machine guns on the wire in front of C, and left six dead. The identification was definite: the regiment facing the Ravi Lancers was the 88th Bavarians. Still Warren wanted more—a live prisoner. It was all going well, Krishna thought, but ... The regiment was as good as Gurkhas or crack British infantry regulars, but...

A white Very light whooshed up into the sky half a mile to the right, and Krishna jumped up to the firestep. Another light hung in the dark night, showing the earth as a rotting green plain, mutilated and laid out for the undertaker. Machine guns clattered, rifles banged, machine pistols fired in staccato bursts. Then the German field guns opened up. The shells burst in yellow splashes of flame on the Ravi trenches opposite the firing. The artillery swept the front line and No Man's Land for five minutes, then stopped. A breath later a machine gun made a long monotonous statement. Silence.

Krishna hurried through the last two bays of his inspection and then hastened back along the trench line to the right end. Mahadeo Singh's patrol was to come back in through the wire in front of B Squadron. They were due at half past twelve. It was about that now.

Warren Bateman was waiting at the appointed place. He peered at Krishna in the gloom and said, 'How was the inspection?'

'Very good, sir, on the whole. There were a number of small things wrong, which I'll put in my report ... Any news of Mahadeo Singh?'

'Not yet.'

They settled down. The CO was smoking a pipe. Now and then his clenched teeth gleamed in the flame of the hurricane lantern set beside the field telephone. Occasionally he murmured something to Shikari, crouched at his feet. He talked a lot to the dog these days, the way other men talked to themselves. Sometimes the hand holding the pipe shook slightly for a moment before he again got it under control. Himat Singh was there, too, a major now, pale and thin. He had only come out of hospital two days before, and returned straight to the regiment instead of taking the two weeks' convalescent leave the doctors had ordered for him. Flaherty, now a captain, was there, silent. The jemadar of the troop in whose sector they waited was standing on the firestep beside the sentry, both seen as dim silhouettes against the drifting cloud rack.

The jemadar leaned down and whispered, 'Someone is coming, sahib.' To the men crouched nearby he muttered, 'Stand-to!' and they stepped silently up on to the firestep, weapons aimed and ready. Krishna joined Warren in the crowded line. Peering intently ahead he made out a low shape, hardly to be separated from the earth. The sentry a few feet to his right muttered sharply, 'Halt, oo go dah?'

'Friend,' a voice gasped. *'Madad dena, bhai.'* The man sounded exhausted, and his voice shook with terror.

'Countersign dena!' Warren Bateman whispered.

'Aii, bhol-gaya, sahib,' the voice quavered, *'madad dijiye!'*

'What the hell's the point of giving passwords and countersigns if the men are allowed to forget them?' Warren snapped. 'What squadron's this patrol from?'

'D, sir.'

'Tell that man to come on in.'

The jemadar hissed an order and the thing came on along the earth, a dark snake turning slowly into a man. The jemadar pulled him into the trench where he collapsed. His right leg ended in a tattered stump below the knee. Now another man was coming in; this one had half his face scraped off by grenade splinters; another, a bullet through the arm. The trench began to stink of iodine as B Squadron's medical orderly cleaned the men's wounds and put on their first field dressings. The next man in was not wounded and Warren Bateman said, 'What happened?'

The sowar spoke in short gasps, 'We crawled out ... through the wire ... the lieutenant-sahib and Sowar Jamundar crawled ahead ... to cover us ... but the enemy were ready ... machine guns ... grenades ... rifles ... artillery ... we were helpless, lying there twenty feet away ... the lieutenant-sahib was killed...'

'How do you know? Who saw his body?'

305

'I, sahib, and three others ... The dafadar said, charge ... We tried ... I reached the lieutenant. His face was ... smashed ... twenty, thirty machine gun bullets into it ... We came back.'

'Who gave the order?' Warren grated.

'No one, sahib. There was no one ...'

Warren Bateman straightened up from the crouched position where he had been talking to the sowar. 'Get these men back to the RAP,' he said. 'See that the Intelligence Officer talks to each of them before he is allowed to be evacuated to the CCS. Send the unwounded back to their squadrons.'

He stood up, glaring towards the enemy trenches. Then he stared at Himat Singh, six feet from him; then at Flaherty, even closer; finally at Krishna Ram. The eyes, dully gleaming yellow, rested. He said, 'Major Krishna Ram, you will take out a fighting patrol tomorrow night and bring back at least two live prisoners. About thirty men from A Squadron. Work out a plan with the IO and discuss it with me at noon.'

'Yes, sir,' Krishna said formally. The CO swung on his heel and walked away down the communication trench, his ash walking stick thumping angrily into the sandbags at every second step.

Major Himat Singh said tenderly, 'I wish the CO had sent me. I'd get the prisoners he wants.'

Krishna said, 'If I don't come back, he will—he will.'

He stayed a long time in the front line, as the sentries were changed, and the bloodstains washed away. The sowars settled back to sleep, but the smell of iodine and the gasping breath of the men in agony remained, as though embodied in the air, to hang for ever about that place.

Krishna started for the rear. Someone ought to visit those wounded men. They'd all be suffering from shock soon. When he reached the RAP near two o'clock in the morning he found Captain Ramaswami in his little dugout office. He said, 'I thought someone ought to see the wounded from Mahadeo Singh's patrol. And the men wounded when that experimental mortar blew up earlier.'

Ramaswami nodded. 'Yes. But someone has already been. The CO.'

'Oh,' Krishna said. He was surprised. From the tone of Warren's voice in the front line, it sounded as though he blamed the men for the patrol's failure.

The black doctor said, 'You must not underestimate him. It is not the sowars who are his enemies. They worship him.'

Krishna sat down. 'They do. Yet we have a sickness rate double that of the Gurkhas or the Punjabis. Why?'

'The men's spirits are being starved,' Ramaswami said promptly. 'I get fevers that are genuine—temperature of 105 or 106 and the man as weak as a kitten—but I can't diagnose them. No malarial parasites, no virus that I can isolate. I keep them here two or three days, the fever drops, and I send them back—but they're not cured.'

'Do you think—' Krishna lowered his voice. 'Do you think that Vedic medicine might help, if you were permitted to practise it?'

The doctor said, 'Yes—not because it is Vedic, but because it is Indian. The men are suffering fundamentally from starvation, as I said. I have been experimenting. The results aren't definite, but the fact is that these NYD fevers go down in a day or less if I put the patient in a ward where I have the Brahmin chanting *mantras*, giving out Ganges water, and putting rice and caste marks on the men's foreheads.'

'The CO allows that?'

'I don't ask him,' the doctor said grimly. 'I have a very efficient spy system and when he is seen coming everyone washes his forehead and the Pandit hides ... Don't bother to see those men. The ones who aren't asleep are in shock by now. Come tomorrow afternoon ... By the way, how long is it since I examined your penis?'

'The week after I came back from leave,' Krishna Ram said.

'Well, that's nearly a month now, isn't it? I need to make one final check to see that no scar tissue has formed, and then you're cleared. And the best way to prove it is to have a woman. It excites the walls of the urethra, and if anything's wrong there, it will discharge ... Drop your trousers.'

He got his instrument, greased it, and gently inserted it into Krishna's penis. As he peered down there was an exclamation from outside, and the orderly cried, 'Sahib, no!' then the door burst open and Major Himat Singh rushed in, crying, 'Doc...'

He stopped, staring. Captain Ramaswami stood up slowly. He said, 'There's a sign on that door. It reads PRIVATE. KNOCK BEFORE ENTERING.'

'I'm sorry,' Himat Singh stammered. He recovered himself and said, 'I brought down a very sick man from my squadron. I'll wait outside.' He walked out, closing the door carefully behind him.

The doctor said, 'Well, I fear that is the end of the secrecy about your little mishap. From what he saw me doing he will know that you have had VD.'

'It doesn't matter,' Krishna said, 'Himat's a good chap.'

'But he worships the CO,' the doctor said.

'Anyway, I don't think I'll last long enough for him to do anything about it, even if he decides it's his duty.'

'What do you mean?'

'The CO's sending me out on a fighting patrol tomorrow night.'

'H'm. That's fine. Dress . . . He sends some officers out a lot.'

'Yes, but I think he hopes they will come back safe. He was very upset about Mahadeo Singh. I may be imagining things, but with me . . . I am not sure.'

'Well, if you're going out on a patrol tomorrow, you'd better get some sleep now. Good night.'

Krishna went to his dugout in the Rear HQ area behind the third-line trenches. The blanket was spread on the camp bed, and a candle shed a golden glow on the rafters and sandbags and the boarded floor. Hanuman hung his gas mask on a nail beside the door, and his equipment on another, then knelt to take off his boots. Krishna sat down at the crude plank table and rested his head in his hands.

He had to bring back two prisoners, alive, from the German trench system opposite. The Germans would be aroused by to-night's performance, and exultant over their success. Ten dead, six wounded, one missing. And for the Germans probably nothing, unless some of the bombs hurled into their trench had taken effect.

It was easy enough to plan his patrol . . . there was just so much length of trench, its shape exactly known; so much wire, all shown on the wire maps. One went one's course, into the muzzles of the guns. Whether one lived or died was pure chance, not skill. But this was what the Europeans called 'Oriental fatalism'. Was that why he had to do it? Because he was an oriental?

He pulled out her letter from the breast pocket of his tunic and read it:

Dear Krishna,

I hope you are well. We have been having dreadful weather

here ever since you left. You must have taken the sun back with you???!!! The work in the factory is very boring, but also quite dangerous if you get careless. A girl in my shed lost two fingers yesterday. She was lucky not to lose her hand. We have been promised a week's holiday beginning on Monday, August the 4th. They are altering the machines or something and there will be no work for us while they are doing it. I miss you so much. Oh, darling, I long for you. I must be a very wicked woman for I can think of nothing but you, day and night, even when I am in bed. I am afraid of losing my hand in a machine because I am always daydreaming!! But I am not really afraid because I would rather lose my hand than lose you. Darling, can you please get leave and come over?

Diana

There was a PS written hurriedly and badly, as though in the dark.

PS We wouldn't have to go to Shrewford Pennel. I have not told anyone there about my holiday yet.

He read it again, although he knew it by heart. Then he took his new fountain pen from his inner pocket—Warren would not allow officers to wear them where they showed—and wrote quickly.

Dearest Diana, We are now in the line before Perouges, and when we are relieved will go into immediate reserve . . .'

That was censorable. Why did he put it in then? Because he wanted Diana to know as definitely where he was as he knew where she was, either in the dingy rooming house, or the noisy factory. Anyway, he was the regimental censor for the officers' mail. He wrote on:

I cannot get back to England unless I am wounded, which may happen. There is a lot of patrolling and there are rumours of a big new offensive. But if I survive this month I am due for 72 hours leave. I will apply for my leave to start at 0700 hours on Tuesday, August 3rd.

He stopped. Then what? Supposing she could get over to France, where could he meet her? And then what? He felt the familiar trembling in his loins. They must have three days undisturbed, to get to know each other, to make love, to walk in peace, arm in arm, as she liked to do.

It was past three in the morning. He went to the door blanket, stirred Hanuman with his foot and said, 'Give my salaams to

Captain Sohan Singh, the quartermaster-sahib.'

The orderly got up, rubbed his eyes, took his rifle and gas mask —and went off. Krishna sat down to wait. Warren Bateman would not think of routing the quartermaster out of bed at 3 a.m. on a personal matter ... but he was English. He, Krishna Ram, was the Son of the Sun, and a prince of ancient India.

The quartermaster appeared in twenty minutes, bowing. Krishna thought, he's not saluting but bowing and making *namasti*; he knows this is not British military business. He said, 'I want a good hotel room in Paris, for three days from August 3rd.'

'Oh, in August,' the captain said with a sigh of relief, speaking in Hindi. 'That is no problem, highness. I was afraid it might be for the next few days.'

'A double room ... make it a suite, in the best hotel in Paris,' Krishna said. He added, 'Some place too expensive for most British officers to go to.'

'I understand perfectly,' Sohan Singh said, rubbing his hands. 'It will be an honour to provide this for my prince. I wish I could do more.'

'I shall pay,' Krishna said.

'There is no need,' the fat captain said. He was on his hunkers now, squatting like a merchant in his store window, an attitude wildly incongruous with his uniform and rank badges. 'There is plenty in my private fund to cover it. You recall, lord, the fund I am building up from the profits of the brothel.'

'Oh.' Krishna had forgotten all about that. He said, 'So that's going well?'

'Very well, lord. And certain other transactions I carry out with our GS wagons, also my operations on the Bourse. We have over a lakh of rupees in the fund now. Some of it is in stocks, but some is in gold ... buried where I can get it if we have to retreat.'

Krishna shook his head wonderingly. Apart from the hundred thousand rupees Sohan Singh had amassed for what he and Krishna might regard as the public service, there would certainly be half as much again for the service of Sohan Singh. Well, he had earned it. He said, 'You have had no trouble with the Military Police over the brothel?'

'None, lord. One sergeant-major stumbled on it by mistake, but he is being well taken care of.'

Krishna said, 'I want you to keep a list of anyone seriously wounded or killed, Sohan. Send a hundred rupees to each one's next of kin in Ravi, at once. And have your father or uncles find out what state each family will be in, with the man dead or disabled. Of course there will be British government pensions for them, too, but we may need to do more. I shall write to my grandfather about this.'

'It shall be done, lord,' the quartermaster said.

'And, if we have as much money as that, give the Brahmin a thousand rupees to spend on his *mandir*.'

'It shall be done, lord.'

'See that all this is done, whatever happens to me.'

'Prince, I pray . . .'

'That's enough . . . give me the address of the hotel in Paris where you have it arranged.'

'I can tell you now, lord. It will be the Meurice Hotel. I have an understanding with one of the assistant-managers there over certain loans I have made to him.' He bowed and *namasti*'d himself out of the room. Krishna Ram picked up his pen again:

I shall be in the Hotel Meurice in Paris from early afternoon that day. Can you arrange to arrive after 4 p.m., when I will be waiting for you in the lobby? You will be known as Mrs. Krishna Ram. Or I will meet your train if you can let me know which it will be. Perhaps you could telephone the hotel, from Boulogne or Le Havre. I believe there is a through line.

He ought to add some endearments, *All my love*, or *Longing to see you*. But how petty that would be, appended to the central thought of the two letters; that she had asked to spend a week alone with him, as his mistress; and that he had accepted. He signed his name, sealed and addressed the letter, and stamped the envelope 'Passed by Censor' with the little rubber stamp on his table.

Then he reflected that officers' outgoing letters were often opened by the Brigade Intelligence Officer, or by the Intelligence staff at Division. And he was going out on patrol. Better not to mail the letter until after that. Take it on the patrol, in his pocket? But if he were killed and his body brought back, his papers would be given to Warren Bateman, who would then see and read the letter, and know what his sister was doing. But he ought to know. Really, he, Krishna Ram, should go and tell him, to his face. It would come to that soon enough.

He put the letter into his breast pocket and buttoned the pocket down. If he came back alive from the patrol he'd give it to Sohan Singh and tell him to post it through channels which would avoid all military censorship. That would be child's play, for Sohan.

Thunder growled all around in the night. Krishna waited, commanding himself not to look at his watch again until he had counted to two hundred slowly. 'We've got to keep it up ... at all costs,' Warren Bateman muttered, at his side. Krishna said nothing. Warren was talking to Shikari. The dog whined and thumped his tail. Warren said, 'They're planning another big offensive ... Krishna, did you hear what I said?'

'Yes, sir ... Do you think we'll be in it?'

'We've got to be. I'll speak to the general. I'll make sure we are ... What time is it now?'

'Two-thirty-five, sir.'

'Five minutes to go.'

The lightning was almost continuous now as the storm slowly advanced from the south-west.

Warren Bateman said, 'One minute, Krishna. Good luck.' He held out his hand. Krishna shook it. At 2.40 a.m., he climbed on to the firestep and started through the British wire, followed by his men in single file. The CO had not liked this part of his plan, of setting out late in the night rather than in the traditional early darkness. 'If you are delayed or lose your way,' he said, 'you'll finish up out there in broad daylight. First light's 0441 tomorrow, you know.'

Krishna Ram had agreed with the danger; but the Germans were always much more alert in the early hours and his plan depended both on their fatigue, and on the fact that many of the trees of the Bois de Perouges were still standing behind part of their line. The British had taken aerial photographs of the trench system and had numbered every sector, from north to south, successively. Each communication trench began a new sector. The Ravi Lancers faced Sectors 74 to 80. The remains of the Bois de Perouges was immediately behind Sectors 76, 77, and 78, with a few stumps of trees standing even in front of the German lines. Krishna had decided that there was no hope of catching the Germans unawares in the front line; but if some of them could be manoeuvred into using the communication trenches, prisoners might be taken there.

The easiest way of doing that was to fake an attack on a sector of the front line. From what Hauptmann von Gerhard had told him, when the British artillery lifted, the Germans sent men up from the rear to the front trenches. To capture one of them he must cross the front line and lie in wait over the communication trench, say a hundred yards back. Here the stumps of wood would help. It was a risky plan, but better than crawling up to alert and ready machine-gunners.

He crawled on in the uncertain darkness. Was that the guns? No, thunder, close to the west now. A large drop of rain landed on the back of his hand. He crawled on. Compass bearing 56 magnetic would take him to the centre of Sector 78. He must be about fifty yards from the German front line now. 0258 hours. He stopped, and the men stopped to right and left. A tremendous explosion overhead made him start half up. As he sank down again, understanding that it was thunder, the rain broke. Lightning seared his eyeballs. A sharp click close behind him was followed by a brighter, longer flash, and a clap of thunder that rattled his teeth in his head, as the bolt struck ten feet from him. The British guns opened up for the ten minute preparation fire which the CO had been able to wring for him from Brigade. Now he had to move fast. The artillery barrage was hitting the centre of Sector 75, a quarter of a mile to the north, his left. He reached the German wire and the sowars started working quickly with the long-handled wire cutters. He didn't hear the snip and click as they cut through, though he was six feet away, so the Germans thirty feet off certainly could not have. He crawled under the wire, his rifle pushed forward, knowing that the patrol was at his heels. He peered over into the trench. No one there. He rose, crouched, and jumped across. One by one the others followed, wraiths in the streaming rain. The artillery fire still exploded close to the north. Shell splinters whined over and a flare rose from the German trenches. Krishna crouched against a tree stump and froze still. The hovering ball threw its pale light on the array of stumps, the slanting rain, and then went out. Krishna hurried on. Twenty paces, thirty, forty. Now left. Check the bearing. 326 magnetic. Ten paces, twenty, thirty ... here it was, the communication trench. The British artillery stopped firing. He was just in time.

He waited. His men crouched ready, three at each traverse. Once they had the men they wanted between two traverses, they'd block off a bay by killing the men front and back, then drop into the bay to get the ones in the trap.

A minute passed. Two. The Germans usually sent their reinforcements forward within half a minute of the ending of the barrage, as the British had discovered, time and again, to their cost.

Three minutes. Four. In the name of God, he could wait no longer. His plan was a precise thing, not a matter of waiting for something to happen. Thank God for the rain and circling thunder. What in hell had happened? The Germans always sent up reinforcements ... To the north-west, about where the next communication trench was, he thought he saw the gleam of a bayonet tip ... and another ... several, in line. A solution struck him and he almost laughed. Too late to do anything about it now. He signalled his men in and they began the return. This time they found two German soldiers patrolling the piece of front-line trench they had to cross to get back to No Man's Land. Krishna signalled two sowars up close. He whispered to them, 'Next time, bayonet!'

The two Germans reached the far traverse, and turned. One began to climb up on to the firestep to look towards the British lines, and Krishna gave his two men a shove. They sprang, rifles and fixed bayonets lunging. The bayonets thrust home with a thud and one of the Germans screamed a terrible cut-off, choking, bubbling scream. By then the rest of the patrol were jumping the trench. Krishna reached down to help up the two men. Another German appeared round the traverse, and a sowar behind Krishna fired but missed. The German whipped up his rifle and fired twice. The two sowars in the trench fell dead. The sowar behind Krishna fired again and the German fell. A grenade flew over the traverse and burst in the trench. Orders were being shouted close by in German. The dafadar of the patrol said, 'Come, lord.'

Nothing could be done for the dead. Krishna turned, ran to the wire, crawled under and set off at a trot back across No Man's Land, his patrol spread out on either side of him—all but the two sowars left in the trench.

He dropped into the Ravi front line and Warren Bateman caught him. 'Well, did you get them?'

Krishna shook his head, 'No, sir ... We were waiting by the communication trench between Sectors 77 and 78.'

'Yes, yes, I know.'

'The German reinforcements went up the one between Sectors

314

76 and 77, two hundred yards to the north-west. I believe they have a one-way system, one communication trench only for forward traffic, the next only for rearward traffic. No one passed in ours.'

Warren said, 'You might be right ... but the reinforcements would eventually have gone back to the rear, down your trench.'

'Perhaps, sir, but probably not until daylight,' Krishna said briefly. He was very tired and suddenly wanted nothing more but to get to bed. He'd lost two men, his faithful servants, for what?

Warren Bateman said, 'Did you hear that, Puran Lall?'

'Yes, sir,' the young man said.

'You follow Major Krishna Ram's plan tomorrow ... They didn't see you on the communication trench, did they?'

'No, sir. And we killed the only two in the front line, who might have seen us coming from that direction, from the rear. But...'

'Not tomorrow,' Warren Bateman said, taking the words out of Krishna's mouth. 'Give them, say two days, to forget all this. The third night from now, Puran.'

'Yes, sir,' the young man said. His voice was without any emotion, either of love or hate, fear or exaltation.

Krishna went to his dugout and said to Hanuman, 'Well, we live, see?' The letter felt warm in his pocket, as though it were her breast pressing into him. He said, 'Tell the quartermaster sahib I want to see him.'

The fat captain came hurrying as the first light spread. Krishna handed him the letter.

August 1915

'R EADY THEN?' WARREN BATEMAN asked as he finished buckling on his Sam Browne belt and sabre. 'Let's start.'

He turned to climb the steps out of the dugout, colliding with a sowar carrying a couple of letters. 'Christ!' he snarled in English—then, in Hindi—'Can't you look where you're going, you clumsy idiot?'

'I'm sorry, sahib,' the sowar said. 'Mail.' He handed one letter to Warren Bateman, the other to Krishna Ram. Krishna's heart bumped and his hand shook with a sudden spasm so that his letter almost fell from it. It was from Diana. He glanced quickly at Warren to see whether he too had recognized the handwriting, but the CO was stuffing his own letter into his pocket with a muttered, 'Bloody tailor. Come on.'

Krishna put his letter into the left breast pocket of his tunic, buttoned it down, and followed Warren Bateman up the steps into the open air. The CO was muttering to himself or to Shikari all along the trench to the rear, and still talking when they stepped out into the open at the rear of the trench system half a mile farther back. It was July 28th, 1915, a brilliant sun shining and the wheat heavy in the fields, that began here and stretched away to the west, only lightly touched by the war.

The regiment's first line transport was drawn up for inspection, headed by Rissaldar Ram Lall.

Ram Lall saluted as the CO walked up, and reported the parade state. Warren Bateman glared at him and said, 'Who are you? You're not the rissaldar-major. I distinctly said that the RM was to ...'

Ram Lall looked from the CO to Krishna Ram, then said woodenly, 'I am the acting rissaldar-major, sahib. Rissaldar-Major

Baldev Singh became ill and was sent on sick leave a week ago.'

Warren shook his head as though to shake off water then muttered, 'Oh, yes. Of course...'

He began the inspection. Krishna, walking close behind him, thought that he was like an engine missing fire on one or two of its cylinders. Sometimes you would never guess anything was wrong. His eye would pick up the general condition of a GS wagon, and the fact that it had a rusty split pin in the rear axle-housing, all in a single sweep, but at the next wagon the horse had an obvious girth gall as big as a saucer, and he didn't see it. His manner, too, altered without apparent reason. At one moment he was cracking a Hindi joke with a young sowar who had done nothing—neither right nor wrong—but stand there stiffly at attention; five minutes later he was viciously castigating a dafadar who had also, apparently, done nothing. 'Take his name!' he snapped.

'*Jee huzoor*,' the acting RM said and wrote it down in his well-thumbed notebook, with a painstaking hand.

That part of the inspection ended, Warren stopped and said, 'Well, time for a beer in the mess.'

Krishna Ram said, 'Yes, sir ... Captain Ramaswami is expecting us at the RAP in ten minutes.'

'Of course, of course,' Warren muttered. He put a hand to his eyes and said, 'It's damned bright today. Like Jacobabad in May. Were you ever in Jacobabad?'

'No, sir ... Shall I take the inspection for you, sir?'

'No! Who the hell do you think you are? I'm the CO of this regiment and I'd thank you to remember it. The men will NOT wear caste marks while I'm CO ... not in Europe. Do you understand?'

'Yes, sir ... Turn left here, sir.'

They started back up the trench system towards the Regimental Aid Post. The regiment was in brigade reserve, occupying trenches half a mile behind the front, but connected to the front by numerous communication trenches. The RAP was in deep cellars of several houses that had once formed a hamlet here and of which no trace remained but piles of rubble and armies of grey rats. The bricks and stones of the shattered houses had gone to the revetting and reinforcing of such places as the RAP, the ammunition store, the quarter-guard, and, a couple of hundred yards away, the whole brigade headquarters complex.

Captain Ramaswami was waiting at the entrance to the cellars. He saluted and Krishna thought, inwardly smiling, that his saluting was getting worse, not better. Warren Bateman returned the greeting smartly, then began his inspection. It was the same as at the transport lines, an affair of fits and starts, of long silences while the CO stood at the foot of a table and stared at the waiting medical orderly, saying nothing; of sudden outbursts. One of these, directed at the dispenser who was showing him how the reserve of morphine was stored, caused the doctor to break into the CO's flooding wrath with a curt, 'It is not his fault. I ordered that.'

Warren Bateman turned on the doctor and for a moment Krishna thought he was going to lose his temper, but instead he suddenly collapsed, growing visibly smaller, like a pricked balloon ... no, like a man turning into a youth, an unsure youth. 'Oh,' he said in a low voice. 'Did you? ... Good, good.' He went on to the next ward, where there were six beds, all that the RAP had, for most sick and wounded were sent back to the first place really organized for dealing with lying patients, the Casualty Clearing Station seven miles to the rear, outside field artillery range.

The CO walked jerkily into the ward and made a joke with the first man. The young sowar's face lit up as Warren talked to him about his home, the fishing, the crops, the animal fair. After five minutes Warren nodded and moved on. He stared at the next man. He turned slowly, looking dumbly at Krishna. His mouth formed words, but none came out. His eyes took on a hunted look. Krishna tried to read what was being said, but he could get no meaning from it. Captain Ramaswami stepped forward, and took the CO's arm. 'This way, sir,' he said gently. 'I have something I must show you.' Aside to his dafadar he said, 'Clear my bed ... This way. Let's have the sleeve up a bit.'

Warren said, 'You know that fourth ribbon of Rainbow's, Krishna?'

'Yes, sir,' Krishna said; he couldn't remember which it was at all, but thought he had better humour Warren for the moment, while Ramaswami was dabbing his arm with cotton soaked in alcohol.

'Do you remember once he was telling us what all the ribbons were, but skipped over that one? Well, I've discovered what it is —Austrian. He's wearing an enemy decoration! And he knows it! Ha, ha!'

'Ha, ha!'

'Ow, what the hell? ... Have I been wounded? Is that a tetanus injection?' Shikari crouched on the floor, whining.

'A touch of fever. We'll have you right in no time. Lie down here.'

'We can use that to blackmail him, eh, Krishna? If he refuses to send us up the line ... keeps us in reserve instead of leading the assault ... eh?'

'Take his boots off. Undo his tie. He'll be asleep in a couple of minutes.'

They stood over the foot of the bed in the tiny cubby hole which was Ramaswami's own billet at the end of the RAP and watched Warren Bateman sinking into unconsciousness. The dog Shikari looked on anxiously. The doctor's face was dark and stern as usual, but there was a softening at the corners of the thick lips.

He turned to Krishna. 'Overwork. He was unconscious on his feet. He's got to have a couple of weeks off ... ten days at least.'

'He'll never go,' Krishna said.

'No. He's the white god, the white father. Without him we black men will go to pieces. Besides, he has to punish us ... He'll wake up tomorrow feeling much better. Then he'll start again, twenty hours a day, driving us hard, himself harder. Two or three days later he'll be back here like this—but worse. There's no knowing what he might do in this state. Shoot a man for having a boot-lace undone. Burst into tears on parade.'

'The men would understand,' Krishna said.

'Yes. But Rainbow Rogers wouldn't ... I think you should go to the general. Give him this report'—he was scribbling on a message form—'and tell him that Colonel Bateman needs two weeks' leave at home.'

'Baldev Singh's there,' Krishna remembered suddenly. 'He'll never allow himself to be away at the same time as the RM.'

'He won't know,' the doctor said. 'If we act quickly he'll be well on his way before he wakes up. Orderly, fetch the CO's orderly to take his dog away and look after it ... Here's my note to the general. Tell him I'll come and give my opinion in person if he wants me to, but it's all there.'

Krishna nodded and set off down the remains of the street, between the non-existent buildings, to Brigade Headquarters. When the staff captain took him into the general's presence Rainbow greeted him jovially. He had apparently come off some sort of a ceremonial parade, for the collar of the CMG hung gaudily round his neck under the lapels of his tunic. He read the doctor's letter with small clucking noises and said finally, 'H'm ... There's going to be another big offensive soon ... but you handled the regiment well enough last time, when he was wounded ... All right. Send him off on two weeks' leave ... two weeks in England that is. You assume command, effective at once. Publish that, John.'

'Yes, sir.'

Krishna headed back to the regiment's lines. At the RAP he told the doctor to get Warren Bateman off, under escort, with his leave warrant. Then he wrote a note of explanation, to be given to him when he awoke, stressing that the general had ordered him to take two weeks' rest at home. Then he returned to his own billet, the letter from Diana suddenly burning in his pocket. He had forgotten it in the tension of Warren's breakdown, but now it was like a fire against his skin.

Alone in the midday dusk of the dugout, candle lit, he opened the letter.

Dearest Krishna, Oh, how wonderful! I will be there. Nothing will stop me. I will arrive in Paris at the Gare St. Lazare, at 4.23 p.m. on Tuesday August 3rd. No one will know I am not still working at the factory. All my love my darling—Diana.

And a dozen Xs. What did that mean? Was it some Christian sign? But the Xs were made that way, not vertically like the cross of the religion of Christ. Tuesday, August 3rd, the day he'd told her his leave would begin, now just four days away. He sank on to his camp bed. He could see her as clearly as though she were standing there in the dugout. She was here, the candlelight glowing in her hair. Now she was sitting opposite him in the train as it left Paddington, after the great day at the Oval, the platform lights passing, at first slowly, then faster, flashing in her face—flash, one eye, the one nearest the platform gleaming, suddenly a red glow in the pupil...

The letter fell from his hand. He was the Commanding Officer. He could not be away from the regiment for 72 minutes, let alone 72 hours. He ground his teeth with despair. That madman, that assassin Warren Bateman had arranged this, pretending to have a breakdown, just so that he could not take the leave that had been promised! He had done it because he knew that Diana was going to join him in Paris. Krishna's hands clenched until the nails bit into the palms.

He relaxed, his head sinking. Of course Warren had not done it on purpose, of course Warren knew nothing. Nevertheless, there it was. He ought to send a telegram off at once telling Diana he could not get away. He could word it so as not to compromise her or let anyone else guess the truth. He ought to warn her that her brother was on his way back to England. Warren was very fond of her. He might go up to London to see her, or ask her to come down to Shrewford Pennel for the weekend; and she would not be there ... But she would, because he must tell her the meeting in Paris was impossible. He must, he must ...

He must go, he must stay ... the words ran like a refrain in his mind, as they had done for three days, hammering behind his words of command, the orders and instructions he gave by day, dripping like a tap when he lay down at night, ceaseless. He must stay, he must go ... but suppose the CO came back suddenly? But there would never be another chance like this. And who could guarantee his surviving the next spell in the front line? He loved her. She was risking so much for him. If he didn't go, she would be alone in Paris ...

The dafadar instructor barked, 'Gun stops, one ... Hand flat on the cocking hammer, check its position ... No, owl, flat, like this ... Position one!'

The four men sitting behind the four Vickers guns wrenched open the top cover of the breech, revealing the lock.

'Lock, position two, unfired round in the top, round in the bottom,' the dafadar cried. The four sowars shouted together, 'Misfire!' They pushed the lock back into place, slapped the covers down, jerked the cocking hammer twice, bent down to look through the sights, sat up, and pressed the thumbpieces.

'Sit up, sit up!' the dafadar yelled. 'Observe the strike! Gun firing all right ... Gun stops, two ... Hand flat on the cocking hammer—flat, flat, you idiot ... Cocking hammer, position three!'

Diana's boat would sail from Southampton. She would be coming via Le Havre as there was no civilian traffic through Boulogne or Calais. Allow eight hours for the crossing, she would be leaving Woolwich ... in the next hour. If he ran off the practice ground here behind the trenches, ran to brigade headquarters, told the brigade major he had a most immediate message for the CO ... he might be able to get a telephone connection through to London in time.

'Round jammed in breech!'

Back and forward, back and forward flew the cocking hammers with clack of steel on steel.

'Round won't extract!'

'Broken extractor claw!' the men behind the guns shouted. The men lying beside them searched frantically in the metal boxes for the replacement parts and handed them up. 'Slow!' the dafadar yelled. 'The Germans would have reached Bombay by now.' The men replaced the claws. 'Change!' the instructor yelled. The men who had been sitting behind the guns struggled to their feet and ran to the rear. The men who had been lying beside the guns took their places at the triggers, four more men doubled up from the row awaiting in rear to take the places of the No. 2s.

'Check guns!' the instructor shouted.

'Carry on, dafadar-ji,' Krishna said, walking away with his swagger cane touched to the peak of his cap.

He must, he must!

At the CO's office he sent for the intelligence reports. Still no threat of enemy movement. The British offensive preparing, but slowly. All quiet on the Western Front, as the London newspapers said. At least on this part of it. Some trouble in the Argonne, in the French sector. And in Italy on the Isonzo. But locally—nothing. Rumours that the 88th Bavarians had been replaced by the 179th Prussians, but no prisoner confirmation. Aircraft report that a heavy battery was gone from the position it had occupied for seven weeks behind Perouges.

The stalemate was complete. The opposing armies were locked like wrestlers trying to find a decisive hold ... but there was none.

He looked at the pile of reports on the table. Petty thefts in all squadrons. That was bad, worse in some ways than the rape-murder charge against a lance-dafadar in B. Government equipment deliberately damaged in C; inordinate waste—could that too have been deliberate?—in A. It was hard to credit such reports in an Indian regiment, where it was in the men's bones to treat their clothing and equipment, and everything belonging to the Sirkar, with a real reverence. Could he leave the regiment even for an hour when it was in this state? He had still nearly two weeks left as CO in which he could try to restore some of the qualities Warren had been steadily ironing out in his demands for military efficiency at all costs.

Flaherty appeared at the door. 'The quartermaster would like to see you, sir.'

He showed Captain Sohan Singh in, then retired, leaving the door open. Captain Sohan Singh waddled in, gave Krishna his version of a military salute and in the same motion managed to close the door behind him without appearing to do so.

'Rations, lord,' he said. 'I am thinking that the men need less *ghi* than they are getting, in this hot weather, but . . .' He launched into a long and tedious explanation, his voice droning. Krishna thought, he expects Flaherty to be listening at the door and is boring him off. Sohan Singh droned without a change of tone into saying, 'And, lord, I think you had better start out now if you are to reach the city at the time you hoped.'

'I can't go,' Krishna said miserably.

The quartermaster said, 'Oh, lord, all is arranged. Here I have the money for your stay.'

'I tell you, I can't,' Krishna said. He stood up and stalked up and down the confined space.

The quartermaster's voice was still a soft drone: 'Nothing will happen here, lord, I know it.'

'The brigadier general . . .'

'. . . will not make an inspection. He inspected us last week.'

'He might come round, to see how I'm doing,' Krishna said.

'Lord, if he does, the doctor-sahib will say you are sick with a mysterious Indian fever. It is like rabies, and lasts four days, and is very infectious during those days. There will be a man wrapped up in bed in a dark room.'

'But . . .'

'Major Bholanath-sahib will give any necessary orders. All will obey them.'

Krishna Ram stifled a groan. Betrayal of trust . . . Diana on her way . . . Warren in Shrewford Pennel, confident that the regiment was in good hands. Or was he? Who or what *did* he have confidence in, really? Was Flaherty listening at the door?

He made up his mind, and said abruptly, 'Very well, I shall go sick—now.'

'Very good, lord,' the quartermaster said. 'Here is five thousand francs. A ration lorry will be waiting in our transport lines at 9 p.m. It will reach Amiens at midnight. Major Bholanath will tell the adjutant tomorrow morning at dawn that you have gone sick and cannot be seen. My clerk will make out your pass and warrants as soon as the adjutant leaves the office.'

'Who will know, who will be in this ... thing?' Krishna asked.

'Myself. The doctor-sahib. Major Bholanath. Hanuman. My clerk. That is all, prince.'

Krishna grinned suddenly and said in Hindi, 'Aii, what a jest if the general should insist on seeing the sick man.'

'A jest indeed,' Sohan Singh said, 'but alas, such jests are beyond him.'

He bowed himself out. Captain Flaherty came in at once, frowning slightly. 'I have that report on the gas training that you asked for, sir...'

Krishna Ram shook his head and stood up, one hand to his forehead. 'I'm sorry,' he said, 'I'm feeling a little off colour. I think I'll go and lie down.'

'Very well, sir,' Flaherty said, standing aside. He looked disapproving, Krishna thought. British COs didn't go sick until they were practically dead, the look seemed to say. British COs carried on until they dropped.

He went to his dugout, told Hanuman that no one was to disturb him until half past seven, and tried to get to sleep. But sleep would not come, as thoughts of Diana filled his mind. She was in the train to London ... in the tube to Waterloo to catch the train to Southampton, walking the gangplank on to the cross-channel steamer, in the train to Paris, arriving ... the train was steaming into the Gare St. Lazare, he saw her in the carriage, the doors opened, she came out ... shyly or running into his arms? ... then a taxi to the hotel, a bellboy to carry her bag, probably snickering behind his pert face, up to the room, and then ...

The bellboy pocketed his tip and gently closed the white and gold door. Krishna Ram turned the key in the lock and faced her. She was wearing a dove grey suit and coat, grey silk stockings and black patent-leather shoes with low, splayed-out heels, and a toque hat with a thin veil. She lifted the veil and he took her in his arms. Her head sank back and her eyes closed. Her face was smooth ... a little tired under the eyes, the teeth big in the wide mouth, a few freckles on her cheek. He kissed her. She smelled of eau-de-cologne and soap and soot. Her lips were opening wide, her tongue slipping into his mouth. He felt no spasm of lust for her. It would come, at night when the light glowed in her creamy skin. Her lips were becoming more insistent, her mouth sucking his tongue from his own mouth into hers, her breath coming deeper in little gasps. She pulled her mouth away from his a moment and muttered, 'Take me ... take me!'

He held her a moment, a few inches away. He had not thought it would be quite like this. He had imagined night, her waiting, a certain fearfulness. But, broad daylight, and the woman demanding? He felt his desire rising, his penis stiffening. She pulled away from him, carefully but quickly laid her hat on the ormolu dressing-table, her coat over the back of a Louis XV chair. He began to undress. She said, her mouth full of hair pins, 'That bellboy didn't believe we were married. I don't care.'

Krishna watched her slip the garters off her thighs and unroll her stockings. She was big, strong, open. She stood, naked but for a petticoat, and held out a little package she had got out of her bag. 'Here, Krishna. One of the girls gave them to me.'

'What are they?' he asked.

'The girls at the factory call them French Letters—FLs,' she said. 'You ... well, you put one on. It prevents the girl getting in the family way.'

He saw the packet contained a dozen rubber tubes rolled into rings. By unrolling them down his penis they would make sheaths to prevent him impregnating her. He said, 'I don't think...'

'Darling, until we're married—please.' She was blushing, now holding her arms crossed over her bosom, as though he could see the breasts through the white linen of the petticoat. He looked down at himself and thought, you have to be stiff to be able to put one of those on, and, in a minute I won't be. Slowly, with naturally lascivious movements she pulled the petticoat over her head. A small brown bush appeared, and a flat belly, then a pair of small high breasts, the areolas large, the nipples small in the centres of them, her face, flushed, large-eyed.

She fell back on the bed, pulled him down beside her and began to kiss and caress him. He took an FL but she put it aside, whispering, 'Later ... oh darling, I *am* frightened ... but then I'm not ...

325

I don't want to be anywhere else in the world, or doing anything else ... Do you know how long a girl dreams of this? I'm thirty ... thirty-one in December.'

'I didn't think that ladies like you were supposed to think about such things.'

'Oh Krishna,' she said, 'I am a woman ... I live in the country. I can't help seeing things, dogs, the bull, our cats ... And wondering, when will it be me, what will it feel like.'

'Not who?' he asked. She had taken his hand and slipped it between her legs. In the cradle of her thighs, deep in the thicket, she bared wet lips that became slippery to his fingers.

'No,' she said seriously. 'How can one think of a person when you don't know who it will be?'

She was a virgin, he realized. A virgin of thirty. There was something indecent about that, as horrible in its way as the monkey-men in gas masks. She had become a woman fifteen or sixteen years ago, and passed all those years waiting—for what? To be deflowered in a Paris hotel by a brown man. How could they allow women to waste, and wait, like that?

Not a brown man but a prince, a Son of the Sun. For a moment he felt a desire to whip her as he had whipped the French whore; but that passed, for his penis rode proud and noble. For her sake he'd stifle its pride in this ill-smelling device. He knelt over her, rolled on the FL and said to her in Hindi, 'Open for your lord. Clasp me!'

She could not have understood what he said, but her thighs opened wide and she raised her pubis. The pink lips parted invitingly and the curly hairs, now wet and glistening, sprang back. He plunged slowly and steadily into her. She cried out sharply as her maidenhead broke with an audible crack, then sighed again, 'Take me, take me!'

The Son of the Sun mounted fully upon her, and made love until his sweat dripped on to her tear-stained, working face. She moaned continuously in an indissoluble mixture of pain and ecstasy.

When he finally rolled off her, and her breathing had returned almost to normal, she said in a low voice, 'I'm sorry I made such a noise. I didn't know it would feel like that.'

'How could you?' he said. His arm was under her neck, her head heavy on his upper arm, her breasts pressing into him. 'Besides, I liked it.'

326

She said obstinately, 'Yes, but I ought to be able to control myself.'

'Why?' he said, but she leaned up on her elbow, kissed him on the forehead, and said, 'Thank you, darling. It hurt a bit, but not as much as I was expecting.' She slipped out from under the sheet and ran to the bathroom. Her buttocks were a little heavy, he noticed, and they did not wiggle as other women's he had known did, for there was not much fat on them; they moved like a man's. She disappeared into the bathroom, and the door closed, but the vision of the buttocks remained. How strong they were, and how white. Through the door he heard the sound of running water, and sighed and turned over to lie on his back. She had smelled of sex for a little while then, and sweat, and the sweetness of his seed, but soon she'd come back smelling of soap and water, and everything would be English and proper again. He thought he'd go and watch her washing, and got up. He realized that the obscene FL was still wrinkled and full on his penis. He took it off and went into the bathroom. She gave a little cry: 'Oh! ... Krishna! I'm ...'

She was sitting on the lavatory and he heard a tinkling below her. He said, 'I had to get rid of this.' He looked around and was about to drop it into the waste basket but she said, 'Here, give it to me.' She dropped it between her thighs into the toilet bowl. She said reproachfully, 'You shouldn't come in here when I'm doing this.'

'Why not?' he said. He bent and kissed her where she sat and cupped her breasts in his hand. 'Sex doesn't stop after we have made love—it begins.'

She was dabbing herself with paper. She said, 'What's that thing for? Another lavatory?'

Krishna looked and laughed, and said, 'I didn't know, either, when we first came to France. It's called a *bidet*, and it's for cleaning your behind—and this.' He cupped her vulva in his hand, pressing a finger gently between her wet lips.

'But how?' she said, at first making as though to push his hand away and then spreading her legs to give him deeper access.

'You sit on it, run the water—either just into the bowl, or there's a vertical spray—then use your hand to soap yourself. Your left hand only, if you're an Indian.'

'The left hand?' she said, puzzled.

327

He nodded. 'This one'—he held it up—'We use it for wiping ourselves, instead of toilet paper.'

'Instead of toilet paper,' she gasped, 'you mean ... ?'

'Yes,' he said. 'We think that toilet paper is really very insanitary. You can only get clean in running water so when we defecate we take a pot of water called a *loti*, and when we have finished we run some of the water over our left hand, and then rub the backside and go on doing it until the hand comes away clean.'

She moved to the basin and began to run hot water. She said, 'Do you do that?'

He said, 'Not now, because the general and Warren ordered us to act like British officers. But I shall again soon ... We also think it's dirty to bathe in a bath, like that'—he nodded at the elaborately decorated bath tub. 'We only bathe in running water, usually a river. A woman will go in wearing her clothes.'

'How dirty!' Diana said.

'But it isn't really. She washes under a layer of cotton. The cotton dries on her, she's clean, and she hasn't displayed herself in invitation to men.'

He held her from behind, again cupping her breasts in his hands. 'Get dressed, and we'll go out and see Paris.'

It was two days later. 'An orphanage,' she said dreamily, 'with a playing field. Two, close to each other—one for boys and one for girls. And two hospitals.'

'All right,' he said, laughing, 'you shall have one hospital and one orphanage. Boys and girls who lose their parents don't need to lose the company of the other sex as well.'

'But there ought to be a special hospital for women,' she said.

'Eventually,' he said, 'but when there isn't any hospital at all, the first step is to get one, not to start worrying about specializing in diseases of women, or of the lungs, and so on ... Hey, a little slower, darling. We're not on a route march.'

The Seine flowed placid beside them, at their left hand. On the towpath ahead a pair of huge horses towed a long coal barge up towards Fontainebleau. Cattle lay in the heavy green of the water-meadows, the dense yellow of buttercups and dandelions carpeting the fields with what seemed to be a reflection of the golden bowl of the summer sky. This was Krishna's last afternoon of leave.

At five o'clock next morning he must catch a train for the front.

She slowed her pace. A diamond brooch sparkled at her breast. It had cost the equivalent of three hundred pounds, and he had almost had to fight her to make her accept it. Mercenariness was not a fault that she possessed; just the opposite—it was hard to give her anything, from an embrace to a brooch, unless he could somehow persuade her it was good for her ... healthy, proper.

The barge was far ahead, no one following them, the nearest house a riverside tavern at the lock ahead, which the horses were approaching. He caught her sleeve and said, 'Let's make love.'

'Here?' she gasped.

'Yes ... quick. I've got those things in my pocket.'

'Oh, Krishna!' But he had her half down in the long grass, and she was lifting her heavy skirt. He tugged impatiently at her white drawers and got them down. 'Oh, Krishna,' she said, again. There it was, the rough triangular copse, the slit he had entered a dozen times, and now was ready for again. With trembling fingers he rolled the FL on to his bursting penis, feeling that it would explode, shooting seed into her face if he had to touch it a moment longer. Then he plunged it into her.

She held his head, murmuring, 'There, there!'

The ecstasy came before he had thrust five times, and he cried out, moaning the name of god in Hindi, for surely it was the divinity who squeezed all his being into his loins and sent it squirting out in these long shuddering pulses. 'There, there!' She was like a mother now, harbouring his head, his tears, his seed.

He lay spent on her. A while later, he did not know how long, she said gently, 'Get up now, darling ... Feel better?'

He nodded. 'Better' was not the right word, but what was? He peeled off the FL and threw it into the river. He watched her pull up her drawers and arrange her dress, then they walked on, towards Fontainebleau.

Fontainebleau. The most beautiful palace in the world, she would probably say. As Versailles was the biggest. The Louvre the best art gallery. The British Museum the best museum. Let her talk. What use was it to tell her of Shalimar or Fatehpur Sikri or the Red Fort, or that place in Cambodia—Angkor Wat? As well try to persuade her, or Warren, to use a *loti* instead of toilet paper. Or that boys and girls were better off growing together, discovering each other, than segregated. Or that orphans might be better regarded as wards of the world, children of all, rather than institutionalized, in some sense prisoners.

After they were married, and he had succeeded to the *gaddi*, there was so much she was going to do. He must have spent half his leave talking about Ravi, because she wanted to know. She was going to be a loyal and hard working Rani, inspecting hospitals, looking after sick women and orphans, holding functions for charity, presiding at baby clinics and sewing bees.

They passed the tavern, and the woman at the lock gates curtsied as they went by. The forest of Fontainebleau swept down to the river's edge and a lone swan glided slowly along under the bank, disdainfully indicating that they might throw him a crumb. A tall black soldier in French uniform passed, his cheeks cicatrized with tribal slash marks, a plump white girl on his arm. The soldier nodded cheerfully, and Krishna nodded back. They were both in uniform, but the man could not be expected to know British rank badges. That was one good thing about the French—they didn't have the same sense of colour superiority that the British did; though, from what he had seen, they were even more certain of the superiority of their civilization. Diana was learning, too, for the continual sight of French women with Negroes and Arabs and squat little men from Indo-China had made her realize that others did not think the way Warren and most Englishmen did. Once, seeing a particularly black soldier sitting with a French girl at a pavement café on the Champs-Elysées, Krishna had said suddenly, 'Are you glad I am not that black?'

She looked at him with her deliberate cow-like placidity, and said, 'I don't know. If I felt the same about you as I do now, I wouldn't care.'

'Yes,' he said, 'but *would* you feel the same? *Could* you?'

She had thought a moment before replying, 'It would be more difficult, because I feel that very black people must think differently from us. You think like an Englishman.'

He said nothing. It had been true once. At least, he had done his best to make it true. But it wasn't true now, and never would be again. But what was the use of telling her that? She would find out for herself in time.

'Tell me about the schools,' she said now. 'What sort of schools are there in Ravi? Who are the teachers? What subjects are taught? What is the compulsory school age?'

She was very like Warren, he thought, asking how many men were on parade, how many NCOs trained as small arms instructors, how many stretcher bearers, how are the gas masks cleaned.

But that night, on the wide bed, with the window open and Paris humming like a mighty animal all around, and the light on, though she had whispered, 'Turn it off,' he mounted between her upraised thighs, and when she gasped, 'The FL, darling!' he had said 'No!' and entered her with powerful determination, and held his seed until she moaned in transport far beyond the therapeutic exercises of the early times, and writhed and bit him like the animal he had at last succeeded in making her, neither English nor Indian, brown nor white, only female. 'There ... there ... there!' he cried at last, the words forced out of him with each spurt of his seed. 'There!'

Let Vishnu decide, for His hands were upon their loins, and upon their fates.

August 1915

T HE TRAIN CLATTERED out on to an iron bridge and
for a moment, between the girders, Warren looked down a
curving reach of the river, where the dome of St. Paul's rode high
above the teeming chimneys and myriad spires of the city. The
train slowed, rode in under a glass arch: Charing Cross. Now at
last, in London, he felt that he was home again. But he saw, as he
stepped out on to the platform, that the trains had brought the war
with them from France. A score of the officers getting out of the
first class compartments, and as many of the soldiers pouring out
of the third class, were lightly bandaged, or limped, or carried one
arm in a sling. And these were only the 'walking wounded', already discharged from hospitals or, like himself, not sick enough
to go to one at all. The train at the next platform was a hospital
train, come up from Folkestone with the seriously wounded evacuated from the field hospitals in France. Few of these would ever
again be fit to fight. He stood, feeling cold in the muggy heat of the
day, looking down into shattered faces obscured by layers of bandage, on to bodies on stretchers, the coverings not concealing that
the body ended at the trunk, at faces already grey with the pallor
of death, at faces without eyes, at eyes glaring out over the abyss
of a vanished face and jaw. Here and there gracious ladies moved
among the stretchers handing out flowers bought from the cockney
flower girls in the station yard, where hospital orderlies were loading the wounded into ambulances for transport to their next, last
but one, resting place.

Warren turned away, trembling. Narayan Singh had his valise
and suitcase out of the compartment and was waiting, the baggage
hefted on his shoulder. The air felt stifling and oppressive. Warren
thought he would suffocate inside one of those smelly boxes on

332

wheels called taxis. Telling Narayan Singh that he had decided to walk, he beckoned a taxi, and said to the driver, 'Take this man and the bags to Paddington, please. Drop them at the booking office. Give him the change from the fare out of this, after you've taken a shilling tip for yourself!'

'Bob's your uncle, guv,' the driver said. '' 'Ere, *chalo*, 'op in, mate.'

The taxi chugged out into the Strand and vanished in the swirling traffic of Trafalgar Square. Warren stayed in the station yard until all the wounded had been loaded into ambulances. The ladies spoke to the wounded, as they waited, and the wounded smiled politely, when they were physically able to do so. The flower girls joked with them and they tried to laugh, if they had anything to laugh with. All the while able-bodied men passed in and out of the station, up and down the Strand, outside the iron railings. Some were in uniform, but most were not. Hulking stevedores from Covent Garden; clerks—mousy, but fit enough to carry and aim a rifle; youths flirting with the flower girls when they should have been in the trenches; older men, but still not forty, paunchy from sitting at desks, when they could have been driving lorries or issuing stores for the Service Corps ... all these people, guzzling, soaking, guarding their worthless hides while the flower of England, the volunteers, lay in windrows in Artois and Flanders, mown by the Spandaus.

He started walking, taut with anger. 'Come, Shikari,' he ordered. 'Keep to heel.' But then he realized that Shikari was back in France, and he was alone. A passing woman looked at him curiously, and he flushed; she must have heard his call to the non-existent dog.

The Admiralty Arch opened up the long vista down to Buckingham Palace between banks of flowers. Pelicans patrolled the sward of St. James's Park, and flotillas of ducks and geese swam on the tranquil waters. He strode on, his swagger stick swinging. His head had begun to ache again. He'd be all right as soon as he was tucked up in his bed in the Old Vicarage for a good night's sleep. It was funny waking up two—or was it three?—nights ago and finding Narayan Singh standing guard over him as though he were a prisoner, or a would-be suicide. Narayan told him, when he was really awake, that there was a letter in his pocket. Had all that really happened, that Krishna had written? He could faintly recall some of it. Still, the brigadier-general's signature on his leave

333

pass was clear enough. And the doctor's brief note; over-work, need to avoid a complete breakdown—the only cure was rest, away from all responsibility.

But how could anyone rest while England lay in mortal danger? Look at this man coming down the Mall, arms swinging, fit as a fiddle—but not in uniform. And there, two more lying on the grass with shop girls, canoodling, while the corpses rotted outside Ypres. And here, a woman in a tilted hat with a wide brim, eyeing him, smiling, inviting. ''Ullo, dearie.' 'Go away,' he snarled at her. 'You ought to be ashamed of yourself.' Sentries stamping on the ground outside the Palace. Buttons in threes, Scots Guards, in khaki. Good boys, they'd be in France soon enough. Every man was needed, every single one, to overcome the Hun. No exceptions, no excuses, no mercy. Up Constitution Hill, the couples rolling together like mating animals in Green Park, the grass stretching away under the heavy-leafed trees to Piccadilly. Apsley House, the Iron Duke on Copenhagen, flanked by his Highlanders and Riflemen and Dragoons. The building of England stood, the banks and palaces and mansions; the trees of England stood, the oaks and elms and chestnuts ... but the people, these people scurrying, lying grinning, were like termites gnawing at the foundations. Undermined by selfishness, self indulgence, failure to uphold the honourable and the good—how long could England stand?

They were looking strangely at him now as he strode up the edge of Hyde Park. They were easing away from him as he passed. He glared back, seeing the evil and the weakness in each, however carefully they tried to hide it. The men to France ... every one of them! The women ... God, for the women, what? There was a man with a red tie at Hyde Park Corner, shouting, and waving his arms, a hundred people gathered, some listening, some talking. Scum! He shook his fist at the speaker and went on. The Edgware Road, Sussex Gardens, denser crowds, the smell of bodies, barrows of flowers, fish on trollies, Jews selling underwear, even a Sikh selling shirts from a barrow. What was he doing here, instead of with a regiment?

'Sahib ... sahib ... here I am.'

He realized he was looking straight through Narayan Singh, standing at attention beside the valise and the suitcase in the Paddington booking office. His head ached more violently, but with the pain came a steadying. He had only to buy two tickets to

Woodborough, sit in the train for a couple of hours, and then he'd be home.

He leaned out of the window of the room, his elbows rested on the sill. It was Diana's room, and he was sleeping in it because Joan said he must not be disturbed at night by her insomnia. This morning, as on each of the five days he had been here so far, his mother had brought him breakfast in bed. After eating he had dozed some more, read *The Times*, and dozed again, until he began to feel restless. Then he got up, washed, shaved, and dressed. The day was bright, white clouds like flocks of heavy-fleeced sheep grazing the sky above Salisbury Plain. Narayan Singh and the slacker, Young Marsh, were weeding the tomato patch. His mother was talking to the rissaldar-major, who was standing between rows of cauliflowers, a trowel in his hand. Ralph Harris was sitting on a bench, sunning himself; there was a worse slacker than Young Marsh, really, for he had been given a decent education, and knew what he owed his country. From an open window downstairs there escaped the wail of a suffering violin, where that sodomite Fuller, or whatever his name was, was teaching Louise. Joan had arranged that. He wouldn't have allowed it himself, if he'd been asked. And if it had been Rodney instead of Louise, he'd have thrown the fellow out on the spot. But those swine were supposed to be afraid of women, even little girls.

He found himself frowning fiercely, and looked back to his mother and the RM. That made him feel better. They were so much of a kind, those two. His mother was twenty-five years older, and that was the reason the RM showed her a deference which would otherwise have been inappropriate. His mother remembered a few words of Hindustani from a time she had spent in India with her brother, old General Savage, donkey's years ago; and the RM had picked up a few words of English in his years with the Guides, and now, of French; but, as Warren knew, they mostly spoke each in his own tongue, and communicated by means other than words. His mother was probably telling the RM how she wanted the cauliflower seedlings set up, and he was understanding, although the words made no sense to him. Another time she had shown him the old church, and talked about its history and meaning, and he had nodded and understood.

His mother went on up the garden, her basket over her arm.

The RM knelt to continue his weeding. He was wearing khaki slacks, ammunition boots, a khaki shirt and turban, and, though still a little drawn from his bout with pneumonia, had begun to insist that he was fit to return to the regiment in France. Farther along, Young Marsh picked up the corduroy coat he had hung on a pear tree at the edge of the vegetable garden, went to Warren's mother, said something, and left. Warren turned away and finished his toilet. Ten minutes later he went down and joined the workers. The RM and Narayan Singh stiffened to attention. His mother held up her cheek to be kissed. Warren stretched luxuriously and said, 'Eleven thirty! I ought to be ashamed of myself.'

'No, Warrie, that's what you were sent here for.'

They strolled together up and down the gravel walk, while the two Indians returned to their digging. 'They are so *good*,' his mother said.

'They're farmers,' he said. 'They miss the soil ... Mother, I wish you wouldn't employ Young Marsh—a convicted criminal.'

'Now, Warrie,' his mother said gently, 'the sentence was reduced on appeal, and then suspended. He only had to pay a five pound fine.'

'Which you or Joan paid,' he said, his voice hardening. 'When I think of the men fighting in France, and this big fit young brute here, slacking ... I don't know how you can do it. If you sacked him no one else would employ him. He'd have to volunteer.'

His mother laid a thin hand on his arm. 'I do know how you feel, but I can't dismiss him for something that's his business, not mine.'

'It's every woman's business, mother,' Warren said. 'If the women of England encourage slackers, what hope is there?'

'It's for him to decide. If they pass a law saying that everyone has to serve that would be a different matter, but now it's for each of us to make up our own mind.'

'And I'd like to know why Ralph hasn't decided to do his bit,' Warren snapped. 'Look at him ... not even working to pay for his keep here.'

'I don't mind that,' his mother said. 'Though I do wish he would find some job to keep him happy.'

'He seems happy enough here,' Warren said, 'as long as no one asks him to do any work.'

'Now have a nice sit down, dear,' his mother said, 'and enjoy the sun while we have it. Tomorrow it might rain.'

Warren moodily watched the RM at his weeding for a time, then said abruptly, 'Put that down, sahib. Come with me.'

The RM obediently put away the trowel, donned his tunic, straightened his turban and fell into step at Warren's side. Five minutes later they were sitting on a bench outside the Green Man, looking across the road at the cricket field, glasses of beer before them.

'No one to play cricket,' Warren said, indicating the shuttered pavilion and the grazing cattle. 'All the men have gone to fight the war ... except Harris-sahib, who prefers to read books, and that other one who works for my mother. A worthless fellow,' he ended viciously.

'As the sahib says,' the RM said.

'Be healthy,' Warren said, raising his tankard.

'Be healthy, presence,' the RM said, and drank deeply. 'This is good beer, sahib, much better than is sold in bottles from Solan and Murree for the *gora-log*.'

'Sahib,' Warren said abruptly, 'we'll be going back to France soon. There'll be a big offensive in the autumn. I heard talk about it at Abbeville and on the ship. The regiment will take part.'

'We will not fail to do all that man can do,' the RM said.

'The Germans are strong, hard, well trained. We have to be stronger, harder, better trained.'

'*Huzoor-sahib!*'

'When we get back we must work at the regiment as you have been working in my mother's garden ... finding the weeds, rooting them out mercilessly. You understand what I mean?'

'Yes, presence.'

'Of any rank, any station! The weak. The cowardly. The careless. The disloyal.'

'Yes, presence.'

Warren drank again, staring across the field at the wooded slope of the land, the Elizabethan chimneys of Pennel House just showing above the trees, the bare breasts of the Plain high and stark beyond.

'England!' he said softly. 'We shall win! At any cost, we shall win!'

The hobbled pony grazed along the grassy bank under the

trees. The trap stood, shafts in the air, where the lane crossed the stream at an Irish bridge. The picnic hamper lay open on the grass and Joan was getting out glasses and a bottle of wine. Louise and Rodney splashed about in the shallows of the river, Louise wearing a bathing dress with flounced skirts to below her knees, Rodney a triangle of blue and white striped cotton. Warren was wearing a bathing suit which was still damp to the touch, for as soon as they had arrived at the picnic spot he had gone into the deep pool for a swim. Ralph Harris sprawled back against a tree trunk, his hands clasped behind his head.

'There,' Joan said. 'It's still cold.'

Warren drank some of the chilled white wine. He, too, rested against a tree. He wished Joan hadn't insisted on inviting Ralph to the picnic. Bees droned heavily among the flowers, swallows swooped low over the water, the river tinkled, and there was the distant hum of an aeroplane from the Royal Flying Corps airfield at Upavon on the Plain.

'Be careful, don't go near the deep pool there,' Joan called to the children.

Warren drank again. Joan was looking less peculiar than usual, though her hair still hung down like a gypsy's. Yesterday, for an afternoon visit to Pewsey, she'd worn trousers. Now she was feminine again, frowning in concentration as she began to cut the bread and spread the butter for the sandwiches.

'Here,' Warren called to his daughter. 'I'll teach you to swim.' He stepped gingerly into the stream. Louise was splashing about in water to her knees. Warren lifted her under one arm and walked out towards the deep water of the pool at the far side. 'No, daddy!' the girl suddenly screamed. 'I don't want to!'

'Oh, let her go,' Joan called. 'She'll learn in time.'

'She'll learn now!' Warren snapped. He held tight hold of the struggling girl as he transferred one hand to her stomach. 'Now, stop it, at once, Louise! ... I've got you. You can't sink. Just pretend you're a...' but the child screamed and struggled and sobbed and would not rest supported on his hand. He shouted at her, 'Then swim on your own, damn you!'

He took his hand away and stepped back. The girl's frantic face disappeared under water, came up again with a terrified shriek, and disappeared again.

'Go like this,' Warren shouted, imitating the breast stroke. 'You won't sink. Come on!'

Joan splashed violently past him, seized her daughter by the hair, dragged her out and up, and floundered back towards the bank, crying, 'There, there, it's all right, darling. You're out now.'

Warren came slowly up out of the water. 'What the hell did you do that for?' he snarled. 'She was just beginning to swim.' Ralph Harris sighed and lit a cigarette.

'She was drowning,' Joan snapped. 'She was in a panic. You...'

The girl stopped her sniffles and ran back to the water. 'See!' Warren shouted. 'There's nothing wrong with her. She's got to learn to swim sooner or later. She's just taking the easy way out. Like some other people here.'

'Do you mean Sam? Or Ralph?' she flared. 'Why should they go and fight in a war that's destroying everything it's supposed to be saving? Cities, farms, cathedrals, churches, libraries ... manners, kindness, charity, love ... all gone. Look at yourself, Warren, inside yourself, instead of just the face in the mirror. Don't you realize what sort of person you have become?'

He shouted, 'I won't have any more of this! Louise *will* learn to swim. And they will *not* wear those ridiculous clothes you put them in. Or lack of clothes. They're the laughing stock of the village. And they *will* be told what to do, and whipped if they don't do it. You're bringing them up like ... gipsies, no better disciplined than puppies.'

'I'm bringing them up according to the Harz-Goldwasser method,' she said angrily, 'which is designed not to stunt but develop the child's creative impulses. You *used* to think it was good, once.'

'To hell with Harz and Goldwasser. Why should my children be filled with bloody Hun notions? And Louise is not to have any more lessons from Fuller.'

'You're being ridiculous,' she said.

'That's what you think,' he snarled. 'But if you won't enforce the proper standards, I will. I'm not going to have my children associate with a sodomite hiding under an alias.'

'He's a gentleman and a scholar,' she stormed. 'How can you be so vindictive? Nothing's ever been proved against him, only gossip by nasty-minded people.'

'People who don't want any of his filthy perversion,' Warren said.

'Your second-in-command doesn't seem to mind,' Ralph cut in. 'Krishna offered him a job in his state any time he wanted to accept.'

'What Krishna Ram does or says is his business,' Warren said. 'He's an Indian. We're English. Fuller will not enter my house again.'

'It's not yours. It's your mother's,' Joan snapped.

The aeroplane buzzed like a giant bee in the clouds. That was the sound of the war, God damn it, aeroplanes humming and buzzing all day up and down, up and down over the trenches in the blue sky.

'Oh stop it, for Christ Almighty's sake!' he yelled.

The children playing under his window awakened him before he had slept an hour. He frowned in annoyance, and thought of shouting to them to be quiet; but he heard the rissaldar-major's voice, and, glancing out, saw that the RM was giving them piggy-back rides. He didn't have the heart to disturb the game, but he couldn't sleep through the noise, so crossed the hall in his pyjamas to the big bedroom at the back, where Joan slept. It was the day after the scene at the river picnic, another afternoon of heavy air, slow drifting clouds and the sounds of late summer. The curtains were open and he went to close them to shut out the strong light. As he neared them, his hands out, he saw his wife slip into the little room at the end of the stables where the groom used to sit and polish the saddlery in the days when they had a groom. The door closed. Warren stepped back instinctively. What was Joan doing there? She had moved quickly, with a glance to right and left as she entered the room. There was nothing in there, as far as Warren remembered, but a table and chair and an old camp bed. There was a little window facing the side. He edged back, looked, and saw that the faded curtains on the little window were drawn. His heart began to pound. He slipped back across the landing and dressed quickly. The children were still playing with the RM. His mother would be resting in her room. Narayan Singh was digging in the tomato bed. Warren went quickly down the stairs and out of the back door. He crossed the brick-paved stable yard on stockinged feet and paused at the door of the little room at the end of the stables. Did he hear sounds, a rhythmic panting, the moans of a woman in passion? Sounds he had not heard from Joan for a long time.

The door would be bolted; but he remembered the bolt—a flimsy affair, the metal rusted from years of disuse, the screws set in rotting wood. He stepped back, then rammed his shoulder into the door with all his weight and strength. The bolt gave way with a rending of wood and he half fell, half ran into the room. A flood of heat, as sensual and achingly bitter-sweet as a massage of the prostate, overcame him.

The man's trousers hung round his ankles, the great gluteal muscles of his bare buttocks rhythmically contracting in the final throes of orgasm. His body, wearing a white shirt, covered the body of the woman under him. Her legs were well clasped round his back, her arms round his neck, her pelvis heaving against his thrusts.

Warren waited. The convulsive movements stopped, the man slid off the woman without looking round, pulled up his trousers and began to fasten his fly buttons. The woman, the lips of her vulva enlarged and wide-spread, dripping out the seed just squirted into her, the blonde hairs wet, was his wife. Slowly she pulled down her skirt, staring him straight in the eye as she did so. Ralph Harris turned round, and said, 'I'm sorry, but I suppose you had to learn some time.'

Warren said, 'Whoring with a slacker. Now I see why he wouldn't go away to fight—or even work.'

'I love him,' she said. She had stood up and was holding Ralph's hand. Her face was mottled and flushing as the blood flowed back into it from the secret parts of her body.

'He is five years younger than you,' Warren said contemptuously. 'Apart from the other things.' He thought, I ought to feel anger, but I don't; only a kind of heat, as of battle, where I have the enemy in the hollow of my hand, the machine guns trained, and no escape for them. She had to be punished, for she had broken the standards and was teaching others, even his own children, to do the same.

She said, 'I used to love you, Warren. Until this war, you were . . .'

'Stop!' he ground. 'We've been into all that before.'

'We'll get married as soon as you divorce her,' Ralph said.

'You won't,' Warren said, 'because I'm not going to let her go.

341

You're not going to marry anyone. You're going to France.' He stared into his half-brother's face. 'You come to Devizes with me tomorrow and volunteer for the army. The infantry. No escape into the service corps and a safe billet at the base for you. The Guards would do you a lot of good. You will volunteer for the Coldstream Guards in my presence, and you will go in, and stay in.'

'Don't be ridiculous, Warren,' Joan said.

'Or,' Warren continued, 'I shall sue Joan for divorce, and drag all this mud into the open.'

No one spoke for a while, then Ralph said, 'I'll have to go, darling.'

'Of course you don't! I don't mind who knows!'

'It would kill mother,' Ralph said. '*He* knows that.' To Warren he said, 'I'll go with you tomorrow, but you must promise to let Joan free. There's nothing left of your marriage. You can't pretend there is.'

'I promise nothing of the sort,' Warren said. 'She is going to stay with me, as my wife, doing her duty in her proper place, as I do mine in mine. All I promise is that I shall say nothing to anyone else about ... this.'

'Leave us then,' Ralph said, his voice hardening, 'we have to say good-bye.'

For a moment Warren hesitated. The nerve of the man, to ask him to leave them alone, to make love again perhaps. But they were looking into each other's eyes and he realized that it would make no difference whether he stayed or went. They were aware only of each other. He went out, closing the battered door carefully behind him, and returned to his room.

The train slid across the flat fields of Berkshire at a steady seventy miles an hour. It rushed over the Thames at Maidenhead and raced through Slough. Warren sat in a first class corner seat, his thoughts passing in pleasant review. Ralph Harris was in the army, at last. Fuller had been told not to appear again. Joan would not speak to him, except in front of his mother, and then only when she had to. Good. Everyone was doing what they must, what was right. His mother had noticed something amiss, and asked anxiously, 'Dearest Warrie ... is there anything wrong between you and Joan?'

'Nothing, mother,' he'd said, patting her hand. 'Nothing at all.'

She had looked at him doubtfully. She knew he was lying, perhaps, but then she knew too that a man's marriage is his own business and no one else's, not even a mother's. She had said, 'Joan's a good girl, really, Warrie. It's this war that has upset her ... and she so highly strung. Think of the number of people she loved that she's lost.'

'There's nothing to worry about, mother,' he had said. And that was the truth. What was there to worry about in the fact that he had put his foot down at last, as he should have done years ago, when he first recognized the way she was heading, towards this arty and dangerous socialist nonsense? She had ruined the marriage so what was left but duty?

The train came to a halt at Paddington and there, as he went out with the RM and Narayan Singh, was Dayal Ram, helping Lady Harriet Symonds out of a taxi. A porter took the couple's suitcases. Dayal Ram saw Warren and saluted. He had a half smile on his handsome face, but it was a smile of superiority, not friendliness.

'Good morning, Lady Harriet,' Warren said. 'Good morning, Dayal.'

'Just arrived on ten days' leave, sir,' Dayal said. His voice was cold.

'And I'm whisking him down to Warwickshire to have a real rest,' the girl said, 'and all the things he can't get in the trenches.' Her smile left no doubt of her meaning. 'Now do excuse us, we only have a minute to catch our train.'

They hurried off. Warren stared after them for a moment. Dayal was going to spend ten days fornicating with an English girl, a peer's daughter at that. He'd have to teach him a few harsh lessons when he got him back into the trenches. And what had Diana been doing? He'd written to her address the day he arrived on leave, but had had no answer until this morning. Where could she have gone, without telling her mother, or why hadn't she answered before? Why hadn't she come down to Shrewford Pennel, knowing he didn't have long on his leave? Ah, perhaps she had known about Ralph and Joan, and guessed that this time it would come to a head, and didn't want to be there when it happened...

He took the RM and Narayan to the hostel for Indian soldiers in Victoria Street and arranged to pick them up there in time to catch the returning leave train that evening. Then he continued in the same taxi to his great-uncle's flat in Kensington.

Major-General Rodney Savage, CB, was his mother's older brother. He was eighty-seven or eighty-eight now, long a widower, and lived alone in a flat on Nashe Street, with his bearer, Ashraf, who was nearly as old as he. Warren wondered, as he waited on the step after ringing the bell, whether he should tell the old man about Joan; but what would be the purpose, except to make clear to him the terrible slackening of morality in England, and surely he must be well aware of that already?

Soon he found himself seated in a big chair in front of the fire, a whisky and soda in his hand. It was a hot day but the old general's blood ran cold, though his eyes still sparkled a fierce frosty blue and when he stood up his back was straight.

'Why didn't you bring your rissaldar-major along, Warrie?' the old man asked. 'You said in your letter that he was with you in Shrewford Pennel ... Speak up. I'm a little deaf these days.'

'I thought I'd see you alone,' Warren said. 'Then I'm going down to Woolwich to see Diana. If you felt up to it, I thought I'd send the RM round on his own.'

'Of course I'm up to it,' the general grumbled. 'When the time comes that I can't talk to a rissaldar-major I won't be able to talk to you ... What does he make of England, eh? Is he from Ravi?'

'No, uncle, he's from the Guides Cavalry.'

'Good regiment, good regiment!'

'And he's a very good man, too ... The richness of the soil here and in France impresses all of them, of course, and the size of the buildings.'

'They have big buildings in India, too.'

'Yes, but ours seem more solid to them, I think, and they are in use. The big buildings in India mostly seem to be ruins, or monuments, or museums ... Of course he doesn't know enough of England to see what a deterioration is going on in our life. I don't really like having sowars come to England ... women accosting them in the street, men and women drunk in the gutters ...'

'They've seen *gora-log* drunk in the bazaars of India,' his great-uncle said.

'Yes, but that's different ... And, when they've volunteered, what can they make of all the able-bodied slackers they see in the streets and shops? I'm afraid they'll go back to India with an impression that we're finished, that we have lost our determina-

344

tion as a people ... that we won't fight ourselves but are hiring them to fight for us.'

The general shot him a quick look under the fierce white eyebrows. 'And you think that's true?'

'From what I have seen, yes, sir.'

The general took a mighty gulp of his whisky and put the heavy cut-glass goblet down. 'Things are changing, certainly ... gals showing their ankles almost as much as they did when I was young, before that German prig Albert had his way. And a lot of the barriers between the classes are breaking down. Not bad ideas as long as something better replaces them. And there are a lot of slackers, yes, but not all the able-bodied men you see about in mufti are slackers. Do you realize two million men had volunteered for the army by last Christmas—four months after the war started? But hundreds of thousands of 'em haven't been called up even yet because of shortage of equipment of every kind ... No, no, we're not finished. When they're really up against it, the people will come through all right. Always have. Always will.'

'I don't know, sir. I wish...'

The general interrupted him, 'One reason for discontent or lack of enthusiasm, that does exist, is the way the war is being fought. Great God, I wish I were young enough to be out there with you and see for myself what's wrong. All we know here is that the generals keep promising, but never perform. The casualties are enormous but where are the results? We are destroying Christendom ... for what?'

'That's what Joan says,' Warren said, involuntarily, the words jerked out him by surprise.

Again a keen look was shot at him. 'Oh. How is she?'

'Well,' he muttered.

'And the children? You have two, don't you?'

'Yes, sir. They're well ... What do you feel about pacifists, sir?'

The general drank again and pulled speculatively at his ear. He said, 'I'm Indian Army, Warrie—like you. We've only dealt with volunteers. That's all we want to deal with, eh? When we're recruiting through the Doab Canal villages, we don't go in demanding why this boy and that boy don't volunteer. We just take the ones that do, and try to send them back so proud and fit and strong that next time we go, more boys will volunteer. I treat every Englishman the same way. If he's not in uniform he has his reasons, and they are not for me to question—as long as the service is voluntary.'

'That's what my mother thinks.'

'Margaret's a sensible girl ... but whether recruiting *ought* to be voluntary, that's a different matter. We've never had conscription in this country and the idea is hateful to me ... but then we've never had casualties on this scale before, and the war going to go on for years, as Kitchener thinks. Perhaps we ought to enlist everyone ... including a few top business-men to help run the war. We soldiers certainly are not doing it very well.'

They talked then of Shrewford Pennel and of old days in India, until Warren looked at his watch and saw that it was time for him to set out for Woolwich. As he got up the general said, 'I've put in a telephone ... in the hall. Tell the rissaldar-major to come along at four. I'm going to have a little stroll and then a nap.'

The old bearer creaked out of a back room and showed Warren to the door, saluting in the old fashioned way, his doddering hand shaking against the dark green puggaree band adorned by the crossed kukris and silver figures XIII of his master's old regiment. Warren found a taxi, and nearly an hour later was walking down a dingy street in Woolwich looking at the house numbers.

The landlady eyed him suspiciously when he rang the bell and announced that he wanted to see Miss Bateman, but her face cleared when he added, 'I'm her brother.' She peered up at him and said, 'Ow yes, so y'are. Look alike as two peas ... 'Ope you wasn't offended like but we carn't afford to get a bad name 'ere, y'know.'

Diana came to her door when he knocked and after a startled pause flung her arms round his neck, crying, 'Oh, Warrie! I'm so glad to see you.' He wondered why she looked surprised, for she knew he was coming.

'There now, 'e's safe,' the landlady cooed, and went downstairs, clucking sympathetically.

Diana looked well, Warren thought, prettier than the last time he'd seen her; younger, too, though she was nearly thirty-one. Her eyes sparkled and she had an air, a new manner. She chattered away, asking him whether he was ready for lunch, and where he wanted to go. As he answered he glanced out of the window at a vista of grimy brick walls and broken windows. God, how ugly, he thought, and turned his eyes inside the room. He caught sight of a photograph in a silver frame on her bedside table. He recognized the frame. It used to hold a photograph of himself in full dress, but now it held a photograph of Yuvraj Krishna Ram and Diana, holding hands with the Eiffel Tower behind them.

He felt again the strange red-hot sensation in the depths of his body that had flooded him when he saw Ralph thrusting into Joan. He said, 'When was that taken?'

She looked around, saw the photograph and opened a drawer as though to sweep it in. Then she stopped, holding the photograph hugged to her breast. 'Oh dear, I meant to put it away before you arrived, but I forgot ... or perhaps I didn't really want to.'

Now he saw the diamond brooch at her breast. 'Is that real?' he asked. The sensations plunging through him were alternately hot and crackling cold, as though he were a part of a line carrying thousands of volts of electricity.

'Yes,' she said, '*he* gave it to me. Oh, Warrie!'—she put down the photograph and clung to him—'we love each other so much! I've never been so happy. We're going to be married and one day soon I shall be the Rani of Ravi. It's so exciting, so wonderful, there's so much for me to do there! *I* shan't just sit in the harem eating sweets and getting fat!'

'You went ... lived with him, in Paris?'

'Yes,' she said.

'When?'

'This week. I'm only just back.'

He turned and walked out of the room and down the stairs, hearing her cry behind him: 'Warrie ... Warrie! Warrie, please!'

August–September 1915

KRISHNA RAM CRAWLED carefully down the side of the shell hole and crouched at the bottom, recovering his breath, until the eight other men of the patrol joined him. The German lines in Sector 76 lay fifty yards ahead. It was near the end of August, and a warm rain was falling. In this area the lines had been stationary long enough now so that, what with harassing fire every night, and covering fire for patrols and small scale attacks, and SOS tasks and defensive fire, the tree stumps had been blown to matchwood; and the ground, which had once been stippled with grass, and wild flowers, and wheat grown from last year's un-gathered harvest, was now just mud—brownish mud, wet, slippery, and cratered with small and large shell holes, littered with corpses, helmets, bayonets, skulls, broken rifles, snakes of barbed wire, sand-bags, and boots with feet rotting inside them. Over all hung the universal smells of lyddite and decay.

This was Krishna's third patrol since the CO came back from sick leave. The first had been a small reconnaissance patrol, such as this, sent out to observe movement in front of Sector 77, where the Germans were thought to be putting up new wire. They weren't, they were doing nothing, and the patrol returned, without incident or casualties. Why had Warren sent him, his second-in-command, on that task? The most bone-headed acting-lance-dafadar in the regiment could tell whether wire was being put out or not.

The second patrol he'd been ordered out on was more reason-able—a full scale fighting patrol to cover the establishment of an advanced listening post in front of B Squadron at the left of the line. Even so, two troops totalling forty men with two of the new Lewis guns was hardly a major's command. The normal person to put in command of such a force would be the squadron leader—Himat Singh, or his senior rissaldar.

Perhaps the CO wanted him, Krishna, to get more tactical experience at the junior level. Perhaps it was something more personal. But that would be peculiarly oriental. It would be ironic if Warren Bateman, in his efforts to turn the men into brown-skinned Englishmen, himself turned into a white-skinned Indian.

He peered around. His men were all here and rested. Time to move on.

He crawled up the side of the shell hole and on across No Man's Land parallel to the German wire, which was on his right. It was strange that he had had no mail since the postcard Diana had sent him from Le Havre, which said simply *All my love, D.* He'd told her in Paris that Warren was on leave in England. Had she gone down to Shrewford Pennel when she got back? Had Warren visited her in Woolwich? Did he know that she had been away from Woolwich? Of their meeting in Paris? If she had told him about that, surely she would have written saying that she had done so. He ought to tell the CO himself. It was shameful to live with such a pretence; also, like all lies and deceptions, it showed fear. He was not afraid of Warren Bateman. He ought . . .

A hand on his boot stopped him short. As he turned his head he heard an exclamation from close in front, and saw the loom of a body no more than six feet ahead of him. A rifle exploded almost in his ear. The dark shape lurched, coughed, and was still. Two more shapes detached themselves from the first, rose, and ran. The sowar behind Krishna fired again but the runners had melted into the darkness. A pistol flare rose into the rain, and a machine gun began to sweep No Man's Land from the German lines. Its fixed line was somewhere off to the left and the bullets ripped high over the crater where the Indian patrol lay.

The sowar who had fired muttered, 'I thought you had seen him, lord, or I would have fired earlier.'

'I saw nothing,' Krishna said. 'You saved me.'

That's what came of thinking about one's private life in No Man's Land, he thought grimly. He'd crawled almost up to the muzzle of the German's rifle—would have done so if the sowar had not fired. Something was trickling down his face. He put up his hand and peered at it—blood from a cut in the forehead. Probably wire in the shell hole, which he'd slid on to or over. Nothing to do but wait now.

The machine gun was joined by another. A shell from a German field gun whistled over to burst close by. The two remaining Germans of the listening patrol must have got back to their line by now and reported the position where the Indians ran into them. But they were as safe here as anywhere, lying on their faces in the mud at the bottom of the shell hole, safe from anything but a direct hit, and the Germans didn't sound very angry, or disposed to fire too many shells.

Diana ... he saw her body, not in the great bed, but in the long grass beside the Seine, dandelions under her thighs and daisies under her head. It was hard to imagine her as his wife. Her relationship to him could not be the same as his mother's had been to his father, or the old Rani's to his grandfather. Diana was both stronger and less influential. Indian women had ways of exerting pressure that you did not recognize until they had had their effect and you had done or thought what they wanted you to do or think; but Diana said, Do this, don't do that ... which gave a man the ability to resist, if he wanted to.

The shelling, after ten minutes' desultory searching of No Man's Land, ceased. The machine guns stopped firing. He muttered to his dafadar, 'Five minutes more, and we'll start back.'

An hour later he was in the RAP, having the long wire cut in his forehead bandaged. He and Ramaswami were alone in the little office. It was near two in the morning. The doctor said, 'There. You'll look very warlike for a few days ... The CO has been making a thorough investigation of the sick list, and the medicines issued. He says it is to check up on whether I am using Vedic cures, but I think there is another motive—to find out whether you were really sick, and confined to your dugout for those four days, as I reported ... You look as if you could do with a cigarette.'

Krishna sat on the edge of the table, swinging his legs. 'No, thanks,' he said. 'I'm over that craving now.'

The doctor said, 'I thought you should know. Might he have come to suspect something?'

Krishna said, 'I don't know ... I was with his sister in Paris.'

'Oh.' The doctor's dark face was grave. 'I didn't know that.'

'I don't know whether he knows. I haven't had any mail since, though she promised to write every other day.'

The doctor said, 'You've been sent out on, how many patrols, since the CO came back from leave?'

'Three.'

'He's trying to get you killed. Which means that he knows about his sister.'

'Perhaps. Though Diana is not really the cause. She's only a symptom.'

'Are you going to let him? There's nothing I can do to save you, but there's plenty you can. He could be found shot by accident any day. Or dead from food poisoning.'

Krishna said seriously, 'Not yet ... I feel that a great battle is coming. It will decide.'

'A battle with the Germans? Or between you and him?'

'Between the Kauravas and the Pandavas.'

The doctor said, 'And he is Duryodhan?'

'Yes. I am trying, like the god whose name I bear, to find a solution without war ... but Duryodhan is determined to fight a decisive battle. It shall be as it shall be.'

It was raining again, with an early autumn wind blowing from the Atlantic across the sodden earth. The wind blew wet on Krishna's cheek and water was soaking the big khaki handkerchief he wore round his neck, and beginning to run down his back.

Seven days since his last patrol. Or was it six? Every other officer of the regiment had been out in between, including the CO himself, so he had no justification, according to European ideas of fair play, to think that he was being picked on; yet he was sure. Warren had told him that the brigadier-general was insisting on more and more aggressive patrolling along the whole of the brigade front. That would be true enough. Some time had passed since Rainbow Rogers got his CMG, and he would be hungry for something more. There were rumours that a Spanish Army delegation studying trench warfare would be willing to swap a high decoration for a really good demonstration of a fighting patrol. Nevertheless, to Krishna, all that was more of an excuse than a reality. If Rainbow hadn't become so keen on patrolling, Warren would have, on his own account. And certainly no one could say he was a coward. He was quite willing to risk his own life to get Krishna's.

He peered at the luminous dial of his watch, shading it in his cupped hand. 0237. He could start back in, say, ten minutes.

It had rained every night that he was on patrol. Was his ancestor the Sun turning his face from him? Or sending his handmaiden to protect him with the sound of her tears? This northern rain

351

made night in No Man's Land very uncomfortable, the air raw and chill, the mud clammy in hands and face and heavy on the boots; but the sounds of the water in the puddles and shell holes, the slap and ting of raindrops on an abandoned mess-tin, the sough of the wind in the jungle of barbed wire, these helped a man to move without being heard and made the German sentries huddle deeper into the collars of capes and greatcoats, less able to identify what they were less able to detect.

He tapped his dafadar on the shoulder and signalled with his hand, 'Back.' The NCO started back with half the men, while Krishna stayed forward with the Lewis gunner and the other half, in case covering fire was needed. Far up the line to the north a star shell threw a tiny glare into the sky. Momentarily the Lewis gunner's brown eye gleamed above the fat, shiny barrel. Then the light faded. Nothing to report, Krishna thought. Four hours on listening patrol, hoping to ambush a German patrol or at least to hear and see and not be heard and seen. All quiet. No casualties, no prisoners. The CO had brought back a German body from his patrol last week, with no casualties or loss to his own men.

The British wire glinted dully in the rain and a sentry challenged quietly. Krishna passed through the gap and slid down into the trench. It wouldn't take long to tell the IO what he had learned on the patrol—nothing.

Half an hour later he walked down three steps, pulled aside a gas curtain, and entered the candle-lit cave of his dugout. He sat on the camp bed, yawning, while Hanuman took off his boots. A British officer would take a tot of rum at a time like this; so would he have, six months ago—two or three tots. But Hanuman handed him a mug of steaming hot tea laced with pepper and cardamom seeds. The warmth flowed into his chilled bones and he yawned again. Pahlwan, the IO, had told him that the CO had not gone to bed but was waiting in his command dugout for the patrol report. Well, now he too could go to bed. Krishna had survived the night. Warren had patience.

A voice at the gas curtain said, 'Prince?' He recognized the quartermaster's voice and called, 'Enter.'

Sohan Singh came in, making deep *namasti*. He opened a little jar and said, 'This will give you a good sleep, lord, with pleasant dreams.'

Krishna saw that the powder in the jar was high quality opium.

He said, 'Oh ... well, I'm not on duty again till noon. Drop some in.'

'In a moment, lord,' Sohan Singh said respectfully. 'At this quality, and in the hot tea, it will act very quickly ... Prince, Major Himat Singh spent two hours with the CO yesterday. Captain Flaherty placed chairs so that the clerks could hear nothing, and he himself waited in the outer office so that no one could get closer.'

'Discussing fighting patrols?' Krishna said. 'Himat's a great expert on them.'

'Lord, Himat Singh will do anything for Colonel Bateman. Even to betraying his own prince.'

'For the sake of the regiment. Yes, I can understand that.'

'With a British officer, it might be so, lord, but he is an Indian. What he is doing is not for the regiment but out of his love for Colonel Bateman ... I think that the colonel may have asked him, on his honour, to tell if he knows of any irregularities that occurred while he was away, or that are still taking place. Such as the private fund you authorized me to arrange. Such as the French women in the barn.'

'And you think he may have done so?'

'It is possible. Colonel Bateman shows nothing, says nothing. His face does not alter towards me.'

Krishna said, 'Very Oriental. Just like you yourself, or your father. Or my grandfather ... Is that all?'

'Yes, lord.'

'Give me the opium ... Hanuman, see that I am not disturbed, except by the colonel-sahib in person, until eleven o'clock.'

'Huzoor sahib!'

It was raining again. This autumn was wetter than last year's, but not as cold. Under the rain the soil here in Artois turned into a peculiar glue-like clay that he had not met in India. It was exactly a year since he had landed at Marseilles with the Ravi Lancers, the flower of Indian chivalry. He could see the lance points gleaming as the regiment, reunited with their horses, trotted out of the docks and up the hill through the streets. The sun was shining that day, and the sea a blue-painted backdrop, the light glittering on the little wave crests as it glittered on the lance points.

Five days since his last patrol. This one was a fighting patrol to knock out a machine gun post on the slope of Hill 93. Hill 93 was no more than a melancholy hump six or seven feet high, but in that flat land it gave the gunners command of a long sector of No Man's Land. Patrols and aerial photographs had shown that the post was well roofed and sandbagged, and well protected by wire. It probably contained eight men and two NCOs, no more, for the photographs showed that it was a round bay, twelve feet in diameter, linked to the front line behind it by twenty feet of trench.

Here was the wire. The machine gun post was close to his right front now. The sentry ought to be standing on the open firestep to one side or other of the roofed gun platform. He ought to be ... but *would* he be, in this rain? More likely, he was crouched over the gun, under cover, peering through the narrow band of the aperture for the gun's traverse. He murmured to the jemadar who was his second-in-command on the patrol, 'Ready?'

The jemadar muttered, 'Yes, lord.'

Krishna crawled off to the right with six men. Straight in front of the post, but to the side of the machine gun platform, which was positioned for the guns to fire in enfilade, two sowars covered the wire in a blanket, and began to cut through, one man cutting and one holding the wire on either side of the cut to prevent it springing back to hit another wire with a distinctive sound. Once the sowar dropped the wire cutters and Krishna tensed, ready to charge, but nothing happened. After twenty minutes of careful slow work they were through the wire. The machine gun post lay ten yards ahead.

Krishna brought his men up close, rose to his knees, and broke into a careful run. He reached the edge of the pit before anyone else, and dropped in a long jump on to the firestep, thence to the duckboarded floor. He heard an exclamation to his left, and saw something move under the gun's low roof, and fired his revolver twice at two feet range. Immediately, from where he'd left the jemadar, the patrol's Lewis gun began to fire in bursts along the German front line trench. Two of his own sowars ran past him down the short communication trench and began to throw grenades. Two more raised the gas curtain covering the dugout in the back wall of the post and threw in four grenades. They burst in a clangour of steel, followed by agonized screams. Steel splinters thudded into the sandbags as Krishna pulled the dead sentry off the gun and fired his revolver into the gun's firing mechanisms.

Then, ordering Hanuman to pull aside the gas curtain, he went into the dugout, revolver out-thrust. A hurricane lantern still burned in a sandbagged niche at the back. Half a dozen German soldiers writhed, groaning, or lay still, on the floor and in bunks at the sides. Against one wall were stacked three cylinders with nozzles. Krishna recognized them at once, from intelligence reports and drawings, as flame throwers. The Germans had used them at the end of July but the British, so far, had not made any of their own. He called up to his men, 'Come here. Take those ... Out now!'

He ran out and climbed up on to the firestep. One by one his men joined him, and passed through the wire. The jemadar and the rest of the patrol came up and they all started back towards the British lines at a slow run. From the German lines there was silence until the patrol was passing through the British wire; then Krishna heard the thud of artillery from the east and with a whistling shriek four shells burst among them, blasting Krishna to the ground.

As he picked himself out of the mud, he called, 'Are you all right? Moti? Chattar Singh?'

No one answered. The jemadar was calling to him from the safety of the trench close ahead, 'Come in, lord. Quick! They'll fire again.'

But Krishna searched along the wire in the mud and darkness until he found first one then another and at last all six of the sowars who had been with him at the machine gun post. They were all dead, two decapitated, two torn in half. The German artillery did not fire again.

Warren Bateman was waiting for him in the trench. A torch flashed momentarily in his face and the familiar voice said, 'Krishna? Are you hit?'

'No, sir,' he said.

'Did you get the machine guns?'

'Yes, sir. Killed the sentry and half the crew. I went into their dugout. They had three flame throwers there. We brought them back ... We had six killed, just now. They're along our wire, here. And the flame throwers.'

'Right. I'll have them brought in at once. Wait for me in my office dugout at rear HQ.'

'Yes, sir.'

Krishna walked along the front line trench until a communication trench opened up to the rear. His boots were heavy with mud and he kept staggering and sliding as he shuffled to the rear. For a moment out there, in the exhilaration of the fight, he had felt eager and young. Now he did not. Nor yet old and cold, nor precisely numb. He felt removed from himself, watching his body trudge down the trench, past the reserve trench line, past the second reserve line, past the RAP, a dim blue lamp outside its gas curtain, to the CO's office dugout. Warren's orderly was there, and two hurricane lanterns burned on the table. A calendar hung on one sandbagged wall, with a framed portrait of King George V, which he had presented to the regiment after his inspection last December. On the other wall hung a hand-coloured photograph of Krishna's grandfather the Rajah of Ravi, and a pair of large maps, stuck with coloured pins and covered with red and blue lines. The desk was a bare table, a hard chair behind it and another in front.

Krishna sat down in one of the chairs, and waited. Ten minutes later the gas curtain parted and the adjutant, Brian Flaherty, came in, saluting, and said, 'The CO will be here in a moment, sir.'

Krishna thought, this is going to be the declaration of war. Anything else could have waited till morning. Warren had been hoping, surely, that the Germans would save him the necessity of this step; but Vishnu looked after his own, and Krishna was going to live. The battle would have to be declared. Four a.m. was a time to catch a man weak and off his guard, particularly if he has just spent three hours in No Man's Land, killed a man, and was splattered with the blood of his comrades, and subjects.

Warren Bateman came in, followed by Flaherty, and Krishna stood up. The CO sat down behind the desk, took off his peaked cap and set it carefully down in his IN tray. Flaherty stood rigid behind and to one side of Krishna. Krishna thought, I wonder why he has brought Flaherty into this? It could be as a witness to some order he was about to give, but it felt like something else, something more personally concerning the struggle between them.

Warren Bateman opened the table drawer and took out a packet of letters. He handed them across the table to Krishna Ram and said, 'These letters are addressed to you. They were intercepted

356

and examined by the Corps Censor . . . at my request.'

Krishna said, 'Did you have reason to doubt my loyalty, or discretion, sir?'

'I had reason to doubt your devotion to duty. Those letters prove that you were in Paris when you were supposed to be here in command of the regiment. You deserted your post without leave. And you lied about it, giving out that you were sick and unable to see anyone. Is this true?'

'Yes,' Krishna Ram said.

'I will deal with that, as a military matter, later. As a personal matter I am telling you that my sister is not going to marry a liar, a man who betrays the trust placed in him. Do you understand?'

Krishna Ram said, 'That will have to be decided by her, sir. As you say, it is not a military matter.'

'You will not marry my sister,' Warren Bateman said forcefully. 'These things that you have done have proved finally what Rudyard Kipling said, *East is east and west is west and never the twain shall meet.* Your ideas of decency and honour are not the same as hers, and I am not going to see her life ruined by a . . . you. Nor have her bear children like Flaherty here.' He looked at Flaherty. 'Are you happy with what you are?'

The burly half-Indian looked startled, then his mouth quivered and he said, 'No, sir . . . I hate it, sir! I often pray to God to make me English or Indian, one or the other.'

Perhaps he's right, Krishna thought. It needed more than wisdom to hold to two cultures, embracing both—it needed love. Or strength. Warren did not seem to know, or perhaps had forgotten, that Kipling's poem continued:

> *But there is neither East nor West,*
> *Border, nor Breed, nor Birth,*
> *When two strong men stand face to face,*
> *Though they come from the ends of the earth!*

Mr Fleming had taught him that, very emphatically.

'You see?' Warren said. 'The subject is not for discussion any more.' He took another sheaf of papers out of the drawer, opened it and spread the papers on the desk. He said, 'Here are statements by Major Himat Singh and Quartermaster-Jemadar Chhota Mall. They state that the quartermaster is misusing regimental funds by investing them in the French stock exchange, and by dealing with various commodities on the civilian market. He is also

running a regimental brothel. Here'—he tapped another paper—
'is his own statement. He says that all this is true, and it was all
his own idea and no one else knows about it. Is that true?'

'No, sir. It was done on my orders.'

'Why?'

Krishna Ram looked thoughtfully into Warren Bateman's eyes.
What did he see, with those eyes and how much deeper with the
eyes of the spirit? He loved India, and Indians, without understanding either. What sort of explanation could Krishna give now,
that would transfuse into Warren's consciousness ideas and thoughts
that had grown up not in the dust of the plains, the heat of the
bazaars—Warren knew all that—but in quiet rooms with the old
Brahmin, with his mother, with the pert girl sent to teach him
love of women, in the inner depths of the temple, from the paintings of past rajahs and their women by the river at Basohli?

He said, 'I thought it was right, for the men. It was according to
our customs in Ravi.'

Warren Bateman said, 'You have betrayed the trust I put in you,
which is not important. You have forced half a dozen men to lie
for you ... the doctor, your orderly, all the officers of the regiment,
except one. But I see that lying is nothing to an Indian, especially
an Indian prince ... But perhaps you care that you have wrecked
the career of and ruined the life of a man who, until you came,
had every hope of a long and prosperous retirement, loaded with
honours. Rissaldar-Major Baldev Singh.'

'The RM?' Krishna said, staring down at Warren. 'He knew
nothing of it.'

'Do you expect me to believe that?' Warren said.

'He didn't,' Krishna said vehemently. 'We knew that he would
do his duty at all costs, so we saw that he was kept in the dark
of anything that was done against your British rules and regulations.'

'What is the rissaldar-major's job?' Warren said quietly.

'To ... to know,' Krishna said. 'Yes. But how *can* he, in a
regiment like this, with its special circumstances? In the regular
army, the officers are British, so the sowars and sepoys turn to
their VCOs, headed by the rissaldar-major. They rely on their RM
to interpret for them to the British ... to translate what they feel
into what the British can understand. But here—we are the same
as the men. Only you and the adjutant are foreign. The men do

not need interpreters. Even so, as the RM is a Rajput, too, he might have learned of what I had ordered, if I were not who I am.'

'And you used that fact to destroy discipline in your grandfather's own regiment? Well, I am going to have Baldev Singh demoted and discharged. I hope you will realize that you alone bear the burden of his disgrace, for that is what it will be.'

Krishna looking into Warren's face, saw a tortured intensity behind the hostile mask. Something terrible had happened to him in England, something that turned the struggle between them into a gouging at his vitals. There was Diana, but it felt like something even more personal. Perhaps he had learned about Joan and Ralph Harris.

But he must not allow the RM to fall a victim to the CO's agony, like a spectator killed by a stray bullet at a duel. He said, 'If you punish the RM, sir, I shall cable my grandfather asking him to withdraw this regiment from Imperial Service.'

Warren Bateman sat back as though he had been struck in the face. His brow darkened. He said, 'You couldn't do that. We are in the war. You want to run away from it? From our duty?'

'Whose duty it is, is a matter that is not clear to me ... to any of us,' Krishna said. He knew he had Warren in a corner now. Warren was Duryodhan, bent on war. If the regiment were withdrawn there would be not war, but peace, at least for the time being. But Warren Bateman was committed, like all the nations drowning in this ocean of mud, to total victory. The puzzled and hurt look in Warren's square face momentarily touched a chord of pity in Krishna. Warren could not really believe that his second-in-command was blackmailing him. Krishna said gently, 'Sir, why don't you request transfer back to the regular Indian Army? It would not be hard to persuade Brigadier-General Rogers to accept me as CO, and you would certainly get another regiment ... a real one.'

'And watch you let this one go to pot in your own decadent way?' Warren snarled. 'The first thing you'd do would be to get it out of France, isn't it?'

'Yes. But that would no longer be any concern of yours, would it?'

'Yes!' Warren shouted, banging his clenched fist down on the papers spread on the table. 'By God, yes! I was appointed to make this regiment as good as any in the Indian Army, as good as the Guides or Hodson's, and I'm going to do it ... Why don't you ask for a posting back to Ravi? I'll see that you get it on the grounds that you are your grandfather's heir.'

'No, sir. My place is here.'

They stared at each other. Krishna saw Warren's thoughts. He was thinking that if he was to have his duel to the death he must accept Krishna's terms. At length Warren Bateman said, 'This private fund has got to stop. The regimental funds must be used only as the PRI recommends and I approve.'

'Yes, sir,' Krishna said. He himself was the President of the Regimental Institutes, and the CO would now approve those items such as special rations, and comforts, and rum for nautches and celebrations, which he recommended.

'The brothel must be closed.'

'Yes, sir.'

'And the rissaldar-major reinstated as the only channel of communication between the men and myself on any matters which do not pass through the normal chain of command.'

'Yes, sir. Is that all?'

'Yes.'

'Then, sir, I request that all ranks be allowed to wear caste marks when not on duty in the front line. That Captain Ramaswami be permitted to practise Vedic medicine on those men who so request. That durbar be reinstituted whenever we are out of the line. That the Brahmin be given money to build, or adapt a building, for use as a temple at any place where we are billeted. That all officers wear the turban at all times. And that new bodyguards be posted to me.'

Warren Bateman tried hard to keep the emotion out of his face; but his cracking knuckles, the set of his jaw and the sweat on his forehead gave him away. He said, 'And you will stay? And the regiment?'

'Yes.'

'I agree. Dismiss!'

October 1915

WARREN POINTED WITH the long staff Narayan Singh had cut for him. 'This is where the village of Fosse-Garde used to stand. It has been totally destroyed. The whole offensive will be centred on Fosse-Garde. The Hindustan Division will be in the centre of the army, and our brigade leading the division. We are leading the brigade ... in the centre.'

The rumble and roar of artillery surged louder and Warren leaned on the staff, waiting for it to die down again. This was the fifth day of bombardment, and, like waves in the sea, the sound waxed and waned without any apparent reason, for the fire from seven hundred guns was in fact continuous and steady.

The roar sank to a heavy muttering grumble interspersed with crashes from a nearby medium battery. Warren let his eyes travel round the half-circle of his burberry-clad officers the other side of the sand model. A light, chill rain fell without cease. He held Krishna Ram's eye and said, 'I may say that in the original plan we were to be held in reserve. But I felt that as the Fusiliers suffered most heavily during the brigade's last spell in the line, and in order to do away with any idea that Indian troops are not as good as British, or have to be protected, or let the British troops do the unpleasant jobs, I asked the general to allow us to take the place allotted to the Fusiliers in the attack, and place them in reserve. The general was good enough to agree, so ...' Krishna Ram's eyes did not blink. Warren stared coldly at the rest of the officers, one by one. Any one of them, except Himat Singh, would betray him at a whisper from Krishna. Himat was the only Indian he could rely on, through thick and thin, the only one who had really learned the lessons he had been trying to teach them ever since he joined the regiment at the campground at Kangrota.

He returned to the sand model. 'As you can hear, the artillery preparation began five days ago and will last until zero hour, the day after tomorrow—seven hundred guns, from 4.5 inch hows up to 9.2s. You might have guessed at the size of the programme from the number of lorries and cart convoys using the roads in the rear areas here. We have the improved model gas masks, and if the wind is right gas may be used by our side, but that will not be decided till the last moment. The artillery preparation will smash the wire in front of Fosse-Garde, destroy all Hun trenches to a depth of one mile, and also destroy his machine gun posts. All four of the regiment's machine guns will be carried forward by the assaulting waves, so that we will be in a better position to beat off the counter-attacks which may be expected after we have taken our objective. Our objective is the eastern edge of Fosse-Garde, an advance of 500 yards from the front line trenches of VIII Corps, through whom we are due to pass at zero hour ... As soon as we have taken Fosse-Garde the Jubbulpore Brigade will pass through us to take the high ground beyond—here'—he pointed off the edge of the sand model to the east—'then the 1st and 2nd British Cavalry Divisions will pass through, and fan out in the German rear areas. The front will be irretrievably broken and a war of movement and manoeuvre will be reinstated ... to our advantage. I will issue detailed orders closer to the time. The attack will begin, as I said, the day after tomorrow—October 12th.'

'Dussehra!' one of the officers exclaimed.

'Oh ... I forgot,' Warren said. He cursed himself silently. He ought to have remembered that. He recovered himself, and said, 'A good omen. We shall make our sacrifices to Kali in the bodies of Huns ... Any questions about the overall plan?' The rain dripped off the peak of his cap in front of his eyes.

Major Himat Singh said, 'We're going to need carrying parties to carry ammunition forward with us, sir. The assault waves can never carry enough, especially if they are going to take the MGs with them.'

Warren said, 'I am going to have each squadron use one of its troops just for that. It isn't more men that we want up there, but fewer men with more fire power.'

Krishna Ram said, 'As the bombardment has been going on so long, sir, the Germans will expect the attack when it comes. Is there anything we can do to regain surprise?'

Warren said, 'I think you can rely on the general for that. Any more?'

Major Bholanath said, 'Is raining, now. Has been raining nearly all days since we left the line. This ground up there clay, very heavy. Horses and mules were not being able to move *before* we left the line. After six days shooting, thousands, millions of heavy shells, *no one* being able to move ... surely not cavalry, sahib.'

Warren said impatiently, 'The weather is certainly bad, but it is not only bad for us. The Hun will find it just as hard to move his reserves as we do to advance. We must impose our will on the enemy, Bholanath, not allow difficulties to overcome us ... Is that all? Remember that this is all top secret and may not be discussed with anyone not present at this meeting. Dismiss, please.'

Warren sat at the rough table in the regimental office, signing his name over and over again. The worst thing about being in the rear areas was the torrent of bumf that descended on you. Lists in quadruplicate, equipment returns, states of men sick, by classes and ranks. It was better up the line ... well, they'd be there again soon enough, barely thirty hours now. His jaw tightened at the thought. This would be the decisive battle ... Fosse-Garde, the turning point.

Captain Flaherty appeared at the door. 'Major Krishna Ram would like to see you, sir ... alone.'

'Tell him to come in. You stay, too,' Warren said. He put down his pen and straightened his back.

Krishna Ram entered, and Warren said, 'Is the matter you want to speak to me about entirely personal—to do with your private life?'

Krishna Ram said at once, 'No, sir.'

Good, Warren thought; a purely private request could only have to do with Diana, and he didn't want to talk about that now. The solution would not come in words but in action, at Fosse-Garde.

Aloud he said, 'Then the adjutant must hear it, to act as a witness to what is said, if necessary. Speak up.'

Krishna Ram stood at attention the other side of the bare table. He looked Warren in the eye, and said, 'Four weeks ago, sir, in return for your promise that you would take no action against the rissaldar-major, I agreed not to ask my grandfather to have this regiment recalled to Ravi.'

'Yes.'

'Apart from wanting to save the RM I wanted to prove to you that we could be good soldiers and still think like—and *be*—Hindu Indians. You wanted the regiment to stay to prove the opposite ... and you wanted me to stay because I have become, you feel, the personification of all that you want to get rid of. You therefore felt it necessary to overcome me in a personal duel.'

Warren sat silent. Allowing Krishna to speak like this was bad for discipline, but what he said was true, no use denying it.

Krishna said, 'I, too, welcomed the duel at that time. But since we came out of the line I have been spending as much time as possible each day in solitary meditation. It has been shown to me, in these long lonely hours, that I am keeping the regiment here to use them as my arms, my weapons in the duel with you. I am risking their lives not for their sakes but for mine, for the sake of my pride ... I hoped for more time to think this through to the right decision, the wisest and most proper for us ... but the offensive has forced me to make up my mind at once. I am sure that I don't want to fight any more here in France, for France or for England. I am sure that the men of the regiment feel the same. I have come to ask that we forget our agreement of four weeks ago. I am surrendering. Please go to the general—I will go with you—and tell him that our morale has gone, and that we are not fit to take part in the offensive. There won't be time to make any big changes before it begins, but we must go into reserve in place of the Fusiliers, not to be used except in self defence. As soon as the offensive is over, we are to be sent back to India—in disgrace, if you wish. If you think you need some proof of the state we are in, I can organize a mutiny, a mass refusal to obey orders ... whatever you think best.'

'And the rissaldar-major?' Warren said. 'You promised to keep the regiment here in order to protect the RM, didn't you? Now you don't care what happens to him?'

'I do care, sir,' Krishna said. 'But I think I can guarantee him a great future out of the army, in our state—I would like to have him as my Chief Minister when I succeed to the *gaddi*—to compensate him for anything you do to him. But in any case I cannot allow one man's fate, neither his nor mine, to cause any more death or disillusion. The regiment must go back to India.'

He looked determined but not hostile, Warren thought, and thinner than before. Perhaps he had been fasting while he squatted crosslegged in solitude, in the Indian way of *bhairagis* and *sunnyasis*. But how out of place in an Artois farmhouse! And how different he had become from the cheerful young aristocrat of the dak bungalow at Kangrota!

Krishna continued, 'The war is becoming more inhuman every day. Our gods are human, and allow for war, but not for mechanical destruction. They are not themselves mechanical and cannot tolerate mechanization. But every day the war forces us to become more machine-like, less human and so—according to our belief— less divine, for the gods that humans worship are themselves, really, human too.'

'Go on,' Warren said, hearing Flaherty's disdainful sniff beside him. Flaherty was so eager to disavow his Indian heritage that he wouldn't accept even what was patently true; and this that Krishna Ram was saying was true enough ... only irrelevant.

Krishna said, 'It isn't only the war ... it is Europe. In trying to learn the European way of making war we have learned European ways of thought. The ties that bind us to our own principles, our own ways of thought, have been weakened, or destroyed. There have been rapes and petty thefts, all entirely foreign to our men. Absence without leave, desertions even ... unheard of before we came here. Lying to escape punishment. Deliberate waste. We have caught a disease, just as my grandfather warned me ...'

'You call Western civilization a disease?' Warren said. Krishna was still at attention the other side of the table, but for the first time since he had joined the regiment, the facts of the difference in their rank, and of his position as Krishna's commanding officer, were not present in Warren's mind. It was almost as when they had first met, at the cricket field in Lahore, and he was interestedly sharing opinions with a member of a different culture.

'Yes,' Krishna said, his face sad. 'It has symptoms ... what that young sowar brought up in durbar—the false Christianity that preaches love, and kills ... that teaches poverty, but takes ... that preaches tolerance, like to Mr. Fleming—and rejects ... the fever that enabled Europe to conquer Asia, and believe that there was nothing to be learned from the conquered ... If we don't go back now, it will be too late. It may be too late already. We, all the

Indian troops here, will take this disease back with us. Instead of believing that a man's inner posture, his relationship with his soul, is more important than his position on earth, many will believe that only victory, self-fulfilment matters ... which is the same as saying, getting your own way regardless of what outrages on the body and soul you have to commit ... This will spread in India, which will not help either India or England. The sowars and sepoys are not political themselves, and never will be, for the most part. But the disease they carry will infect all India. The politicians will not act like Indians any more, but like Europeans. There will be political crimes, that India never knew ... murders, assassinations, poisonings, the killings of women and children ... I beg you, sir, let us go now.'

Warren said, 'Is that all?'

'Yes, sir.'

Warren drummed his fingers on the table, looking out of the broken window of the little room while he marshalled his words. At last he said, 'What you said about Europe is partly true. My old CO, and the Commissioner of Lahore, both thought it would be dangerous to bring Indian troops to France, for different reasons. But the war hadn't really started then. We took it lightly, being cocksure of the outcome. Here in France we learned in suffering that the outcome was not predetermined ... that it depended on our beating the Germans to their knees, smashing them in battle, face to face. We cannot achieve victory without hardening ourselves ... but we do not have to remain hard afterwards.'

Krishna made a gesture of disagreement but Warren said, his voice rising a little, 'It is true! So, after we have won, you can go back to your old ways. But first, we must win, or the world to which we return will be a different one.'

'It will be anyway, sir,' Krishna interjected.

'A German world, which we will not tolerate ... We are going to win. You are going to help. The effect on your soul, or whatever you call it, or on the souls of other Indians, matters as little as the fact that you or I may be killed the day after tomorrow. I hold you to your promise.'

'Very well, sir,' Krishna said. 'I suggest, sir, that you make sure that your orderly is always armed, and covering your back, wherever you go. The news of the offensive has pushed some of the men ... and officers ... to the end of their tether.'

'And you're encouraging them to get rid of me?' Warren sneered.

'No, sir. The trouble is that some are not thinking of me as they used to, as a Son of the Sun, but only as your second-in-command, and assistant. The ones who are stretched near the limit will not confide in me.'

He saluted and went out. As the door closed behind him, Warren said, 'What did you make of that, Flaherty?'

'About what you'd expect,' the captain growled. 'Wouldn't it be wiser to send him back to India, at once, sir? He says the men just think of him as the second-in-command, but it's not true. He can twist them around his little finger. And the officers even more so.'

'It might be wise,' Warren said, 'but I'm not going to do it. I'm going to show him, in battle, that he's wrong and I'm right ... I'm not going to sign any more papers. I'm going out. D Squadron are playing hockey, aren't they?'

'Yes, sir ... But wait till your orderly can get his rifle, please, sir.'

At midnight some change in the rumble of the artillery brought Warren upright in bed out of sleep. He sat there a while in the darkness, listening. The ground shook as always, the broken panes in the window rattled as always. The sound of the guns almost, but not quite, drowned the hiss of the rain on the tiled, patched roof. Each time the near battery fired, Warren said under his breath, 'There! Take that! Bloody Hun!' seeing in his mind's eye the machine gun post pulverized, the smashed bodies, the avenues of wire being ripped to shreds. After half an hour the guns still thundering like distant surf, he went back to sleep.

He awoke to a formless screaming that sent his hands grabbing for the revolver in the equipment slung over the head of his bed. Then a sharp explosion seared his eyeballs with yellow flame, bits of something smashed into the brick wall over his head, and the window blew out with a tinkling of glass. For a second longer things fell or bumped or rattled. Then, in the silence, he heard a long low breathing, a bubbling breath that became a rattle, a sigh, and died. Beyond, a voice called, *'Sahib! Colonel Sahib! Ap thik hai?'*

He jumped up, and switched on the flashlight he kept on the

stool beside his bed. A big khaki hump lay sprawled in the doorway, in a spreading dark pool of red. He bent over it as his orderly ran in, a hurricane lantern in his hands.

Warren turned the twisted head on the floor up a little and saw that it was Captain Flaherty. He was dead, his chest and stomach blown out. Distinctively waffled metal shards stuck out of the walls, or lay on the floor. Flaherty had been killed by one of the new British grenades. The orderly knelt in horror beside the dead adjutant, facing Warren across the body.

At length Warren said grimly, 'Tell the woordie-major to send a party to clean up this room now, and prepare a burial party for ten o'clock.'

The guns still shook the earth and sky. It was three in the morning, and someone had tried to murder him. Flaherty had had the room across the hall of the little house. Perhaps he, too, had been kept awake by the guns, and had seen someone creeping up the street, to drop a grenade through a broken window, or roll one in through the doorway.

On an impulse Warren pulled on his boots and greatcoat, crossed the street, and entered Krishna Ram's billet. Hanuman lay sleeping across the door. He sat up, rifle in hand, when Warren stirred him, ordering, 'Out of the way!' He followed Warren as Warren entered Krishna's room, where a hurricane lantern was burning. Krishna Ram was sitting crosslegged on the bed, his palms joined. He looked up, as Warren came in.

'You keep late hours,' Warren said.

'I was meditating, sir.'

'Did you hear an explosion just now?'

'The guns?'

'No. An attempt to murder me. A grenade in my room.'

Krishna Ram said, 'I'm sorry.'

'Flaherty's dead, trying to save me.'

Krishna muttered, '*Dand*, just as the Rawal warned me.'

'What are you talking about?' Warren asked belligerently.

'Something a Brahmin warned me about before I left India— that some of my people might resort to force before I felt compelled to do so myself ... This is what I was talking about in your office, sir. This, that has happened, *could* not have been done by anyone in the regiment a year ago. It—the seed or foetus of it—was not in them then. It has been put there. Please, sir, go to the general. It's not too late.'

Warren said, 'When we come back from the attack—if we do—you will find out who murdered Flaherty, and report to me. Meantime, I'm appointing Sher Singh as adjutant, and Dayal Ram to D Squadron.' He swung out and back to his own room, where he watched a party with buckets and cloths clean up the floor.

Twenty-four hours later the Ravi Lancers were in the communication trenches, moving up. Warren, at the head of the regiment, had thought that surely a path would have been cleared in front of them; but in these first hours of Z Day the trenches seemed to be full of ammunition fatigues, sappers, signallers laying wire, gunner observation groups, and ration parties. He would shuffle twenty paces forward, then stop for ten minutes. Then on again. The rain fell steadily out of a dark and windy night. The bombardment, on which 890,000 shells had been expended so far, continued at the steady pace that had characterized it from its beginning a week ago. Perhaps this was the surprise which he had assured Krishna Ram that the Army Commander would have up his sleeve—to continue the bombardment, to which the Germans must by now have become numbingly accustomed, and attack out of it with no further warning.

The wind was in the south, and there would be no gas; but a group of his men were carrying, strapped to their backs, two of the three German flame throwers captured by Krishna's last patrol. The third had been used up finding how they worked. He ought, as Flaherty had nervously reminded him, to have sent the weapons back to brigade; but he had said, 'I'm damned if I will. It isn't as though Intelligence didn't know that the Germans had flame throwers. These *we'll* keep, and use.' That would give the enemy a surprise, all right; it might turn the tide in some critical situation.

He plodded forward. Who had tried to kill him that night? Not who had thrown the grenade—in dealing with Indians that was always unimportant—but who had told him, guided him, to do it? Not Krishna; he wanted to overcome Warren alive: triumph over a dead man would have no savour. Pahlwan Ram or Sher Singh, perhaps; they could summon the nerve to do it, if they thought it would save their skins; in the desperation of their funk they would not realize that it was too late for that, with the attack definite and the regiment committed to it. Of the VCOs and men ... very difficult to say. There were too many of them for him to be certain that none was harbouring some secret grudge or hate or fear.

Three o'clock and the attack due to begin at five. He inched forward again. An hour later a white face peered at him and a Canadian voice said, 'Ravi Lancers? Where's your CO? ... This way, sir.' The soldier led him to the dugout of the CO of the battalion they were to pass through for the attack. The Canadian colonel was about the same age as himself. 'Have a snort,' he said. 'Is this goddamn rain ever going to stop?'

He handed Warren a mug half full of whisky, adding, 'I don't envy you fellows.'

'We'll do it,' Warren said confidently.

The other looked at him curiously. 'You think so? I think the Limeys are putting you into the mincer ... Hell, of course you *are* a Limey. Well, drink that down and I'll show you the ground.'

Three-quarters of an hour later Warren left the Canadian colonel and went to his command post. Sher Singh was nervous and forgetful as his adjutant, and he wished he could have appointed almost anyone else; but at a time like this the better an officer was, the more he was needed with a squadron.

Krishna Ram came up the communication trench that started immediately behind Warren's position. 'The regiment's all up and ready, sir,' he said.

'Ten minutes to go,' Warren said. The bombardment suddenly doubled, trebled, stepped up to a shattering intensity. The torrent of steel exploded close in front. Curtains of yellow and red flame shook and flashed along the German trenches. Steel splinters whined back overhead and the drone and roar of the incoming shells sounded like a hundred trains rushing simultaneously through an underground station. Shikari began to fidget and whimper at Warren's feet.

'This will tell them we're coming,' Krishna shouted.

'Get to your post!' Warren said.

Krishna Ram tramped away. He turned at a few paces, and said, 'We're all in the arms of Kali now. The feast of Dussehra has begun ... Good luck, sir.'

'Good luck,' Warren repeated automatically. He stooped down and cuffed his dog savagely. 'Sit still! Quiet!' Shikari whimpered more loudly, shaken uncontrollably by the thunder of the artillery fire.

Two minutes to zero. The trench was crowded with men, his own ready near the firestep, trench ladders in place, the Canadians pressed back against the parados. The flame thrower detachment was ready in the next bay to the right.

By the glare of the explosions he saw it was zero hour. He blew his whistle, picked up Shikari, lifted him on to the parapet and followed, running quickly up the trench ladder. As he stepped off on to the shattered earth beyond the parapet, Shikari turned and jumped back down into the trench.

'Come here!' Warren shouted. 'Heel! Come here ... you bloody coward!'

The little dog cowered down, whining. Warren drew his revolver, his head bursting with anger. No one was going to escape, no one, no one. In a bright flash he aimed and pulled the trigger. The fox terrier's head dissolved into a pulp. Warren turned and began to walk forward. His boot sank three inches into the mud at the first heavy step. A German machine gun began to fire.

October 1915

THE MACHINE GUN stopped after firing half a belt, and Warren plodded forward. The first wet streamers of light lining the darkness ahead silhouetted the bowed shapes of sowars trudging ahead of him, distorted pack animals with gas masks, packs, equipment, extra slung cotton ammunition belts, rifle, bayonet and entrenching tool. The ground became increasingly less solid as they entered the zone into which the British artillery had fired a million shells. The pace, instead of the one hundred yards in two and a half minutes which had been allowed for, slowed to a hundred yards in four minutes, or five. The creeping barrage of howitzer fire moved faster than the infantry, gradually outdistancing them. The advance was not at an even pace over the apparently level plain that had shown through the periscopes but a slipping and stumbling, now sliding ten feet into the bottom of huge craters, now splashing through two feet of water in the bottom, then struggling up the other side. Warren shouted at the gunner subaltern beside him, 'Bring the barrage back closer, Bruington.'

'I can't, sir,' Bruington said. 'We're going slowly here, but look...' He pointed, and Warren saw that some of his men were far ahead on the right. He cursed, but there was no way of slowing them; nor were they doing anything wrong; somehow they alone had managed to keep to the ordained pace. Then, even as he watched, they went down to a man, as though a scythe had swept through long, waving grass. Star shells were bursting in the livid sky and clear ahead, close, Warren saw the gleam of barbed wire ... new, unrusted wire. The machine gun bullets clacked closer in double, quadruple, uncountable hammering streams. My God, he thought, there must be a score of guns firing, apparently untouched by the tremendous bombardment. His men were going down to

372

right and left, either wounded or diving into shell craters or pressing themselves flat into the mud to seek shelter. The advance stopped.

The advance stopped all along the line. Warren went on a few more painful paces and then jumped down into a crater as machine gun fire slashed and spurted all round him. Geysers of muddy water shot up, soaking him to the skin and fouling his trench cap. Pahlwan Ram, Sher Singh, various orderlies and trumpeters and the gunner party followed him into the huge crater. 'One of the trumpeters killed, sir,' Pahlwan Ram said. He was trembling, his face pale and his eyes staring at a point past or through Warren; but there was nobody there.

'Can we get through on the field telephone?' Warren asked.

'I'm trying, sir,' Sher Singh muttered.

'Our artillery line's been cut,' Lieutenant Bruington said. 'They're starting counter-battery and harassing fire.'

Then Warren realized that there was a continuous murmur and rustle of shells passing overhead, from the Germans towards the British. Faintly he heard the distant explosions in the British rear and gun areas.

'Through to brigade,' Sher Singh said. 'The general's on the line.'

Warren seized the headset. He was lying on his back against the steep slope of the crater, his back towards the German lines. The rain slanted into his face and the clouds were turning a darker violet as the light increased.

'How are you doing?' The general's voice was tinny and hiccupy as though the wire was being rapidly broken and rejoined while they talked.

'Held up, sir ... About two hundred yards short of our objective.'

'Held up? How ... possible.'

That last word must have been 'impossible', Warren thought. He said, 'Machine guns, not knocked out. Must be twenty firing at the regiment now. Uncut wire ahead.'

'... impossible! ... seven days ... heavies ...'

'The wire's there,' Warren shouted. 'I've seen it.'

'What ... you ... do?' the general said. He sounded desperate, as though it were he, not Warren, lying in a hole with machine guns

373

sweeping the ground above as systematically as mowers on a lawn, and shells bursting all around.

'Try to get forward,' Warren said.

'I'll ... heavy artillery support,' the general said.

'If they didn't knock out the machine guns in seven days,' Warren said, 'they won't do it in half an hour now.' His eye swept the collection of filthy human beings crouched and lying in the crater, and fell on a dafadar with a heavy metal canister on his back. He said into the phone. 'Wait a minute, please, sir ... Bruington, what direction is the wind?'

The artillery officer scrambled up the crater wall, put out a finger into the storm of steel, and said, 'South.'

'Can you put down smoke along the German front?'

'For about ten minutes. We don't carry much smoke shell.'

Warren returned to the telephone. 'Sir, I'm going to attack the nearest machine gun posts in half an hour. We'll need smoke. The artillery line is cut. Will you please put our FAO through to the gun position via your exchange?'

'In a minute,' the general said. 'How many casualties have you had, Bateman?'

'I don't know. We're all pinned down in shell holes or out in the open.'

'This ... decisive battle,' the general said, '... cisive ... stand? All our futures ...'

Warren said, 'I understand, sir.'

He gave the handset to Bruington and sank back against the wall of the crater. He had a clear mental picture of No Man's Land, the expanse of shell holes, the barbed wire gleaming in thick rows ahead, the humped ruins of Fosse-Garde. The enemy machine guns stopped, all at once. Shells continued to crump and burst all round. Krishna Ram came over the lip of the crater and slid down in. Warren looked at him speculatively. Perhaps the moment had come.

'I've been to both forward squadron HQs,' Krishna said. 'They have each had about thirty casualties, nearly half killed. They won't be able to advance until those machine guns are knocked out, sir.'

Warren nodded without speaking. The squadrons had lost about a third of their strength. He switched his mind back to No Man's Land, the position of the squadrons, the positions of the Boche

374

machine guns. Ten minutes later he said, 'Galloper, bring Major Himat Singh here.'

'I'll get him,' Krishna Ram said, 'I know where he is.'

'No. You stay here. Show the galloper.'

The galloper ran off, low crouched, and Warren returned to his planning. Soon Major Himat Singh tumbled into the shell hole. Warren said, 'Himat, Krishna, Bruington—listen. Sher Singh, make notes so we can confirm details if necessary. Pahlwan, listen carefully ... We will knock out the German machine guns with flame throwers. At zero hour C Squadron on the left will advance. The purpose of this is to draw the German machine gun fire to that flank. At zero plus four the artillery will lay down a smoke screen just in front of the German lines in front of B Squadron. At zero plus six, when the smoke screen will be fully effective, B Squadron, with the flame throwers—all under command of Major Krishna Ram—will advance. Their task is to destroy the German machine gun posts. The smoke screen will end at zero plus fourteen, so the task must have been achieved by then ... The success signal for the wiping out of the machine guns will be red over red Very lights, to be fired by you personally, Krishna. On that signal C and the remainder of the regiment will again advance at the double to seize all original objectives. And, Bruington, please open up on the German support trenches with HE and shrapnel on the success signal. Zero hour will be ... 0730. The time now is ... 0705. Synchronize. My headquarters will remain here until we move forward to the captured enemy trench. Any questions?'

'The enemy wire, sir?' Himat Singh said.

'It's there and pretty thick,' Warren said. 'Concentrate your wire-cutting teams. Remember you'll be in smoke ... Pahlwan, go and explain the orders to Major Bholanath, in person. Go on, for God's sake! Just run from shell hole to shell hole. They're not going to waste ammunition on one running man.'

'The shelling ...'

Pahlwan stopped. Warren realized he was glaring at the lieutenant like a wild animal, teeth bared. Pahlwan scrambled up the side of the shell hole and vanished. Sher Singh was looking at Warren as though a fiend of his nightmares had taken shape beside him. Was he imagining it or were the others in the crater huddling farther away from him, as though he was marked by an infectious disease. Even Bruington was looking at him with ...

what? Fear, compassion, hatred? What else was there to do? What else could he have done with the wretched dog?

The minutes passed slowly. The only voice was Bruington's, shouting into the telephone. Finally Bruington looked at his watch and scrambled up the front wall of the crater. 'C Squadron's moving, sir,' he called down.

Warren struggled up to join him, and peered to the left. Lines of sowars were emerging like burrowing animals from the waste of mud. They moved heavily forward. After a long slow count of twenty the German machine guns opened fire. Men fell, to vanish into the earth, but the uneven lines kept moving forward. A gleam of steel flashing in the gloom must be old Bholanath leading them with drawn sabre, as he always did. Men were going down faster now. Warren ground his teeth in anxiety. He should have allowed them less time to advance without smoke cover; the object of drawing fire was already achieved.

Shells whistled low overhead and burst with peculiar hollow puffs. 'The smoke, sir,' Bruington said.

The white cloud thickened rapidly. C Squadron sank into the mud. The German machine gun fire slackened as their targets began to be hidden from them. To the right B Squadron rose from the earth and moved briskly forward, sharply silhouetted against the white smoke. Bayonets pointed forward, the burdened figures began to run. They disappeared into the smoke.

There was a pause of two, three minutes. Suddenly in the smoke, a tongue of orange flame licked out forty feet along the ground; and another to the right of it. Flames grew and spread like blossoms in the rainy morning. Dim on the light wind, above the syncopated crashes of the German artillery, Warren heard an unearthly scream. A whole patch of earth over there seemed to be on fire. Flames glowed again in the smoke, accompanied now by a frantic crescendo of bomb blasts and the staccato bark of rifles and light machine guns. Three, four minutes passed.

'Smoke screen ending now, sir,' Bruington shouted. The shells ceased to whistle overhead.

Out of the thinning smoke cloud on the right rose a red point of light. It burst into a red star, followed five seconds later by another.

'The success signal!' Warren yelled. He blew a series of sharp blasts on his whistle. To right and left the Ravi Lancers were out in the open, advancing steadily. B Squadron was past the machine guns, C again moving on the left. Here was the wire, and nothing more than desultory rifle fire from straight in front. The Germans had relied too much on those machine guns, keeping everyone else out of the front lines, which must now be almost unoccupied. The wire cutters went click, snip, the wire sprang back. The trenches which were the first objective loomed ahead. Warren jumped down in as Narayan Singh behind him shot a German soldier as he was aiming at Warren.

Warren shouted, 'Fire the DF tasks without further orders if they counter-attack, Bruington. I'm going to see the squadrons.' To his signaller he said, 'Tell A and D Squadrons to come up ... commanders here. Pahlwan, come with me.'

Then, his orderly at his heels and the Intelligence Officer lagging behind, he ran to the left along the trench, his revolver drawn. There was no one in the first bay, two dead Germans in the second, and in the third, sowars of the regiment, led by Major Bholanath, advancing towards him.

He shoved his revolver back in its holster. 'Well done, Bholanath! We have the whole of our first objective now. I'm going to see if we can get forward to the second objective before the Huns have recovered. Get a telephone line strung along this trench to RHQ as soon as you can.'

He hurried back, past his own headquarters, and on towards B Squadron. He soon met men of the squadron, and a little farther, Himat Singh. He found him leaning against the sandbagged parapet of the trench, retching and vomiting. From somewhere close by there was continuous shrieking, without cease but with no other pattern, crawling up and down the scale, now wailing soft now piercing loud. Two sowars were also vomiting in the trench, a flame thrower pack thrown down beside them.

'What's happened?' Warren said.

Himat Singh motioned up with one hand. 'One of the flame thrower men, the dafadar, hit by a bullet ... It exploded on his back ... that's him, dying.'

Warren climbed up and saw, twenty feet away, a man, or what had been one. He was wearing boots, puttees, and trousers from the knees to near the crotch. Above that the clothes had been burned off him, revealing a blackened piece of smoking steak. The head was grotesque, like a chestnut left too long in the fire.

The flames had burned through the wall of his stomach, revealing long stripes of blue and red entrails steaming in the fire that still licked all over him. The shell of the flame thrower canister rolled and clanked on top of the sizzling meat as it jerked, giving out continuous shrieks.

'This is not to be borne,' one of the vomiting sowars in the trench cried in Hindi. He climbed up beside Warren, levelled his rifle at the screeching horror, muttered, 'May God forgive us,' and fired. His hand was shaking so much that he had to fire three times, the meat jerking to each impact, before it fell silent.

Himat Singh gasped, 'Krishna was right, sir ... Oh my God, you should see the German machine gunners ... they're all like that. Out there, in the gun pits ...'

Warren said, 'Pull yourself together, Himat ... We're going to advance to the final objective as soon as I can arrange supporting fire. Get a line to me and stand by to advance.'

'Yes, sir,' Himat said dully.

Warren hurried back to his RHQ. The field telephone line had been brought forward and was working. He got Brigadier-General Rogers on the line. 'We're on our first objective now, sir,' he said, 'and we're going forward to the final objective as soon as I've fixed the supporting fire. But, sir ...'

'Yes? What is it?'

'We won't take the objective without more casualties. The regiment will be very weak. We must have a battalion, at least, come up to take over the position, if it is to be held against counter-attacks.'

'The cavalry will pass through you,' the general said.

'Not if the Germans counter-attack, sir,' Warren insisted.

'There are no more troops in hand,' the general said. 'You must hold the objective yourselves. Do you understand?'

'Yes, sir,' Warren said. Gently he put the handset back in its cradle, his teeth grating.

Soon Dayal Ram and Puran Lall arrived, their squadrons spread out along the trenches to right and left. By then Warren was ready. He gave out his orders, to some of the commanders in person, huddled in the trench at his headquarters, and to some by the field telephone. At nine o'clock the Ravi Lancers advanced again, this time with A and D Squadrons leading, B and C in reserve.

Twenty seconds after A and D Squadrons moved out behind a

creeping barrage of howitzer shells, Warren knew that the attack would not reach its objective. Once again, machine guns were stopping the advance. As he leaned on the parapet, his binoculars to his eyes, he saw the sowars moving very slowly over the torn waste between the German front and support trenches, where the heaviest of the preparation fire had landed; then, out of the cratered landscape came the unseen streams of machine gun bullets. Men went down ... he saw Puran Lall running on for a time alone on the right, his revolver drawn, firing. Then he too dropped —no, jumped, and vanished. Both squadrons sank into the earth. The only advantage of the state of the ground was that men could find cover almost anywhere, in the innumerable pits and holes and craters.

With his binoculars Warren searched for the German machine guns. They were somewhere in the rubble of bricks, barely three feet high, that had been Fosse-Garde—somewhere, but where exactly? It had to be exact, or even heavy artillery could not knock them out. The flame throwers were used up and no more available. Gas? The wind was wrong. The machine guns had to be knocked out. If not one way, another. There could be no advance without that.

He said, 'Sher Singh, I'm going forward to A Squadron. I'll be back as soon as I've found out where the Hun machine guns are.'

Doubled up, he ran forward until he reached the place where he had seen Puran Lall disappear, and slipped down beside him.

'We've got to get those machine guns,' he said.

Lieutenant Puran Lall said, 'I'm going to try now.' His level eyes were hard as agate, deep rings under them, his mouth thin and bitter. He looked about forty instead of barely twenty; and a murderer, instead of a gay young blade.

'Where are they?' Warren said.

'I've located two. The right corner of the rubble. Right, two degrees. Something dark. They're beside that, in some sort of a pit, covered over. I can see the flicker of the nozzle flames when they fire. In the binoculars you can see the water jumping in the puddle just in front of them, to the muzzle blast.'

Warren peered at the dark spot. It was about a hundred yards away, and the guns firing in enfilade. The bullets kicked up water and mud in a long line across his front. A hundred yards—in this soil—would take two minutes even for a man charging light ...

379

Before he could stop him Puran Lall was out of the shell hole, running hard, revolver in one hand, a grenade in the other. The machine guns continued to fire in enfilade. They would be on fixed lines, ready for British use of smoke. It would take the gunners a few seconds to loosen the clamps for a swinging traverse. He grabbed the rifle from a sowar beside him, aimed carefully at the spot where he thought the machine guns were, and fired. Puran Lall ran on. After a pause the guns began to fire directly at him. Warren fired again. Puran Lall, still thirty yards from the guns, threw his grenade as he ran, with all the strength of his arm. He ran on, now firing his revolver. As the grenade burst the guns stopped firing. Rissaldar Chaman Lall, beside Warren, shouted, 'Lieutenant-sahib *pahunch-gaya*! Advance, *jawan*!' He stood up and all round the sowars crawled out of their holes and continued their advance.

A new storm of machine guns opened up from the left, at least four guns. Chaman Lall doubled, coughed, and fell before he had gone ten paces. Man after man went down, silently, or with a groan, to lie crumpled and still, or twist and writhe, crawling towards shelter. Puran Lall came running back. As the last effort to advance died Puran Lall fell into the shell hole he had left barely two minutes earlier.

'I'll get them,' he shouted. He began to run out of the crater towards the new threat. Warren caught him—'Come back! You don't know where they are, or anything. You've got no covering fire! And they're farther off ... behind the next German trench, I think.'

'I'm going, I'm going,' Puran Lall screamed.

Warren held him tight. 'You're trying to get yourself killed!'

'Why not?' the young man shouted. 'My brother dead, for what? So you can blow down your own churches ... slaughter children in ships ... burn the living as though they were ... aiiih.' He put his head in his hands and sank down, weeping.

Warren waited. He could not get back to his HQ until the machine gun fire slackened. He felt numb and tired. Puran going, Himat weakening. Krishna was winning, his presence steadily undermining all that had been built.

Half an hour later he touched Puran Lall on the shoulder, as he sat staring across the crater, his revolver in his hands, and said, 'Hold tight, Puran. I'll get D Squadron on to those machine guns.

380

Look out for German counter-attacks. Do you hear?' He shook the lieutenant lightly.

Puran Lall said, 'I hear.'

Warren started back, walking fast from shell hole to shell hole. Bullets clacked around him but they were not aimed at him, rather it was the firing of German gunners sweeping No Man's Land from positions well behind, not seeing their targets. Then one bullet came very close, and it was isolated, not one of a stream. He flung himself flat.

The next bullet hit him in the upper left arm, striking with the force of a sledge-hammer and jerking him round where he lay. Then, through a shock of pain that seemed like an electric flash in the centre of his brain, he saw the firer ... an Indian, turbaned, aiming at him from his own trench, the face hidden behind the cuddled rifle butt. A communication trench ran past a few feet to his left and Warren jumped down into it in a long stumbling leap, as the marksman fired again. He fell against the back wall of the trench with another grating of pain. His left arm hung loose, the bone broken. He drew his revolver, ran down the trench, turned the corner and looked up. There, sprawled on the old parados, was Captain Sher Singh, still peering down the sights of a rifle. Two VCOs were in the trench watching the captain. Warren glared at them, his revolver jerking. Slowly they raised their hands. Sher Singh on the parapet looked round then, saying something in Hindi. He saw Warren and started convulsively. Warren said, 'Come down. Leave the rifle.'

From the next bay he heard Pahlwan Ram talking to Krishna Ram and Bruington.

'Why were you firing at me, Sher Singh?' he said.

The man's handsome face was grey under the brown skin. From a sudden uncontrollable movement of his body Warren thought bowels and bladder had emptied, from fear.

'I ... I ...'

'Why?' Warren turned to the VCOs.

'He told us you had gone mad and were going to get us all killed, sahib,' the jemadar said.

A stench of diarrhoea filled the trench. Warren, aiming at Sher Singh's stomach, pulled the trigger. 'You fucking sodomite,' he said. The heavy bullet blasted the officer against the back wall of the trench. He clasped his hands to his belly, swung slowly, and fell, screaming as he rolled on to his face. Someone shouted in the next bay and men appeared, rifles ready. The scream ended in a bubbling gasp.

Warren said, 'Rissaldar Chuni Ram ... Jemadar Dial Chand ... You knew he was shooting at me?' His arm ached steadily.

'No, sahib,' one said, but the other said, 'Yes, I knew. I thought he was right ... That you had gone insane.'

Warren fired again, aiming at the speaker's heart. The rissaldar fell without a sound.

'Sir! What ... ?'

Warren ignored Krishna, beside him now, and said, 'You jemadar-sahib, are reduced to sowar. Go and tell Major Himat Singh that. And why.'

The jemadar said, 'Major Himat Singh is dying. The rissaldar-sahib had just taken over command of the squadron.'

'Where's Himat?' Warren demanded.

'In the next bay but one,' Krishna said. 'A shell burst in the trench close to him ... But you're wounded, sir.'

Warren ran along the trench, returning his revolver to its holster as he ran, misery in his heart. Himat gone, the only one he could trust. He found the major lying on a German stretcher, a ground-sheet over his body, an orderly at his head. Warren dropped to one knee beside him. 'Himat ... where are you hit?'

'Stomach, sir. I'm going.'

'No, no!' Warren cried fiercely. 'Don't leave me! You'll be all right!'

'Dying,' Himat said. He coughed feebly. Blood trickled down his chin and on to the ribbon and rosette of the DSO.

His hand reached up and Warren, turning, found Krishna Ram at his elbow, kneeling beside him. The dying man took the prince's hand and held it tight. 'You were right, lord,' he gasped. 'We should have stayed ... in India ... I'm sorry ... I betrayed you, lord ... Forgive me.'

'It doesn't matter,' Krishna said. 'Lie still.'

'Take ... the regiment ... home!'

'You, too?' Warren cried, wounded to the depths.

'Yes, sir ... All we have learned is strength ... and ugliness ... not virtue.'

The major's other hand was gripping him like a claw. Warren

tried to free himself but could not. A rattle began in Himat Singh's throat. In a moment he was dead.

Warren stayed a long minute, kneeling. Then he stood up. He said, 'Krishna, I'm going to attack again as soon as we can arrange the fire support.' He reached his headquarters in the next bay.

'The *jawans* are exhausted,' Krishna said. 'They're at the end of their tether.' His voice rose. 'Do you think *this* would have happened'—he pointed at the corpse of Rissaldar Chuni Ram, now on the parapet—'unless they were stretched beyond reason? Do you know how many casualties we have had? We've taken half our objective, which is more than anyone else did ... more than anyone would have believed possible this morning.'

'It's not enough,' Warren said. 'If we don't attack, the Germans will. And if this regiment doesn't go forward, it'll go back. That's the state of its morale, thanks to you. *Jawan*, give me that telephone.'

He sat down on a pile of sandbags. 'Put me through to brigade headquarters,' he said.

'There's no communication beyond our rear headquarters, sahib,' the young signaller said.

'There hasn't been for quarter of an hour,' Krishna said. 'The rissaldar-major said he thought the Germans had counter-attacked on both flanks and were in behind us.'

'Is he all right?' Warren said.

'Yes, sir. And Ramaswami, with the advanced aid post he'd brought up to rear HQ. And the Pandit-ji. The quartermaster's there, too. He'd come up with the extra ammunition and seems to have been trapped ... stretcher bearer, here, help me put the colonel sahib's arm in a splint.'

Warren waited, sitting still, his head nodding, while they cut off the sleeve of his tunic and made the splint out of a stick of wood found in a dugout, bandaged it, and put his arm in a sling. 'Take some morphine, sir,' Krishna said.

He shook his head. 'We're going to attack again. If you can drown a sowar in peacetime, just to make a good show on manoeuvres, it shouldn't bother you to lose every man in the regiment in a real decisive battle ... Is there no way you can get through to the guns, Bruington?'

'I'm afraid not, sir.'

Krishna Ram said, 'It isn't necessary. We are not going to attack.'

For a moment Warren did not understand what was being said. Then he started forward, his hand going to his hip, but as he looked up he realized he was staring down the muzzle of Krishna's revolver. Krishna said, 'I'm sorry, sir, but you are relieved of your command. Pahlwan, cover Lieutenant Bruington. Take his revolver. Hanuman, cover the artillery signallers...'

The young gunner subaltern quavered, 'My God, sir, what are you doing?'

The trench reeked of fear and urine and wet wool and death.

'Colonel Bateman is temporarily insane, because of his wound,' Krishna said. 'I am assuming command ... Don't worry, I'll tell the general as soon as I can get through to him.'

Warren experienced a slowly spreading emptiness in the pit of his stomach, half agony, half ecstasy. It was exactly the same sensation as had come over him when he saw Ralph's buttocks thrusting between the spread thighs of his wife. He turned slowly on the prince. Krishna was pale, his face splashed with mud, the wet tunic clinging to him. The rain continued to fall without cease. Warren said, 'I am in full possession of my senses. You are fomenting a mutiny.'

'I say you are insane, sir. But not only you. Everyone fighting here in France. We are getting out.' He took the revolver from Warren's holster and reached out to hand it to a trumpeter. Warren leaped at it, but as his hand touched it Hanuman's rifle jerked down. The butt smashed against Warren's wrist, knocking the revolver out of his hand. He stood swaying, the wrist hanging in throbbing agony. 'Are you going to obey my orders, sir?' Krishna said.

'No, you treacherous swine!'

'Guard the colonel-sahib, Hanuman. See that he does not get possession of any weapon.'

Jee han huzoor.

'Signaller, tell the quartermaster-sahib and the rissaldar-major-sahib to come here at once. Pahlwan, take command of B Squadron ... But first order all squadron commanders to send out patrols to establish the present position of the Germans in front and to the flanks ... and, from B and D Squadrons, to the rear ... Stretcher bearer, give the colonel-sahib morphine. Hold him, Hanuman. I'll help. There ... Lie still, sir.'

384

October 1915

S UNSET WAS INVISIBLE in the rain, the yellowish tinge
subtly leaving the light and then the light itself, grey-green,
fading slowly into darkness. It stopped raining. Artillery grumbled
from in front and behind, flashes lit the horizon all round, growing brighter as night advanced. The earth trembled continually
but no shells fell among the trenches held by Krishna's men.

Krishna, in a German dugout which faced the wrong way, its
door protected by the original gas curtain, studied a trench map
spread on a crude table. The Ravi Lancers were surrounded. If
the Germans knew that they had a pocket of British troops between
their advanced and rear elements they had done nothing about it.
A few German carrying parties had tried to use the communication
trenches but had been beaten off without difficulty. Their artillery
had made no attempt to fire and no patrols seemed to have been
sent to find out the situation. The Ravi Lancers remained in a
sort of hollow square—A and D Squadrons forward in old German
reserve trenches; in the centre, Regimental HQ and the machine
guns in German front line trenches; to the rear, B and C Squadrons
in what had been the British front line.

This state of affairs could not last long, Krishna knew. Either
the British would launch a counter-offensive to regain what had
been lost, or the Germans would attack to wipe out the lodgment.

'Galloper,' he said, 'I am going to hold a panchayat here at eight
o'clock. Tell Captain Ramaswami, the quartermaster-sahib, Rissaldar Ram Lall, and the Pandit-ji to attend ... Rissaldar-major-sahib,
will you take part?'

The rissaldar-major said, 'It would be improper for me to do so,
Yuvraj.' He was sitting on one of the bunks against the back wall,
his hands bound behind his back with field telephone cable, for

Krishna had placed him under arrest as soon as he came up from the rear, knowing that his duty would compel him to support Warren Bateman. Also, in arrest and bound, no British authority could later accuse him of complicity in anything that happened in the regiment. On the next bunk Warren Bateman was propped up with sandbags, his face greasy-white even in the yellow light from candles stuck in bottles.

'You don't even have the guts to give orders, but call a panchayat,' he muttered weakly. 'You claim you're commanding, don't you?'

'This isn't a matter for a command decision, sir,' Krishna said. 'I shall hold the panchayat here. You are welcome to give your opinions during it.'

He went out into the trench. His bodyguards, squatting outside the gas curtain, rose and made *namasti* as he appeared. Was there a moon trying to rise? It might be important later, but not now. Later, too, he'd look at the squadrons. A machine gun was in position above, the gunner hunched in silhouette behind the thick barrel. '*Sab thik hai, jawan?*' He spoke to the dim shape.

'*Thik hai, huzoor.*'

To the right was a stretch of trench where the Germans must have once had a battalion headquarters at the least. It contained several big dugouts, which Krishna had ordered taken over for the Aid Post. He ducked under the tarpaulin covering the entrance to the centre one, and paused, chilled by the sight. The colour was red-brown, mixed of earth and blood. The floor was densely covered with men, blood seeping through bandages and from open wounds. Blood ran from the table where Captain Ramaswami, shirt-sleeved in the chill night, operated fast. Legs and arms piled up in the far corner and even as Krishna watched a sowar staggered by with a load of them bloody in his arms, to take them outside. Orderlies removed the man Ramaswami had been operating on and carried him out to one of the other dugouts. Another man was lifted on to the table. Ramaswami cut his tunic, looked at the mess of entrails revealed, and shook his head. The orderlies took the man out.

The doctor looked up and saw Krishna. Sweat ran down his dark coarse skin and his eyes were bloodshot. He said, 'Dussehra, prince! See how your goddess Kali shows her love for her children!'

'This isn't the work of Kali,' Krishna said bitterly. 'She is human, this is the work of a factory ... Is the CO going to lose his arm?'

The doctor shook his head. He was making long slits in a man's forearm as he spoke, the man grey of face, staring with wide open eyes at the hurricane lantern swinging from a stick over his head. 'It's a simple fracture of the humerus. The arm may heal a little short, as the bullet blew a piece of the bone clean out.' He wiped cloth and mud out of the strongly bleeding wound under his hands. 'Iodine and bandage!' he called. 'Next! ... I hear we're surrounded. Why don't we surrender?'

Krishna said, 'That's what we're going to discuss at the panchayat. You can come, can't you?'

The doctor gestured at the patiently waiting wounded. Krishna said, 'I think it's important. Please come.'

The doctor said, 'You're exhausted. Get some sleep.'

Krishna went up the dugout steps into the trench, breathing deeply of the damp air. Yes, he was tired; but there was not much more to endure. He returned to his own dugout and lay down. 'Wake me when the members of the panchayat come,' he said, and closed his eyes.

He had thought, as soon as he shut out the scene actually before him, that visions of the Aid Post and its mangled humanity would come, or memories of the broken bodies he had seen above ground, churned into the mud of Artois; but what came to him were visions of Diana Bateman ... smiling at him as they walked on the Plain ... tossing her head, her short curls shaking in the wind ... talking of what they would do together in Ravi when he became the Rajah. She was so innocent, not of sexuality or sin, but of other values than the ones she had been brought up to. She was innocent of doubt. He wondered how she would have fared if circumstances had forced her into the same self examinations and re-evaluations that had faced Warren since he joined the Ravi Lancers. Then he saw her naked, her arms up, and he thought, she may be carrying my child, a son of the Sun. Surely she would have told him somehow if she was. There was nothing about that in the letters that Warren had given back to him. But perhaps she was sure, from his actions in Paris, that he wanted a child, and would only write if to say that, alas, she was not pregnant.

He was sure, suddenly, that she was pregnant. She thought that he wanted the child, and would be delighted by the revelation, which she wanted to make to him from her own lips—for it was to be a moment of joy for both of them.

He turned over, opening his eyes. What would he really think, if that was the truth? What would he say? What he actually did was the least important, for what would matter in any future life he might live with Diana, would be the inwardness of his feelings ... and that he didn't know.

One by one the members of the panchayat came down the steps. One by one they squatted round the walls. Krishna, squatting in the centre, looked at them, one by one—fat Sohan Singh, his jowls trembling—but from what? He wasn't physically frightened. The doctor, black, dead weary, bloodstains on his sleeve, officially a Christian, really almost an atheist, and mentally farther from Krishna's Rajput Hinduism than Warren Bateman lying on the German blanket there. The Brahmin, also trembling a little, but because he was physically afraid; he had put a caste mark and rice on his forehead. Rissaldar Ram Lall, clean shaven, tall, his Sam Browne gleaming, the belt buckle like the sun, the ribbon of the IOM red and blue on his chest. Himself ... he looked in the broken piece of mirror some German had hung from a roof beam, and saw a haggard unshaven man, dark eyes fiery in a dirty face, hair long and black hanging down under the mud-stained turban. He said, '*Pandit-ji*, say a prayer for us.'

The Brahmin joined his palms and intoned in Sanskrit, praying, 'O Lord Vishnu, whom we worship, and Lord Krishna, his avatar, give guidance to our prince here, earthly presence of Krishna, Son of the Sun, and to us, his subjects and servants, in our present difficulty.'

Krishna raised his head and put his palms flat on the ground in front of his knees. He said, 'You know the situation. What are we to do? Let the Brahmin speak first, concerning how the holy books and ancient custom might guide us.'

The woordie-major stuck his head round the gas curtain at the top of the steps. 'Prince, a German officer came into A Squadron under a white flag. They have sent him here. He refuses to speak to anyone but the commander.'

'Bring him in.'

The German officer who came down the steps was young and blond and held his head arrogantly. He said in clipped English,

'Who is the commander here?'

'I am. Major Krishna Ram.'

The German clicked his heels and bowed. He said, 'I am authorized by Colonel von Stalwitz, commanding the Imperial German troops in the immediate vicinity, to accept your surrender. You will be permitted the honours of war.'

Krishna found a smile. 'You mean, we can keep our sabres and rifles?'

'The honours of war means that you may march to the rear carrying your arms. In a safe area you will pass before a saluting guard of honour of not less than one full platoon commanded by an officer, with guidon. Once you have marched past, you will surrender your arms, of course.'

'That is the correct way, is it?'

'Yes, major.'

Krishna said, 'We have not yet decided what to do. I was just about to discuss it with these gentlemen.'

The German's wondering eyes took in Sohan Singh's flabby jowels, the Brahmin looking like a beggar on a cold day, Krishna's own unkemptness. He said insolently, 'I thought you were the commanding officer. Is it a Workers' Council that I am negotiating with?'

Krishna said patiently, 'No. Now you may go.'

'But what answer . . . ?'

'None, yet.'

'Never surrender,' Warren Bateman's voice was a croak from the corner. 'Tell him to go to hell.'

The German said, 'Colonel von Stalwitz will feel free to begin action against you immediately after my return.'

Krishna said, 'Very well, though, as I said, we have not yet decided. Until we do, we shall defend ourselves, and you will lose many men . . . That is all,' he added peremptorily.

The German, after another hesitation, again bowed, clicked his heels and went up the steps and out.

Krishna turned to the Brahmin. 'Now, *pandit-ji.*'

The Brahmin said, 'Prince . . . the Rawal of Basohli told me, when he selected me as the pandit to accompany you over the Black Water, of the talk that you and he and your august grandfather had had in the temple the night you proposed that the regiment be offered to the British Sirkar. He told me that the sending of the regiment was like the sending of Lord Krishna, your namesake, to Hastina as an ambassador to find out whether it was to be peace or war between the two kingdoms. The new things we have learned, the battles we have taken part in, the defeats we have suffered, the victories we have achieved through such as Himat Singh—all these are as nothing. They are no more than the playing of light and shadow upon the question, and the question was—peace or war, between them and us. We have seen much that is good and noble. More, far more, that is ignoble, debasing of man and god alike. I say therefore that the answer we take back to Ravi is ... war. We shall not surrender any more to their ideas. They shall force nothing more on us. There shall be no union or accommodation between us.'

Krishna Ram said gently, 'I understand, *pandit-ji*. But how shall that decision be interpreted in the matter before us now?'

The Brahmin said, 'It is of no consequence. Fight. Surrender. It does not matter. Our embassy is ended. Soon or late we shall return to Bharat-desh, and inform our sovereign of our thoughts.'

The doctor said slowly, in the halting Hindi he had acquired during his fourteen months with the regiment, 'You mean ... total rejection of the west? Their medicine and science, too?'

'Yes,' the Brahmin said.

'Government? Engineering? Farming? All that the sowars have been studying, hoping to adapt to conditions in Ravi?'

'Yes,' the Brahmin said firmly. 'There can be no compromise. Either we follow the light of the Lord Vishnu or we follow these foreign gods. We cannot do both.'

The doctor said, 'I cannot go quite that far ...' A whistling shriek presaged the burst of a shell somewhere close by. One of the candles went out in the shiver of air from the explosion. Sohan Singh relit it. The doctor continued almost without a break, 'I am a Christian, you know ... I think that we who have seen so much here, and learned so much, have a duty to tell the rest of our people about what we have learned, to enable them to separate what is good from what is bad about the European way of life. They—our people—are so uneducated that, if not advised, they must take all or nothing. It is our privilege to be able to show them how to make distinctions ... It is therefore imperative that we survive in order to carry this knowledge back to India. I am for surrender.'

Krishna glanced at Sohan Singh, who spread his fat hands. 'Yuvraj ... as for this embassy, I agree with the *pandit-ji*. I have learned nothing from the merchants I have dealt with. I came ready for the honesty the Christians talk of, and I was prepared to be honest myself in turn ... but they act no differently from the greediest Basohli bazaar thief. Nor are they very intelligent. I have amassed over two lakhs of rupees for the regiment with no exertion and no risk, not from my acumen but from their stupidity, and greed.'

'And half a lakh for yourself, I don't doubt,' Krishna said dryly. 'What do you advise here?'

'Surrender,' the quartermaster said. 'Thinking that this might happen at some time, I long ago prepared ways of transferring some money into Germany. Wherever they imprison us, we and the sowars will be well looked after.'

From the gloom Warren Bateman muttered hoarsely, 'Treason! There must be no surrender.'

Krishna said, 'Rissaldar-sahib?'

Rissaldar Ram Lall leaned forward where he squatted with the rest of them. 'We are fighting men,' he said. 'We cannot return to our homes and say we gave up before we had to. Who knows what may happen tomorrow? We must hold on here.'

Krishna looked at Warren Bateman and said, 'I presume you would continue to fight, sir?'

'Of course I would,' Warren said. 'And when you are court martialled, as you certainly will be, it will be for cowardice as well as for mutiny if you order a surrender now.'

'Rissaldar-major-sahib?'

'As I said, lord, I do not think it is proper for me to take part in this panchayat since it is being held against the orders of the true commanding officer.'

Bateman broke in, 'Speak, sahib. You may be able to save them from a greater disgrace.'

The rissaldar-major said, 'As the presence orders ... My lord, sahibs assembled—as to this talk of an embassy, I understand only dimly what is meant. I was a servant of the Sirkar while this was being discussed in Basohli. But I understand enough to say that unless there is a mighty change of heart in all India, it will serve nothing to try to reject what the English and the others have brought. Does anyone here know a peasant who, being offered a ride in a motor car, will walk? Or, being shown a tap with running water, will insist on carrying water half a mile from the well? He who preaches keeping to all our old ways must act upon the minds and hearts of Indians, not against the inventions of Europeans. It is in my mind that our first task is neither to accept all nor to reject all that the Europeans have brought, but to decide each case on its merits. But, as men, we must prove that we can stand level with them. I, who have eaten the Sirkar's salt, cannot stand level with anyone if I fail now in my duty. Our clear duty is to fight. If help comes, so much the better for our wives and children. If not, we shall go to join the army of the Sun.'

'Not today,' the Brahmin said gloomily. 'Indra has hidden his face from us for the past seven days.'

'Which was the duration of the war in heaven,' Krishna said. Another shell burst in No Man's Land, but closer. He continued, 'My friends ... subjects of my grandfather ... citizens of Bharat-desh ... as you have all agreed, our embassy to the west is ended. We have tried all the methods which the wisdom of our ancestors laid down ... *Sam*—we have spent thirteen months asking, seeing, observing, discussing ... *Dan*—we have given our blood, our money, our labour, our very lives to Europe ... *Bhed*—we have created a rift among them, for some think one thing about us and some another. Perhaps the rift would have become deeper if we—I am particularly to blame—had not turned at last to *dand*, physical force. As my grandfather warned, we came here young and will return old, having learned much that we would prefer to have remained innocent of ... It is time we went back to our own earth, our own sun. As to what we do when we get there, I stand like a cow on four legs—one is the word of the Brahmin—utter rejection; and one is the word of the doctor; and one the word of Sohan Singh; and one the word of the rissaldar-major. Where then is my heart? My head? It is my opinion that we must get back to Bharat-desh and there decide, as we face each problem, which is the proper leg to stand on for that moment, that problem ... As to what we do now, I think we shall not surrender here, because we are decided that we shall no longer surrender there, in Bharat-desh. Shall we then simply hold on here, hoping that the British will rescue us? No, because that is what we must not do in Bharat-desh. We must rescue ourselves in order to be free. We will fight our way out.'

'Lord,' Rissaldar Ram Lall said doubtfully, 'there will be no artillery support.'

'We have seen many attacks,' Krishna said. 'Did the artillery ever destroy the wire, the machine guns? No, we must rely on our own ways, of speed, and stealth. We will carry no weapons but the bayonets. We will move by dark. *Pandit-ji*, look to your astrological tables and tell me when the gods will that we move.'

'I do not have them with me, lord,' the Brahmin said, 'but your highness is surely aware that tomorrow is your birthday. You were born at ten minutes before noon. Of a certainty, that will be an auspicious moment.'

'But, *pandit-ji*,' Krishna said jovially, 'that's broad daylight. And the Germans won't wait that long ... Hold! I was born in India, was I not?'

'Of course, lord,' the Brahmin said wonderingly. 'In Basohli.'

'Don't you remember how they kept changing the clocks on the ship?' Krishna said. 'Five and a half hours altogether ... take five and a half hours off 11.50 and you get 6.20. I was born at 6.20 a.m., French time.'

'As the presence pleases,' the Brahmin said dubiously.

Krishna said, 'Which is half an hour before first light. We shall move at that hour. And the men certainly need some sleep. So be it. What is the strength of the regiment here, now?'

'Three hundred,' Sohan Singh said.

Krishna said, 'Let every man be asked personally whether he wishes to come with us, or stay here to surrender to the Germans after we have gone. Let every man who comes with me tie the handkerchief round his right wrist ... I will give orders to squadron commanders here in half an hour.'

The quartermaster said hesitantly, 'Prince ... I have a thought ... I may be out of my proper senses, but...'

'Speak up, man,' Krishna said testily, 'what is it?'

'It is the second day of Dussehra. I had brought up some sets of nautch clothes, with the extra ammunition. I was going to get some of the best dancers dressed, and let them dance, to a little music, in the Aid Post, in the reserve trenches, in the dugouts, so that the men would have a little something of Dussehra, and...'

'By the eyes of Vishnu, you are right!' Krishna exclaimed. 'You were going to suggest that some of us wear the costumes! Yes! Distribute them, as many as you have, to the men who will be around me—my bodyguards, Hanuman, the rissaldar-major-sahib.'

'It will make you more conspicuous,' Rissaldar Ram Lall said doubtfully.

'I hope so,' Krishna said. 'Now, let us pray in silence.'

He bent over, palms joined, and prayed, then rose to his feet. The members of the panchayat filed out, making *namasti*. Warren Bateman said, 'You're mad.'

Krishna replied, 'No, I am just coming to my senses.'

At five o'clock in the morning Krishna arose and went out. He waited till his eyes had become accustomed to the darkness, but after five minutes still could not make out the shape of the sentry at the end of the bay. The air was thick, wet and motionless. He realized that a dense fog had settled on to the land. He stripped to the Indian testicle bag he had taken to wearing instead of European underpants, and ceremonially washed from head to toe in water which Hanuman poured into his hand from a big German container. The Brahmin watched, praying.

When he finished, Krishna returned inside the dugout, where Hanuman and the two bodyguards dressed him in the white ceremonial costume worn by the character dancing the part of his namesake the demi-god Krishna in the epics. A huge tinsel sunburst decorated the front of his red turban, and a smaller one, representing the Sun of Ravi, shone on the left breast of his yellow silk tunic. The sword stuck through his sash was an ancient Rajput blade, heavily curved, that was much used in the dance. Krishna felt the edge, and gave it to his orderly. 'Sharpen it, Hanuman. We are not going to dance with it today.'

He turned to the watching Brahmin. 'Are you staying here, *pandit-ji*?'

The Brahmin fell on his knees. 'Lord, is there permission?' His voice quavered. 'I am not a man of war, but I would a thousand times rather come with you, reciting prayers at your side as we Brahmins did in olden times at the side of the Kings of Ravi, than that you should turn your face from me afterwards, because I did not come.'

'No, *pandit-ji*,' Krishna said, pulling the man gently to his feet, 'your prayers will be heard from here, as well as from my side, if the Lord Vishnu wishes to hear them at all. Put on my *tilak*—red today.'

394

That done, he walked on down the trench. Outside the Aid Post he found Sohan Singh also in white, and said, 'Are you coming with us, Sohan, or will you stay here with the wounded?'

'And spend the next ten years in a prison camp in Germany?' Sohan said. 'I would lose a crore of rupees! Of course, I might be able to bribe myself out as soon as I could get my father to send money from Basohli.' He shook his head and his jowls wobbled. 'But I could not count on it. The commandant of the camp might be impervious to bribes. Some such people exist. No, lord, I will come with you.'

'Good ... Are the men eating?'

'What they have, lord, and some bread the Germans left behind. Also German schnapps, a tot for each man.'

Krishna went down into the Aid Post. Captain Ramaswami was sitting on the operating table, drinking something out of a mess tin. 'My goodness,' he said, looking at Krishna's finery. 'We are going to re-enact the Mahabharta in Artois! ... This is the schnapps. It's good stuff. Have some.'

Krishna waved it away, smiling. 'No compromise! ... The Brahmin will be staying with you here, and about twenty fit men from the squadrons, who don't want to come with us. Soon after first light put up a white flag and surrender to whoever the Germans send in.'

'I should come with you,' the doctor said. 'Though I don't think you have a hope of getting through.'

'Why not?' Krishna said. 'Vishnu has already given us a dense fog, to go with our white clothes. We shall continue to obey him, not the European gods—the machines, the guns. We have proved again and again that weight of metal does not achieve results ... We are not going to stop for wounded, doctor. You stay here. You will be able to practise your profession in the prison camp. Perhaps they will even let you out to help the women. There must be a great shortage of doctors in Germany, too.'

Ramaswami said, 'Is that an order?'

Krishna said, 'It is my wish, as Prince of Ravi.'

The doctor said sarcastically, 'Your wish is my command. Very well, I will do as you want ... What about Colonel Bateman?'

'Is he fit to move?'

'Yes,' the doctor said. 'He's in slight shock, but he can move, provided it isn't too far, and too long. But...'

'Then I will take him with us.'

'I was going to say you would be wise to leave him here with me. Then he cannot give evidence against you until the end of the war. No one's going to take any action then.'

'That's the reason I must take him with me,' Krishna said. 'We can't be free unless we do what we must do, openly.'

'You're mad, Yuvraj,' the doctor said gruffly. 'But perhaps India needs some madness to survive. Good luck.'

'Thank you.' He shook the doctor's outstretched hand and returned to his dugout.

He knelt beside the bunk where Warren Bateman lay, his eyes open. The colonel was muttering, 'Joan ... I could understand ... hurt as much as I thought ... But you, Di ...'

The rissaldar-major, sitting on the next bunk, said, 'He talks to himself much, sahib.'

Krishna shook Warren gently and said, 'Sir ... sir ...'

The eyes opened wider and Warren sat up, gasping, 'Di!' and then, after a pause, 'What is it? Are the Germans attacking?'

'We shall be moving soon. I'm going to have the rissaldar-major untied to go at your side, and there will be four sowars to help carry you if you become tired. Rissaldar-major-sahib, look after the colonel-sahib at all costs.'

'I shall, sahib.'

'Keep close behind me. We'll be with A Squadron. I had intended to keep the squadrons well spread out, and separated, but with this fog I'm ordering them to keep concentrated. Dress in these clothes. May Parmeshwar guard you, sahib.'

The RM, freed, began to change. When he was ready, the handkerchief tied around his wrist, he drew his sabre from its scabbard, and said, 'We are ready.'

Six-fifteen. Krishna passed down the trench in the swirling fog, his sword on one shoulder. As he passed, the men, all in white here, fell to one knee and, reaching out, touched his foot or the hem of his tunic. Their faces, pearled with moisture, were eager and uplifted as though they had taken drugs, though they had not.

Six-twenty. Silently Krishna climbed out of the trench, compass in hand. The bearing of the retreat was 270 magnetic, due west. The fog seemed to carry its own light within it, for he stood in an eery white glow, sensing the white-clothed men coming up out of the trenches and spreading out in tight lines to right and left.

He began to move. He could reach out and touch the nearest men on either hand, but the fog deadened all sound. The massed ghosts, naked bayonets or sabres in hand, drifted silently, like the fog, over the muddy, churned earth. The ground was littered with corpses from the attacks on Fosse-Garde, dead brown faces upturned in the fog, in some places so thick that he had difficulty not treading on them, rifles abandoned and broken, wire coiled across shell holes, here bodies jumbled where a heavy shell had burst in a crater full of men, humped rubble of bricks, arms sticking out of sandbagged revetments, the trail of a German gun long broken and abandoned. They came to wire, which Krishna thought had been in front of the old British second line; but it had been cut in many places by shell fire and perhaps by German assault parties, and not repaired, for now it was facing the wrong way. The sowars drifted through with little more difficulty than the fog itself. The trench was occupied only by a sleepy sentry, who had no time to sound the alarm gong before a sowar slid his bayonet into his neck. Then they were up and out the far side. Guttural shouts arose behind, quickly swallowed. A machine gun close at hand began to fire, but Krishna thought it was firing the wrong way. Some stirring of the fog, as though by a giant hand, warned him that light was coming. They passed another line of trenches, this one unoccupied, or perhaps the men in it were all asleep in the dugouts and had posted no sentries. Now they must be near the end of the old British trench system. How far had the Germans penetrated? They certainly had not had time to dig more trenches beyond whatever they had captured.

The ground began to shake to heavy artillery fire to the right, the north. The fire seemed to be coming from British guns. Perhaps they were launching a counter-offensive. It would be the normal time of day to do so.

A helmeted, grotesquely masked figure appeared, another beside him. A machine gun loomed nearby. Krishna and the rissaldar-major charged silently, six others with them. The Germans' yells of terror were stifled in the masks, and choked off as they died, heads rolling and blood spouting over the ground. Krishna kept steadily on. Why were the Germans wearing gas masks? There was no gas in the air.

He understood: a slight west wind had sprung up, which would enable the British to use gas. In this fog the gas would not be detected until too late. All this was to the Indians' advantage, for no one could see well through those masks.

A battery of mortars appeared in the strengthening light, dug into shallow pits. Masked infantrymen lay asleep all round, fully dressed. The Rajputs swept forward as whistles blew and the Germans leaped for their weapons. A mortar man died over the barrel of his mortar, rifle shots exploded and here and there Krishna saw a Rajput fall. A German towered up, rifle in hand. Krishna stepped aside, swung his sword, and the man's arm fell off at the elbow. Hanuman jumped in with his bayonet in his left hand; an officer aiming a Mauser fired one burst into the ground as he died. The Rajputs glided on into the fog. Five minutes later Krishna dimly made out a column of men looming up ahead and to the right. By now the light was strong but the fog persisted. The column was German infantry moving east over broken ground. The British artillery fire was getting heavier and closer. Krishna signalled his men to sink to the ground. The Germans were going towards the rear. It might be a normal relief movement, or it might be that the British were indeed attacking somewhere to the north and the Germans were adjusting their tenuous line. The column passed, perhaps five hundred men. Rifle fire from behind, a little later, made Krishna think that the column might have run into one of the other Ravi squadrons ... but they were in a hurry and would only have fired at any Lancers who got in their way.

He signalled his men to advance once more. The breeze blew more strongly into his face and the fog began to thin. The sun was trying to rise. Behind him Warren Bateman was being supported by two sowars as he stumbled forward.

They came upon German infantry, lining the edge of a shattered wood, facing the other way. The Lancers fell on them, momentarily as irresistible as Arjun's legions of the sky. Sabres and bayonets slashed and thrust. The fighting became hand to hand. Krishna saw Lieutenant Puran Lall's sabre sweep almost completely through a German officer's body at the waist. Then a German soldier thrust his bayonet into the young officer's heart. Puran Lall fell, turning, a smile on his face, the first Krishna had seen there since his brother was killed.

'On!' Krishna cried. 'On!'

For a moment the fighting was intense around him. One of his bodyguards fell to a rifle shot, and the trumpeter to an officer's Mauser. Hanuman's bayonet dripped in his hand, staining his white garment. Krishna slashed down one last man and then he was through, out of the wood on an open field, unmarked by shell fire, the wet grass firm underfoot. 'Close up,' he called. 'Keep formation.' The tendrils of fog closed in behind, and the machine gun fire sent after them ceased.

Ten minutes later a shot from in front cracked close over his head. He saw a man in khaki uniform kneeling behind a low wall, making ready to fire again. The man had slant eyes and was wearing a wide-brimmed hat. It was a Gurkha, a look of amazement clearly visible on his round face. 'Friend, *dost, dost*!' Krishna called, his hands raised. Slowly the Gurkha stood up.

Brigadier-General Rainbow Rogers, seated at a rough table in a battered railway station building at Contamines, said, 'Sit down, Krishna, sit down. Feel better now?'

'Yes, sir,' Krishna said. 'Twenty hours' sleep is enough for anyone.'

The general shuffled an army signal form in front of him. 'It appears that you brought out 240 all ranks. Do you know how many you started from Fosse-Garde with?'

'Two hundred and eighty.'

'Great heavens, you had heavy casualties in the battle, then. But afterwards you only lost about forty, fighting your way out through a German division. A remarkable feat of arms, and one that reflects the greatest credit on you ... and your officers and men, of course. And wearing fancy dress! An extraordinary idea, I must say, but it seems to have caught the Germans off guard ... though I am not sure that you wouldn't be liable to be shot as spies if the Germans had caught you. Being out of uniform, you see. You won't do that again, will you?'

'No, sir.'

'Good. I think I can promise you a DSO within a few days. Get yourself some uniform as soon as you can.'

'Yes, sir ... We left about forty more wounded, who couldn't walk, in the Aid Post,' Krishna said, 'with Captain Ramaswami and our Brahmin.'

'Poor fellows. Well, the war is over for them, eh? The front disintegrated just after I last spoke to Colonel Bateman. The

Germans broke through on the right and all communications were cut. No one knew where anyone was. Our dispatch riders found themselves in the middle of German columns, and we captured a German colonel who thought he was five miles on his side of the front. Terrible state of affairs! No form, just a mess, changing every moment. I didn't know where any of my brigade was ... except you.'

'We would never have got out if the situation hadn't been so fluid,' Krishna said.

'Quite. Well, it's stabilized now, thank God. The forward troops are digging the new trench lines now. We've lost some ground here, gained some there...' He put his monocle carefully in his eye and looked at Krishna. 'How was Colonel Bateman at Fosse-Garde? A little—overwrought, eh? That wound must have been very painful, and of course he had been working himself unmercifully for weeks before the battle.'

'He was tired, sir, but in full possession of his faculties.'

'H'm. Wouldn't you say that his wound had temporarily rendered him unfit for command?' The general's eye gleamed meaningfully behind the glass.

Krishna hesitated. It was such an easy way out, and the general obviously wanted him to take it. But there must be no more lying. 'No, sir,' he said firmly.

The general said petulantly, 'Oh, very well. You know that he has made extremely serious charges against you?'

'I know he was going to, sir.'

'Mutiny. Disobeying the lawful order of your superior officer. Cowardice in the face of the enemy. Disgraceful conduct.' He tapped the table top. 'Here's his deposition, signed and witnessed, and supported by another one from Rissaldar-Major Baldev Singh. This means a court martial, Krishna. A very serious scandal involving your grandfather's state, and the Indian Army as a whole.'

'I know, sir, but I think it will lead to good in the end.'

The general said, 'Be reasonable, Krishna. No one wants a scandal. General Glover told me to do all that I could to hush this whole thing up. You did very well getting your regiment out of Fosse-Garde in obedience to my orders.'

'Your orders, sir?' said Krishna, startled.

'Yes. When the Germans broke through on the right I sent an

order for you to retreat to this area, Contamines, as fast as possible.'

'We never got it.'

'But you were carrying out my intention when you, h'm, took command, don't you see?'

Krishna said, 'I imagine the court martial will have to decide on that, sir.'

The general snapped, 'Oh, very well. But it can't be held until Colonel Bateman is fit again. He's being evacuated to England tonight. I'm sending the rissaldar-major on leave, too, as I think it would be better if he were out of your regiment until the court martial. Meantime, consider yourself under open arrest.' He let the monocle drop on its cord.

'Yes, sir ... Sir, I think it will be best for all concerned if our regiment is returned to India and mustered out of Imperial service.'

The general said, 'Do you want me to forward that request officially? ... Because, between you and me, there is a strong chance that the Indian infantry divisions will be pulled out of France as soon as shipping is available, and sent to Mesopotamia.'

Krishna said, 'I think my grandfather would ask that we be returned to Ravi.'

The general said, 'I quite agree. The 44th Lancers must be over their anthrax long since and General Glover would like to have them back. No offence, you know, but in Mespot they'd be mounted, real cavalrymen again. As for your regiment, you've lost so heavily that the general is returning the 8th Brahmins to my brigade, and taking you back as divisional troops ... but he told me he won't use you except in real emergencies.'

Krishna said, 'Then I may take it that we will be sent back to Ravi at the first opportunity?'

'Yes, I think so.'

'I shall notify my grandfather accordingly, sir.'

That was it, he thought. The general was standing up. By now there were four rows of ribbons on his left breast. He would do anything for more of them ... risk his life ... or see that the Ravi Lancers were sent home to Bharat-desh. Krishna said, 'I have heard from many sources of your heroism at Fosse-Garde, sir. As we are now leaving your brigade, I ask you to honour us by accepting membership in the Royal Order of the Sun of Ravi.'

The general's long face reddened with pleasure. 'Why, that's very good of you, my boy. The Royal Order of the Sun of Ravi, eh? What is the, er, ribbon like? And I suppose there's a cross to go with it?'

'Not a cross, sir,' Krishna said, 'we are Hindus. A gold and enamel sunburst, to be worn as a collar, with a yellow and white ribbon. My grandfather will send you your collar as soon as possible, but meantime...' He unfastened the tinsel brooch from the left breast of his silk tunic and said, 'Here, sir ... On behalf of His Highness Sir Sugriva Valadeva Yudisthir Bhishma Pandu Abhimanyu Satrughna Krishna Vishnu, Surya-ka-Chora, Knight Commander of the Order of the Star of India, I bestow upon you the Royal Order of the Sun of Ravi.'

He pinned the brooch on the general's tunic. The general saluted, his back rigid, the monocle glinting in his eye.

Major Bholanath lay sprawled on a broken bed in what had been the mayor's house of Contamines. His white moustaches were curled up, and protected by a handkerchief tied round his head. He was wearing khaki riding breeches, army socks and a flannel shirt, and he was smoking a hookah of hashish. His orderly squatted at his feet blowing on the charcoal in the bowl of the hookah. Krishna, wearing no Sam Browne belt but otherwise fully dressed in an ill-fitting uniform, sat on a bench beside him. The sound of music, Indian music, drifted through the village from the town square, where the regimental band, their instruments brought up from the base, were playing for a dance while the massed sowars, all in uniform, watched a dozen dancers, ceremonially dressed and garlanded, shuffle and gyrate over the cobbles.

'You're the commanding officer now,' Krishna said.

'Very well, prince,' the old man mumbled, the words coming out slowly and luxuriously. 'Tell me what you wish. It shall be done.'

'And we'll be sent back to Ravi soon.'

'Good ... though I shall be sorry not to fight these Germans some more ... they are good warriors ...'

'I hope we have had our last casualties. There have been enough. Six hundred and twenty killed and wounded since we came to France—for what?'

402

'Who have gone ahead "along the mighty steps"?' old Bhola-nath mumbled. 'Colonel Hanbury was the first. He should have been tending his garden long since.'

'He was younger than you, uncle ... Himat, I wish he had not had time to think again, at the last ...'

'Sher Singh ... Bateman-sahib gave him his desserts, saving me the trouble.'

'What do you mean?'

'It was he who killed the half-caste, Flaherty, meaning to murder the colonel. My rissaldar found out ... Then there was Mahadeo Singh—well, he died as he would have wished, though in a place far from his home.'

'The Heavenly Twins ... one knowing the glory and one the bitterness.'

'The black doctor. He was a good man.'

'He and the *pandit-ji* aren't dead, only prisoners.'

'What difference? ... So many good rissaldars and jemadars. Aiih, we shall have much teaching to do when we get back to Basohli.'

'Mind that you see that the regiment is properly purified after crossing the Black Water, uncle.'

'Have no fear ... but you will be back with us by then.'

'Perhaps. Perhaps not. It will depend on the court martial.'

'There will be no court martial. The British will find some way of preventing it ... You forgot one more good man destroyed by this war.'

'Who's that?'

'Bateman-sahib. But he did not go down before doing what he set out to. He has changed us, all of us.'

'He is not defeated yet,' Krishna said sadly. 'There is yet more that he can do, and will.'

November 1915

THE THIN NOVEMBER sunlight gleamed along the bare arms of the oak trees in the woods, and hoar frost lingered in the shadowed grass under the cottage walls. The furrowed land swept up through misty distance to the brow of the Plain, elms standing in silhouette, stark guardians of the crest. Faint from the valley Warren heard the sound of a hunting horn. At his side, Diana said, 'They're drawing the Bohun copses.'

Warren said, 'I didn't know there was any hunting this year.'

'It's difficult,' Diana said, 'with the hunt servants gone to the army and taxes so heavy, but so many officers on leave said that a day's hunting was all they longed for, when they were in France, that the Master has arranged one day a week ... Warrie, I'm pregnant.'

They walked on in silence along the canal bank, the spaniel Fudge trotting beside. It was Saturday and she had only arrived late yesterday evening to spend the weekend at Shrewford Pennel. Before that, once or twice while he was in hospital, she had come to see him, but had not mentioned—this. Warren knew he ought to say something but no words would form.

'Krishna will be able to come as soon as the court martial is over, won't he?' she said.

Warren said, 'If he wants to ...'

'Oh, Warrie,' she said, 'you think he doesn't want to ... marry me?' She sounded miserable, and frightened.

He said, 'I thought he did, at first ... and I was against it. I told him so. I thought it should not be allowed ... because the marriage would not succeed. You would not be happy. There is too much difference in your ways of thought ... your backgrounds ... what you think important ... your religions, if you like.'

He walked on, sucking on his pipe. Fudge was not as affectionate as he used to be, Warren thought. Did he know, or guess, what had happened to Shikari? Well, he wouldn't make that mistake, of trusting even a pet dog, again.

Diana said, 'But you've changed your mind? You think we should get married?'

'If you are pregnant, yes,' he said dryly, 'though you may have to get a divorce or separation later ... But I'm not sure now that Krishna wants to marry you. Because you are English ... European. He is turning away from everything Western. At first he blamed me personally for all the bad things of this war, the unpleasant things that can't be avoided—then he found the sin to be in all Europe, in all our way of life. You are part of it.'

It was Diana's turn to keep silent. They walked a mile along the canal bank and turned. The cry of the horn came sharper on the damp breeze, blended now with the falling whistle of an express rushing down the vale.

Diana said, 'What sentence do you think they'll give him?'

Warren said, 'The prosecution will ask for the death sentence'—he heard her intake of breath—'but as he is, what he is, I'm sure it will never be carried out. Or, perhaps, imposed ... My God, Diana, I wish I could let the whole thing go, pretend it never happened, so that he could marry you and you both go off to Ravi and live happily ever afterwards. But I can't.'

'I know you can't, Warrie,' she said, laying her hand on his arm. 'You must do your duty.'

She understood, he thought. Did Krishna? Did any of them know the meaning of duty?

Diana said hesitantly, 'Of course, I don't really know him very well.'

'No,' Warren said. 'Nothing like as well as I do. It's a pity, but I don't see how you, or any woman, can know the man she thinks she wants to marry. You don't live with them before you're married, though that fellow Goldwasser suggests in his book that there should be some arrangement of the sort ... legally, with everyone's approval, for six months on end, he proposes.'

Diana said, 'I wish Krishna and I could have done that. I was—I *am*—so lonely. Thirty-one years old. Paris was so exciting ... But I love him, I love him,' she finished defiantly, as though to reassure herself.

After a time she said, 'I feel that I am being torn apart. Krishna, whom I love, is going one way, and you, whom I worship, are going the other way. I think I understand why each of you is doing what you are doing. But I have to make a choice, don't I ... What am I to do, Warrie?'

He couldn't answer. He didn't know.

They walked on. From outside the silence between them might have been taken for their old companionable quiet, a lack of need to exchange words, that there had always been; but it was not. Warren walked enclosed within a circle of his own thoughts, which Diana only touched where her unhappiness touched a similar chord in him. What had happened to her? What would become of her? These thoughts made him shiver, but not for her sake; for his own, because the formulation of the idea forced him to ask the same questions of himself.

When they turned into the drive they saw their mother standing outside the little greenhouse, a pink slip in her hand. The rissaldar-major stood in front of her, holding her elbows. Warren broke into a run. His mother's face was pale, and there were tears in the corners of her eyes, but staying there, held. He took the telegram form from her hand as she sank her head on the rissaldar-major's shoulder. Warren read the telegram, hearing the RM's muttered Hindi words of comfort. The War Office regretted to inform them that Guardsman Ralph Harris had been killed in action.

'He was not a soldier,' his mother said, raising her head.

And I sent him, Warren thought. Is that what she means? I killed him? Joan was in the house somewhere. He could see the children through the drawing-room window. Millions of people who were not soldiers had died, and more were going to. Diana had her arm round her mother's shoulders, and the RM had stepped back.

'We did all we could for him, didn't we?' his mother said, her voice choking.

More than all, Warren thought, especially you, my mother, taking into your house and your heart your husband's bastard.

His mother said, 'He was the only one who needed me. Now he's gone ... What am I to do?'

Warren stood silent. Again, he could not answer, because he did not know.

His mother went into the house on Diana's shoulder. Now he had to tell Joan. That would be the worst of all.

He found her in the sewing-room, letters before her, the machine idle, cloth scattered on the floor. He squared his shoulders as though going up into No Man's Land, and said, 'Ralph's been killed in action.'

'I know,' she said, her fingers touching the letters. 'One of these is from his platoon commander and the other from a guardsman who'd been his friend in training. I suppose a telegram's just arrived? It must have been delayed ... Ralph and the guardsman had only been in France two days. The letters were addressed to Mother, but I opened them. I had a feeling...'

'Do they say how he was killed?'

She laughed, a bitter humourless laugh. 'Yes,' she said. 'The officer says he was killed instantly, while doing his duty, by a stray German shell. The guardsman says he was hit by shell splinters while he was on the latrine, and died in agony six hours later.' She laughed again. 'How would it have been, Warren? You've seen it all ... his bowels blown out? His brains running out of his head?'

'I'm sorry,' Warren said. She was looking directly at him, the large eyes larger, wider, the pale hair luminous round her face.

'Not a very noble end,' she said. 'One to match his beginnings.' He had thought she would cry, but there were no tears.

He said, 'He was doing his duty.'

'Thanks to you,' she said. He looked wonderingly at her. What did she mean?

'We've hardly spoken for three months, have we?' she said.

'No.'

'First you were in France, then hospital ... I've been thinking. I didn't love Ralph. I hated the war. But it's winning. You know, I could go and kill Germans, myself, thinking of Ralph, blown to bits on a latrine ... Krishna's beaten you, hasn't he?'

'The court martial will decide that,' he said, his voice harsh.

'Don't you see,' she insisted, 'he will have got his Indians out of Europe, whatever the court does to him? That's the point, isn't it? A rejection of all that you have been trying to teach.'

Warren didn't answer. It was impossible to accept what she

407

said, and face the consequences, without further mental preparation, as though for an assault.

She said, 'Here, the war's winning, Warren. Everything flows into it, it flows out into everything, everybody ... Some time ago I had to admit to myself that I didn't love Ralph. Before that I knew I didn't love you. So apparently I don't love anyone, only hate ... What's to become of me, Warren? Tell me, tell me!'

Her hand was on his, crushing, clawing like a drowning woman's. He pulled himself free and went out, the memory of her hand burning like a blister on his wrist. His head ached sharply, as it used to before they sent him home the last time. What was to become of them? Diana. Joan. Mother. England. India. Mankind? He could hear only the crushing thunder of artillery, without cease, surrounding him so closely that it was inside him as well as outside; and the universal crackle of machine guns.

The rissaldar-major was in the greenhouse, dis-budding chrysanthemums. He straightened as Warren came in. Warren said, 'We return to France the day after tomorrow, sahib.'

'*Jee, huzoor.*'

'I heard a pheasant in the wood as we were coming back from our walk. We'll go shooting. In half an hour.'

'*Jee, huzoor.*'

The RM was looking doubtfully at him. Perhaps his eyes were wild, or there was something distraught, undone, about his manner. The RM looked as though he were going to say something, then his mouth closed. He must want to ask how he could retain the trust of the Ravi sowars when he had helped put their godling, their Son of the Sun, into a British gaol ... or against a wall, facing a firing squad of beef-eating British soldiers. There was no answer. No answer to anyone.

Warren went to the gunroom, took his favourite twelve-bore in its case, and a box of cartridges, and walked out of the back door and across the little bricked yard to the stables. He went into the room where he had watched Ralph making love to Joan, sat on the bed, and took the gun out of its case. He wiped the gun clean with a slightly oily rag, then loaded both barrels with No. 5 shot. Was that Krishna peering in through the little window? The door was not barred. How could he let Krishna get away with it? How could the young Indian, believing he was reliving the *Mahabharata*, have been right, and he himself wrong?

He heard the sound of boots outside. The RM was coming, looking for him. The black mouths of the twin barrels were Krishna's dark eyes, understanding.

November 1915

KRISHNA STOOD AT the graveside, head bowed, sleet falling from a grey sky. He could not see the coffin very clearly for his eyes were dim and swollen.

For a thousand years in Thy sight are but as yesterday, when it is past, and as a watch in the night.

Joan Bateman stood at the foot of the open grave, opposite the vicar intoning the service. Old Mrs. Bateman was at her right, and Diana at her left. All three women were in black, heavily veiled. Krishna could not see whether they were weeping or no but he thought not.

I will lift up mine eyes unto the hills; from whence cometh my help?

Beside him the rissaldar-major's Sam Browne belt gleamed with an unearthly luminosity, and the hilt of his sabre glittered in the crook of his left elbow. Sir Tristram and Lady Pennel were there, and Old Marsh and a dozen villagers, some of whose faces Krishna recognized from the cricket match of his first visit.

Out of the deep have I called unto thee, O Lord; Lord hear my voice.

Mr. Fleming was there, in the uniform of a private of the Royal Engineers, standing at the back of the little crowd, looking at no one.

Unto Almighty God we commend the soul of our brother departed and we commit his body to the ground; earth to earth, ashes to ashes, dust to dust...

Sprinkling of earth, patter of the wet earth on the coffin, becoming white from the falling sleet.

Almighty God, with whom do live the spirits of those who depart hence in the Lord, and with whom the souls of the faithful, after they are delivered from the burden of the flesh, are in joy and felicity; We give Thee hearty thanks for the good examples of all those Thy servants, who having finished their course in faith, do now rest from their labours.

The drifting sleet thickened the air so that, beyond the bare arms of the elms outside the churchyard there was no vale, no Plain, no distance. Nothing existed outside the group round the open grave, and the curved arm of the churchyard wall protecting them.

Amen.

The service was over. Warren's mother was kneeling in the mud beside the grave, Diana and Joan standing beside her. The rest were drifting away. Mr. Fleming passed close at Krishna's side and he said, 'Mr. Fleming . . . sir . . .'

The tutor walked on, his head averted. Krishna's hand dropped. He ought to have expected it. He turned again, to look down at the coffin. He joined his palms in *namasti,* and recited to himself, in the Sanskrit in which he had been taught the epic.

Woe to us! Our eldest brother we have in the battle slain,
And our nearest dearest elder fell upon the gory plain,
Not the death of Abhimanyu from the fair Subadra torn,
Not the slaughter of the princes by the proud Draupadi borne,
Not the fall of friends and kinsmen and Panchala's mighty host,
Like thy death afflicts my bosom, noble Karna loved and lost!

The women were leaving the churchyard now, passing under the lych gate and the little wicket on to the Old Vicarage grounds. Slowly Krishna followed, the rissaldar-major a pace behind him.

Mrs. Bateman was sitting in the drawing-room, alone, her veil raised, mud at the knees of her long black skirt. As he had thought, there were no tears in her eyes. She sat very upright beside the small coal fire burning in the grate. Krishna said, 'Mrs. Bateman . . . I loved him, too.'

'I know,' she said. 'I don't blame you for . . . anything. It is the war. I . . . we . . . all thought that it would be the Germans but . . . there are other enemies.'

Krishna said, 'Mrs. Bateman, I want to ask Diana if she will marry me.'

Diana came in, her veil off, her eyes red and suffused with tears. She was still dabbing at them with a handkerchief as she closed the door behind her. She saw Krishna and stopped, her

411

face draining. Her mother said, 'Krishna wants to ask you to marry him.'

Diana's breathing came heavier, and she clasped her hands before her breasts, the little handkerchief crushed in them. She said, 'You killed Warrie!'

Mrs. Bateman said gently, 'Krishna didn't kill Warren, dear.'

'He did! ... I never want to see you again.'

She turned and ran out of the room.

'I'm sorry,' Krishna said. Mrs. Bateman's head was bowed and now, he thought, though he could not see, that she was weeping. He said, 'Good-bye, Mrs. Bateman. May the rissaldar-major come in?'

The bowed head nodded, without words. Krishna went out and nodded at the RM, who was waiting outside. He went forward, and Krishna carefully closed the door behind him.

Joan Bateman was in the dining-room, laying the table, the children Louise and Rodney helping her. She looked up and said brightly, 'Are you staying for lunch, Krishna?'

'No,' he said, 'the RM and I have to catch a train.'

'I'll drive you to the station,' she said.

'You'll miss your lunch ... Can't Young Marsh do it?'

'Young Marsh?' she laughed. 'He's volunteered for the Navy. When he heard that Ralph had been killed, he went off, the next day. The war's getting us all, isn't it? If it's not patriotism, it's vengeance. Not for you, I suppose. For Warren, it was duty. For some, shame. I'm head of the Shrewford Pennel Women's War Work Association now, you know ... I suppose you won't be court martialled now.'

'No. General Glover ordered my release as soon as he heard about the CO—Warren ... Good-bye, Mrs. Bateman.'

'Good-bye,' she said. She bent her head and went on putting knives and forks beside the place mats on the polished mahogany table. The grandfather clock in the hall struck twelve.

The train swept silently towards London, the whirling sleet smudging the window and blocking out all sound of their passage through the early dusk. The carriage heating had failed and Krishna sat huddled in his British warm, the rissaldar-major opposite. He wondered whether Diana was pregnant with his son, who should have been the next heir to the Kingdom of Ravi. He would never know now.

The rissaldar-major said, 'Lord...'

'Yes, sahib?'

'The regiment is returning to India?'

'Why do you ask?'

'It is in my mind, if so, that I must request transfer to another regiment, which is staying. I cannot return to my home until this war is won, for the sake of the word I gave Bateman-sahib.'

Krishna Ram looked out of the window, but saw only his reflection in the blurred wet glass. After a while he said, 'I think, sahib, we will all stay ... I meant all that I said at the panchayat at Fosse-Garde, when we were cut off. But back in India, in the beginning, we gave our word to serve to the end, and now we must keep it—for we can no longer ask Colonel Bateman's forgiveness and understanding. We can only earn them ... The Indian infantry divisions are leaving France, but the Indian Cavalry Corps is staying, and I shall see that we stay with it ... For the rest, for that which we decided at the panchayat—and for India—there is time.'